A STORY FROM THE FILES OF ALEXANDER STRANGE

FLORIDA MAN

J.C. BRUCE

Florida Man
A Story From the Files of Alexander Strange

Copyright © 2020 J.C. Bruce

ISBN: 978-1-7342903-8-7 (Hardback)
ISBN: 978-1-7342903-2-5 (Paperback)
ISBN: 978-1-7342903-3-2 (eBook)

Library of Congress Control Number: 2019920365

This is a work of fiction. Names, characters, places, and incidents are a product of the author's imagination. Locales and public names are sometimes used for atmospheric purposes. Any resemblance to actual people, living or dead, or to businesses, companies, events, institutions, or locales is completely coincidental.

Book design by Damonza.com
Website design by Bumpy Flamingo LLC

Printed by Tropic Press in the United States of America.

First printing edition 2020

Tropic Press LLC
P.O. Box 110758
Naples, Florida 34108

www.Tropic.Press

Books by J.C. Bruce

The Strange Files

Florida Man: A Story From the Files of Alexander Strange

Get Strange

Strange Currents

To Sandy, Kacey, and Logan

"Never assume. If your mother say she loves you, kick her smartly in the shins and make her prove it."

—Edward H. Eulenberg, City News Bureau of Chicago

PROLOGUE

If I had read Shirley DuMont's diary earlier, some of this might have made more sense at the time. Even so, if her words are to be believed, the unbendable trajectory of fate cannot be altered and nothing we did—or attempted to do—would have changed the outcome.

Fate. The ancient Greeks believed destiny revealed itself in the form of three white-robed entities called the *Moirai*. Even the gods feared them. Shakespeare referred to them as the Weird Sisters, from the Nordic *Wyrd*. Thank you, Will and Norsepersons. News of the Moirai doesn't have the same ring as News of the Weird.

That's my job, reporting weird news. It's often silly and speaks to the absurdity of the human condition: A Florida woman who bit a camel's testicles when it sat on her. The Florida man who got his head stuck in a fence while spying on a neighbor. An undergarment-free teacher who performed cartwheels in front of her adoring students—while wearing a dress.

But sometimes pursuing weirdness takes us to less trivial places, where our contemporary understanding of reality collides with the inexplicable. It is the height of arrogance—and ignorance—to dismiss evidence that is plainly before us merely because it doesn't conform to the laws of nature as we, ourselves, have defined them.

There was a time, after all, when it was understood by everyone in the world that big rocks fell faster than small rocks. It was simply common sense. Until a guy named Galileo said, "Oh yeah? I'll bet you a pizza it ain't so." Which is how Galileo got fat and science was invented.

No such thing as ghosts? Can't speak with the dead? No one can predict the future? And exactly how do you know that? For certain?

Shirley DuMont wasn't crazy. At least, I don't think so. But crazy things were happening to her she couldn't explain. And we still can't.

But that didn't mean they weren't real.

I only discovered this entry from her private journal after the events in this narrative played out. But I will share it with you here. Perhaps, forearmed with this snippet, some of the occurrences that will unfold in the following pages will acquire a clarity that eluded me while I was embroiled in them.

She wrote:

Once again, I am trying to stop Alexander Strange. In previous lives, I have locked him out of my shop, refused to enter his car, assumed different personae—all to no avail. I'm trying something different this time: I'm letting go, throwing myself to the fates.

We shall see what we shall see.

—Alexander Strange

CHAPTER 1

Near the River Styx

I wanted to get to Florida in the worst way, so I arrived in a coffin.

I wasn't dead, not yet. But I knew death was lying in wait, stalking me, ready to pounce. Death was lurking in the shadows outside the beams of the hearse's headlights as we roared across the state line, as if the Grim Reaper himself were in pursuit.

Or is it herself? Do we really know the Grim Reaper's gender? Maybe Grimmy is an it. Whatever, my plan was to outrace her, him, it for as long as I could.

Most souls are blissfully unaware of the moment their mortal coils will unwind, a comforting ignorance allowing us to pursue daily life with a kind of mad denial of the inevitable. Unavoidable, sure, but not imminent. But I had been warned my time was nearly up. I would soon kick the bucket, buy the farm, cash in my chips.

A palm reader in New Orleans told me so.

And why would I give credence to a French Quarter fortune teller, you might ask? You're a college-trained journalist, you could note. It's your job to second-guess charlatans, to sniff out liars. That's what my journalism professors did their best to beat into me: Trust no one.

But try as I might, I can't seem to be cynical enough. It's an awful professional failing, I suppose. In my defense, however, you had to have been there, to have seen the soothsayer's stricken look as she glanced at my palm. How the blood drained from her face. How the beads of perspiration blossomed on her forehead. The way she sucked in her breath as if she'd seen a ghost.

She said she saw death, but she was a little vague on how or where. Would it be in the Gunshine State, my current destination?

After all, I was already in a pine box.

Well, that's a tad euphemistic. It was, actually, a metal casket, an impressive number from the Downer Collection, a Silver Acqua coffin made of chromium stainless steel with a continuously welded bottom, chemically treated to resist rust and corrosion and featuring a special watertight seal guaranteeing the deceased would remain nice and dry even if water tables rose with climate change. I knew this from reading the sales literature in the back of the hearse.

And why was I in a hearse if I had yet to reach my expire-by date? Because hitchhikers can't be choosers, and when you're standing on the edge of a busy interstate highway with your thumb out, you take what you can get.

The sun was dipping below the horizon in my rear view mirror when my engine died. I was driving an aging maroon Chrysler Sebring convertible with more than 200,000 miles on the odometer, fleeing Phoenix and the furnace of the Sonoran Desert for the tiny island town of Goodland in sweltering southwest Florida.

My destination was a converted fishing trawler owned by my Uncle Leo—Maricopa County Superior Court Judge Leonardo D. Strano to you. It would be my home and office as I began a new career working for a start-up online news service.

The Sebring's demise was undramatic. One instant, I was barreling along Interstate 10, top down, buffeted by the cool breeze of twilight. The next instant, the engine simply stopped turning over, as if it had suffered a stroke or a heart attack—a fatal case of internal noncombustion.

Fortunately, I was cruising in the outside lane and was able to glide off the roadway onto the grass before some passing semi steam-rolled me.

I tried calling AAA on my cell phone, but it seemed I had stalled in one of the inconvenient stretches of interstate unplugged from the myriad cell networks, all of whom advertise the fastest connections and the most reliable networks covering ninety-nine percent of this great land of ours. Evidently, I had discovered the lost one percent.

I was west of the Alabama-Florida state line and traffic was brisk. I wrestled my enormous suitcase and smaller gym bag from the back seat, then tried to raise the rag top, but it wouldn't budge. Thankfully, there was no rain in the forecast. I positioned myself at the edge of the highway and stuck my thumb out, facing an onslaught of hurtling sedans, SUVs, pickups, eighteen-wheelers, a growling peloton of Harleys, and, in short order, a black and chrome meat wagon.

I should mention I wasn't hitchhiking solo. Uncle Leo's fifth wife, Sarah—or as I liked to call her, *Numero Cinco*—had given me her dog, Fred. She'd discovered caring for a crotchety old judge and a bouncy, energetic puppy more than she could handle.

Fred is a Papillon. If you are unfamiliar with the breed, imagine a collie that's been shot with a shrink ray, but sporting enormous ears that when raised look like furry wings, hence the name: Papillon is French for butterfly.

He's a fine traveling companion and at eight pounds Fred's so small I didn't fuss with pet-friendly motels on my journey—just tucked him inside my gym bag and smuggled him inside with me wherever I settled for the night. I hoped his presence on the edge of the interstate would be a plus. After all, your average highway serial killer posing as a hitchhiker wouldn't own a sissy dog like Fred, would he?

Whether that was the reason or not, the kid piloting the hearse took pity on me and pulled behind my stalled car. The corpsemobile sported a vanity plate reading: DIRT NAP. I walked over, and a teenager who barely looked old enough to drive lowered his window. I leaned down.

"Dirt nap? Really?"

He laughed. "Yup, my daddy, he got a funny sense a humor. We own the funeral home back in Bay Minette." That was nineteen words and about forty syllables. We were, after all, in the deepest Deep South.

"Bay Minnow?"

"Minette. It's right on the Styx River."

I felt a chill tingle my spine and my heart skipped a beat—a premature ventricular contraction. I get them when I'm stressed, which is stressful, but my doctor tells me they are benign.

It took me a moment, then I asked, "Styx?"

"Yup. See that ahead there?"

I turned around and the hearse's headlights painted a bridge over a small stream.

"That's the Styx River," he said. "Flows all the way back to Bay Minette."

"So, we're about to cross the River Styx? In a hearse?"

"Yup," the kid drawled. "Just like in that Greek mythology. I've studied up on that since I plan to take over from daddy when it's time for him to cross. We lay 'em out in the parlor on the west bank of the river and take 'em over to the cemetery on the other. We got 'em crossin' over the River Styx two, three times a week, sometimes more when bidness is good."

"People just dying left and right in Bay Minnow, huh?"

"Ummm. So, you got car trouble?"

"Yeah, it died on me. You heading to Pensacola?"

"Sho nuff. Got a box in the back to deliver. Funeral home there's workin' a double, a murder-suicide, and they run outta matching caskets. I got one and they need it, like, yesterday. Hop in."

Hopping in meant climbing into the rear of the hearse as the passenger seat was crammed with several wooden crates stacked atop one another, each stenciled in black lettering with "Hydrol Embalming Fluid" on the sides and tops.

The kid met me at the rear of the deathmobile, opened the door, and said, "We ain't got far to go, about ten minutes out, so you make yourself comfy."

"Uh, you saying you want me to sit in the coffin?"

"Sure. I take naps in 'em all the time. Best seat in the hearse."

I don't do well in confined spaces. And a coffin definitely qualified as closed-in. Fortunately, I wasn't taphophobic—a condition plaguing people terrified of premature burial. Mine was ordinary claustrophobia. But if it were for only a few minutes, I figured I could suck it up. So I hoisted my suitcase and gym bag into the hearse, then climbed in after them. After I was settled into the casket, the kid handed Fred to me.

Was I in the coffin destined for the murder victim? Or the suicide? I didn't ask, and I guessed the kid behind the wheel neither knew nor cared. But one of them would find their eternal resting place slightly used. Maybe even with a few stray Papillon hairs.

I had no idea where Fred and I would spend the night once we arrived in Pensacola, how quickly my car could be repaired, or if I would finish the remainder of my journey with my thumb out continuing to rely on the kindness of strangers. But I had been warned: I'd better enjoy life while I could.

I relished the idea of awakening on each of my remaining days to the peaceful sounds of the marina and the gentle rocking of the *Miss Demeanor,* Uncle Leo's trawler. How many mornings would I have left to enjoy? The psychic's divination of my palm did not offer much in the way of specifics. So I needed to celebrate every sunrise, every sunset, every Cuba Libre until the end.

But it didn't feel like it would be tonight. For no reason other than the denial of our mortality that allows each of us to carry on. But it would be just too clever to croak while traveling in a coffin, too convenient, too ironic by half. No, I felt confident Grimmy would be occupied elsewhere for the time being.

I held Fred in my lap. He seemed antsy, as if he detected something outside the range of my own senses that disturbed him. Maybe he did. I'd never been inside a hearse before. I sniffed the air. It smelled of the silk lining of the coffin, of metal, of upholstery, and something else, but I couldn't quite place it. Maybe a little embalming fluid? I scratched Fred behind his enormous ears, which seemed to settle him down.

"It's all good, buddy. We'll be out of here in no time."

Then the kid hit the gas and the carsophagus shot onto the highway. The G-force from the acceleration rocked me backward into the coffin, and as the hearse fishtailed onto the interstate the lid slammed down.

CHAPTER 2

New Orleans, Two Days Earlier

I'M NO STRANGER to games of chance, and Uncle Leo and I had once spent a wild weekend at Harrah's Casino and Hotel in New Orleans in the hope—indeed, expectation—that Lady Luck would smile upon us.

It was a graduation present, a well-earned reward after six grueling years of beer pong, competitive swimming, and video games at the University of Texas where I finally matriculated with a degree in journalism and a couple of medals from splashing around in the pool.

Unlike most of my peers who remained crushed under the ponderous weight of college loans, I accepted my sheepskin without that cruel burden thanks to Leo's generosity. And he'd done more than pay my way through college—he'd saved my life.

I was orphaned as a youngster when my drug-addled mother drowned in a cave during a sit-in to save an endangered species of spider. An Austin real estate developer planned to pave paradise and put up a parking lot. Specifically, asphalt for a new shopping mall that would be sited atop the small cavern, arachnids be damned. Mom and several of her Earth First friends hatched a scheme to thwart his rapaciousness and began rotating vigils inside the cave, playing chicken with the bulldozers.

During one of Mom's shifts in the middle of the night, the heavens opened and the raging waters of a flash flood swept her away. Her body was never recovered. Nor, for that matter, the corpse of the eyeless Braken Bat Cave Meshweaver she tried to protect.

Leo, my mom's brother, took me in, eventually adopted me, and put me through school. He'd also spotted me two hundred dollars to wager at Harrah's poker tables upon college graduation, which with skill, patience, and cunning I parlayed into precisely zero dollars in less than two minutes—a feat for which the blackjack dealer congratulated me as possibly setting a casino record. But I was younger then, and it stood to reason I would do better now that I had the benefit of an additional five years of life experience and had matured into a hardened veteran of the newspaper wars.

I'd worked for a paper in Arizona, the *Phoenix Daily Sun*, a job my uncle helped me get. I wrote a column, *The Strange Files*, a play on my name, Alexander Strange, and descriptive of the oddball characters and events I wrote about: A dog owner shot by his collie when he carelessly left his pistol on the couch; a burglar who broke into a farmhouse only to be greeted by the owner's pet tiger; a color blind counterfeiter caught because he used the wrong ink. Stuff like that.

My newspaper, which had been on the edge of extinction during my entire time there, had now joined the ill-fated Braken Bat Cave Meshweaver and swirled down the drain. But while the paper might have been out of business, my editor and a few other ink-stained wretches were not out of ideas. We'd launched an online news service called Tropic ⑥ Press where I would continue to write my weird news reports.

I suppose I could have stayed in Phoenix, but Uncle Leo offered me the use of his boat, and the idea of living in Florida intrigued me. It was, after all, the home of Florida Man, the online meme synonymous with weirdness. Widely viewed as the Candy Land of crazy, I wondered why, exactly, was Florida home to so many weirdos. Was the state a magnet for the off-balanced, or was it something in the water that turned normal people nuts, or was the whole Florida Man phenomenon just a self-fulfilling stereotype?

Why not go there and find out? The state would provide a bottomless well of source material for the *Strange Files*, and I could research the larger question of what made Florida men and women so prone to zany behavior. And the idea of living in the subtropics held a certain romantic attraction, as did living in a marina. Maybe I'd hook up with Travis McGee and we'd swill some Boodles together. Or perhaps the ghost of Hemingway would inspire my writing. And then there was the element of danger—would I be at risk of becoming a Florida Man myself? Could it be contagious? Constant vigilance would be my byword.

The road trip from Arizona to Florida was a straight shot eastward on Interstate 10 until it collided with I-75. Then I would plunge southward toward the Everglades and Goodland, my destination near Naples. I planned one stop in Florida along this route, dinner with a friend in Gainesville where she had founded an alternative newspaper called *The Agi-Gator*. Like newspapers elsewhere, hers was also in dire financial straits and was circling the drain. "We're planning a party for our final edition," she'd told me. "Me and my remaining staff of two."

Before arriving in the Sunshine State, however, New Orleans beckoned. I'd decided to invest a small portion of my modest savings on a return bout at Harrah's with the goal of erasing my earlier ignominious defeat at the tables and, perhaps, even growing my bankroll to make life in the tropics a little more comfortable.

Diversification is the key to a successful investment strategy, so I also decided to buy a lottery ticket while in the Big Easy. But a question loomed: Should I let the computer pick the numbers randomly, or should I determine my own fate? And if I chose the latter strategy, what numbers?

I pondered this vital question as Fred and I strolled Royal Street, which parallels its more famous and raunchier French Quarter artery named for Kentucky's most famous—and delicious—beverage.

It was lunchtime, too soon to check in at the hotel and too early to start drinking (although that was not inhibiting the revelers on Bourbon Street one block over). Also, I needed to park Fred in our hotel room before I could hit the blackjack tables and the bar. And I had to do it discretely since Harrah's, while a splendid establishment for humans, frowns on four-legged guests.

I noticed an attractive African-American woman standing in front of a shop, wearing an over-sized purple dashiki over tight black jeans, a red turban, and yards of beads. Both of her forearms were sleeved in odd symbols that looked vaguely like hieroglyphics. She was leaning against the door frame, sucking a Kool, and scanning the passing throngs of tourists through pink wraparound shades. A scarlet neon hand decorated a large portion of the shop's window. A plaque over the door read:

Madam Jazzabelle
Licensed Chirologist

Fred and I crossed the street and approached her.

"You Madam Jezebel?" I asked.

She blew a cloud of smoke in my direction. "It's Jazzabelle. J-A-Z-Z. It's New Orleans. Get it?" She scowled when she said it, but was that also the hint of a smile? Was there a name for that? A *scile*?

Some people might have felt foolish asking if Jazzabelle was her real name. But my years as a reporter have taught me sometimes the best questions are the ones you're afraid to ask because they might make you sound stupid. So, I did.

She snorted. "What? Are you stupid?"

"You tell me, you're the mind reader."

She flipped the butt onto the sidewalk and fished a new coffin nail out of the box she was holding. "I don't read minds, sonny. That's impossible. But for a Jackson, I'll examine your hands and we shall see what we shall see. Bring your mutt." She turned around and retreated into the dusky confines of her establishment. And after a moment's hesitation, I followed.

I think she knew I would.

"What exactly is a chirologist?" I asked. "A fancy name for palm reader?"

She shook her head as she led me to a small, circular table covered in an ornately embroidered red and gold silk cloth. "Palm readers are charlatans," she said. "They say they study the influence of the planets, including Pluto, which isn't even a planet anymore. A chirologist—a certified chirologist such as myself, mind you—focuses on the five elements of nature—earth, air, water, fire, and chi."

"I thought chi was a drink at Starbucks."

"That's chai, spiced tea. Chi is the life force."

"The Force? As in…"

"Yeah, like that. The Force."

Fred reached up and placed his front paws on her legs. She smiled, bent down, and scratched him behind his ears. He smiled back at her and let his tongue loll out of his mouth. Fred can be a bit of a showoff.

"You here to party or just passing through?" she asked without bothering to inquire if I were a local.

"Driving to Florida," I said. "Starting a new job."

She leaned back and nodded. "I don't think I've ever been." She removed her sunglasses and looked me over. Her brown irises were speckled with gold, giving her a faint lupine aura. A little spooky.

"Where'd you get those shoulders?" she asked.

"Did a lot of swimming in my youth."

"Youth!" It came out as a shout and quickly devolved into a coughing fit. "Youth. Give me a break."

I'd been trying to guess her accent—or lack thereof. She wasn't Cajun. She sounded Midwestern, maybe Detroit or Cleveland. Now I wondered about her age. Forty? Certainly not much more than that.

She seemed to read my mind, even though she'd denied having

those powers. "Forty-three," she said. "That answer the question you wanted to ask?"

"I was going to say thirty-eight."

She did the laugh-turned-hacking-cough thing again.

I put my fist to my forehead, closed my eyes, and said, "Karnak sees a future. A future with you in chemotherapy if you don't quit the Kools."

"I see a future where you're twenty dollars lighter." She tapped the center of the table with a long, turquoise fingernail, and I plopped down the cash.

"Let's see."

She reached out, palms up, a signal for me to do likewise, then clasped my outstretched left hand and gazed at my palm. But not for long. In a few seconds, her eyes sprang wide, stricken in terror, and she began perspiring furiously.

"What?"

"I see death," she whispered, hoarsely.

"You see dead people? That's a line from a movie."

She shook her head. "No, not dead people. That's impossible." She squinted her eyes as if she were in great discomfort. A rivulet of sweat coursed down her right cheek. She was breathing heavily, almost gulping for air.

"I see... I see... I see death. Very soon. There will be a crossing."

"Crossing?"

Her doleful eyes bore into mine. "When we die, our souls are escorted to a great river and we must pay Charon to cross over."

"Okay, but before I do that, you got any lucky lottery numbers?"

She shook her head. "May I know your name?" she asked, her voice barely a whisper.

"Uh, Strange. Alexander Strange," I said.

"Hmm. But not always, surely."

How did she know?

She rose from the table and said, "Goodbye, Alexander Strange."

Then she turned, took a step, faltered briefly, righted herself, then strode through curtains in the back of the room. I sat there stunned momentarily, then, for reasons known only to him, Fred began barking. Which was uncharacteristic behavior. Fred almost never barks. Except when he's angry. Or he's hungry. Or, as it turns out, when he's annoyed by mysterious chirologists.

Feeling a little discombobulated, I grabbed his leash and walked toward the door. As an honorary member of Cynics Anonymous, I knew I should blow off her prediction. But she seemed so sincere, so alarmed, so sweaty. And what was with that bit about Strange not always being my name?

I was blinded by the bright sunshine when I stepped out of the dimly lit shop onto Royal Street. What a bummer. I never should have stepped foot inside her little parlor of buzz kill.

There was a small rush of air and then a loud slap as the door slammed behind me. Scared the crap out of me. Fred, too, who began yelping again.

Rude!

I turned back to the door and twisted the handle, prepared to give Madam Jazzabelle a piece of my mind, but it was locked. I rang the bell. Nothing. I knocked. No answer. I knocked again, this time with additional vigor. Still no response.

I hate it when I don't get the last word.

So I was crossing over, was I? And soon. But she hadn't said exactly when, a critical omission. She'd left me hanging—although, of all the ways to go, hanging would not be at the top of my list. Bullets, poison, woodchippers—none made my hit parade of ways to check out, either. Perhaps in my sleep at the age of 103?

Which is when I remembered who Charon was—the boatman from Greek mythology who escorted the dead across the River Styx into Hades. The River Styx, where the mother of Achilles dipped his infant body to make him invulnerable, but held him by his ankle, which went untouched by the empowering waters. Hence the Achilles heel.

Odd story, but were the beliefs of the ancient Greeks any weirder than other religions? Pick your creed from the overflowing menu of human imagination. Have fun with it. I hope it gives you comfort. But don't push your superstitions on me. Not that I don't have my own beliefs. For instance, at that moment I believed it was time to check into Harrah's and beseech yet another set of deities—the poker gods.

I looked both ways before crossing the street. Good thing or a guy pushing a Lucky Dogs cart would have mowed me down.

Maybe that's how I was supposed to cash in my chips—crushed under the wheels of a hotdog vendor, buried under an avalanche of mustard-soaked sausages. But what if Madam Jazzabelle's warning had somehow altered that fate, changed the space-time continuum? Maybe I was now in a parallel universe. Maybe my troubles were over.

Maybe I needed that drink.

CHAPTER 3

Pensacola, Two Days Later

HERE'S AN IMPORTANT tip for those of you inspired by this narrative to consider travel by coffin: If the lid accidently slams shut on you, don't panic like I did—it doesn't lock. Oh, there's a locking mechanism, but it has to be keyed from the outside.

I discovered this, to my great relief, approximately eleven nano-seconds after I found myself trapped inside the casket. The lid crashed down, enveloping Fred and me in absolute darkness and relative quiet as the hearse rumbled toward the Florida state line.

Panic-stricken, I pushed upward, momentarily terrified the lid wouldn't budge. It was heavy—the casket was metal, after all—but it swung open.

"Holy fucking fuck!"

The kid heard that and started laughing his ass off. "Kinda gives ya the jibblies the first time, don't it?"

I glanced out the windshield and saw an enormous blue and white Welcome to Florida sign fly past. Irrationally, I felt relief in leaving Alabama, as if the rural Florida panhandle were any less *Deliverance* country.

But I had crossed the River Styx and was still breathing.

"You call for a tow?" the kid asked.

"I tried, but that's a dead zone back there."

"Nuh uh. Check your phone."

Like some teenager would know more about cell phone technology than me. I wrenched my iPhone from my back pocket and checked the screen.

"No signal."

He shook his head and held up his own cell phone. "You sure it's workin'? I got four bars."

I took a closer look. It wasn't that I had no signal, I had no juice. I pushed the power button and held it down. Finally a faint red line appeared on the screen inside the thin outline of a battery. It had run dry. Which was weird because I had the phone plugged into the Sebring's cigarette lighter throughout the trip. And why hadn't I noticed that before?

I looked at the kid again. "So, my car dies, and my cell phone wasn't charging. Got an idea what that could mean?"

"Alternator."

"Not the flux capacitor?"

"Alternator." Deadpan. Like he'd never seen *Back to the Future*.

"Name Marty McFly ring a bell?" I asked.

"He play for the Saints?"

"No, the Pinheads. Can you call Triple-A for me?"

"No problem." In a few minutes he'd made all the arrangements. Fletcher's towing would be on the road within the hour to pick up the Sebring and they'd deliver it to a place called Mike's Automotive, which they said was open seven days a week and would have me back on the road in no time.

"Mike's Automotive, they're reputable?" I asked the kid.

"Absolutely. He's my cousin."

Why did I feel a major hosing coming on?

We were in Pensacola now and I asked him if he knew a cheap place to stay near the car repair shop. A few minutes later, I was in the lobby of a Motel 6 on Pensacola Boulevard where the desk clerk assured me I was within convenient walking distance of Mike's Automotive and a liquor store, and that dinner could be procured at a Whataburger across the street.

I took Fred for a brief stroll, then set out his bowls of food and water. I locked up the motel room and hazarded the traffic on Pensacola Boulevard to the hamburger joint. I ordered a world-class jalapeno cheeseburger with fries and a Diet Coke. I wolfed down the chow, then took the Diet Coke for a walk to the liquor store where I picked up a pint of Bacardi. I'd walked back into my motel room when my iPhone, now charging on the nightstand, began buzzing.

"Sir," the tow truck driver said. "Just to let you know, you may have a problem."

"Like what?"

"Like your trunk either blew open or was broken into."

"My trunk?"

"Yes, sir."

"Oh, shit. Did you see a Vulcan in there?"

CHAPTER 4

My LAPTOP WAS frozen on the scene in *Wrath of Kahn* where Spock is staring through the glass of a radioactive chamber and he tells James T. Kirk, "I have been and always shall be your friend." Then he dies.

That and the bit in *Spider-Man 2* when Peter Parker is pulled into the runaway train by the passengers whose lives he's saved ("He's just a kid.") never fail to choke me up. If I'm ever on Broadway and cast in a role requiring the spontaneous generation of tears, recalling either of these scenes would do the trick.

I was left alone a lot as a boy, and I watched the old *Star Trek* reruns over and over again. Spock was my fave. I liked how steady he was. I admired his imperturbability. My life was chaos. His was orderly. I wanted to be like him, cool, calm, capable.

It's good to have stretch goals.

One of the happiest days of my young life was the Christmas my mom gave me a life-size cardboard cutout of Spock, phaser on hip, issuing his split finger "live long and prosper" salute. A few months later, she was transported to the hereafter along with a blind eight-legged member of *Cicurina venii*.

Mom was gone, but I had Spock. He accompanied me from Texas to Arizona when Uncle Leo took me in. Spock traveled with me back to Austin when I went to college and where he was even inducted *in honorarium* into my fraternity. He was my roommate in Phoenix when I took a job at the *Daily Sun*. And because I was afraid the wind might blow him out of the car with the top down, he'd been stowed away in the trunk.

And now he was missing.

The phone call to the Florida Highway Patrol did not go well.

Me: "I need to report a kidnapping."

FHP Dispatcher: "Where did this kidnapping take place?"

Me: "In my trunk. On Interstate 10. About a mile west of the state line. But my car was in the eastbound lane so the kidnappers must be in Florida by now."

FHP: "Are you saying someone was kidnapped from a truck?"

Me: "Not truck. Trunk. His name is S'chn T'gai Spock." (Okay, I admit, I was showing off a bit there.)

FHP: "Spock. As in Mr. Spock?"

Me: "The one and only."

The dispatcher then lectured me on how filing a fake police report was a felony, to which I retorted that Spock really was stolen from my car, to which the dispatcher replied that stealing cardboard did not constitute a kidnapping, which led to a disagreement about Spock's sentience, and I was finally transferred to a non-emergency number where I was put on interminable hold.

So I called the Alabama Highway Patrol, told them my car may have been broken into, and they asked where it was, and I explained it was in Pensacola, to which the dispatcher suggested calling the Florida Highway Patrol.

So, having received no satisfaction from law enforcement, I figured I would need to take matters into my own hands. Spock was out there somewhere. If I could make contact with him, maybe he could tell me where he was being held. I should note that would be a first. In the long history of our relationship, Spock has never spoken to me. Not once. I use him as a sounding board, and he always listens patiently. But he is a clever Vulcan preferring to let me figure out things on my own. But, perhaps for once, given we were in a desperate situation here, maybe he'd help me out.

It occurred to me that if I had an image of him to look at, then maybe somehow he could channel a message to me. Which is why I had *Wrath of Kahn* playing. That was ridiculous, I know, and it might be fair to point out that some rum and Cokes were involved, but I figured I had nothing to lose. And I was sad.

Before she drowned, my mom grew concerned about my attachment to Spock and asked the school psychologist to talk to me. I saw multiple shrinks at a variety of schools. Homelessness will do that for you—provide an ever-changing panoply of settings from which to experience life, introduce you to fascinating people with unusual histories, and provide you with a chance to test your resourcefulness from time to time in defending yourself against those individuals.

Shrink: "Alexander, your father doesn't live with you, does he?"

Me: "I don't know who my father is."

Shrink: "I'll bet it would be nice to have a dad to talk to, wouldn't it?"

Me: Shrug.

Shrink: "So you talk to Mr. Spock instead?"

Me: Shrug.

And so on.

Spock was a talisman, a good-luck charm, the psychologist told my mom. Your son is merely going through a phase. He'll outgrow it.

Ha! I showed them.

I poured another drink with the remains of the rum. Were Spock in the room he would disapprove of my overindulging. He can be a bit of a prig, despite his fondness for Romulan ale.

"You probably didn't even put up a fight, did you?" I said to his image on my laptop.

I waited a for a reply, but the only sound was the hum of the air conditioner and my breathing.

"I thought Vulcans were supposed to be tough."

Still no reply.

I took a sip of my drink. Then another. Spock continued to stare out of the radioactive window. Kirk still looked stricken.

What would James Tiberius Kirk do in my situation? He wouldn't abandon his friend, that's for sure. Kirk famously refused to accept the no-win scenario. He'd figure something out.

I chugged down the last of the rum and Coke, set the laptop on the nightstand, and turned out the light.

Tomorrow, as soon as my car was ready, I'd drive back to the Styx River crossing. I'd look around. Maybe Spock had simply been blown out of the trunk by a passing semi and he was lurking in the weeds. Failing that, I'd contact some locals. Maybe I'd put an ad in the paper. Post something on Facebook. Call up the local radio station if there was one. Perhaps offer a reward. But I certainly would not do nothing.

It was good to have a plan.

"Good night, Spock," I said and closed my eyes.

He didn't reply, but Spock was never big on pleasantries.

CHAPTER 5

New Orleans, Two Days Earlier

THERE IS THIS overused joke that we tell in newsrooms: The three things you never ask a journalist to do are add and subtract.

That's slightly hyperbolic. After all, how could reporters check their bar tabs without addition? And those numbers can add up quickly.

Not only was I able to add and subtract, I could even multiply and do both long *and* short division. But I quickly discovered in college that I wasn't destined for a career in any occupation involving the need for calculus (which ruled out the sciences and engineering) and statistics (which ruled out social work) or spreadsheets (which ruled out business). This was not because I found them too challenging. It's because they are BORING.

But I could card count. Which is a useful skill at the blackjack tables, especially playing at an establishment that uses single decks of cards. That's the good news. The bad news is that few casinos do that anymore. Multiple decks are mixed together with automated shuffling machines making card counting harder and statistically (I suppose) less likely to work.

Still, of all the games of chance, blackjack offers the best odds of beating the house—if only marginally—assuming you know basic strategy (when to hit, when to hold, when to double down, when to split the cards in your hand, etc.) and with even rudimentary card counting your odds of winning—over time—improve. I say over time because as every gambler knows, winning and losing can be streaky. Bet heavy when you're on a heater then walk away from the table before giving it all back.

But as they say in the military, no plan of battle ever survives contact with the enemy, and my strategy for the evening vaporized when I stepped onto the casino floor and saw the sign outside the poker room that read:

Texas Hold 'Em Tournament

I referred to games of chance earlier. Blackjack, roulette, baccarat—these are all forms of gambling. On the other hand, poker—especially Texas Hold 'Em—is a game of skill. A game of psychology. True, you need to understand the odds, but the most important factor is understanding the players. Anyone who has ever watched *World Poker Tour* on TV understands this.

I approached the attendant at the poker room's reception desk and discovered play was about to begin. Buy-in was a reasonable $200, but it was a no-limit game, so I would have to be careful managing my limited cash supply. I took a seat at the table, stacked my chips, and hoped for the best.

Four hours later, I walked out of the poker room with ten black one-hundred-dollar chips in my pocket, flush with my winnings and a sense of redemption. I walked my new-found money over to the nearest blackjack table, one with a twenty-five dollar minimum bet, sat down at an empty seat, and put two black chips on the table.

I drew a two and a seven. Dealer showed a queen. I had no idea how the cards were running, and the conservative play would be to simply hit, but, no, with a snoot-full of Cuba Libres, I doubled down. That meant I had four-hundred dollars at play, forty percent of my poker winnings on one hand. I was feeling lucky.

Sometimes it's is better to be lucky than smart. I drew an ace, for a total of 20. A player to my left had blackjack, ace and ten, and was paid out. Two other players stayed with their hands. The final player hit and busted. The dealer flipped her hold card. It was a king. Twenty points. We'd tied.

I pulled my chips off the felt while the dealer slipped the cards into the auto-shuffler. Should I try again? Or should I not risk the vengeance of the poker gods by being greedy? I rose from the table and took my four black chips and cashed them in. The vibe felt off. And I had already been fortunate. Time to take Fred for a walk and call it a night.

I'd stashed Spock in my room's closet, still folded in half (he's cardboard and travels easily) but kept the door open in case Fred needed company. They get along. "Well team," I announced as I entered the room, "Lady Luck was good to me tonight."

Spock ignored me. Fred was sound asleep. What duds.

After learning from Madam Jazzabelle that my time was nearly up, it was nice to have some extra cash in my pocket—a much needed and well-earned morale boost. In a drunken moment, I thought I might wander back into the French Quarter, bang on her door again, flash my cash, and tell her, "Not bad for a dead man, huh?"

But that would be stupid. And immature. Even arrogant. Only an asshole would do something like that.

Which is how I found myself on Royal Street fifteen minutes later, ignoring my better judgment, which apparently I had used up by leaving the blackjack table when I did.

Oh, I told myself I had a different reason for venturing into the night. I'd recalled that lottery ticket I was going to buy. How that was the reason for visiting Madam Jazzabelle in the first place. The drawing wasn't until the next day, but a karmic instinct told me I should get it in New Orleans, not on the road somewhere else. I'd go with random, computer-selected numbers, since old Jazzy had been no help on that front.

I did exactly that—five Powerball tickets; predicted jackpot $67 million.

Walking back toward the hotel, I worked out some quick math in my head. After the deduction for taking a cash payout instead of the 30-year annuity, and after taxes, the actual take-home would be a paltry $25 million. Still, better than a sharp cliché' in the eye.

I decided I would split the loot with Uncle Leo. After all, I wouldn't have a dime in my pocket were it not for him. That would leave me about $12 million. If I invested wisely and earned, say, five percent interest on the untouched capital, that would bring in about $600,000 a year. Yeah, I could get by on that. Live in a marina, work on my tan, maybe take up golf. That's what all the rich guys did.

But that would be boring, wouldn't it? No, even with the cash flowing in, I'd need something entertaining to occupy my time. Maybe I'd buy out my partners in the news service. Instead of writing about weird news, I'd be a publisher. Which after a few seconds' consideration also sounded boring—hiring and firing, paying bills, grubbing for subscribers and advertisers. Yuk.

So maybe I'd start a foundation. Do something genuinely useful. Create a school for orphans, or build affordable housing, or find a cure for gingivitis. My imagination rolled like that until I came to the corner of Canal and Royal streets. I glanced up Royal and was surprised to see the street was ablaze with flashing lights.

Like a moth attracted to a flame, I walked in the direction of the strobes until I found myself outside Madam Jazzabelle's shop. The pulsating lights were atop a white ambulance emblazoned with the words: New Orleans EMS.

CHAPTER 6

New Orleans, The Next Day

UNIVERSITY MEDICAL CENTER is about a mile from Harrah's Hotel and Casino near the Interstate 10 overpass on Canal Street, a not unpleasant walk in the early morning, which is what I was doing, I'm not entirely sure why, carried along by some indefinable impulse—more than curiosity, perhaps concern, maybe some odd sense of connection.

They'd hauled Madam Jazzabelle out of her little parlor of prophesy on a gurney and rushed her away in the ambulance, lights flashing, but no sirens for some reason. I hoped it wasn't because she'd already given up the ghost.

I'd called the hospital later that evening to check on her status, but they had no record of anyone in the ER by the name Jazzabelle. No surprise there. So I took a stab at calling someone who might help me at the *Times-Picayune*, the NOLA daily, so named for the price of the newspaper when it was founded in 1837—one picayune, a Spanish coin equal to about six cents.

I got lucky. Madam Jazzabelle, a.k.a. Shirley DuMont, was a colorful and much-written-about New Orleans personality who, in various incarnations, had been a street dancer, a nearly successful candidate for city council, the winner of a Mardi Gras "Best Breasts" contest sponsored by a Bourbon Street saloon, and had, prior to becoming a Royal Street oracle, been the proprietor of the Little Shop of Whores, a museum celebrating the world's oldest profession that was shut down after a rare New Orleans vice squad raid when, prosecutors alleged, the shop's back rooms were discovered being used for what were described as "demonstration studios." Hence the "madam" in Madam Jazzabelle.

The night-shift guy on the *Time-Picayune* city desk said DuMont learned palm reading while serving time in the county lockup. And that when she was released, her fans held a massive GoFundMe drive and raised enough money to set her up as a French Quarter soothsayer.

After hearing that, I absolutely had to check on her. How could any journalist specializing in weird news pass up the chance to interview an oddball character like her? She was a column waiting to be written. I only hoped the next story about her, by me or anyone else, wasn't an obituary.

In the morning, I called the hospital's admissions office, flim-flammed them a bit by saying I was her nephew, and eventually was given the room number of Shirley DuMont who had been admitted the night before and was now in Patient Tower 3. The hospital had three color-coordinated buildings, and Shirley's was purple. Somehow that seemed right to me; orange and green, the colors of the other two towers, were clearly insufficiently exotic.

I snuck Fred outside in my gym bag for his morning bathroom break, hung the Do Not Disturb sign on the door when we returned, and strode out of the hotel and up Canal Street toward the hospital.

The massive Adler's jewelry store clock overhanging the cobble-stone sidewalk said it was 9:05. Checkout was at 11:00, ample time to pay a visit to Madam Jazzabelle, throw my belongings into a suitcase, then continue my journey to Florida.

A slender middle-age man wearing a fedora was sitting on the sidewalk and picking an electric guitar in front of the VooDoo Mart, strumming melodies from the Beach Boys. I dropped a couple of bucks into his jar. I grew up listening to Uncle Leo's vast collection of old tunes. Unfortunately, I have this irresistible compulsion to rewrite the lyrics in my head. They become earworms that take me hours, sometimes days, to shake off.

The Beach Boys lyrics were especially easy to rewrite and I used to amuse my high school friends with my revisions of their hits—although some of my pals pretended not to like my singing voice. But I knew they were only kidding because of Jo Jean Jackson. Jo Jean was the hottest girl in my class, way out of my league, but she thought my voice was godlike. One day I was singing a Monkeys rework right before the start of class and I overheard her tell a girlfriend: "Sweet Jesus, Zander's doing it again." Now that was music to my ears.

Across Canal Street at Rampart, the historic Saenger Theater advertised that Cody Jinks was playing that weekend and Weird Al Yankovic would be on stage soon thereafter. A red and gold streetcar turned onto Canal Street and a banner on its side noted that French Quarter Phantoms was "the #1 Haunted Tour" in the city.

I'd never taken a haunted tour of any ranking in any city. I didn't believe in ghosts and goblins. Bill Murray and the rest of the Ghostbusters killed them all dead as far as I was concerned. You want to make the case for zombies, UFOs, vampires, deities who walk on water, be my guest. I'm a sucker for good stories. I'll listen. But the burden of proof is on you.

I crossed North Clairborne Avenue where an encampment of homeless people rested, permanently enshadowed by the I-10 overpass. I counted a dozen tents and lean-tos and as many people milling about. Discarded clothing littered the area and drifted onto the sidewalk in heaps, like seaweed on an untended beach. From their tents, the denizens could gaze across the manicured lawn that served as a grassy moat between the interstate highway and the gleaming new University Medical Center.

I walked over. A man and woman younger than me were sitting on the ground outside their small red and gray tent. I leaned down beside them and handed them a twenty-dollar bill.

"What's this for?" the guy asked.

"It's for you, dude. I've been here."

When I was young, my mother and I couch-surfed and stayed in homeless shelters in the Austin area for a couple of years until she finally found a real job and she was able to rent an apartment. It's the first permanent roof over my head that I recall. It was small and dingy, but I had my very own room. I was in heaven. That was the Christmas Spock came into my life, the best present my mother ever gave me.

Then one day she left me alone in that apartment, told Spock he was in charge, and went to meet her maker trying to save an eyeless spider, as if a bug were more important than her only child. Her last words to me before she left were, "I won't be long, Alex."

What a liar. Not that I'm bitter or anything.

And I shouldn't be. Not really. Things worked out well, actually, thanks to the kindness and generosity of my mother's brother. I was lucky. Not everyone is.

I entered the hospital through automatic sliding glass doors at a rear entrance near the parking lot. A uniformed guard in the sally port nodded at me, but didn't ask for identification, so I strolled through the second set of automated doors unchallenged.

To the left of the entrance a couple of hospital employees in surgical greens were drinking coffee in an alcove identified as the Resident and Student Dining Area. To the right, a short hallway led to elevators to Patient Tower 3.

I paused as the elevator door slid open. I won't say I broke out into hives, but staring into the confined and menacing space did not lower my blood pressure. Damned claustrophobia. Plagued with misgivings, I courageously walked in and placed my back against the rear of the ominously empty car. As the door closed before me, I began practicing my relaxation breathing, inhaling deeply, exhaling slowly.

Did you ever try NOT thinking about being crushed to death in a collapsing elevator car? It doesn't work. I could feel myself begin to perspire. The walls were closing in. Was the ceiling descending? And then, after an eternity, my heart hammering, my breathing accelerated, the doors finally, blessedly reopened and I stepped out.

I was on the third floor.

The 'vator disgorged into a small reception area where a large woman sat behind a counter guarding the entrance to the patients' rooms and nursing stations. She was middle-aged with the broad shoulders of a linebacker and gray hair that drooped off her head like a sagging clump of Spanish moss. And she was scowling into a computer screen. Perhaps she was engaged in important hospital business. Or maybe deciding upon her cafeteria options—would it be the steamed peas and onions or the Italian wedding soup? I waited patiently. She didn't look up. Maybe I was invisible. I looked down at my hands. I could see them. But perhaps invisible people can see themselves. Finally, I cleared my throat.

"Yes?" she asked without looking up. An economy of words. No "may I help you?" No "how's it goin?" Not even a "what the fuck do you want?" Only "yes."

Was it Shakespeare who said, "brevity is the soul of wit"? Take away her glower, her mossy hairdo, her apparent disinterest, and perchance underneath it all was a humorous, delightful woman with an outgoing personality ready to burst from behind the bleak curtain of her protective disguise and engage in a round of witty repartee. I decided to give her the benefit of the doubt.

"Hello to you, too. I'm looking for a patient. Shirley DuMont."

She glanced up from her computer screen, her scowl deepening, forming furrows Grand Canyon-deep across her face. Then she crossed her arms over her enormous chest. "So's everybody else."

Ah! Progress.

"I do apologize if I've taken you away from critical tasks at your station, ma'am, but I have an appointment with Ms. DuMont."

Now she was giving me curious. I was winning her over, I could tell.

"You a lawyer?"

I was wearing my Midget Handjob tee shirt, cargo shorts, and deck shoes. If she'd asked if I were delivering pizza, it might have made some sort of sense. But lawyer? Maybe lots of Louisiana attorneys wore obscure rock band tee shirts. Or maybe this was her hidden wit bubbling out from her dim exterior. I went with it.

"How'd you guess?"

Now, that's not a lie, actually, is it?

"Well, good luck with that," she said. "She's gone."

"Gone as in discharged?"

"No, gone as in skipped out. And it's not the first time."

Now that was interesting. I leaned down, casually rested my palms on her counter, and said, "Really?"

You could almost hear the rusty gears grinding inside her unlubricated skull. She gave me a long stare, a bit of a squint, and finally said, "You're not a lawyer, are you?"

Hmmm. So much for the "wit" theory.

"Would you believe pizza delivery guy?"

Blood rushed to her face, and while I'm sure it was my imagination, her head seemed to swell. She swiveled in her chair, which let out a mournful groan as she turned, and called to a nurse who'd walked into the lobby holding an iPad. "Shelly, can you step over here?"

Shelly, in contrast to her colleague, was young, slim, articulate, and her green eyes shined with intelligence.

"Hi," she said. "Can I help you?"

"Hope so," I said. "I came to see Shirley DuMont. I was at her shop yesterday—you know, Madam Jazzabelle's?"

She nodded cautiously.

"I went by last night and saw the ambulance, called the hospital, and was told she was here. I felt badly about that and thought I'd drop by. Not sure why, really, but something just, I don't know, something kind of compelled me to come by—if that makes any sense?"

I was giving her my *aw shucks* treatment, and I was sure she saw through it, but she couldn't fight off a quick smile.

"Anyway," I continued, "your *endomorphic* colleague here said she's left the building and it seems to be a habit, and I was wondering what the heck that's about."

She shook her head. "We can't talk about patients."

"Even regulars like her?"

"Even regulars like…" Then she caught herself, frowned, and she did the arm-crossing thing, too.

"Okay, I'm going to level with you," I said. "Everything I told you is true. But there's more. She read my palm and seemed shocked. Said she saw death. And it's been bugging me. So, well, here I am."

Shelly continued staring at me for several beats, then said, "Death."

"Yes."

"Your death?"

"It was my palm she was reading."

"Well, if you feel a serious case of deadness coming on, come back and see us."

She seemed to be cutting off our conversation, which was disappointing. After all, I'd been giving her my best 200-watt smile and my practiced, relaxed, and open body language. Maybe it was the Midget Handjob tee shirt.

"You know, rejection can be extremely damaging to a guy's self-esteem."

"I'm sure you're used to it."

With that she turned to her iPad and began memorizing the screen. I knew it was pointless to linger, so I retreated to the elevator bank. But before I punched the down button I spotted an exit sign and navigated my way to the stairs, thus eluding that death trap.

So Madam Jazzabelle was AWOL. Maybe she was back at work. Since I would pass Royal Street on my return trip to the hotel, I decided to swing by. The streets were crowded with tourists, and shopkeepers hung outside their doorways like carnival barkers hoping to lure visitors—and their dollars—inside. I walked to the front door of Madam Jazzabelle's palace of palmistry and tried the handle, but it was locked. I knocked several times to no avail. I was feeling a sense of *déjà vu* all over again.

I wandered into an antique shop next door named Vieux Carrie' Curios and struck up a conversation with the proprietor, an older guy with white hair, a Clive Cussler goatee, and a dense Cajun accent who tried to sell me an old microscope, or he could have been asking me if I wanted a vasectomy, hard to tell, Cajun being only slightly more intelligible than Mandarin.

I struck out at three other shops along Royal Street, where at least they spoke English but had no useful information on Madam Jazzabelle. At least none that they would share to a nosey stranger. The clock was ticking and I was becoming concerned about checking out of the hotel on time. I'd done all that I could do.

It's a short stroll from the corner of Royal and Canal streets to the casino entrance. I'd struck out at the hospital and at Madam Jazzabelle's. Maybe I could make it a trifecta and lose a few drachma in the casino en route back to my hotel room. It's a shortcut, really, so beelining through the casino really wouldn't take any longer even with a quick stop to, as they say on Wall Street, improve my financial position. That's what I told myself.

There were three gamblers squatting at a Caribbean Poker table, two were middle-aged women, one in jeans, another wearing baggy green shorts, both sporting fanny packs. The third player was an older man with thinning hair whose circus tent of a fishing shirt failed to hide the beach ball he'd apparently swallowed for breakfast. I pulled out my wallet and sat down, promising myself that I would play only one hand. Win or lose, that would be it, then I would get Fred and go.

"Oh, cool wallet," the woman in the baggy green shorts said. It's made of blue translucent plastic with an embroidered red and gold Superman emblem.

"Watch out," fishing-shirt man said. "This guy"—he was nodding at the dealer—"he's made of kryptonite."

"Change one hundred," the dealer intoned as he took my cash.

35

Then he shoved over three green twenty-five dollar chips, four red five-dollar chips, and a stack of white one dollar chips. His hands did not appear to be green, nor did they glow. I concluded Beachball Belly didn't know as much about kryptonite as he'd like people to believe.

I bet one dollar on the Jackpot spot and played a green chip on the ante. I drew a pair of Jacks with a seven, eight, and nine—all of unmatched suits. The dealer showed a four of diamonds. A pair of Jacks isn't the worst hand. I deposited two twenty-five dollar chips on the felt and hoped for the best. The dealer revealed a pair of threes, a two, and a seven. I had doubled my money.

I scraped my chips, left four whites for the dealer, and took the rest to the cashier. I would leave New Orleans a winner. To hell with Madam Jazzabelle and her dire prediction of my fate.

There was a commotion outside my room when I returned to the hotel. The housekeeper was knocking on the door despite my Do Not Disturb sign. As I approached, I could hear Fred barking inside the room.

"Do you have a dog in there?" she demanded, all frowny and disapproving.

"Don't be silly."

"Then what's that sound?"

"Oh that? That's my alarm clock." I dug into my wallet and pulled out a fiver. "Here. Sorry for the confusion. I'll be out the door in a jiffy."

I slipped the key card into the lock and looked over my shoulder. She was hovering, ready to catch me lying.

"Oh, look," I said, gesturing down the hall. "Somebody's ripping off your cart."

She didn't go for the head-fake, so I cracked the door, scooted in, and slammed it shut. If there's a Guinness record for blowing out of hotel rooms, I set it.

CHAPTER 7

Pensacola

I WAS TEN thousand feet above the planet Oa when my power ring began vibrating, making an unusual buzzing noise. Was it out of juice? Was I about to plunge to an ignominious death, an embarrassment to the Green Lantern Corps? I awoke with a start.

But the buzzing persisted.

The sound was coming from the Motel 6 nightstand. I glanced over and my iPhone was illuminated with an incoming call. The time was 6:30 a.m.

I snatched the smart phone off the table and saw that the number was from the 352 area code. Probably a robocall, but I clicked the green ACCEPT button anyway.

"This better be good."

"It's Tess," a small, female voice said. Tess Winkler, my friend, the journalist I planned to visit in Gainesville. I'd met her years ago at a wild party in Austin involving prodigious quantities of alcohol and other recreational activities. She'd been in town visiting a mutual friend at the student newspaper, *The Daily Texan*. We'd stayed in touch ever since.

"I need you," she said.

"You and countless women across America."

There was a pause. "I'm in jail."

That should have been a surprise, I suppose, but I knew of at least two previous occasions Tess had found herself behind bars. The first was an underage drinking bust during her freshman year at the University of Florida. More recently, she'd been detained by police when her roommate, a woman named Amelia Duffy, disappeared and the cops received an anonymous tip there was blood on her kitchen floor. The tipster said that if the blood were tested it would match Duffy's' DNA.

And it did.

Tess had returned home from a three-day weekend to discover her roommate missing, a small pool of dried blood near the kitchen sink, and yellow crime-scene tape blocking her door as cops and lab techs milled about her small two-bedroom bungalow in southeast Gainesville.

They'd hauled her off to the police station and held her overnight, but released her the next day when her alibi checked out. Her story: She was visiting friends in Tampa. Cops confirmed it with a few phone calls.

That was a year ago. Duffy was still missing.

"Who'd you kill this time?" I asked.

"I punched a cop."

It took me a few beats to process that, and when she didn't elaborate, I asked: "So, this cop, he deserved it, right?"

"No. He was breaking up a bar fight. I wasn't trying to hit him, but his face got in the way."

When I'd promised Tess I'd stop by on my way to Goodland, I hadn't anticipated that visit taking place at the Alachua County Jail. It was only going to be a quick detour, mourn the folding of her newspaper, then off to my new life in the marina.

Now this.

"So, you need bail or something?"

"My first court appearance is this morning. I'm lawyered up and she says if we can convince the judge it was all a misunderstanding, I should be able to make bail."

"And if not?"

"Under Florida law, aggravated battery of a law enforcement officer carries a minimum mandatory prison sentence of five years."

"Great Caesar's ghost!"

"Yeah. But my lawyer's pretty smart, and it's not like I sent the cop to the hospital or anything."

"Glad you pulled your punch."

Early morning sunlight was creeping through the motel window's curtains. A truck rumbled outside my door. People were chattering in the parking lot. Like it or not, the day had begun.

"So, you in Florida yet?" she asked.

"I'm in Pensacola. Had a little car trouble. I'm getting it fixed today, although there's a complication."

As soon as I said that I felt foolish. In my defense, I hadn't had any coffee yet and it takes several cups of caffeine to clear the sleep from my brain.

"Of course there's a complication," she said. "It's you."

"Forget it. I'll deal with that later. I'll get there as soon as I can. If you make bail, I can reach you on your phone, right? If you don't answer, I should assume you're still in the hoosegow? And what's your lawyer's name in case I can't reach you? And what do you need me to do?"

"It's a better interviewing technique to ask one question at a time," she said. Tess sounded tired. "And, yeah, that's why I called. I need your help with something. I'll fill you in when you get here."

"Why not now?"

"They record all the calls, I think."

That sounded paranoid, but I went with it.

"Alright. I think I need a new alternator, then I can be on my way."

"That's your complication?" she asked. Apparently there was no imminent threat of the turnkeys ripping the phone out of her hands.

"No, and this is stupid, but the complication is Spock. He's missing."

"Missing? How?"

"Look, you've got bigger fish to fry with…"

"Are you kidding? It's Spock. He's, like, your best friend, right? Where is he?"

"You really want to talk about this now?"

"Yeah, tell me about it. As soon as I hang up, they're taking me back to my cell. How the fuck do you lose a Vulcan?"

I filled her in on my car troubles, how the wrecker guy said my trunk had been popped or maybe blown open.

"So, the last time you saw Spock was when you put him in the trunk?" she asked.

I started to say yes, an automatic response. That's where Spock had traveled the entire trip. Then a random synapse sparked and I paused. What was that? It took a few beats, but eventually my cranial hard drive spit out the answer.

"Oh, fuck! You know what? I may have left him in my room in New Orleans. I was in this big-ass hurry to get out of the hotel. I remember throwing my stuff in my suitcase, hiding Fred in my gym bag…"

"Who's Fred…"

"My dog. He was spooked. I think it was the maid's vacuum cleaner out in the hallway, and he was barking, and the maid was pounding on the door, and the thing is they don't allow dogs at Harrah's, so I was shoving him into my gym bag…"

"Gym bag?"

"Yeah, he's little. And, dammit, dammit, dammit, I must have left Spock in the closet. What an idiot."

"Some friend you are. Poor Spock."

"Sweet baby Jesus."

"Don't go blaming Jesus for your troubles." She was laughing, although I certainly didn't see anything funny about the situation. Hers or mine.

"Oops," she said. "I gotta go. Find me when you get here. And get Spock!" That was a shout, and the line went dead.

A hot shower, two cups of passable motel coffee, and three phone calls later I learned that Mike's Automotive would be working on my car that afternoon. If it was the alternator, it would eat up a sizeable chunk of my poker winnings and the Sebring would not be available until late in the day. A receptionist at Harrah's confirmed the brooding presence of a Vulcan in their lost-and-found closet. And I learned that the nearest rental car dealer was right across the street next to Whataburger, something I had failed to notice the night before.

By nine o'clock, I was on the road with a tall cup of coffee in the rental's cup holder and a Whataburger Breakfast on a Bun on my lap. It's a six hour round trip between Pensacola and NOLA. With any luck I'd be back right about the time my car was ready.

As I entered I-10 westbound, I reflected that if the Sebring hadn't died, if Tess hadn't called, Spock might have been lost forever. Isn't it fascinating how random events can alter the course of your life? That's what I was thinking as I, once again, crossed the River Styx.

However, I was wrong about that. There was nothing random about it. Nothing whatsoever. It was always going to happen. But I wouldn't discover that until much later.

CHAPTER 8

New Orleans, The Return Trip

I HAD JUST cleared the tunnel under the Mobile River, an hour into the drive back to NOLA, when my phone lit up and I saw I had an incoming call from Uncle Leo.

"Twenty-four hours a day, seven days a week, this is Alexander Strange."

"Don't you get tired of that joke?" Leo asked.

"Guess not."

"So, you make it to Goodland yet?"

"Nope, had a little detour. Car broke down outside of Pensacola. It's in the shop. Now I'm in a rental heading back to the Big Easy to pick up Spock."

"Spock's in New Orleans?"

"Would you believe me if I told you he was too hung over to travel?"

"I don't know. Are you likely to say something that absurd?"

"Would you believe I had to blow town in a hurry and forgot him?"

"Okay, let me hear it."

I related the entire shaggy dog story including my encounter with Madam Jazzabelle, my winning night at the casino, and the odd conversation that morning with Tess Winkler.

"What's this Winkler woman want from you anyway?" he asked.

"Not entirely sure. She needs help with something, but she was vague about it. Said she couldn't tell me because the phones in the jail might be bugged."

"You bet your ass they are. And if she was worried about that, it sounds sketchy. Look nephew, you don't need my advice—and I'd stroke out if you ever took it—but you sure you need a distraction like this? Now of all times when you're trying to get your career restarted in a brand new place with a brand new company?"

Leo's a born worrier. But I knew his heart was in the right place.

"It'll be fine, Leo," I assured him. "I've got my priorities straight."

That earned a snort. "I know all about the priorities of guys your age. I may be old but my memory's still intact."

There was commotion in the background and then a woman's voice came on the line. It was my cradle-robbing uncle's latest wife, Sarah.

"Hi, Mom," I said. It annoys the bejesus out of her when I call her that. But it is technically accurate. Since Leo adopted me, and they're married, it does make her my stepmother. Even though she's only fifteen years older than me and could easily pass for thirty.

"You have to do that, don't you? You must hate me. But I'm not going to let you ruin a perfectly good morning. Leonard is taking me to brunch and I see a mimosa in my future. I only wanted to check on Freddie."

I didn't hate Sarah and she knew it. But I did needle her. Maybe I needed to dial that back a little.

"I'm in the car right now or I'd Facetime you and let you say hello. But he's doing fine. He's a good little traveling buddy. I'll send you some pictures next time we stop."

"Thank you, Alexander."

Leo came back on the line. "Gotta go. Watch your back down there. It's Florida. Everybody's fucking nuts."

We hung up.

Earlier on the trip, I'd tuned into talk radio to catch up on the news. The first item turned out to be disappointing. Six warehouse workers in Fayetteville, Arkansas had won the lottery. So much for my dream of living a life of philanthropy. I knew in my heart of hearts that they, unlike me, would squander the money. Probably blow their winnings on red plastic pig hats and season tickets to the Razorbacks. They would never, ever even try to find a cure for gingivitis.

Scanning the dial, I also stumbled onto a broadcast by the Rev. Lee Roy Chitango on his *Oh God, Oh God Radio Network*. Today the Sermonator was calling on Congress to enact a law that would require all atheists and homosexuals to be registered, like sex offenders. "For the sake of the God-fearing Christians who founded this great nation we need protection from these wolves in cheap clothing." Never mind that Thomas Jefferson was an avowed deist, like many other Founding Fathers. And, come on, everyone knows that *Canis lupus* is a sharp dresser.

Back on the news station, a customer at a Publix supermarket in Safety Harbor returned to her car to find a shopping cart chained and padlocked to her roof. "Twice last week you failed to use the cart corral. Your misbehavior has been avenged." It was signed "M.M." Which callers to the radio station said stood for Mister Manners. And "M.M." had struck the previous week outside Orlando by Super Gluing shut the windows of a pickup truck that he alleged had been playing music too loud.

And in Fort Walton Beach, south of Interstate 10 in the Florida Panhandle, police arrested a 37-year-old man for attacking a mattress with a bedpost claiming that zombies were hiding inside. He was turned in by his girlfriend, whom he was holding hostage "for her safety," but who escaped by jumping out a second-story window where she broke her ankle, but was able to call the cops. By the time the police arrived the zombies had fled.

All of these news reports were an inspiration.

"Yes!" I shouted, startling Fred in the back seat. "This is awesome."

"Gerrrufff," he responded.

"Fred, this is going to be great. We're going to have a field day in Florida. Leo was right. These people are fucking crazy. They'll write my column for me."

I had only been on my cross-country road trip for a few days, but already I could feel the itch to get back in front of the keyboard. Florida! My kind of place. No offense to Arizona or any of the other forty-nine states, but if you were going to be in the business of reporting on the news of the utterly and completely weird, you needed to be in the land of the hanging chads, God's waiting room, where it's never too hot for Kevlar vests. The punch lines were endless.

I pulled into Harrah's right at noon and strode into the lobby where I was escorted to a room where the hotel staff keeps lost-and-found items.

Spock was folded in half and seemed unperturbed to be resting in the darkened closet. No greeting, and I didn't expect one. But no admonitions, either. After our years together, I think he's gotten used to the occasional curveball in our relationship.

Now I had him propped up in the back of the Ford rental, pinned to the seat by my huge suitcase. Figured he might as well enjoy the view as we returned to Florida with no danger of him blowing out of a rental hard top. Fred was snoozing beside him.

I pulled out of the hotel loading zone, my intention to make my way straight onto I-10 and back to Pensacola, but somehow I found myself drawn, like a planchette on a Ouija board, in the direction of Royal Street and Madam Jazzabelle's place.

She'd been rude to me. And she'd conned me with that Styx River nonsense knowing I would literally cross the river while driving to Florida. Apparently, she was also a world-class hypochondriac, or so I gathered from the hospital staff. I imagined regular trips to the ER every time she broke out in a sweat.

I'd asked Siri about that as I was driving back to New Orleans.

There's a condition called hyperhidrosis, a medical term for excessive sweating, which can be caused by alcohol abuse, diabetes, infections, lymphatic tumors, and other terrible maladies. There also was a disease in the Middle Ages called English Sweating Sickness, nearly always fatal, that scientists now think was caused by a hantavirus. And some people simply sweat a lot.

Or perhaps she really did see something in my palm, and my literally crossing the Styx River near the Florida state line was merely a coincidence. She said she'd never been to Florida. Maybe she'd never heard of the river, either. I hadn't. But those thoughts did not brighten my day as it could mean she actually did see something dreadful in my future.

Then again, if she were prone to over-reacting, as the nurses seemed to feel, maybe she got it wrong and my death wasn't imminent after all.

Perhaps just serious injury.

Or maiming.

See, you have to look at the bright side.

I pulled up to Madam Jazzabelle's, parked illegally, and saw movement through the shop's window. I told Spock to keep an eye on Fred and stepped out of the rental car. Her front door appeared different in two respects: One, it was not only unlocked but slightly ajar. And a white legal-sized flier had been posted on the door displaying a large headline that read:

EVICTION
NOTICE

I pushed the door wide and stepped inside the gloomy interior. "Yoo-hoo. Grim Reaper here. Anybody home."

Jazzy stepped out from behind the curtain at the back of the room, looked me up and down, then allowed herself a brief smile. Her pink wraparound sunglasses were propped on her forehead and her curly ebony hair was a spray of confusion that framed her face. No turban this morning.

"Still heading to Florida?"

"Been there and returned. Thought I'd stop off and let you know I figured out your Styx River trick."

She cocked her head. "Trick? What trick?"

"There's an actual Styx River between here and the Florida State line."

"And that's what you thought I was talking about?"

"That's what you implied."

"That's what you inferred."

"Inferred. That's a sophisticated word for a French Quarter palm reader."

"Chirologist. And I wasn't always reading palms down here, sonny. At least I don't think so."

She started to say something else, but paused. She gazed at me dolefully for a few seconds with those lupine eyes.

"Nobody, me included, knows what happens to us when we pass," she said. "Pearly Gates? The River Styx? It's the ultimate unknown." She reached her hands out to me, like she wanted to examine my palms again, but I stepped back.

"Okay," she said. "But what I told you, about seeing death…" Again she paused. "I wouldn't lie about a thing like that."

"That's comforting. Not."

"The truth often isn't. And truth telling is often lonely business. Which is how I can help."

"Help, how?"

"Help by coming with you."

With that, she stuffed what appeared to be a journal into a canvas briefcase, looked around the shop as if she were leaving it for the last time, then picked up a paisley carpet bag lying atop the circular table where she had divined my fate.

"You saying you need a ride?" I asked.

"In the worst way."

"Ever travel by coffin?"

She ignored that and marched out the door. I followed.

"This your ride?"

She didn't wait for an answer. She opened the passenger-side rear door and crammed her bags on the floor in front of where I had Fred strapped in on the back seat. She patted him on the head, closed the door, then climbed into the front passenger seat.

She was so assertive, and utterly confident that I would go along with all this, that I just stood there transfixed. Charmed, really.

She stared up at me through the open passenger door and lowered her sunglasses onto her face. "Come on. We need to get going."

She glanced around, her brows furrowed. Any moment she'd break out in a sweat again and I'd be rushing her to the hospital. I climbed in behind the wheel, cranked the rental, and we pulled away from the curb.

"You know," I said, "I only came by here on a whim. What would you have done if I hadn't shown up."

She scanned me through her rose colored glasses.

"I knew you'd come for me. You always do."

CHAPTER 9

Gainesville, Florida

Tess Winkler swung open the door to her white clapboard bungalow in southeastern Gainesville. She wore a wide smile that gleamed in her porch light but froze when she saw I wasn't alone.

"Alex," she said. "I didn't know you were bringing a friend."

It had been nearly a decade since I had last seen her in person—although we corresponded regularly on social media. She'd been nineteen, drunk, and laughing. She wasn't laughing now. She had a fatigued look, probably from lack of sleep overnight in the jail. The right arm of her eyeglasses—storm-window thick—was held in place by a bandage of masking tape.

Tess reached out and offered her hand to Jazzy. Her fingernails, polish-free, were chewed to the nubs. "Hi," she said. "Name's Esther, but everybody calls me Tess."

Jazzy stepped past me and took her hand. "Hi. Aquaman and I only met recently. I was in a jam and he gave me a ride."

"Aquaman?" Tess frowned. "That what you call yourself now?"

"Uh, I've no idea where that came from."

Jazzy glanced back at me. "He was on the swim team at Texas. I give everybody nicknames."

How did she know that? When we first me, I'd told her I swam.

But I hadn't said where. Nor anything about swimming competitively. It never came up during our drive.

We'd made two stops en route to Gainesville. The first was in Pensacola where I turned in the rental and reclaimed my Sebring. As I feared, much of my poker winnings were now in the hands of the owner of Mike's Automotive. I'd left Fred's car seat in the convertible when we'd abandoned it at the state line. He hopped right back into his elevated, sheepskin perch as soon as I opened the door to the convertible. And Jazzy and I followed.

We stopped again outside Tallahassee for gas and burgers—and a cigarette break for her. She offered to buy the gas, but I told her I would expense it and slipped the receipt into my backpack. Then she'd asked me how far south I was heading, wondering if we'd end up anywhere near Key West. I wasn't driving that far, I told her. But on Marco Island, where the town of Goodland is located, she could catch a ferry. She liked that. I also told her I planned to stop in Gainesville, that I had a friend who'd asked me for some help.

"You seem to be in the habit of helping people," she said.

Not a question, a statement. As if she knew me so well. And apparently she knew enough about me to know where I went to college. Madam Jazzabelle, woman of mystery.

Tess invited us in, then told Jazzy, "Any acquaintance of Aquaman's is welcome here. You got a name?"

"Shirley. Shirley Dumont. Although he's taken to calling me Jazzy."

"Jazzy is it?"

Tess was giving me a curious look.

"Madam Jazzabelle. It's her business name. Until this morning, she operated a fortune teller's..."

"...chirologist."

"...chirologist's shop in New Orleans. She's a palm reader."

"Chirologist."

"I know the difference between a chirologist and a palm reader," Tess said. "Studied up on it when I was in college."

"You studied palm reading…"

"… chirology…"

"…in college?"

"At *The Agi-Gator*. We had this brainstorm, trying to figure ways to make some extra money to keep the lights on. We published a guide to weird places in Florida. There's a village, the Cassadaga Spiritualist Camp, not far from Daytona Beach. We had a lot of stuff about tarot cards, palm reading, mediums, all that crystal-powered malarkey."

"Have you ever had *your* palm read?" Jazzy asked, slightly edgy, apparently taking umbrage at the malarkey remark.

"It's on a long list of things I intend never to do." She pointed down a short hallway. "You can have the guest room on the left. Alex, I'll make down the couch. It's a sofa-bed."

I'm an experienced couch surfer, so that was no problem. Although I would be lying if I denied that I'd wondered—before Jazzy interloped—what the sleeping arrangements might turn out to be. It had been a long time, and it had been only one night, but the question was inescapable.

The guest room was her missing roommate's old digs. She hadn't sublet the place since Amelia Duffy disappeared. If the choice were the guest room or the couch, I was happier with the couch. Not that I believed Amy's old room was haunted or anything. I am, after all, an enlightened 21st century skeptic. As noted earlier, until evidence is presented to the contrary, I don't believe in ghosts, vampires, or that the Miami Dolphins will ever again win the Super Bowl.

Still, it felt creepy, so I was happy for Jazzy to have the guest room. Maybe she could channel Amy and discover where she'd disappeared to.

Tess must have seen the look on my face. "It's not fucking possessed. Lots of people have slept there."

"Any of them survive?"

That earned me an exaggerated eye-roll. I returned the favor with a clownish wink.

She helped me unload the car while Jazzy loitered on the porch to catch up on her nicotine. I set Spock up in the guest room. "Keep an eye on her," I told him. "Report any suspicious or paranormal activity."

Then I took Fred for a walk around the neighborhood of older homes, cafes, and bail bondsmen—all college town essentials. Tess's house was within walking distance of the historic Hippodrome Theater, which at that time was featuring a production of Alfred Hitchcock's *North by Northwest*. And, I learned later, her newspaper office on Main Street was only a few blocks away.

When Fred and I returned, I poured the remains of a bottled water into one bowl and dog food into another, then set Fred's car seat by the sofa-bed with his blanket. When I got to Goodland, I'd get him a real doggie bed. Meanwhile, he seemed to like the car seat perfectly fine.

Jazzy had lingered on the patio during all this and finally re-entered the house and announced she hadn't slept much in the hospital and was going to crash. Why was she hospitalized? What was with the urgent need to blow town? No answers yet. I tried to ask during our drive, but she deflected my questions. Well, tomorrow would be another day.

Tess and I settled across from one another at her circular kitchen table. It was a retro dinette set with chrome edges, a white laminate surface and four matching chairs in white and red vinyl with chrome legs. Uncle Leo has a similar table in the little dining nook off his kitchen. He says it reminds him of Ozzie and Harriet, whoever they are.

She poured herself a cup of coffee and added a dribble of milk from the fridge.

"You drinking coffee this late?" I asked. "No offense, but you look like you could use a little shut-eye."

She laughed. "Yeah, didn't get many Zs at the jail. But I can drink caffeine all day and fall right asleep. Some sort of genetic mutation, I think."

I had a glass of tap water. Not because it was my first choice for an evening beverage, but after her DUI bust, Tess didn't keep booze in the house.

Tess, like Jazzy, was a petite woman. Long, light-brown hair framed her round, freckled face. Her taped-up glasses were the same shade as her hair—a nice bit of color coordination. She was dressed casually—tan shorts, white flip flops, and a loose-fitting black t-shirt with white letters that read:

FEMINISM

n. the radical notion that women are people.

"Nice tee," I said.

"Same to you. Never heard of Jesus Chrysler Super Car."

"Arizona band."

"Music any good?"

"No clue. I'm just into obscure rock band tee shirts."

She grinned briefly then reached into a bowl of sugar cubes on the table and dropped one into her cup launching concentric rings of amber coffee waves that radiated to the cup's edge, then bounced back. I didn't realize they still made sugar cubes. Maybe it was a Florida thing. I remembered reading that sugar was big business here.

"So," I said. "You made bail?"

She set her cup on the table, leaned back, and ran her fingers through her hair.

"Released on my own recognizance." She shook her head. "Get this. There's this Florida law that says anyone involved in a brawl can't file assault charges because when you get into a fist fight you have to expect to get punched."

"But it was a cop."

"Yes, but he was off duty and out of uniform. Actually, he may not have a uniform. He's a detective. Anyway, my lawyer thinks she can get the charges dropped."

I took a sip of water. It tasted terrible. I remembered how awful Florida water can be when it's unfiltered. Chalky.

"So what was the fight about?"

"Amy's brother…"

"Amy?"

"Amelia. Amelia Duffy, my disappeared roommate?'

I rolled my hand, a dismissive signal for her to continue. Like I should have known which of all the world's countless Amys she was referring to.

"His name's Darnell. Darnell Duffy. Everybody calls him D2, which sort of sounds like shorthand for R2D2, except not. Anyway, he's Amy's older half-brother and he believes I'm the reason she became a lesbian, that I converted her or something, me being a *dyke* and all. And he blames me for her disappearance.

"Dyke? Did I miss the memo on that?"

She smiled, briefly and, I thought, a bit coyly. "I recall—barely recall—a drunken evening in Austin that might have led you to believe otherwise."

She barely recalled because she was shit-faced. As was I. Also, our romp in the hay, as it were, did not set any endurance records. She didn't know this because I had been too shy to admit it, but she was my first. That's right, eighteen and still a virgin. But she fixed that for me in all of thirty seconds, if it even lasted that long.

"Don't tell me. I ruined you for other men."

"Not entirely. But… hmmm… I don't talk about this much, but while I don't like the word *dyke*, D2's not entirely wrong."

"Which part? The converting Amy to lesbianism part or the disappearance part."

"Neither. My sexual orientation part. We're both baseball fans, so I don't have to tell you what a switch hitter is."

"That you? A switch hitter?"

"Well, I haven't been up to the plate in quite a while. Pretty much been on the bench. And I'm happy with that, by the way." She looked at me over her coffee cup. "At least for now."

I nodded. Message received.

"Anyway, yeah, D2 wasn't all wrong."

This was an unexpected disclosure given our own one-night encounter lo those many years ago. But, I am nothing if not a liberated, 21st century, cosmopolitan sophisticate, so I said:

"Huh."

"Took me a while to come to grips with it. Spent some time in counseling at the university. I think that's why I fell into the bottle, trying to cope with the confusion. Finally got myself figured out."

"Well, score one for the other team."

She chuckled. "Well, both teams, actually." Then, playfully, she put on a little frown and said, "I hope this doesn't change anything."

I took that as my clue to express my disappointment, to reaffirm how desirable she was, and to offer a little harmless validation.

I lowered my head and sighed. "I'm crushed, really. I had all these hopes…"

She leaned back in her chair and smiled. "I asked for that, didn't I? But be serious for a minute."

I nodded. "Life's short. Find happiness where you can. How's that?"

"Nice. Thank you."

While I had wondered what might happen, if anything, when we reconnected, I was hardly crestfallen that she'd decided to bench herself, as she put it. I was a little surprised she had shared all that, but I was pleased she had enough confidence in our relationship to open up. But I wanted to return to our earlier conversation.

"You were talking about Amy and her robot brother, D2."

"Half-brother, technically. Darnell came first, two years before Amy. Different dads, neither in the picture. Their mom was a mess. Heavily into drugs. Prostitution, too, if the rumors were correct. Darnell and Amy were never close, she said. Lots of sibling friction. Amy took after her mother, especially the drug-use part. We argued about that a lot. With my history of alcohol abuse, I was sympathetic and I genuinely wanted to help Amy, but she was a wreck. Darnell was pretty fucked up, too, and he's turned into a world-class bigot. Hangs with a really rough crowd. Anyway, he assumes that since Amy and I became roommates we must have been lovers."

"And you weren't?"

"Nope. Not my type." She took another sip of her coffee. "Honestly, I don't know if I can define my type. Can anyone? I mean, you either click with someone or you don't. We didn't. At least, I didn't. And her being a stoner was a real turn-off for me. I worked hard to get sober, and people who are out of control bug me."

"Okay, but this D2 guy, he thinks otherwise. Since Amy lived here you had to be a pair and he believes his sister was following the straight and narrow until you had your unnatural ways with her. Or some such?"

"That's pretty much it. Lesbians are a scourge. Gay men, too. And let's not even talk about transsexuals. Darnell made all that very clear and very loudly that night, how cursed—(she pronounced it *curse-ed*)—we are in the eyes of Jesus. The Reverend Lee Roy Chitango says so, therefore it's gotta be God's own truth."

"That's when you hit him?"

"I didn't hit him. He was in my face. He's a stocky guy—not nearly as tall as you, but he's got some meat on him. And he was hovering over me, all intimidating. And he was drunk and definitely *loco* in the *cabeza,* wide-eyed—I'm thinking PCP or meth, but who knows? Anyway, some dude stepped in and shoved him away from me. D2 took a swing at him and missed—it was a terrible punch, slow and sloppy—but the dude backed into me when he dodged it and I fell into a table and knocked over some drinks, and a chick at the table—I think she thought he hit me—she jumps up and goes after him with a beer bottle, protecting a fellow sister and all—did I mention this is a biker bar?—and D2 dodges her and lunges at me again, and it was pretty chaotic at that point, and I took a swing at him and connected with this other guy's face. Who, as it turns out, was this off-duty cop."

"And you were probably the only sober person in the bar."

"Right. I was there waiting to meet a friend of mine. She used to work on *The Agi-Gator* when we were in college. She's one of the founding members, like Amy—it was an all-female cast, the six of us at first. She said she needed a drink. She needs a drink a lot. Actually, after all this, I may start drinking again. Anyway, I agreed to meet her at the Thunder Hog. Then this shitstorm erupted."

"Cops arrest this D2 guy?"

"No. He managed to sneak out while I was apologizing to the cop. I mean, I didn't really hurt him seriously, just a split lip, but I did knock him on his ass."

I gave her raised eyebrows.

She set down her coffee cup and curled her bicep. "I work out."

"Dyke."

She grabbed a sugar cube and threw it at my head. Missed.

"Yep. Definite anger management issues. But you throw like a girl."

She threw another one. I didn't dodge it this time, let it plink me in the forehead, and when it did she covered her mouth and guffawed.

"I need the name of that cop."

Talking with Tess felt natural and unselfconscious. While our real-life encounter had been long ago, I was reminded how we'd managed to stay friends over the years, not only because of the things we had in common, but because of the easy way we could talk with one another.

Our families had roots in the Cincinnati area, which made us both long-suffering Reds fans. She was one of the few women I knew who actually understood and enjoyed baseball. Some of her favorite memories from childhood were at the ballpark. I never went, but Mom regaled me with stories of when her dad would take her to see the Big Red Machine.

(That was before she ran off to become a Deadhead and then got knocked up in a pup tent on the twentieth anniversary of Woodstock.)

Tess and I belonged to several journalism organizations together, too, including Sigma Delta Chi, and we both were contributors to reporters' blogs. And we were dead-even in Word Chums.

Of course, no relationship is perfect. I was Heinlein; she was Asimov. She was Silva; I was Sandford. She was Marvel; I was D.C. The Green Lantern could totally kick Iron Man's ass, I told her, once. She conceded the point but incorrectly argued Carol Danvers would stomp Kal-El. Stuff like that.

She took her coffee cup to the kitchen counter and poured a refill. I leaned down and snatched the sugar cube off the floor, and tossed it to her. She blew the dust off and dropped it into her cup. "Three-minute rule."

Then she reached into the back pocket of her shorts and pulled out her cell phone as she sat back down at the kitchen table.

"D2 is the least of my worries, actually. Here's why I might need your help. Check this out."

I was actually busy checking out her legs. Her shorts were short and her calves and thighs bore evidence of her time in the gym. Strictly a dispassionate anatomical assessment, you understand. It's what reporters do—assess.

She opened her text message app and handed the phone to me:

> *What Amy took*
> *Now is mine.*
> *Want it back?*
> *One piece at a time.*
> *Play my game;*
> *Follow my clues.*
> *Don't call the cops*
> *Or you will lose.*

I looked at Tess and she was staring at me intently.

"This isn't a joke." I said it as a matter of fact, not a question. "Nothing funny about it at all."

I slipped my reporter's notebook from my back pocket and transcribed the message word for word.

"You recognize the sender's phone number?" I asked.

She shook her head. "Tried to look it up but struck out. So, what do you think?"

"I'm no expert, but that could be some of the worst poetry ever written."

CHAPTER 10

THE WOMEN WERE still asleep when I arose shortly after sunrise. I'd slept in my running shorts, so I slipped on my shoes and a tee shirt to take Fred out, but he was nowhere to be found. I peeked around the kitchen and living room to no avail, then quietly padded into the hallway by the bedrooms and whispered his name.

I heard a "gerrrufff" and the plop of paws hitting the carpet in Tess's bedroom. She'd left her door open and Fred came bolting out. He had a huge smile on his little face, tail wagging, eager for his morning walk.

"Traitor!" I whispered.

He cocked his head, evidently unfamiliar with the word. "Guys have to stick together, dude," I told him.

"Gerrrufff."

That settled, I leashed him and we headed out to explore the neighborhood in daylight. Calling it seedy would be unkind, but it would be fair to say that it represented the very finest in affordable housing. Turn left out of her front door and there was a fire station two lots down. Across the street a vacant gravel lot and a couple more houses, her size, small, but aquamarine in color and surrounded by a picket fence unburdened by fresh paint. Lawn mowers and edgers seemed well rested in this corner of Gainesville. And who among us has not traversed cracked sidewalks with a few potholes?

Fred and I crossed the gray asphalt street in front of Tess's to that sidewalk, overhung with sagging phone and electrical wires, and which in short order led to bustling Main Street with only a handful of boarded-up storefronts. A real estate agent would describe the area as "ripe for gentrification." A college student—or a struggling alternative newspaper editor—would call it ideal.

When we returned to the bungalow, I rinsed out Fred's bowl and gave him some fresh water from the tap. He trotted over, sniffed, then expressed his unhappiness.

"Gerrufff."

"Yeah, I know, it smells bad."

I rooted through the refrigerator and found a bottle of Dasani, which according to the label tasted pure and crisp thanks to reverse osmosis and the infusion of a proprietary blend of minerals, never mind all the plastic killing the whales.

I replaced the water in Fred's bowl with the Dasani, and he eagerly lapped it up. Fred, apparently, was unconcerned about the wellbeing of cetaceans.

The women had not stirred, so I tightened the laces on my running shoes and trotted back outdoors, put in about thirty minutes at a light jog meandering about the city and eventually landed at a little café called Maude's not far from Tess's place. I stepped inside, bought a bag of assorted bagels, and returned to the bungalow at a dead sprint. I was panting and sweating by the time I stepped through the door.

"I brought provisions," I said to Tess, who was filling the filter basket of her coffee maker.

She looked up and a brief smile flicked across her lips. Her hair was tousled and she wore pink flannel pajamas decorated with tiny white polka dots, which perfectly accompanied her fuchsia bunny slippers.

"Were you able to sleep?" she asked.

"Like a corpse."

"She didn't keep you up?"

I shot her a puzzled look.

"She was shouting and screaming throughout the night. Sounded like she was having terrible nightmares. At one point, I looked in on her, and she was on all fours, crouched in bed like a cat, whimpering. I whispered to her, asked if she was alright, but she didn't answer."

"Huh."

"I can't believe you slept through that."

"I could sleep through a nuclear bombardment."

While the coffee brewed, I rinsed off in the shower, threw on a fresh tee shirt and a clean pair of shorts. I didn't bother shaving. I was on a four-day personal grooming rotation. At day three, I was sprouting serious scruff. By day four, a well-defined Captain Jack Sparrow goatee would emerge. Then I'd restart the cycle beginning with what I liked to think of as the young Anakin Skywalker look.

Tess was sitting at the kitchen table when I stepped out of the bathroom. She looked up, rubbed her chin, and asked, "You going for the I-sleep-in-a-carboard-box look?"

"I've been told it's adventuresome."

"You're a journalist. You should know when you're being lied to. And what's with the nasty dog?"

I'd thrown on my vintage Faith No More tee shirt, the one with the snarling werewolf that looked as if it were about to eat your face.

"Scares off the zombies."

"There are no zombies in Gainesville."

"See."

I sat down and snagged a bagel from the bag. Blueberry. My fave. I try for a portion of blueberries and broccoli every day. Blueberries are brimming with antioxidants. And if you eat enough broccoli you'll never die. After Jazzy's palm reading, I needed to double down on the cruciferous veggies.

"Speaking of dying, Jazzy hasn't come out yet?" I asked.

Tess looked at me curiously. "We weren't speaking of dying."

"Oh, sorry, I was using my inside-the-head voice."

I grabbed an empty mug from the drying rack by the sink and poured myself some coffee. I found milk in the fridge and added a dash.

"So, how well do you know this woman?" Tess asked.

I glanced back in the direction of the guest room down the short hallway. The door was still closed. I told Tess how I'd met Madam Jazzabelle, a.k.a. Shirley DuMont, her prediction that I might soon be crossing over, how I did, indeed, cross over the River Styx—more than once now—and how I tried to track her down at the hospital and at her Royal Street shop after I had seen the ambulance the night before. And how she was packing up in a panic and how she hornswoggled a ride with me to Florida.

"She stepped into your car? Didn't even ask? And you let her?"

I digested that for a few moments, grappling with what I believed she was really trying to say. "Yeah. And I brought here uninvited, this woman I don't know anything about. That was thoughtless."

She scrunched her nose and cocked her head. "Oh, I don't mind that. You wouldn't believe some of the whack jobs who've crashed here. It's just, well…" She took a sip of coffee and gathered her thoughts. "I guess we're still learning things about one another even after all these years. I suppose I'm a little surprised, you helping a complete stranger like this. That's quite gallant of you." She pronounced it *ga-lont*.

I shrugged. I knew I hadn't been chivalrous. Jazzy basically hijacked the ride. But if Tess wanted to feel that way about me, who was I to argue?

"He's a regular Sir Freelancealot," It was Jazzy. She was dressed in her standard outfit: oversized dashiki, black jeans, turban. And she was perspiring. Even so, that was a clever pun.

Tess cocked an eye. "I'm surprised you're up. You had a restless night."

63

"Horrible Dreams."

Jazzy pulled up a chair, extracted a bagel from the bag, and took a huge bite. We were quiet while she made a production of chewing it, canting her head and smiling through closed lips while masticating.

"Thanks for the fuel," she finally said. "I needed that. We've got a busy day ahead of us. Things are going to get a little hairy."

"Really?" Tess said. "You know this, do you?" And then her cell phone chirped.

Tess redirected her eyes away from Jazzy to the phone on the table and snatched it up.

"It's a text message." She stared at it for a minute then said, "Mother fucker." She pronounced it in two words, with emphasis on the second. Somehow that made the expletive even more powerful. She slid the phone over to me:

> *All is ready*
> *For your arrival.*
> *What's at stake*
> *is your survival.*
> *Meet me at*
> *The hollow tree.*
> *That's where we'll start*
> *Our little spree.*
> *Hop. Hop. Hop.*
> *Don't be late.*
> *We start our game*
> *At half-past eight.*

There was no name attached to the sender, only a phone number. I compared it to the earlier text she'd received, but the number was different. I assumed the douche bag was using a succession of pre-paid cell phones—burners. Once again, I transcribed the message in my notebook.

Jazzy watched impassively as I scribbled. When I was done she said, "I take it this isn't the first time."

"Yeah, there was one before." I handed her my notebook. As soon as I did, I realized I might have overstepped, that even though Jazzy was sitting right there and she had overheard the entire conversation, that Tess might not want her involved. I glanced her way, but if she were perturbed by my indiscretion it didn't show.

While Jazzy was reading, I said to Tess, "Well, we can agree on at least one thing."

"Which is?"

"His poetry's even worse this time."

"Give me a break."

"You don't think so?" I bit off another chunk of bagel "I thought it cryptic, and the meter is strained, and it's a bit cliched, no?"

"Goddammit, be serious."

I sipped some coffee to wash down the bagel, set the mug down, and looked directly into her eyes.

"He's got your number, doesn't he?"

"What's that supposed to mean?" Thankfully she didn't have heat vision or I would have dematerialized into a heap of Alex ashes.

"It means he knows what a wuss you are."

"WHAT!"

She sat upright in her chair, her shoulders stiff and her fists were clenched.

"You know, like that time you told me about, when you caught the assistant volleyball coach spying on his players in the showers, how he threatened to sue you. You remember how you folded."

"I didn't fold!"

"Okay, but how about the time you wrote that story about the dean of students, how he phonied up his resume and he was going to expel you. You remember that retraction you wrote?"

"You know perfectly well I did no such thing." She was calmer now. She'd figured out where I was heading.

"Of course you didn't. You know why? Because you don't let anyone push you around."

Her shoulders relaxed and she leaned back in her chair and brushed a strand of sun bleached hair off her forehead.

"Whoever this diphthong is, he's trying to rattle you. Don't let him. You are the cage rattler. Not the…" I paused for a millisecond, scanning my mental hard drive for the right word, came up blank, then went with… "rattle-ee."

"You do know that diphthong is not an insult."

"It is if I say it is."

She rolled her eyes.

"Anyway, you get where I'm going with this. He's trying to intimidate you. Fuck him. This is cowardly. I've got a couple hours before I have to hit the road. Let's figure out who this asshat is, where he is, then track him down and kick his ass. Then we can get some lunch. How's that?"

She nodded and a smile spread across her face. "You and me."

"Right."

Jazzy said, "All four of us."

Tess glanced at her out of the corner of her eye. "Four?"

Jazzy guzzled the rest of her coffee. The bagel was gone, too. "The three of us and one more. I saw it last night."

"Last night?" I asked.

Jazzy nodded. "I have these spells. Sometimes at night, sometimes during the day. They make me sick. That's why I went to the hospital. My blood pressure spikes, my heart goes crazy, I break out in sweats. They're like these horrible attacks of *déjà vu*."

"So, you're saying you really can see the future," I said.

"I don't know what to call it. I get pictures, images in my head, about things I know haven't happened but they have a feel to them, like when you dream about things you've done but you know they aren't real."

"Wait a minute," Tess protested. "This is too much. I've got these bizarre text messages, this guy who's stalking me over the phone, now you with this crazy talk. I'm overloaded."

Jazzy reached out, her palms up, a signal for Tess to do likewise. Tess opened and closed her mouth soundlessly a few times, like a guppy gasping for air, then reached out and let Jazzy take her hands, a gesture that seemed so disconnected from the irritation she'd been showing, so submissive, that I think my mouth must have fallen open, too.

I imagined Jazzy was about to tell Tess her future, but she didn't. She simply clasped her hands and squeezed them reassuringly.

"I can't explain it," Jazzy said softly. "These visions. They're like flashbacks in a movie. All I know is that when I have one of these attacks, things happen. And I know they happened before and no matter what I do they will happen again and again."

"Have you gotten medical attention?" Tess asked. Her tone was neutral, unsarcastic.

"Several times. They know me well at the hospital. I've been diagnosed as schizophrenic, multiple personality disorder, manic depressive. I've had a pharmacy-full of drugs. I don't blame you for thinking I might be insane. I don't even know anymore. I've pretty much given up trying to control it."

"Jazzy," I asked. "When did you see me before?"

She shook her head. "As far as I know, I never saw you until the day you walked into the shop. Then I had an attack. It started as we were sitting together. I had all these images of you flood into me." She smiled faintly, released Tess's hands, and wiped beads of perspiration from her forehead with a napkin. "That's how it happens."

"And that's how you learned I swam for the University of Texas?"

She shook her head. "No. I googled you after you left. You gave me your name, remember."

That explained it.

"A moment ago, you mentioned four," Tess said. "What did you mean by that?"

Tess had gone from showing open irritation with Jazzy to appearing, if not sympathetic, at least civil. It might have been a show, of course, a demonstration of good interviewing technique to draw her out. But it seemed genuine.

"There's another woman," Jazzy said in response to Tess's question. "She'll be joining us. Making four. She's tall, raven haired…" Jazzy stopped, cocked her head.

And the doorbell chimed.

CHAPTER 11

THE WOMAN AT the door was tall, raven haired, and agitated.

"We gotta talk about this dipshit and his poetry," she was saying as she stormed into the living room. Then she froze when she spied Jazzy and me.

"Bristol," Tess said. "This is... uh..."

"Call me Jazzy, that's what the Strange Man does."

I'd been Aquaman yesterday, now I was the Strange Man. Maybe I'd acquire a new appellation every twenty-four hours, the inaugural member of the Nickname a Day Club. Should I now come up with a new nickname for Madam Jazzabelle? No. I liked Jazzy. It suited her somehow.

Bristol stepped over and offered her hand. When she took it, Jazzy twitched.

"Oh, did I shock you?" Bristol asked.

"You've no idea."

Jazzy turned to me. "I'll be on the porch. I need a smoke."

Bristol's eyes followed Jazzy out the door, then she turned and shrugged. She was taller than Tess and Jazzy, probably around five-eight and was full-on goth—black lipstick, black nails, her skin-tight yoga pants and long-sleeved blouse, both black. She'd added a dash of color with her gold nose ring. Maybe they don't make them in black, but that's speculation on my part having never been in the market for piercings of any sort.

She looked up at me. "Jeez, they grow 'em big where you're from." Then her eyes slid down to my tee shirt and she said, "Woof!"

She turned to Tess. "Does he bite?"

"Not unless you ask nicely."

She curled her left hand and held her knuckles up to my nose, the way you would approach a strange Doberman.

I thought about licking her fist, going along with the gag, but who knew where her hands had been?

"Bristol." I said. "Like Palin? She a drama queen, too."

She frowned and withdrew her hand. "Bad dog."

I looked at Tess and she rolled her eyes.

"She who you met at the biker bar?" I asked.

Bristol jumped in. "Yes. And I'm the friend who showed up at the jail to post bail. And I'm the friend who was by her side last year when the cops accused her of killing Amy. And I'm the friend who was with her when she got her a…"

"BRISTOL!"

She froze, then rolled her eyes at Tess. "Sorrrrry."

"So, Bristol," I said. "You know about the texts. Any thoughts?"

"Oh, a guy shows up and suddenly he's in charge, that it?"

I glanced at Tess, shrugged my shoulders, and sighed. "I can't work in these conditions." I could put on the drama, too.

"Tess grabbed my arm. "Ignore her."

Then she turned on Bristol: "I can't handle any theatrics today, Bristol. Be fucking normal, would you?"

"Whatever." With that she dropped onto the living room sofa, folded her arms, and stared up at me. She pouted for a couple of beats then stuck out her tongue. Which was kind of funny, I suppose, but I ignored her.

Jazzy walked back into the house, glanced in Bristol's direction, then strolled into the kitchen for more coffee. She'd missed most of the dramatics. Or maybe she'd seen them all before in one of her visions.

Bristol Krueger was one of six women who founded *The Agi-Gator* during Tess's freshman year in college. They'd wangled some sort of business start-up grant aimed at encouraging female entrepreneurs, cash they needed to get off the ground. Now, that cash was long gone.

Ironically, the DUI bust that landed Tess in jail was one of the earliest stories the off-campus paper reported. Tess felt an ethical duty to do so, to prove nobody, not even members of the newspaper's staff, would get preferential treatment.

Amelia Duffy, her eventual roommate, was also a founding member, a junior specializing in web design and social media. Bristol, like Tess, was a writer and editor. Tess said the three other women had been seniors when the paper was launched and no longer lived in Gainesville. One had been the business manager and the other two were advertising salespeople.

Tess told me earlier that she had contacted Verizon to trace the first voicemail's originating phone number, but hit a brick wall. She also used several online directories that list cell phone numbers, but they, too, came up blank. She concluded our mad messenger must be using burners.

Jazzy wandered back into the living room, the smell of cigarettes radiating off her like poison gas. Bristol scrunched her nose and waved her hand in front of her face. Jazzy either ignored her or was oblivious. She snatched a pillow off the far end of the couch and propped it against a bare space on the living room wall next to Tess's stereo cabinet and plopped down, ignoring the two occasional chairs in the room. Then she wrapped her legs in some sort of yoga pose and leaned back.

Tess handed Bristol her cell phone. "Check out the latest."

Bristol read the text message, shook her head, and handed the phone back to Tess.

"When I find this fucker I'm going crush his larynx."

"Take a number," Tess said.

"Bristol, any ideas who could be doing this?" I asked.

She shook her head. "No idea who this dick is."

"Dick," I said. "So we're assuming it's a guy?"

"Women can be dicks, too," Bristol said.

"If you say so. Let's see if we can break it down." I read the verse aloud, to ensure we didn't miss anything:

> *All is ready*
> *For your arrival."*
> *What's a stake*
> *Is your survival.*
> *Meet me at*
> *The hollow tree.*
> *That's where we'll start*
> *Our little spree."*
> *Hop. Hop. Hop.*
> *Don't be late.*
> *We start our game*
> *At half-past eight.*

I turned to Bristol and Tess. "The dick by whatever gender wants you to show up somewhere at 8:30 tonight. At least I assume it's tonight and he didn't mean this morning. Got any clue where he's talking about?"

Bristol waved her hand dismissively. "Oh, that's obvious."

Tess looked at her, her eyebrows raised in curiosity. "Oh, yeah?"

"Sure. Hop. Hop. Hop. That's the clue. He's talking about the Devil's Millhopper. What else?"

Tess bounded from the couch and began pacing the small living room. "Of course. And the hollow tree. You know where that is, don't you, Bristol? It's on that path to the boardwalk. An old hickory tree, right there on the trail."

"Hang on," I said. "What's a Devil's Millhopper?"

"It's a huge sinkhole, not far from here," Tess said. "There's a state park built around it with boardwalks and stairs that lead all the way to the bottom. There's a lake down there. And it's haunted."

"Yeah, it was the first stop on our *Weird Tour of Florida*," Bristol said.

"The weird what?"

"A magazine we published," Tess said. "I mentioned it last night, remember, when we were talking about palm readers? There are all these mysterious places in Florida that are either haunted or have strange histories—all tourist traps, of course. We printed this really cool magazine with the ten most bizarre places to visit in Florida. Devil's Millhopper, right here in Gainesville, it was on the list."

Tess stepped over to a small desk in the corner of the living room where her laptop computer lie buried beneath a mountain of bills, letters, magazines, and newspapers.

"I think I've got one here," she said as she fished around the detritus on her desk. In a few moments, she extracted something from the bottom of the pile.

"*Voila!*"

It was a tabloid-sized magazine printed on newsprint in full color. A bold red headline—*WTF: Weird Tour of Florida*—dominated the cover. She turned to the 24-page publication's centerfold to reveal a map of the Sunshine State with ten locations enumerated:

1. Devil's Millhopper
2. The Devil's Schoolhouse
3. The Fountain of Youth
4. The Last Resort Bar
5. Cassadaga Spiritualist Camp
6. Ashley's Tavern
7. Spook Hill
8. Skunk Ape Research Headquarters
9. Our Lady of Clearwater
10. Gravity Research Foundation

She handed it to me and I read portions of the article about the Devil's Millhopper aloud.

"It's a huge funnel-shaped hole in the ground reminiscent in shape to a grain hopper." I lowered the magazine and looked at Tess. "Do people really know what a grain hopper looks like?'

"Just read. You can edit it later."

The story said the ravine was five hundred feet across, twelve stories deep, and a half-mile in circumference in northwest Gainesville, making it one of the largest sinkholes in Florida, a state replete with these cavities in the earth that open up without warning and swallow houses, roads, and people.

There are many legends told about the Millhopper, including one in which Satan lusted after an Seminole princess and he sucked her straight into the earth, creating the Millhopper in his wake. Other folk tales say the devil still uses the sinkhole as a gateway to hell.

Scientists, citing what they call facts, say that in reality it's merely another sinkhole, albeit an enormous and ancient one. The state's bedrock is limestone and is very porous and prone to cave-ins, adding to the list of thrilling ways you can meet your maker in the Sunshine State along with hurricanes, sharks, lightning, deadly plants, poisonous toads, alligators and crocodiles, panthers, bobcats, Burmese pythons, lionfish, red tide and other toxic algae, malaria, dengue fever, flesh-eating bacteria, parasitic nematodes, and the Skunk Ape, to name a some of the non-human threats.

"Well, I see why this made your top ten list," I said. "Should we call 911 now?"

"No," Tess said, her voice sounding a little strained.

"Why not? Call the cops. They stake the place out. Nab this fucktard, and we all go out for cocktails."

Bristol began bobbing her head up and down when I mentioned cocktails, but Tess shook her head again.

"Because he told us not to?" I asked.

Tess's lips were tightly closed and her face was flushed. She couldn't have looked more anguished if she'd swallowed a nematode. Apparently, she liked the idea of calling the cops as much as I liked elevator rides. Maybe even less. Which meant what? That she was holding something back from us? If so, why?

"I need to sit down." She collapsed back onto the couch beside Bristol and ran her hands through her hair. Bristol patted her on her knee and said, "It'll be alright."

Tess looked at her. "I don't see how."

"Why not call the police, Tess?" I asked again, which I knew was annoying, but, hey, I'm a journalist. Being annoying is practically the job description.

Tess buried her face in her hands, then looked up at the ceiling.

"Here's the thing. Months after Amy left, I discovered something—something very private—was missing from my room. I went half-crazy trying to find it, and finally concluded that Amy must have stolen it. In his first poem, this guy says he has it. He says…"

She paused for a beat and reached out to me. "Can I see your notebook for a second?"

I slipped it out of my back pocket and handed it to her. She flipped through the pages, found what she was looking for, then continued.

"He says in the first poem that if I want it back I'm going to get it *one piece at a time.*

"I have to get it back. It…" She paused thinking about what she wanted to say. "It could be devastating if it got out."

Bristol leaned away from her, a frown growing on her face, and took a fresh look at her friend. Apparently this was news to her.

"Like what?" she asked.

"Like I don't want to talk about it."

"Is it a naughty photo? A selfie? Is it…"

Tess reached over to Bristol and covered her mouth. "I don't want to get overly dramatic, but this could get ugly."

Bristol considered that for about half a second after Tess withdrew her hand then said, "Drama? I love drama. I'm in."

Then Tess turned to me. "Alex, can I talk you into sticking around for a bit? I know you've got to get a move on, but I could use your support. I'm not gonna lie, this has me a little upset."

What I might have said was: "If only I could but you know my calendar is packed and I've got this heel spur and there're columns to write and rum to drink and bad habits to foster and I'm conflict averse and I hate poetry because I don't understand it and my boss won't let me and who'll watch Fred and I promised Jazzy a ride..."

Or at the very least I could have insisted that Tess answer a few basic questions. She'd told Bristol things could get ugly. What did that mean? This thing that was stolen by her old roommate, whatever it was, it came in pieces? Didn't she owe us all a few more details if she wanted us to drop everything and help her out?

Yep, those were all logical questions. And, after all, what did I owe her? We hadn't seen one another in years. Sure, we had history. Sure, we were friends...

Ah, there it was. We were friends. And she'd asked for my help. And you are either worthy of friendship or you are not. How many true friends do any of us have in a lifetime? Were I in need, what would my expectation be of someone I considered a friend?

And did I need to be gone in a big hurry, anyway? What for? To kickstart my new life in Florida writing funny stories for people's amusement? Funny stories versus a woman asking for my help? What kind of diphthong would turn his back on her?

So, I answered:

"If only I could but you know my calendar is packed and I've got this heel spur and there're columns to write and rum to drink and bad habits to foster and I'm conflict averse and I hate poetry because I don't understand it and my boss won't let me and who'll watch Fred and I promised Jazzy a ride..."

Jazzy threw the first pillow at me. Then Bristol. Tess just stared at me, waiting for me to get serious.

"Whatever. But when we catch this turdsack, I get the first punch, okay?"

Tess said, "Deal."

Jazzy didn't wait to be asked, she morphed into Lisbeth Salander mode. "How'd he get your phone number? Would it have to be somebody you know really well?"

Tess nodded. "Good question. I've thought about that. I have over five hundred people on my contacts list. My cell is on my business cards, and who knows how many people have one."

"But since he mentions Amy," Jazzy said, "and how she took something from you, and how he now has it, it must be somebody who knew the both of you. That has to narrow it down."

"Right. I thought of that, too. When the police interrogated me after Amy's disappearance, they asked about people we knew in common. I gave them a list. I thought I kept a copy, but I dug around my files yesterday when I got back from the jail and couldn't find it. So, without telling him why, I called the detective on the case and he said he'd look."

"He want to know why you were asking?"

Before Tess could answer, Bristol jumped in: "Cops never took it seriously. The only reason they paid any attention at all was because of that anonymous tip about blood in the kitchen."

"Because Amy was an adult, and adults go missing all the time," Jazzy said. "So they don't get worked up about that sort of thing. That it?"

"Right," Tess said. "But even though they eventually matched the blood to Amy's DNA, using samples they got from her room, there were no signs of real violence, a struggle, forced entry, or anything else indicating she was kidnapped. The blood was by the sink. There wasn't that much. She could have cut herself peeling a potato."

"They find a knife with her blood on it?" I asked.

Tess shook her head.

"They ever figure out who phoned in the tip?"

She shook her head again. "I've thought about that a lot. It would have to have been someone in my house. It wasn't broken into. I guess I've imagined it was Amy, herself, fucking with me."

"It was a female who phoned in the tip?" I asked.

"Yes."

"What about her family?" Jazzy asked. I was impressed with her questions. She might be disturbed, but that didn't mean she wasn't perceptive.

"Amy's mom raised her and Darnell until she died of an overdose," Tess said. "Single mom. No dads around. D2 was in high school, Amy in junior high. After their mom's death, Amy and Darnell were separated and put into different foster homes until they turned eighteen. They only reunited, if you want to call it that, a couple of years after Amy graduated from college. They were never close, and I think Amy found her brother repellent with all his white supremacist, anti-gay ranting. There might have been a great aunt out in California somewhere. Amy mentioned her, but I don't think they ever even met."

"So, Amy goes missing," I said. "She has no family to press the police other than her idiot brother who might not even care. She have anyone else close?"

Tess shrugged. "Me, I suppose. Although, that relationship was at the breaking point. I always figured she just took off when I was out of town because she wanted to get away from it all, wanted to leave without any more confrontations. I never really did believe—I still find it hard to believe—anything bad happened to her."

Jazzy said, "It looks like she took all her things. There's nothing in her old room."

Tess shook her head. "Amy was a complete slob. Clothes on the floor. Bed never made. We had separate medicine cabinets in the bathroom. Her's was always overflowing and crap was constantly falling out. She could have packed some things and I wouldn't have known the difference, but the bulk of her stuff was here when I got back. Of course, that added to the suspicion that she left in a hurry, maybe involuntarily. I figured she might return, but, of course, she never did. I called Darnell several times to come get her things. He ignored me. I figured I'd have to box it all up and give it to Goodwill, although I dreaded sorting through it all, and, frankly I just shut the door to her room and left it untouched for months. Then D2 finally showed up and cleared it all out."

"What about her car?" I asked.

"Missing, too."

"So, it's plausible she simply took off."

"That's what I've always assumed."

"Sounds to me, if it weren't for the blood, nobody would have given this a second's thought. But somebody called the cops. And you think that might have been Amy?"

Tess nodded. "She was one of those passive/aggressive types. I could see her taking a parting shot, getting even. Making my life miserable for a while. And I can't think of anyone else who could have known about that blood."

"Unless somebody really abducted her," I said. "Found a way into the house—maybe somebody Amy knew and she let him in...."

"Or her," Bristol, said.

"Yes, or her. We've no idea, do we? Anyway, that would explain why she left all her belongings."

Tess said, "Yep. That's why it looked suspicious."

"But then why tip the cops? That's inconsistent. And why's someone contacting you now?"

She shrugged. "Great questions. I don't know."

We let it lie there for a minute, then Jazzy asked what we probably all were wondering:

"So, the popo had to ask you about your relationship with her, right? You tell them you two were on the outs?"

Tess shook her head, eyes downcast.

"You okay?" I asked.

She shook her head again, then exhaled loudly. Before she could speak Bristol interjected: "It's ancient history and has no bearing, you don't need to go over all that."

"No, it's alright," Tess said.

She ran her hand through her hair again. She was doing that a lot. "Amy developed a thing for me. At first I thought she was messing around, but after a while it was pretty clear she was serious. It got uncomfortable because I wasn't interested. I told her she was becoming obsessed. That it wasn't going to happen."

She paused for a moment, thinking about what she was going to say—or perhaps not say.

"Here's the thing. I liked Amy. I think everyone liked her. But she was falling apart. She was drinking too much—and I knew all about alcoholism—and she'd started doing drugs. I never really knew what, never saw her taking anything here at the house, but it made her really weird, and I grew increasingly uncomfortable around her. It's like I told you before, Alex, whatever it is that makes two people click, it wasn't there for me."

She chewed her lip for a few seconds then continued: "Anyway, we had a, uh, frank conversation about all of that, about her pestering me, about how I thought she needed to get some help. I'd needed help. I knew sometimes you can't do it by yourself. But if I had needed it, she *really* did. And I told her as much. I told her if she didn't get her shit together she'd have to leave, that I couldn't stand being around her like she was."

"How'd she take that?" I asked.

"She got hysterical. Denied she had a problem. Called me a bitch, which is completely unfair because of the many things I am, I totally suck at being a bitch."

She smiled at that. We all did.

"Anyway, to make my point, I might have had a few sleepovers I now regret. That really upset her. It was tense. And when I got an invite to visit a friend in Tampa, I couldn't get out of the house fast enough. And when I got back, well, you know what I found."

"And you kept that from the cops," I said.

Bristol jumped in: "I told her to. It was absolutely not in her interest to go talking about that. All it would do is make her look even more suspicious."

"Unless the cops sniffed it out on their own…"

"Yeah, but they didn't."

Tess said, "I knew that anything I told them would end up in an investigative report somewhere and there was no upside for me in that. So, yeah, I kept my mouth shut."

And she was still keeping quiet about something, which would make helping her complicated.

"Getting back to calling the cops about all this," I said. "Amy was the subject of a police investigation when she went missing. Now you've heard from an anonymous caller making threatening noises and referring to her. How is this not something you absolutely have to tell the police? Aren't you concerned about what the consequences could be if you don't?"

Tess exhaled and said, "I just can't. But look, I mentioned that I called the detective originally assigned to the case. He's an older guy, I remembered that, and it took a few calls to track him down. His name is Frank Demerest. He's retired now, still here in town. I was able to reach him yesterday about his case notes. I was hoping, without telling him so, that they might be of use. Anyway, it was kind of an odd conversation."

"How so?"

"Well, he seemed a little embarrassed. At least that's what it sounded like on the phone. He asked if I was recording the call, and I told him no. Then he said, 'Okay, here it is: We never should have jailed you. It was bullshit. There was never enough blood for that and no evidence of foul play.' That's what he said."

"What does that mean?" I asked.

"It means that the case was never elevated to anything more than a routine missing persons case. An adult missing person. Given that, I don't think I have to call 911 now."

"Back up," I said. "This detective, he said detaining you was 'bullshit,' his words? Then why'd they do it?"

"He wouldn't say, exactly. He said he was sorry it happened. Then he said something to the effect that it was 'orders from headquarters.' We'd done some stories in the paper questioning arrest practices of minorities—driving while black, that sort of thing. The newspaper is not exactly loved by the police department."

Jazzy laughed. It was the first time I'd heard her do that. "Girl, you really know how to stir up trouble."

Bristol was red faced. "Goddammit. It was harassment is all it was, those pricks."

She might have been a drama queen, but there was a part of me that admired the way she came to Tess's defense.

"We got distracted from the earlier question of who knew you and Amy," I said. "You shared that with this detective, back when Amy disappeared?"

"I don't remember all the names I gave him, there were quite a few, actually. We dealt with a lot of people at the newspaper, some were personal friends, many were simply people we knew in the course of business or at school together. I don't know who all he might have contacted. That's what I was hoping he'd be willing to share."

"And nobody springs to mind?"

She shook her head. "Nobody who would do something like this."

"What about Amy's brother, what's his name, D2?"

"Darnell? I can't say no for certain, but I doubt it. He's not coy, and this all sounds too subtle for him. I mean, he was all about starting a rumble with me in the bar the other night. Of course, there's no secret he doesn't like me. But despite his drinking and drug abuse, he does manage to hold down a pretty good job at a local car dealership. I'm told he's a hard worker. But he's pretty direct. A tire iron would be his style. Not free verse."

We were quiet for a few minutes, having exhausted our questions in this rambling gab fest. There really only seemed one path forward.

"How late's the park open?" I asked.

"I'll look it up," Bristol said. A few taps on her iPad and she had the answer: "Five o'clock."

"How hard would it be to sneak in there?"

"Not hard at all, I would imagine," Tess said. "The park's not much larger than the sinkhole itself and there are streets nearby. It would be easy enough to park a car outside the park where it wouldn't be noticed. We could walk in."

"Bristol, can you check and see what time sunset is tonight?" I asked.

She began pecking away again on her iPad. "Sunset tonight is 7:34 now that we're in Daylight Savings Time."

"So this asshat says we need to be there at 8:30," I said. "It should just be dark. You guys know the lay of the land. Could we sneak in there, hide nearby and catch him—at least grab a photo of him? Is there any place to hang out unseen near this tree?"

"I think so," Tess said. "It's very woodsy."

I checked my watch. "We've got some time before the park closes. When it does, do the park people, rangers or whatever they're called, do they all leave?"

"No idea," Bristol said.

"Why don't we go now?" Jazzy asked.

"Now?"

"Sure. Park a car nearby but outside the park, like you said, walk in, get a ticket or whatever's required, then hide until dark. They'd never know we were still there, would they, if the car wasn't in the parking lot?"

Tess's head bobbed up and down. "I'd rather be doing something than nothing. Sitting around like this, I feel like I've got a bullseye on me."

"Okay," I agreed. "We need a camera with a long lens. And a flash. Anybody got one?"

Tess said, "Yes. We can run by the paper. We keep a couple of pool cameras for use. Mostly they're point-and-shoots, but we've got a good Canon, an 80D, and some long glass that a photographer friend donated to us. Camera has a built-in strobe."

"Will your puppy be okay by herself?" Bristol asked. That was thoughtful.

"It's himself. And, yeah, Fred will be fine. I'll take him for a walk before we head out. He'll be good until we get back. Spock will watch out for him."

Bristol shot me a curious look, but Tess waved her off.

"He has a pet Vulcan."

CHAPTER 12

The Devil's Millhopper

"Get away from me, bitch."

That was Tess, swatting a mosquito buzzing around her head. We were hunkered down thirty yards from a hollowed-out pignut hickory tree, deep in the weeds, sprawled behind the fallen trunk of an ancient live oak that helped hide our position.

"How you know it's a chick?" I asked.

"Males don't bite and they don't bug you like females." She shot me a hostile glance. "And no wise cracks."

"The thought never crossed my mind," I lied.

We'd followed Jazzy's suggestion that we seclude ourselves in the woods of what is officially known as Devil's Millhopper Geological State Park and to do it before the park closed. We'd staked out the drop site where the obnoxious—and I sincerely hoped soon-to-be ass-kicked—poet said we'd find a clue.

Getting to the park involved a few stops first. While I walked Fred, Tess ran by the *The Agi-Gator* to pick up the camera, then stopped at a nearby CVS for bug spray and bottled water.

"You do know it takes 450 years for those things to decompose and that they're killing the whales and dolphins," I said, nodding to the water bottles.

"Straws are worse, and I reuse these."

"You mean that bottle in the fridge, it was filled with tap water?"

"Yeah, why?"

Poor Fred.

After we piled into Bristol's car for the trip to the Devil's Millhopper, Tess complained that her stomach was rumbling, which launched a debate about who wanted what to eat, with Jazzy suggesting pizza, Tess insisting on something vegetarian, Bristol pleading for red meat, and me advising that broccoli is the key to longevity. This prompted Bristol to belittle me for what she called "sissy food" while I remained smugly confident that my regimen of cruciferous vegetables would allow me to join the ranks of the centenarians—assuming I didn't get killed by an insane rhymester first.

We finally settled on the One Love Café, close to the park. I eschewed the Manly Man sandwich in favor of the Girly Girl, which was exactly the same except it had chicken instead of beef. I also ordered a side of organic veggies from Swallowtail Farms that included broccoli, cauliflower, rutabaga, carrots, beets, turnips, and collard greens. Jazzy ordered an avocado flat bread, Tess a black bean burger. Then we all stood around, hungry and impatient, while Bristol made a show of interrogating the college student at the order counter who had introduced herself as Tiffany and told us she was studying hotel/restaurant management.

Bristol: "So, on the Manly Man, can you get the beef rare?"

Annisa (cheerfully): "Certainly."

Bristol: "Now, the menu says this comes with a spicy special sauce. Is there garlic in that special sauce, because I really don't like garlic, in fact I might be allergic to it."

Tiffany (concerned): "I'll doublecheck on that for you."

Bristol: "Now, the bacon, I like it crispy. Is it crispy?"

Tiffany (eyes flitting about for a help or a self-defense weapon): "I'll be sure to mention it to the chef."

And so on.

At one point, Tess put her hand on Bristol's arm, but she shrugged it off.

"Hey, I'm driving. I should get what I want."

I looked at Tess. She looked at me. "Any place nearby we can dump her body?" I asked.

Bristol: "Very funny. Don't forget who's driving."

Jazzy: "Yeah, you mentioned that already. We're *soooo* in your debt. What would we do without you?"

It went on like that for a little while, too.

When the food finally arrived at our table on the sprawling patio, Bristol dissected her sandwich, peeling off the slice of bacon and dangling it over her plate.

"See this," she said, wobbling the flaccid strip of fatback. "Not crispy."

Bristol seemed ready to walk her food back inside and give the poor student at the counter a piece of her mind. But I suspected that by then Tiffany had taken a sabbatical, perhaps changed majors, maybe to criminal justice where she could carry a gun in case she ever ran into any more Bristols.

I pulled my Girly Girl apart and extracted my slice of bacon, which was crisped to perfection. "Here, Bristol," I said. "You can have my meat. My meat is firm. My meat is hot. My…"

That launched the predictable caterwauling, Bristol getting her I-Am-Woman-You-Are-Pig thing going, Jazzy rolling her eyes behind her rose-tinted wraparounds, and Tess shaking her head mumbling, "Bristol, Bristol, Bristol."

All of which helps explain why, when we finally spread out in the woods near the drop site, Bristol found her own tree apart from Jazzy, Tess, and me. She also insisted on using the camera, saying she was the most qualified.

"She still work at the paper?" I whispered to Tess.

She shook her head. "Real estate agent."

"So, she's the most qualified to have the camera, why?"

"She's driving."

"Oh, yeah."

The hollow tree was not far down a dirt path from the park's visitor center, which houses the rangers' small office, a gift shop, bathrooms, and park information kiosks. We'd looked into the hole in the base of the hickory, a cavity large enough for a person the size of Tess or Jazzy to partially curl into. There was nothing in there besides a few rocks, bark, decaying wood, and leaves. No message in a bottle, no hidden immunity idol, no horcrux.

We then moseyed down the trail, all innocent, surreptitiously checking our surroundings to ensure nobody was lurking in the weeds spying on us. Then we skedaddled into the underbrush.

That was the exciting part. Then we faced several hours of nothing-to-do until it got dark. Bristol was about ten feet away, the camera with its telephoto lens resting on a small log, aimed at the tree. She was prone, propped on her elbows, and sullen.

Tess, Jazzy and I took turns peering out over the live oak trunk we were snuggled behind, and when we weren't on lookout, Tess and I played with our cell phones. Jazzy apparently didn't own one, which made her the only untethered person I knew. A small part of me envied her.

My phone was on silent mode, but it lit up with an incoming call. It was from Edwina Mahoney, the founding editor of Tropic © Press and my boss. I let it roll over to voicemail, and in a few minutes I punched the voicemail button and read the transcription:

Alex, checking in. Hope your trip to Florida has gone well. Give me a shout when you get a chance.

That was it. No emergency. I'd call her back later and confess this misadventure I'd stumbled into. I knew I'd catch a ration of shit for it. Edwina is adamant that my column, *The Strange Files*, has to be a daily feature of the news service. It is, she said, one of the "hooks" in our marketing plan. And she can't abide distractions that get in the way of that.

I had a backlog of evergreen columns already written that she was using while I was on the road, but the supply would run out soon and I'd need to get back to work. But I was in Florida now, the epicenter of crazy, where there should be plenty of raw material.

I switched over to one of several news feeds I monitored and began copying and pasting links for future use.

- A Gulfport, Florida man had been arrested for filling a squirt gun with his own urine and shooting a woman who was walking her dog. He told police the woman had allowed her pet to poop on his yard and she had failed to pick it up and dispose of it properly. "I'll do it again, too, if she doesn't stop it," he told police.

- Florida had been ranked Number 1 in the country for fraud and Number 4 for identity theft. But a new report showed that for a change the latest victims weren't senior citizens, but millennials. Florida's conmen, it seemed, were equal opportunity grifters and were now picking on my generation.

- Police accused a substitute teacher of spreading "human fecal matter" on grills and picnic tables at a Sarasota park while wearing gloves and a face mask. All to sabotage a little girl's birthday party. She faced a third-degree felony rap.

But the zaniness wasn't restricted to Florida.

- A Wilmington, North Carolina man had been arrested for animal cruelty for not caring properly for his pet goldfish.

- And a Spanish woman was hospitalized after suffering a severe allergic reaction to sperm. She arrived at a hospital covered in hives, vomiting, and suffering from shortness of breath. Police said she had unprotected sex with her male partner involving "oral ejaculation."

I rolled over and showed that story to Tess. "Now this is what I'd call a ratched date," I whispered.

She read it, then pointed to the bottom of the story. Turns out, the woman's partner had been taking penicillin, and she was allergic to it. Doctors guessed the antibiotic must have become concentrated in his semen.

"This is terrible," I said. "I'll never take penicillin again."

"You ever have the clap?"

"Of course not. I practice safe sex."

She nodded. "So I recall."

"Shhhh." It was Jazzy.

We scrunched deeper into the weeds as we heard footsteps approaching. I glanced toward Bristol. She nodded and gave me a thumbs up. We were ready.

It was hard to make out precisely who was on the trail from ground level looking upward from the forest floor through the weeds and ferns, but the footsteps were coming from the direction of the Millhopper.

Was it our poet? Or merely the last of the tourists returning from a trek more than one hundred feet into the earth and the cool, damp mini-ecosystem created by the enormous sinkhole? It was nearly five o'clock, the park's closing time.

We heard voices. Plural. They were female. And they weren't speaking English. Sounded maybe Japanese. Surely, that wouldn't be our guy.

We relaxed. By we, I mean Tess, Jazzy, and myself. However, the fourth member of our entourage, the self-proclaimed most qualified photographer, suddenly leaped to her feet and charged toward the trail, camera up in her face, the barrel of the long, white telephoto lens jutting forward like the snout of a thick cylindrical weapon an Imperial Stormtrooper might brandish.

She was making a terrible racket as she crashed through the under-brush, but over that thrashing I could still hear the click and whir of the camera as she held the shutter release down. I rose to my knees in time to see a startled Asian woman, wrap her arms around her terrified young daughter as Bristol tripped on a vine and face-planted at the base of the hickory tree, blocking the dirt path.

The woman and little girl stood riveted in place, unsure of what to do with this large, clearly insane, woman in the middle of the trail. I ran up, looked back in the direction from which Bristol had run, and yelled, "Cut!"

"Sorry if we startled you," I said to the woman. "We're filming a movie." That didn't get a reaction so I asked, "Do you speak English?"

When she didn't reply, I made a circle with my left hand and held it up to my left eye, and then cranked my right hand in a circle next to it, the universal sign indicating motion photography.

"Ah!" the woman said.

"Yes!" I said. "It's a *Star Wars* sequel. *Attack of the Morons*."

Bristol was on her hands and knees, struggling to her feet. He glasses had fallen off and were lying in the dirt in front of her, but they appeared unbroken.

"Okay, let's try that shot again," I said cheerfully to my imaginary film crew in the woods. I helped Bristol up and gave her a gentle shove toward the direction where we'd been hiding, turned and waved goodbye to the woman and her daughter, then followed Bristol back into the woods.

I could hear the mother and daughter chattering as they left us. Then laughter. That was good. Maybe they wouldn't report us to the park rangers. Maybe the rangers had already gone home. Maybe we could still salvage this calamity.

Back in the weeds, Bristol was slumped over, head down, sniffling.

She looked up at me, the tears streaming down her dusty face morphing into rivulets of mud as they dripped off her chin. "Why?" she sniffed. "Why do I always have to mess up?"

Everybody's the star of their own story. Some people crave the hero role more than others. If it had been our guy, Bristol *would* have been the champion instead of the fool. She threw herself—literally—into the part, but the script called for a clown not a paladin.

I sat down beside her. I can't stand it when women cry. It makes me feel guilty, as if it were my fault and my responsibility to staunch the sadness, apply some sort of emotional tourniquet. I remembered feeling that way as a child when my mom was out of it, me thinking I should do something to help her, but I couldn't. Maybe someday I'll talk it all out with a shrink. Someday. But Bristol needed help now.

She had a twig lodged in her hair. I pulled it free and handed it to her. "Nice camouflage."

She examined the stick for several heartbeats, then dropped it.

"Bristol, this is a tense situation. You ran over there on instinct. Cut yourself a little slack. Some people might have frozen. You charged straight ahead. That shows you have courage."

She looked up and forced a small smile.

"And stupidity and poor judgment and lousy footwork. But you got game, girl. Nobody can say you don't."

She stuck her tongue out at me for the second time that day.

"Shake it off. We're all good here."

She looked into her lap, picked up the camera, and raised it to me like a penitent child returning a stolen toy.

I shook my head.

"No. You're still the most qualified. Come on, hide over here with us. We should stick together."

CHAPTER 13

THREE-AND-A-HALF LONG, BORING hours later, it was dark and we were tired, restless, and eaten up by mosquitos and no-see-ums. The mother and child Bristol startled were the only passersby we'd encountered.

To help kill the time, I'd tried drawing Jazzy out about her condition and why she was in such a hurry to flee New Orleans.

"I saw the eviction sign on the door," I said. "What was that about?"

"That's what they do when you don't pay the rent."

"Oh, I'm sorry. Business slow?"

"Nope. Business was good. Lots of marks—I mean customers. I didn't pay the rent."

"How come?"

"I knew I'd be moving on."

And that was as much as I got about that. Shirley DuMont, a.k.a. Madam Jazzabelle, woman of intrigue.

I shared the story about my misadventure on Interstate 10, how I ended up crossing into Florida inside a casket. This perked her up.

"That explains it," she said.

"Explains what?" Tess asked.

"How he survived crossing the River Styx. He was protected by the casket. It was metal."

"But he went back over the river again when he returned to New Orleans," Bristol pointed out.

"Yes, but that was the opposite direction."

"But what about the latest trip, returning to Florida the second time. Didn't you cross the River Styx again?" Tess asked.

"Yes. But he was with me then. My aura protected him."

"Well, I hope your aura keeps protecting us," I said.

Jazzy nodded. "It will." Then several seconds later added, "For a while."

It had turned 8:40. The stars were out and it was growing chilly. I was glad I'd changed out of my cargo shorts into jeans—a precaution I'd taken before we left, figuring it would provide added bug protection.

This was Tess's show. I'd stay here all night if she wanted. But, finally, she threw in the towel:

"Time to call in the dogs and piss on the fire."

I'd heard that expression before. Even used it. But it seemed odd coming from her.

"Can women do that?"

"It's only a figure of speech. Don't be so literal."

We used our cell phone flashlights to work our way out of the weeds and back onto the trail. Tess was the first to approach the hickory, and I heard her cuss under her breath when the light illuminated the base of the tree.

"What'd you find?" I asked.

"Not a goddamned thing."

I aimed my phone's flashlight at the hollow in the tree and nothing seemed to have changed.

I crouched down and ran my fingers through the detritus hoping to find a package of some sort buried beneath the dirt and leaves. But there was nothing but a few rocks and bark chips.

"I am so pissed," Tess said. "We're getting tooled around."

Most of the pieces of bark were small—nickel and quarter

sized—but one was a bit larger, perhaps the size of a playing card. Could our mad poet have used it to scrawl a message? I brought it up to the light and turned it to see both sides.

Nothing.

The stones looked as if they had been kicked into the hollow from the pathway, most were pebble sized. A couple were larger, one the size of a misshapen ping-pong ball, a couple of flat rocks suitable for skipping on the lake at the bottom of the Millhopper. Then I noticed the top of a larger stone poking through leaves at the back of the cavity. I dug around it with my fingers until I could get a grip on it and pulled it out. It was gray, the color of wet concrete, and when I grasped it I noticed something else: It had a flat bottom.

"Ah, ha."

"What is it?" Bristol asked.

I held it in my fingertips and aimed the flashlight at the bottom of the rock. It revealed a rectangular plastic plug. This was no ordinary stone. This was an artificial rock designed to hide a key. But in this case, I was sure it would hold a clue.

"I'll be damned," Tess said. "We've been here all night, and that damn thing was sitting there all along."

"I find this fucker, I really am going to crush his larynx," Bristol said.

I reached into the back pocket of my jeans and extracted a white handkerchief. Yes, that's old fashioned, unmillennial. But my Uncle Leo had drilled certain survival habits into me as a boy. "You never know when you'll need to sop up blood," he'd said.

Now we were preserving evidence.

I lowered the stone into the handkerchief, careful not to touch it any more than necessary.

"Do we read this now or later?" I asked.

Tess said, "Let's wait until we get back to my place. We can do it there with less risk of smearing fingerprints, if there are any."

Bristol had parked her car at a Wells Fargo bank on Northwest Fifty Third Avenue across from the park. Instinctively, I glanced behind us from time to time as we trekked out, wondering if a poetic madman might show himself. If he was there, he was wearing his cloak of invisibility.

We were quiet on the ride back to Tess's house; tired, but eager to discover what the poet had written.

We gathered around the kitchen table, and Tess used a pair of tweezers to pry off the rubber stopper that sealed the bottom of the rock. Then she extracted a folded slip of white paper from the hollow interior of the stone. She held it up, like a coroner displaying a bullet removed from a corpse.

The message was hand printed with a black felt-tip marker in tiny lettering on the back of a half sheet of paper. On the opposite side of the sheet was what appeared to be a legal document of some sort.

"What's this?" Bristol asked. The wording seemed to be boilerplate for some sort of contract. I caught a glimpse of a few phrases such as "confidential information," "past, present, future business," "third-party source," "obligations under this…" before Tess set the note on the kitchen table, contract-side down, revealing the latest poem:

> *I got the goods*
> *As you can see.*
> *Original only,*
> *I promise thee.*
> *Collect all ten*
> *And you'll be done.*
> *So complete the rhyme;*
> *Let's have some fun.*
> *Stanza one*
> *I'll now show:*
> *YOUR PRIZE AWAITS*
> *SO DON'T BE SLOW.*
> *Find your way*
> *To Stanza Two—*

WTF

It's two, too.

I looked at Tess and said, "I'm going to transcribe this. But while I'm doing that, can we break this down? Let's start at the top. What does he mean by 'I got the goods'? Is he talking about this sheet of paper, the legalese on the back?"

Tess didn't say anything. She sat frozen, expressionless.

"Tess, the thing that was stolen. Was it a legal document, is that what we have here?"

Her arms were crossed against her chest squeezing herself, clearly uncomfortable. She paused to compose her answer and finally said:

"You can tell it's a legal document, yes. It was five pages long. This looks like the bottom half of one of those pages, I can't tell which one. If he's tearing each of the five pages in half, then I guess that would come out to ten, which has to be what he means in the poem when he says collect all ten."

"And it sounds like he's saying this is the original, that he didn't make copies, like we should believe that." I said.

She nodded. "He can't. It's printed on security paper. If you try to copy it, the type is obscured by a hidden message embedded in the paper."

"For real?" Jazzy asked.

"Yes. It's readily available. You can buy it online."

"So this is the original, that's good," Bristol said. "But original what? Is it a contract? A loan? You owe him money? What the fuck is this?"

She asked the question I wanted to ask, but I was happy to let her fade the heat for saying it out loud.

Tess said, "It's complicated. I just can't talk about it."

Her face was flushed and her voice tight. I felt badly for her. But she was making it difficult to help her. She was asking us to trust her, but wanted to keep us in the dark. Ordinarily, trust is reciprocal. Whatever she was hiding, it must be some kind of grim.

Somewhere deep in my lizard brain a primordial instinct was stirring. It was a scratchy feeling, synapses irritated. An intuition that was warning me to raise shields, there was an anomaly on the long-range sensors. Something was very, very wrong.

Fred must have felt it, too. He'd been asleep, but now he was at my feet and he started whining.

"Sorry," I said. "Fred's talking to me. I probably need to let him outside."

I leashed him and we walked out the door.

"Hey, pal, sorry about leaving you alone all day today. It's been kind of crazy."

"Gerrufff."

"Yeah. I hear you. This is all kinds of weird. Especially for you. All these strange new smells, new people. I can tell you're upset."

We walked over to a mailbox and Fred let loose. He was pretty much a once-a-day pooper, and he'd gone that morning, so I figured his excretory needs were satisfied for the evening. But I wanted him to get some more exercise, and I needed to stretch my legs, too, after all that time lying in the woods.

Fred's not a straight-line dog. He meanders. Stopping. Sniffing. In the daytime, he might chase a lizard, but they're way too fast. Squirrels, he ignores. Probably understands that he can't climb trees. Tonight, we simply strolled, taking it easy, breathing in the cool evening air. There was the scent of honeysuckle in the breeze. I could feel a slight mist on my skin and looked up and noticed a faint halo around the streetlight across from Tess's house. It was quiet.

What was in the legal document that Tess was so anxious to hide? I'd never seen her this upset, stricken. Of course, I'd only been around her for a little while, but, still, she was acting like she'd stroke out any minute. As soon as we'd transcribed the note, she'd carefully refolded the document—no mean feat using tweezers—and pushed it back in the little key rock. Then she dropped it into a drawer in her desk and locked it.

"There's some weird shit going down Fred. I'm worried about Tess. It's like a pressure cooker in there. You and me, we're going to have to stick around for a little while, make sure she's okay. You good with that?"

"Gerrufff."

"Atta boy."

I heard footsteps behind me and spun around, startled.

It was Tess.

"I heard what you said."

"She's been spying on us Fred."

She stepped over to us, bowed her head briefly, then looked up into my eyes.

"I know it's a pain, me being so secretive. Thanks for trusting me."

"I told you I would help." The words came out flat, unemotional.

She hesitated. "I know what you said. And I also know what you haven't said."

"Trust is a two-way street, Tess."

"I get it. And I'm sorry. Please, bear with me."

She held out her hand and I took it.

"There's something else I wanted to say. Today, in the woods, what you did with Bristol. You were very kind. A lot of guys wouldn't have been. I wouldn't have been. I was about to let her have it, but you picked her up when she was down."

She put her arms around my waist, pressed her head against my chest, and hugged me.

"Thank you for being my friend."

CHAPTER 14

Gainesville

BRISTOL WAS STABBING the centerfold of the *The Agi-Gator* magazine with her index finger when we returned to the kitchen. "Look at this, I think I've figured something out."

"What is it?" Tess asked.

"Our poet says there will be ten clues, each in two-line stanzas of some bizzarro poem we have to piece together. He's already given us the first stanza. So, simple arithmetic, there are going to be nine more stops to gather all the clues, right?"

"Okay."

"Then he says the next step is *two, too*. The line before he refers to *WTF*." She stabbed the magazine again. "Tess, he's referring to the number on the *WTF* map. And check it out. We selected ten places to visit. He's started with number one on the map, here in Gainesville at the Millhopper. Next is number two, which if I'm right would be The Devil's School. Which means we can plot out where he will be taking us. It's pretty obvious, isn't it, that he's following this map?"

I picked up the magazine. The Devil's School was in Jacksonville, over on the Atlantic Coast. "So what's this douche bag doing? He wants to run you ragged, lead you all over the state on a scavenger hunt?"

"So it would seem," Tess said.

"Each of these places on your map has a number, like Bristol said. Out of curiosity, what was your thinking behind that? Did you rank order these things on some sort of weirdness scale?"

Tess rubbed her eyes. "That was our first argument."

"Whose argument?"

"Me and Amy. Amy wanted to do exactly what you said, Alex. Apply some sort of means test, rank these in order of craziest to least crazy or vice versa. I wanted to make it more user friendly, list them in a logical sequence and include the best routes to get there, this being a travel guide."

"And the other girls," Bristol said, "they wanted to sell advertising, maybe to nearby restaurants, whatever, and they argued we should list them in order of who advertised the most. And you went fucking nuts over that, said it was unethical."

Tess sighed. "Yes. What an idealist I was. Fighting for the ethical ordering of haunted houses for fuck's sake."

"So how'd you resolve it?" I asked.

"Badly," Tess said. "We wanted to make it a top ten list even though we had about fifteen places we liked. So I wrote the names down on slips of paper and drew them out of a hat, one by one, and that's how we got to ten and how we assigned numbers to them."

I looked again at the map and the numbered locations. "Uh, I don't understand. Now that I look at this more closely, these actually seem like they *are* numbered in a logical travel sequence, starting here in Gainesville, then shooting over to the East Coast, then down to near Naples, then back up."

"Yeah, about that. The more I thought about it, the more it seemed stupid. So, without telling anyone, I switched it to the way I wanted in the first place. That was the real reason Amy and I fought. She went berserk when the magazine was printed. The other girls were unhappy, too. The only one who stuck with me was Bristol."

"I see."

That's all I said: "I see." Now is that judgmental? She thought so.

"Hey, chill out. I was fucking nineteen years old."

I thought about Bristol's theory. It seemed as good as anything to go on, but I worried maybe it was a stretch to assume too much about where this wild goose chase would ultimately lead.

"I'm not sure two stops establishes a pattern," I said. "But for now, at least, I say we assume she's right."

Bristol tossed out a not-too-shabby Elvis impression: "Thank you. Thank you very much."

That was all fine, but there were still a pair of elephants in the room: Who was behind this and what was Tess hiding?

"Let's circle back to what you told us earlier," I said to Tess. "After Amy vanished, you discovered something private and important was missing—and now we know it's this legal document. You still thinking Amy ripped it off?

She nodded her head.

"Okay. There are four of us in this room and, fortunately, one of us knows what's missing. I'm not trying to pry the details out of you, but can you at least tell us this: Is it something that could be used for blackmail?'

She eyed me for what seemed like a minute. I assumed she was calculating a response. But all she said was, "Yes."

"It could be used to blackmail you?"

"It could."

I played a hunch. "And someone else?"

She hesitated again then nodded. "Yes. It could be damaging to someone who doesn't deserve it."

"So you're trying to protect someone?" Seemed obvious, but I wanted to hear her acknowledge it.

"That's right."

"Okay, then. If Bristol's right, our mad poet wants to drag us around Florida using this map. He knows the map is your creation. And he had to get the legal document from Amy. Whether Amy is directly involved with this or not, she's crucial to figuring out who is behind this, right?"

Bristol said, "You're mansplaining. The more important question is why doesn't he just get to it, the blackmail part?"

I ignored the mansplaining gig. It helps me to talk things out aloud. Usually Spock is my sounding board but, as usual, he was making no contribution to the conversation. I wouldn't say he's anti-social, but he can be exceedingly unsocial sometimes.

"It's like he's extracting a pound of flesh, first," I said. "Getting revenge for something."

We all thought about that for a bit, then I asked Tess:

"Who hates you this much?"

"It's all I can think about. It's driving me nuts. I mean, the first person I think about is Amy, obviously. But, hell, I don't even know if she's still alive. Or where she is. And if it's her, why the hell has she waited so long to do this? It doesn't make any sense at all to me that it could be her, but it has to be someone who knows—or knew—her."

Bristol said, "Here's a thought: What if Amy and this asshole are working together? Maybe Amy's behind this, trying for some psychotic reason to get even with you, Tess. Maybe this poet person, whoever he is, maybe this is *his* bright idea. Maybe he only recently found out about this stuff Amy ripped off. That would explain the time gap."

Maybe. Maybe. Maybe.

Without knowing what Tess was hiding, how valuable was all this speculation? Still, as shots in the dark went, Bristol's sounded pretty reasonable. She might be a drama queen, but she wasn't stupid.

"I'm feeling like I don't have a lot of options here," Tess said.

"No options?" I asked. "Meaning you're thinking about playing along with this insanity?"

"I don't see an alternative."

Bristol groaned. Jazzy nodded her head. Whether that meant she agreed, or she'd heard it all before, or she was bobbing along to some silent tune she was playing in her head, I didn't know.

"How's this sound?" Tess said. "It's about an hour and a half to Jax. Let's roll in the morning, find the next part of the poem. If he says the next stop after that is—What? St. Augustine and the Fountain of Youth, right?—well, then I think we can feel confident about the pattern. I'm thinking we have to take this one step at a time. That make sense?'

"What choice do we have?" Bristol said.

The obvious choice was to call the cops, but I didn't argue. It was clear Tess wouldn't go along with that. And doing something was usually better than doing nothing. Certainly less boring. Jazzy neither objected nor endorsed it, she was staring at the kitchen ceiling through her pink wraparounds.

"You with us on this, Jazzy?" I asked.

She slowly lowered her head, theatrically removed her sunglasses, and looked at me. Her pupils were dilated, her brown irises a thin rim.

"One of us should stay here."

Tess asked, "Another vision?"

Jazzy turned to face Tess and a brief smile flitted across her lips. "No. Just a hunch."

"Meaning?" Tess asked.

"Meaning we know whoever this poet is, he's been right here in Gainesville. For all we know, he could be looking at us through the window right now."

Instinctively, I glanced out the kitchen window, which was pointless. The glass was black with the night. What did I think I would see besides my own reflection?

"I don't think we should leave your home unguarded," Jazzy continued. "I started worrying about that while we were in the woods. We were gone a long time. How do we know he hasn't already been in here? Maybe he's bugged the place. Maybe he's listening to us right now. Or he's taken something? Or who knows?"

None of that had occurred to me, and I was, once again struck by Jazzy's intelligence. Or maybe my lack thereof.

"I'll go outside," I said. "Reconnoiter. Maybe you all could take a look around the house, see if anything is out of place or if anything is missing. See if you can find any hidden cameras."

"How do you do that?" Tess asked.

"Got a flashlight?"

She nodded. "Several."

"Shine them around, everywhere. If you get an unusual reflection, it could be a camera lens. It would be tiny."

"Sounds paranoid to me," Bristol said.

"Even the paranoid have real..."

"Yeah, yeah, yeah."

I walked out the back door and circled the yard. Nobody jumped out of the bushes, and nothing seemed out of place. Then again, how would I know if anything had been moved or disturbed? But there weren't any broken flower pots, no ladders propped against the walls, no threatening sonnets spray-painted on the clapboard siding. I did shine my iPhone flashlight on the windows. They were all shut, appeared to be locked, and there were no suspicious marks that hinting they'd been pried open or otherwise tampered with.

I extended my surveillance around the block, but again, saw nothing out of the ordinary. Of course, there'd been nothing unusual earlier when I'd taken Fred for a walk.

But when I returned to the house, the women were all standing in the living room waiting for me. They were not wearing happy faces.

"Check out Amy's old room," Tess said, her voice strained.

I looked down the short hallway. The door was open. I stepped inside the room and froze.

CHAPTER 15

SPOCK AND I have been together a long time, and in all those years I've never known him to have demonstrated an affinity for jewelry. Which is why the ring dangling from a delicate gold chain around his neck stood out. The loops in the chain were small, the ring was a plain band with writing engraved on it, and the necklace draped the front of Spock's blue uniform shirt down to the Federation emblem on his chest.

"Is that supposed to be funny?" I asked when I returned to the living room.

Nobody was laughing.

"That ring," Tess said. "It was a friendship ring Amy gave me when she moved in. I thought it was kind of squirrely that she did that and I never wore it. In fact, I put it up and only noticed a few months ago that it wasn't in my jewelry box. No idea where it had gone. I assumed I'd lost it. Until now."

I didn't have to be Dirk Gently to grok the implications.

"Somebody's broken into your house," I said, stating the obvious. But was it obvious?

I tried to recall our movements about the bungalow when we'd retuned from the Devil's Millhopper stakeout. Not that I'm the mistrusting type, but could one of the three women I was facing in the living room have done this before we left or after we returned?

Jazzy, once again, seemed to read my thoughts.

"I didn't do it."

Both Bristol and Tess whirled to face her. The thought never having crossed their minds that one of them could be implicated.

Then they turned to face me.

"You don't think…" Bristol started, then choked it off. Tess said nothing, stone faced.

"Tess, you deadbolted the door when we left the house. I saw you do it. The back door was locked?"

"Yes. I checked. I always check."

"And the front door was still locked when we came back?"

"Yes."

"Alright. Who besides you has a key?"

"I do," Bristol said.

"And my landlord," Tess said.

I hadn't realized Tess was renting the house. For no valid reason, I thought she owned it. Not that it mattered, but it was further evidence of why you should never assume.

"Any keys hidden outside, under the doormat, inside a hollow rock?"

Tess shook her head.

"Amy had a key, right?" I asked, mechanically running down the list of possibilities.

"Yes."

"You change the locks?"

"Of course."

I glanced at my wristwatch. Mickey's little hand was on the 10, his big hand on the 3. Yes, I wear a wristwatch. A lot of people only use their cell phones these days, but I've got this thing about being on time. I could blame it on working for a newspaper, the emphasis on deadlines. But, really, it's genetic. Uncle Leo is a fanatic on the subject.

Ask any lawyer who's ever been late to a hearing in his courtroom. And the new asshole he acquired.

"Is it too late to call your landlord?"

Tess didn't hesitate. She dug into her back pocket, pulled out her cell phone, then called. While it was ringing, she tapped the screen to put it on speaker.

Tess: "Hello, Marv, it's Tess. Sorry about the hour. You still up and at 'em?"

Marv: "Yep. Eating Cheetos and watching *Die Hard*. If this is about your overdue rent, you can pay up in the morning, no need to bother me at home."

Tess: "Not about the rent, Marv. It looks like somebody broke into my house. But he must have had a key because there's no sign of forced entry, no broken windows or anything, and I always lock the doors."

Marv: "Really?"

Tess: "Marv, could someone have gotten hold of a key to this place?"

Marv: "Lemme look."

There was a rustling sound on the phone, the faint clinking of metal on metal, then he came back on the line.

Marv: "I keep all my rental keys on a ring here, and they're all accounted for. But I also have duplicates at the office."

Tess: "Is there any way we can check there?"

Marv: "You mean right now? Bruce Willis is about to throw that guy out the window onto the cop's car. It's one of my favorite scenes."

Tess: "You got a pause button?"

The speaker was quiet for a few seconds while Marv did something in the background.

Marv: "Good suggestion. Be there in ten minutes."

Tess: "On my way."

She turned to Bristol, who by then was slumped on the couch. "Come on, girlfriend. You're with me. Alex, you and Jazzy stay here, watch the place, okay?"

"Sure."

Tess turned to the door, then glanced back. Bristol was still sitting motionless on the couch. "You coming?"

Bristol was staring at nothing, lost in her own head, utterly still. Maybe she'd been shot with a freeze ray.

Tess placed her hands on her hips, impatient. "What is it, Bristol?"

Bristol slowly refocused, then stood up and walked over to Tess. She grabbed Tess by her shoulders, the way a mother might pin a disobedient child while she chewed her out. "You listen to me," she began.

In a seamless movement, Tess crossed her arms in front of her body then swung them rapidly upward into Bristol's forearms, breaking her grip.

"What the fuck's with you?" Tess growled, taking a step backward.

"I'll tell you what the fuck's with me. This isn't funny anymore. You're being physically stalked." She stopped and glanced back and Jazzy and me. "We all are. Who knows how dangerous this asshole is? Where he might show up next? We have to call the cops. If you don't do it, I will."

"Goddammit, Bristol. We've been over this. I can't call the cops. I just can't."

"Bullshit."

Tess took a step toward Bristol, and she, instinctively, stepped backwards, bumping the backs of her legs against the coffee table.

"I get it, Bristol. You're scared. Me, too. But no cops. You understand? You're here of your own free will. I won't blame you if you bail. Go ahead. It's all good. You didn't sign up for this shit. Take off. No hard feelings."

Jazzy jumped in and said, "Ladies, we really don't have time for this."

At which point Tess whirled on her and shouted, "You stay out of this!" And for an disturbing moment I thought she might lunge at her.

If Tess and Bristol wanted to duke it out, that was no business of mine, but Tess's aggression toward Jazzy alarmed me and I did something every man with a healthy sense of personal survival knows never to do—I inserted myself into a cat fight. Stepping between them, I said:

"Girls, girls, girls."

Around 40,000 years ago, the last caveman who interrupted an argument between two females was involuntarily removed from the gene pool—probably after receiving a sharp stick in the eye. Surviving generations of males have instinctively known to stay out of it. But Jazzy had grown on me. And there was a vulnerability about her that aroused my protective instincts. And when Tess turned on her I acted without thinking. Which was successful in refocusing Tess's anger away from both Jazzy and Bristol, but now I was in the crosshairs. I had this vision of having my eyes clawed out or other sensitive areas of my person damaged, so I said:

"Hey, we're all under a lot of stress here. Can't we just get along?"

That got me an eye-roll from Tess and Bristol stuck her tongue out at me.

Then Bristol turned to Tess and said, "Don't worry. I'll stick with you." And after a moment the two women hugged.

Drama over. Just like that.

"We're leaving," Tess announced summarily without further comment and walked out the door with Bristol on her heels.

"Bye, Felicia," Jazzy said under her breath.

After I deadbolted the door, I turned back to Jazzy. She was shaking her head.

"For the record, when we got back from the woods, I didn't go into Amy's room. I saw the look you were giving everyone. It wasn't me."

I nodded. "There were four of us in the house. Any of us, theoretically, could have put that necklace on Spock. But neither you nor I would have any clue about that ring, which leaves only Tess and Bristol. And I don't think either of them did it."

"I don't either. They were both shocked when we saw it."

"What about you, Fred? You sleep through all this?"

"Gerrufff."

Then I had a stray thought. It was stupid, and I knew it. The sort of plot point a TV show might use. Fred's gregarious. If someone entered the house, he would have run over. He's not much of a watchdog, but he does have this habit of jumping up on people's legs to say hello. What if he scratched the perp, snagged some fibers. Wouldn't that be cool?

I sat down next to him and took his front paws in my hands. I'd clipped his nails before our journey so they were short, and he'd been on enough walks that they were no longer rough but smoothed from abrasion on parking lots, sidewalks and streets—not to mention the shoulder of Interstate 10.

His claws were clean. There went my CSI moment.

I wandered back into Amy's room. Spock was still standing motionless with his new adornment.

"Nothing to share about this?" I asked.

Spock kept his thoughts to himself.

I returned to the kitchen where Jazzy was sitting at the table, leafing through the *Agi-Gator* travel guide.

"You see any of this in your visions?"

She looked up. "Not this specifically. But it has a familiar feel."

"What kind of feel?"

She blinked a couple of times and ran her hands over her turban. "Dread."

CHAPTER 16

Jacksonville

EVER TRY DRIVING at high speed while scratching your insect-ravaged ankles? I don't advise it. Especially on an interstate in the passing lane. Which is what I was doing when I heard Jazzy suck in her breath and I looked up just in time to avoid running up the tailpipe of a Cadillac plodding along well below the speed limit.

No-see-ums are a kind of microscopic fly in the biological family *Ceratopogonidae*, which is Latin for "irritating little ankle biters." The female no-see-ums have ferocious jaws that gnaw tiny holes into human skin. You don't feel that violation going on when they're at work chewing on you, but the next day the itching is outrageous. They are blood suckers who need the protein to lay eggs to generate millions more no-see-ums to plague naïve dumbasses like me who lay about in the woods at night becoming irresistible sources of food for itsy-bitsy vampires.

I'd heard of no-see-ums, but until now had never experienced how irritating their bites could be. Welcome to Florida.

"You're probably allergic," Jazzy said. "You have reactions to bee stings?"

"Got nailed by a wasp on my forearm last year. Looked like Popeye for a week."

"You're allergic. You should pee on it."

"Pee. On. It?"

"Works every time."

I recalled a *Survivor* You Tube video in which one of the female castaways gave a dude a golden shower after he was stung by a sea urchin. The ammonia in the urine was supposed to help with the pain or some such.

I glanced at Jazzy and she was staring straight ahead, eyes shielded as usual behind her pink wraparounds. Was that a hint of a smile?

"Or maybe we can stop at a drugstore for some cortisone," she said.

Water droplets began sprouting on the Sebring's windshield and I flicked on the wipers. The Weather Channel was forecasting periodic thunderstorms throughout the day. Jazzy and I had pulled out of Gainesville early after sloshing down coffee and devouring a bag of doughnuts that Bristol delivered. We needed the caffeine and sugar. It had been a short night.

The knock at the front door had startled Fred awake and he began barking. Only seconds before, the rooftop flashers from a pair of Gainesville PD cruisers began strobing the front window. We were all awake, sitting around the kitchen table. Tess was sipping coffee. Bristol and I were chugging Stump Knocker pale ales, a local brew that she had snagged on their return trip from the landlord's office. Jazzy was hydrating with tap water unmindful that it tasted like chalk.

"Who the fuck called the police?" Tess hissed. "We talked about this, goddammit." She was giving Bristol the death stare.

Bristol raised her hands in self-defense. "Jesus, Tess, not me. When could I? I've been with you all evening."

Tess glared at me and I gave her death stare right back. "Don't even."

A pair of cops in a navy blue uniforms with matching ball caps stood at the door. "Are you Tess Winkler?" the taller of the two asked.

"Yes, officer. What's this about?"

The cop had his hand resting on his sidearm. "Did you call 911 with a report of a burglary?"

Tess shook her head. "No, I didn't. You got the right address?"

The cop read off the street address. "Dispatch received an anonymous call saying there's been a break-in at this address. Are you saying you did not make that call?"

"I've made no calls to the police," Tess said, blocking the doorway, her hand resting on the door handle as if ready to shut it in the cop's face.

The uniform was looking past Tess into the house. Bristol and I had wandered over to stand behind her. Jazzy hadn't moved from the kitchen table. The cop turned his attention back to Tess and spoke in a lowered voice. "Is everything alright here?"

The other cop was talking into his shoulder mic. I couldn't make out what he was saying, but shortly thereafter a third cruiser pulled up at the curb and another uniform got out. The cop on the mic motioned him to three-sixty the house, and the new arrival fired up his flashlight and began circling the yard.

"Do you mind if we come in, make sure everything is okay?" the cop at the door was asking.

"Everything's fine," Tess said.

The cop was unconvinced. I wasn't sure, but it seemed like standard operating procedure. Domestic calls are the most dangerous for police. And Tess wouldn't be the first woman who tried to block a cop from entering a residence because somewhere behind the door or in another room a crazed husband or drugged out boyfriend was lurking, maybe with a piece.

They faced off for a few more heartbeats, then Flashlight Cop joined them on the front porch. "Clear on the perimeter," he said.

"Ma'am," the cop was now saying, adopting a conciliatory tone, "I'd feel a lot better if we could make sure you are okay." I spotted his name badge. It said FRINK.

"Look, I didn't call 911."

Microphone cop was talking over his shoulder radio with dispatch. He clicked off and said, "Ms. Winkler, did you speak earlier this evening to a Marvin Mannheimer?"

"Yes. He's my landlord."

"He called back. Said he felt guilty about not leaving his name. Said he did it because he figured you would be upset. But he's worried about your safety. He's the one who called in the burglary report."

Tess folded. "Fine." She swung the door open and with a sweeping motion of her hand gestured them in. "But I have to tell you this is much ado about nothing. Come on in, I'll show you. Someone played a prank on me. No biggie."

She glanced at the three of us, making sure we got the message, as if she hadn't already made that incontrovertibly clear: We were to say nothing about the mad poet,

The cops were unamused by what they discovered in Amy's old room. They called in a pair of Forensic Crime Unit investigators and they all stuck around until 2 a.m., taking statements, lifting prints, shooting photos, and collecting fiber samples—all things I'd seen before on television. Unlike on TV, the crime scene technicians didn't skulk around the house with guns drawn, which was a little disappointing. After observing the techs at work for a few minutes, it was clear to me that a career in watch repair might offer more excitement.

While DNA tests take time, fingerprints can quickly be matched on the Automated Fingerprint Identification System, or AFIS. To eliminate ours from any other prints they might discover in the house, the techs printed each of us. They said they'd have results back in less than twenty-four hours.

I told one of the investigators, a young woman in her mid-twenties, about my brilliant insight that she should check out Fred's claws. "He might have scratched the perp."

"Perp? Nice."

That was about the time we were escorted out to the lawn where legions of *Ceratopogonidae* lay in wait, licking their miniscule chops as the human blood-donors came traipsing onto the grass where they were lurking, readying their attack, the thirsty little psychopaths.

While we milled about outside swatting the bugs we could see—mosquitos—the crime scene techs bagged the necklace and ring dangling from Spock's neck and lifted prints from his surface. Fortunately, they didn't haul him off to the evidence room for safe keeping. Spock had already spent too much time in closets this week.

Officer Frink, preparing to leave, promised Tess she would be hearing from one of the department's detectives first thing in the morning.

"Is this normal procedure for a burglary call?" I asked him. Maybe because Gainesville was a medium-sized town they got amped for things like this, but in any large metropolitan area, illegal entries hardly warranted calling out the cavalry. In some cities, you filled out a form online and the cops never showed.

He gave me the dead-eye stare, then answered: "No."

He turned to Tess: "Frank Demerest sends his greetings." Then he left.

Demerest, Tess reminded us a little later, was the detective who had been in charge of investigating Amy's disappearance. "I guess he thinks he owes me."

Before the cops had arrived, Tess told us the trip to the landlord's place proved inconclusive. He kept the keys to his rental properties in the desk of his small real estate office, Tess said, stashed in separate marked envelopes in one of his side drawers. He owned or managed a dozen rentals, and all twelve envelopes were where they should have been. Although, he admitted, the drawer was unlocked.

The number of keys in each envelope varied, from a high of three, to a low of one. There were two in the envelope labeled with Tess's address. He couldn't remember how many should be there, the numbers changing as keys were lost or additionals were requested.

Someone could have pilfered a key, he acknowledged. He was in and out of the office a lot. But the thief would have needed to know where to look. He had a fulltime secretary and a part-time office assistant, both of whom would have had that knowledge. The full-timer was a woman who had worked with him for twenty-two years. The part-timer was a community college student who covered the office on Saturdays and who had only been there a few weeks. He promised to check with them on Monday.

Tess said Marv seemed concerned for her safety and insisted that he would get a locksmith out to her house first thing the next day. He also urged her to call the police, but she waved him off. Or so she thought.

Until the locksmith showed, somebody needed to stick around the house. Which is how Jazzy and I ended up driving to Jacksonville, leaving Tess and Bristol to guard the bungalow, babysit Fred, and wait to hear from the detective that Officer Frink promised would be contacting her.

Jazzy had borrowed a pair of big Bose headphones and an ancient iPod from Tess. She was listening to—what else?—jazz. She'd stuffed the iPod into her shirt pocket, a loose-fitting, paisley blouse, sleeveless, showing off the hieroglyphics on her arms.

While she entertained herself, I scanned the radio for news. I once again stumbled across the Rev. Lee Roy Chitango, this time ranting about the evils of birth control and morning-after pills and how doctors who performed abortions should be executed—all in the name of being pro-life, of course. Then he switched to the government conspiracy surrounding childhood inoculations, how kids were being implanted with tracking devices and how the vaccines were the source of autism.

And about all those chickenpox and measles outbreaks? Could they not be attributed to a reduction in parents vaccinating their kids? "No, my children," the good reverend intoned. "That is God's punishment for the wicked."

Evidently Jazzy heard Chitango's ravings through her headphones and slipped them off. "That man is dangerous. He's anti-science. He'll get people killed."

"A soothsayer who believes in science?" I couldn't resist teasing her.

She wagged her finger at me and scowled. "You don't know me. You don't know what my life has been like these past few months with these visions, these nightmares. Believe it or not, I *do* believe there is a scientific explanation. But I don't know what it is. Neither do my doctors. But something is going on."

"Oh, sure, sorry. I was just…"

"Don't be ordinary. You're smarter than that. Keep your mind open. The world needs scientists to find the truth. And the world needs journalists to tell the truth. Journalists have great power…"

"Right. And with great power come great responsibility. I saw the movie, too."

"Don't be so cynical. It may be a line from a movie, but it's still true."

She was staring at me, maybe waiting for me to offer a sarcastic comeback. But I understood her point.

"You know the story about Galileo, don't you?" she asked.

"You mean how the Pope threatened to kill him for saying the Earth orbited the Sun?"

She bobbed her head. "There's that, but I was thinking about his experiment at the Leaning Tower of Pisa."

"Where he dropped a big ball and a little ball to show that they'd hit the ground at the same time?"

"Yes, that. You do realize that until then everybody—and I mean everybody—knew the big ball would hit first. Even Aristotle said so."

"And nobody ever thought to actually take a look and see for themselves."

"Right. That's why Galileo's called the father of modern science. I believe in science. And I believe there is a scientific explanation for my visions. I don't presume to know the answer myself. But I don't—and you shouldn't—close the door on a possible answer just because it's out of the ordinary."

"Point taken."

She was quiet for a bit and I waited for her to continue lecturing me. But she changed the subject.

"I've wanted to ask you ever since you walked into my shop. It's about your name. Strange. That a stage name?"

"You mean like Jazzabelle?"

"Yeah, like that."

I get that question a lot and I was weary of telling the story. But there was time and I figured if I shared a little, maybe she would, too. I, too, had questions I wanted answered.

"It's like this. My mom's real last name was Strano. It's Italian but my family traces its roots to Switzerland. But she hated it. She was a Deadhead, wanted a more hippy-dippy moniker, so she started calling herself Alice Sunshine."

"Sunshine," Jazzy mused. "Nice."

"Nice unless you're a little boy getting ready to enter the first grade and kids are already picking on you because of your stupid name."

She nodded. "Sunshine. Not cool."

"Very uncool. On multiple levels. Mom was, uh, confused when she signed my birth certificate, filled in her own name where mine should have gone. The upshot is that on my official birth record I'm Alice Sunshine. But she always called me Alex. And Uncle Leo got the name problem legally fixed for me later."

Jazzy slipped off her pink shades, glanced at me with a mischievous smile, and started to say something.

"Don't even."

She eyed me for a second, blinked, then put her shades back on.

"So, Mom says, 'What's in a name?' And she invited me to pick whatever name I wanted to use when I went to school."

"And you picked Strange?"

"I actually suggested Strano. I knew that was Mom's—and my

Uncle Leo's—real last name. But she said no, that I would eventually hate it. She knew something I didn't at the time, which is that *strano* in some circles is a vulgar term for an anus that becomes enlarged through homosexual sex."

"Good grief."

"Yeah. Dodged a bullet there. Anyway, I asked her what the name Strano meant in Italian, if it had an English translation. She said it did. It translated as Strange."

"So this isn't a Doctor Strange thing?"

I laughed. "No. Although I get that question from time to time. I was a D.C. comics fan growing up. Not Marvel. I actually never heard of Doctor Strange as a kid. But I did know about Adam Strange. He was an archeologist who was being chased by natives in the jungles of South America when he jumped off a cliff and was captured by a tele-portation beam from the planet Rann. He flew around with a rocket pack and a ray gun and was this amazing hero. I did like those comics. Later I realized they owed their lineage to Edgard Rice Burroughs."

"I know him. Tarzan, right."

"Yes. But also John Carter, Warlord of Mars. He was a soldier transported to the Red Planet where he fell in love with Deja Thoris."

"I saw the movie."

"Most people hated it."

"Most people are wrong."

I glanced at her. She shrugged.

"Sometimes being right is a lonely business."

I liked the movie, too. I made a fist and we knuckle bumped.

"Your mother," Jazzy said. "Where is she now?"

"Her body was never found."

She pulled off her shades and stared at me. "What do you mean?"

I told her the spider story, how Mom was washed away, her body never recovered.

"She left you. And you were all alone? For how long?"

I don't talk about my history very often, and on the few occasions that I've shared that story nobody had ever asked about what happened to *me* while Mom was gone. It was always about the stupid spider. Once again, I was impressed with Jazzy's perceptiveness and empathy.

"When Mom left, she locked the door behind her after telling Spock he was in charge. Spock was always in charge. I was too little. She told us not to let anyone in. Under no circumstances were we to answer the door. That it could be dangerous.

"I was so used to Mom being gone, coming home late, drunk or stoned, or both, I didn't take her seriously.

"Later, when she'd been gone for a few hours, there was banging on the door. And a man shouting. It was loud and insistent. I became very frightened and hid in my bedroom. That's when I started worrying, wondering where Mom really was. I remember thinking I should have told her not to go. To stay with me. But I didn't. She used to call me her "brave little man." I didn't want to let her down. I didn't want her to know how much I hated it when she was gone.

"Later that night the banging started again. It was dark, the lights were off, and I snuck into the bathroom to hide. I was terrified. I dragged Spock in with me. I locked the bathroom door and spent the night there. I remember crying. And feeling guilty. I had this awful sense that Mom wouldn't be coming back and somehow it was all my fault because I failed to ask her not to go.

"I spent all the next day in the bathroom, locked up with Spock. By the time the police showed up I think I was delirious. I know it doesn't make any sense, but from time to time I still have these uncontrollable flashes of guilt—that I should have done something to protect her. And don't even get me started on how I can't stand to be in confined places anymore."

I stopped and realized I'd just told Jazzy more than I'd ever shared with anyone about that day and night. Even more than Leo. It was cathartic. But why now? And why with her? I glanced over at Jazzy and her eyes were glassy. She touched my shoulder. Her hand felt warm. She held it there for a few moments, then finally said:

"I am so sorry, Strange Man. So very sorry."

Then she slipped her headphones back on and stared straight ahead out the windshield.

We were quiet for a few minutes and I wondered if the relief I felt in talking to her, that small unburdening of my soul, at all resembled how confessionals felt. If so, I could understand why people did it. Why people went to group therapy, joined AA.

I tapped Jazzy's earpiece and she turned and lowered it.

"My turn to ask questions. Before New Orleans, who were you?"

She tugged the headphones all the way off, set them on her lap, and stared out into the rain through the metronomic beating of the windshield wipers.

"If I told you, you wouldn't believe me."

"You just lectured me a few minutes ago about keeping an open mind."

She smirked. "So I did. Okay, here's the story. It's not long. I woke up one morning lying on a cot in the back of the shop on Royal Street, behind the curtains. I have no memory of anything before that."

I'd asked, so I went with it. "You don't recall getting busted for running a brothel? Learning how to be a licensed chirologist while in jail? None of your history? Not even winning that contest for displaying the best breasts at Mardi Gras?"

"Nothing."

"So how do you even know your name?"

"Oh, Shirley DuMont? When I awoke, there was a journal lying on a little TV table by the cot. On the first page was my name, my address—the address of the shop—and, of all things, my blood type."

"Blood type?"

"Yes, it's rare. AB-negative. Only one in two hundred people have it."

"Well, I suppose that would be important to know. But are you saying you may not be Shirley DuMont, that you're not the real Madam Jazzabelle? Is that why you had to skip town in a hurry?"

"I'm telling you that I have no memory of who I am or what my life was like before I awoke that morning in the shop."

"So, let me guess, you went to the hospital…"

"And I got lots of tests. CAT scans, MRIs, blood work. When I started having these visions, some of doctors thought it might be related to my amnesia, others thought I might be suffering from other neurological disorders, hence the pills and the shots, none of which did any good."

"So can you really read palms?"

She snorted. "I can read. That's a miracle, I guess. I didn't forget how to do that. But, no, I can't read palms. Did you really think I could?"

I shrugged. "I neither believe nor disbelieve. As you said, I'm a journalist. I'm interested in the truth."

She patted me on my thigh. "That's the spirit."

I felt my quadricep muscle bunch up when she did that, as if it had been stimulated by an electrical current. Weird. But what wasn't?

"One more question."

"Okay."

"We talked about this a little bit before. When I first met you, and you read my palm, you said you saw death. Did you make that up, or did you have a vision? I remember you sweating, like you say you do when you have these spells. Was that for real?"

She was quiet for a few ticks, then she said, "Yes, that was real."

"So when am I supposed to die?"

She'd put her shades back on and I couldn't see her eyes clearly, but her brow was furrowed and her face seemed to have sagged. Her voice was hushed when she spoke.

"I said I saw death. I never said whose death I saw."

She slipped her headphones back over her ears and stared out the windshield. Conversation over.

I pulled off Interstate 10 at Stockton Street, the windshield wipers whopping furiously, then followed Siri's directions on my iPhone as we navigated a series of Jacksonville back streets near the intersection with I-95. Forest Street. Park Street. Penninsular Place. Then finally we were idling in the downpour outside a chain link fence guarding 699 Chelsea Street—The Devil's School, or, as it is more formally known, Annie Lytle Elementary, long-abandoned.

Legend has it that the school's janitor used to drag unsuspecting innocents to the basement where he burned them alive in the boiler room. Other stories told of a principal, a deranged cannibal, who kidnapped naïve children sent to detention, then gutted and hung them on meat hooks in a special locker until dinner time. It is acknowledged as Jacksonville's most haunted place.

"You think the legend is true?" Jazzy asked mischievously. "You believe he ate all those kids?"

"Yes," I said in my best Arnold Schwarzenegger impression. "But they were all bad."

That was probably in terrible taste, but you never know what's going to work until you try it out on a live audience, right?

She didn't laugh. Then again, if her memory had been wiped, maybe she had no recollection of *True Lies*. Or any other movies. Or history. Or how to mix a proper Cuba Libre. No wonder she rarely spoke. She had to relearn everything.

"When we get done with all this," I said, "there are some movies we need to watch."

"Like *True Lies*?"

"You've seen it?"

"I believe I have."

"How could you know that?"

She shrugged. "Another mystery."

"Huh."

"Do that again, that Arnold impression." She pronounced it *Ah-nold*.

"*Hasta la vista, baby.*"

"You're pretty good, you know that?"

That was a first.

Chelsea Street bent into Penninsular at the I-95 overpass. Trucks and cars roared overhead. The fence blocking off the decaying brown-brick school was topped with barbed wire and decorated every few feet with ominous black and orange signs—Halloween colors—warning NO TRESPASSING. Some of the building's windows were boarded up, others wide open, some intact. It was a derelict that ordinarily would have been demolished, but preservationists had talked the county into declaring it a historic landmark, the goal being to restore it. But decades had passed and it sat deserted, rotting.

And haunting.

"So, Madam Jazzabelle, here we are. There's no way in without risking arrest for trespassing or getting cut up on barbed wire. You think our poet expected us to sneak in, prowl around this hulk's insides? It could take hours. Or days. And, uh, is this a hurricane?"

I had no umbrella in the car, nor any other rain gear—hey, I'd just arrived from the desert southwest. Not that it mattered. If I'd tried to pop an umbrella in that tempest, I would have been whisked away into the heavens like Mary Poppins.

"I'll stay in the car," Jazzy said. "Make sure the air conditioner is running, that it stays nice and dry and cool while you go exploring." With that, she adjusted her seat to a half-recline, slipped her headphones back on, locked her hands behind her head, and sighed.

The rain was blowing sideways, propelled by furious gale-force winds. I checked the radar on the Weather Channel app and we were in the heart of an enormous thunderstorm that showed no sign of abating. Lightning strobed the sky overhead followed instantly by a crack of thunder that shook the car.

"That was close."

Jazzy didn't stir. Stoic. Or maybe she had already foreseen these events and was untroubled. Surely she would have warned me not to step out into the fury of this squall if I were going to get struck dead by lightning, right?

I inched the car along the chain-link fence, hugging the muddy curb, hoping to find either a way in or some sign the mad poet had been here. If he had left a clue for us, where would it be? I pulled up across a side entrance to the schoolhouse. Ten concrete steps led to closed double doors, each with more NO TRESPASSING signs affixed. Someone had propped a makeshift plywood ramp atop the right-hand side of the steps for reasons that eluded me. Why would an abandoned building need a handicapped entrance or a delivery ramp? At the base of a pair of white Tuscan columns flanking the steps were two signs. The one of the left read *Annie Lytle School*; the one on the right read *EST. 1917*. The steps were free of debris. No out-of-place hollow rocks with hidden messages inside awaited us in the shelter of the molding overhang, best I could tell through the torrent of rain.

At the end of Chelsea Street, where it abutted the interstate overpass, a yellow Caterpillar crane sat abandoned inside the fence. There was a chain-link gate blocking a gravel access drive alongside the overpass, a handful of orange and white construction barrels, and a green outhouse topped with a white roof.

I drove closer and could see piles of construction material stacked in the shelter of the overpass, all part of some repair project, I surmised. I also noticed a gap between the gate guarding the construction area and the schoolyard fence. At first, I thought that might provide an opening I could exploit. But then I realized it merely led to the construction area, not the school property, which remained fenced off.

The rain continued hammering the ragtop in rapid staccato drumbeats. I would be drenched if I stepped out into this maelstrom. The entire expedition was beginning to feel like a clown fiesta.

Jazzy pulled off her headphones and asked, "What's that?"

She hadn't changed position, still reclined, and I had no idea what the "that" was she was referring to.

"Could you be more vague?" I asked.

I heard what could have been a small grunt and she rose a few millimeters forward in her seat and pointed to her right.

I followed the aim of her finger and saw nothing but the blurry image of an oak tree at the edge of the fence through the rain-streaked window. The leaves on the tree were dancing a ragged jig in the wind and the tree's massive limbs were waving crazily, threatening to fly off and crush unsuspecting innocents in nearby convertibles.

"You see it?" she asked. "Blowing around, hanging from that bottom limb?"

I spied a splotch of blue, but I couldn't make out what it was. I leaned over Jazzy to get a closer look. My right arm brushed her chest—I swear it was entirely accidental—and I realized how she might have won that Mardi Gras contest.

"Oh, sorry," I said.

"They're just boobs."

I leaned over some more, careful to avoid physical contact, straining to bring the flash of color in the tree into focus.

"Is that a parrot?"

CHAPTER 17

Gainesville

TESS AND BRISTOL were seated at the round kitchen table with two men. One of them could have been a contestant in the Jeremy Renner look-alike contest if Jeremy had gotten old, fat, and bald. He was wearing a Hawaiian shirt, khakis, and sandals—the northern Florida luau look. The other guy was younger, probably in his early thirties, wearing jeans, a golf shirt, and a Glock. He also sported stitches on his upper right lip.

Tess looked up as we entered the house and said, "Somebody's been playing in the rain."

I was still damp from my sprint to retrieve the parrot. I'd wrestled off my tee shirt before exiting the car, figuring I could use it as a towel when I returned, then charged out into the thunderstorm, leaped onto the fence, reached through the strands of barbed wire, and tore the parrot free from the length of string dangling from the limb.

If only it had been that easy. What really happened is I slid off the fence twice before securing a grip on the slippery wire. It took several tries to snag the parrot, which was bobbing spasmodically in the wind as if it were on meth. I scratched myself on the barbed wire and nearly tumbled off the fence when a thunderclap burst overhead, a lightning strike so close I could smell the sharp scent of ozone in the air. And it took a few tugs before I could break the string without tearing the bird's head off.

I dropped my backpack holding the soggy parrot onto the kitchen counter and turned to Tess's guests. The older of the two men stood up and stuck out a paw speckled with liver spots. "Frank Demerest." Jazzy and I shook his hand. The younger guy stayed seated and waved at us.

"Turner. Jack Turner."

"You walk into a door?" I asked.

"My face got in the way of a fist."

I glanced at Tess and she shrugged.

I looked back at Turner. "You arrested her for that? That little bitty cut?"

He started to speak, but Tess jumped in. "He didn't arrest me. It was the uniforms who showed up. The bartender called 911. And when that happens somebody goes to jail."

Turner said, "I've already told your girlfriend not to worry. I'll make sure the charges go away."

"Girlfriend?" It was involuntary.

Tess was shrugging again. "Don't ask me."

Turner turned his gaze on her for a few seconds, as if he were taking her in for the first time. Then he turned back to me. "No?" Then he rose from the table and gave Tess what I'm sure he thought was a killer smile. "Good."

"Detective Turner was just getting ready to leave when you two arrived," Tess said, ignoring his remark, or at least pretending to. "I'll fill you in on what he told us, but the long and the short of it is there were no surprising fingerprints."

Although it sounded like Turner wouldn't mind getting his fingerprints on Tess.

"Locksmith come?" I asked.

"Yes. We're all secure now."

Tess rose to her feet and escorted Turner to the front door. "I appreciate you coming out in person."

He nodded back at Frank Demerest, who remained at the kitchen table. "He says jump, I say how high. You have my card. If you need anything—anything at all—just call."

Tess closed the door behind him.

"Anything at all?" I said. "Give me a break."

"Knock it off," she said. "You're not jealous and we both know it."

She was right. But there was something primal there, some Neanderthalian instinct deep in my lizard brain that found his attentions toward Tess irritating. You can take the man out of the cave, but you can't take the cave out of the man. Or something.

I was no longer dripping, but felt like a damp sponge and didn't want to sit down and ruin the furniture. I nodded to Demerest. "Tess said you retired."

"Gone but not forgotten."

"So it seems."

Tess returned to the table and pulled up a chair. "More coffee, Frank?" she asked, all chipper and innocent.

Demerest put a hand over his cup. "Maybe in a second." We were all quiet, each wondering who would be the first to speak. The detective finally broke the silence.

"When that call came in last night, Molly—one of the dispatchers—gave me a ring. It's no secret we were hard on you when your roommate disappeared. Like I said, it shouldn't have happened."

Tess said, "We're good."

He nodded, thoughtfully, putting on his good-cop face. "I was on the force for more than thirty years. You learn to read people. It's part of the job, maybe the most important part." He paused, studying her, then continued. "You're a smart woman, Tess. And you know that I know you're hiding something."

Tess sat motionless, waiting to see where he was going with this. It wasn't much of a wait.

"You've got two choices, Tess. You can tell me all about it, and I can try to help you. Or not, in which case our slate is clean and I'll walk out of here."

I'd been all for calling the cops in the first place, but Tess had made it clear she didn't want the police involved. But she was hesitating, chewing on what he said.

"She should trust you, why?" I asked, buying her some time to frame how she would respond. Also, I was curious what he would say.

"You've no reason to *distrust* me," he said. "and I might be helpful."

"Why would you bother?"

He rose from the chair. I thought he was headed out the door, but, instead, he walked his cup over to the coffee maker and refilled it. Guess he changed his mind.

"I've been retired for six months," he said. "You know what? Retirement's boring. I don't fish. I don't play golf. And I refuse to end up fat and drunk and zombied out in front of a television like some guys." He took a sip. "Don't mind the fat and drunk part, but TV's bad for you. So, you know what I did? I called the Third Eye, put in my application."

You'd have to live at the bottom of the Devil's Millhopper, not to know about Third Eye Investigators. The Third Eye is a well-known— legendary, really—detective agency based in Boise, Idaho. They are headquartered there, of all places, because Idaho is one of the few states that doesn't require PIs to be licensed. That loophole has allowed the agency to hire not only former cops but also mercenaries, hackers, special forces operators, journalists, and even a few psychics.

The Third Eye made headlines when its operatives found the remains of D.B. Cooper, and the agency publicly committed itself to tracking down Jimmy Hoffa's final resting place, although they hadn't made good on that yet.

The Third Eye is actually a fanciful appellation, a capitalized nick-name. The agency started out as Investigative Inquiries of Idaho. The news media and pundits began calling the outfit Triple I and it evolved into its current handle. They eventually changed their name to Third

Eye Investigators. I admired the name. It evoked a sense of the mystical. And they do employ psychics, after all. Maybe Jazzy could get a job with them, too.

Tess said, "So what are you saying?"

"I'm saying I'd like to help you. You would be my first client. I can arrange a special discount offer extended to brand new customers."

"Which is?" That was Bristol, who had been uncharacteristically quiet, but now seemed intrigued about talking to an actual, real-life private eye.

"Doughnuts. I prefer chocolate-covered with my coffee."

"I'm on it," Bristol said, as if the matter were settled. And evidently it was.

"I can afford doughnuts," Tess said.

"Come on Jazzy," Bristol said. "I know this great place."

Jazzy looked up, surprised to be included. She shrugged. Said, "I like doughnuts." Then walked out the door with Bristol.

"And what Tess tells you, it stays confidential," I said, putting it on the table.

"Correct. But first, let me get something out of my car. I'll be right back." Then he put his index finger up to his lips, the signal to stay mum until he got back.

Tess looked at me wide-eyed.

I pulled out my notebook and wrote:

"Bugs?"

She rolled her eyes and couldn't help herself. "Fucking great."

Demerest was back in a minute holding what looked like a walkie-talkie. He began strolling around the house with the device. Fortunately Tess's place was probably under a thousand square feet and it didn't take long.

"You're clear."

While he was snooping about with his bug detector, Tess brewed a fresh pot of coffee, and we all sat down at the kitchen table.

"Okay," Tess said. "Here's the rundown." She spent about five minutes walking Demerest through the highlights. She pulled out her phone and showed him the poems she'd received via text message. I flipped open my reporter's notebook and showed him the transcription of the message we'd found in the hollow rock at the Devil's Millhopper. Tess told him it seemed she was being directed along the trail of the *Weird Tour of Florida* and let him browse through the magazine.

"And you don't know who is doing this?" he finally asked.

"No."

"And do you have any sense of why someone would want to do this?"

"No."

And there it was. I had wondered if she would share the deep, dark secret she was holding back, or at least let him know there was something out there that someone might be able to hold over her. But she didn't.

And he didn't buy it.

"No, Tess," he said. "There has to be more to this. I can't help you if you don't come clean."

She ran her hands through her hair and bit her lip. "You're right. I believe something was stolen from me. Something that if it got out could be damaging."

"Do you know who took it?"

"My best guess is Amy Duffy. Before she disappeared."

"Who are you protecting?"

"I'm not going to tell you."

Demerest gave her a dead-eye stare.

"Welcome to our world," I said.

He broke off eye contact with Tess to glance my way, then returned his focus on her.

"Is this a legal issue, or an ethical issue?"

"It's a personal issue, Frank, and I won't discuss it. If you can't live with that, I get it, and we can call it quits."

"Can I have his doughnuts?" I asked.

He looked at me and grinned. I could imagine Genghis Kahn with the same expression right before he eviscerated one of his captives. He raised his Hawaiian shirt exposing a roll of fat and a .38 holstered to his hip. I assumed it was a warning—in jest, of course. Surely.

"I didn't get this belly by letting anyone steal my doughnuts."

A few minutes later, Bristol and Jazzy returned with a bag full of chocolate glazed, chocolate cake, and chocolate sprinkles.

"Uh, that's a lot. Are they all for him?" I asked.

Bristol shook her head. "We get three each. For now. Consider it a down payment, Frank."

Demerest didn't answer, his attention clearly captured by the scent of lard and sugar and dough. He reached into the bag, extracted a chocolate glazed, and took an enormous bite.

The women joined him. While they were munching, I retrieved the soggy parrot from my backpack.

"Here's what we found in Jacksonville," I said.

"A parrot?" Tess asked.

"A talking parrot." It was eight-inches tall, plush, with a black beak and feet, a yellow breast, and, blue body and wings. "It's battery operated. You can see the switch. It records and replays what it hears, like a real parrot. Found it hanging from the limb of a tree by the schoolhouse."

"How do you know how it works?" Tess asked.

"We googled it. According to Amazon, you talk to it, the wings and the body shake—supposed to be a popular with kids—and it plays back whatever it's told."

Tess said, "Have you played it yet?"

"Yes."

Jazzy and I had concluded it would be stupid not to hear what the bird had to say while we were still in Jacksonville. What if the recording had directed us to someplace nearby? We'd feel foolish if we took off without finding out. Of course, we'd feel even worse if turning it on while it was soaking wet screwed up the recording, shorted it out or something. But we'd decided it was a calculated risk worth taking.

"Here we go," I said, turning on the switch.

"Graaakkk. Ahoy mate," the parrot said in a cartoonish voice. "The ring? You like it? Poor Amy. You broke her heart. Graaakkk."

There was a brief pause then, still in full parrot voice, "Here's stanza two so you won't be blue:

"CUT AND PASTE
"AND IT WILL SHOW.
"Graaakkk."

I glanced at Tess and saw the shocked look on her face.

"What?"

"That parrot screeching. Amy used to do that."

CHAPTER 18

"THAT DIDN'T SOUND like a woman to me," Demerest said.

"It's that squawk the parrot made, that *graakkk* noise," Tess said. "That was one of the things Amy did. One afternoon, we'd put the paper to bed, and she blurted out, 'Graaakkk, it's happy hour, Amy want a cocktail.' We all thought it was hilarious. Bristol, you were there weren't you? Don't you remember?"

"Amy squawking like a parrot? No. I missed that, thank God."

That confused me. "Tess, you're saying that was an expression Amy used. So, maybe she made the recording?"

"I'm just saying, that, yes, that parrot screeching reminded me of her."

"Frank, the bird takes the words that are recorded and alters them to sound like a parrot," I said. "I read about how it works online. Do you think there's any chance the original voice that was recorded could be recovered?"

He shook his head. "Don't know. Even if I were still at the department, we'd send it off to FDLE."

"What's FDLE?" Jazzy asked.

"Florida Department of Law Enforcement. It's where we would send our DNA samples for identification, too."

"Can The Third Eye do it?" I asked.

"I'll find out. But even if we can recover the original, we'd need another voice print to compare it to unless the voice was recognizable."

He turned to Tess. "You have a video or anything with Amy's voice on it?"

"I don't know. Amy never did any podcasts or videos for the paper. It's possible I've got her voice on my phone, from a video I might have shot, but I usually don't save those sorts of things."

"Anything on YouTube?" I asked.

Bristol picked up her iPad and began searching. After a few minutes, she shook her head. "Don't see anything yet. Not on YouTube, Vimeo, or Facebook."

"Keep looking," Demerest said. "If we can get a recording of her voice, that could be crucial."

"Frank, based on the little we've shared with the police, is there anything they're likely to do?" I asked.

He leaned back in his chair and scratched the back of his bald head.

"The question is, has there been a crime committed? Offhand, I'd say that we've got illegal entry. We've got stalking, which is a misdemeanor, but advances to a felony if a threat is involved. But we don't have a suspect. And then we'd have to give the police the details you're holding back, Tess, for them to take an interest."

He drummed his fingers on the table, then continued:

"But it doesn't change the fact that *someone* is stalking you."

"Which leaves us where?" I asked.

"The real problem is that without a threat this is merely low level harassment. They'll keep the file open, but, really, they've got better things to do. Unless this nitwit does something dangerous."

"What about the fact this asshole has used the telephone system to convey this harassment?" I asked. "Does that make it federal?"

Demerest shook his head. "If you're thinking about bringing the FBI into this you're wasting your time. Oh, they'd open a file. They always open a file. But they won't do anything. There are state laws that make it illegal to use a two-way communications device in the commission of a felony. But the only way to give the police a suspect is to tell them the whole story."

"So what do you suggest?" Tess asked.

"I suggest you tell me what you're hiding. It didn't escape my attention that you didn't show me the original of the note you found at the Millhopper. I can't do you a lot of good without the complete picture. But I'll be patient for a while. Until then, call me if you hear from him again."

Then he reached into his back pocket and pulled out a folded sheet of paper. "You asked for the list of people you and Amy knew in common," he said to Tess. "This is a copy of my notes about the people I got in touch with. I don't think it will be very helpful, but here it is."

He handed it to her and she gave it a scan. Then a sigh. "Yeah, I don't see anyone here doing this, but thanks. It was worth a try."

Demerest picked up the parrot and walked toward the door. But as he reached for the handle he paused and looked back at me.

"Tess tells me you're on your way down to Naples, that right?"

"That's why I'm here. I'm moving to a little town called Goodland."

"Any chance you can stick around, at least for a couple days?"

Before I could answer, he looked at Tess and said, "Look, don't take me wrong. I'm not trying to get all chauvinistic on you or anything. From Jack Turner's face, it looks like you can handle yourself. But, I'd feel better if he was here."

He didn't wait for either Tess or me to reply. He swung the door open and walked out.

Shortly thereafter, Bristol departed and Jazzy wandered outside to smoke a cigarette. When we were alone, I signaled Tess to join me at the kitchen counter.

"You probably didn't notice it, but there was a slice in the little parrot's belly and this was hidden inside."

I pulled a small, clear plastic resealable bag from my backpack and handed it to her.

"What is it?"

"I didn't unseal it, Tess. I assume it's another piece of that legal paper we got before. Figured you should look at it and then decide if there was anything you wanted to share. I'm trying to be respectful of your wishes here, but I've got to say, I agree with Demerest. It isn't easy helping you while wearing blindfolds."

She pulled the baggie open, grabbed the tweezers, and extracted the piece of paper. Like the previous note, it appeared to be a half page of a legal contract. There was no handwritten note this time on the other side. I only caught a glimpse of the text, but it looked like routine legal boilerplate to me. It could be a real estate contract, a car rental agreement, a lawsuit—anything—for all I could tell from the small type.

"Another piece of the contract or whatever it is?" I asked.

She nodded. "I'm not ashamed to say this has got me a little jittery."

"You'd be crazy if it didn't."

She looked up at me. "So, what Demerest asked. You good for a few more days?"

At that point, how could I say no?

CHAPTER 19

THE NEXT TEXT arrived at midnight, but Tess had silenced her cell phone and didn't discover the message until she woke up. I had rolled out early and gone for a run. Now we were back at the kitchen table sipping coffee. Jazzy was still in her room. Tess had a serious case of bed hair and looked as if she hadn't slept a wink. I still hadn't shaved. If the grooming police showed up, we were in deep shit.

The message, from yet another phone number, read:

> *Follow my lead,*
> *To more hauntin'.*
> *Splash a bit*
> *Near the youthful fountain.*
> *Your next clue*
> *Is in the shit*
> *Ain't no horse;*
> *Ain't no bit.*

"The youthful fountain?" I said. "He must be talking about the fountain of youth. It's on your list. There such a thing? Ponce DeLeon really find it? Why haven't I heard about this?"

Tess rolled her eyes.

"It's a tourist trap in St. Augustine. Of course the whole town is a tourist trap. Lots of whacky stuff there. A haunted fort. Haunted jail. You know, I find this guy, I'm going to strangle him with my bare hands if for no other reason than to spare the world from this godawful poetry."

"He could be the fourth worst poet in the universe," I agreed.

"Fourth worst? Who's worse?"

I'd been googling awful poetry. I ticked them off: "The worst, according to the infallible internet, is Paula Nancy Millstone Jennings. Then the Azgoths of Kria, and the Vogons."

"Why does all that sound familiar?"

"*Hitchhiker's Guide to the Galaxy.*"

"Oh, yeah. Wasn't there that godawful poem the Vogon recited, so terrible his major intestine strangled him or something to spare all Creation."

"Something like that. Here, you'll like this, well you won't." I'd looked up an excerpt of Paula Nancy Millstone Jennings on a *Hitchhikers Guide to the Galaxy* fan page. It was a six-line poem about dead swans in a stagnant pool. It was as wretched as it sounds. I could barely get the last lines out without laughing. Tess was smiling, too, and for a moment the stress that weighed us down was lifted.

"I wish Douglas Adams wasn't dead," she said.

"I'm sure he'd agree."

"I was eleven when I read the book. I thought it was brilliant. I was halfway through *The Restaurant at the End of the Universe* when he died. It was so disappointing."

"For you and him both."

She gave me smirk then said, "You know he was really tall, even taller than you."

"Probably what killed him. Lack of oxygen at that elevation."

"Are you ever serious?"

"Live up in my altitude and you'll know all about serious. Some days I can hardly catch my breath up here."

She slugged me in the shoulder.

"Throw on some clothes and we'll take a walk," I suggested. "Fresh air might do both of us some good. Maybe we can channel Zaphod Beeblebrox and he can help us divine what our mad poet means by shit and horses and bits."

Fred began hopping on his hind legs, his dance routine that translated from Papillon means: "Get me to some grass or you can forget about all that house breaking."

In a few minutes, she had finished tying her running shoes—a pair of purple Nikes with silver swooshes—as I attached Fred's leash. "Come on," I said. "Maybe we'll catch this asshat snooping around your yard and we can take turns beating him to a pulp."

We really did walk around her property before heading out. Tess said everything looked normal, no sign that anyone had disturbed her flower pots, nor her bike chained to the front railing of her porch, nor anything else amiss. Fred found nothing to growl at, but did decide one of Tess's flower pots needed watering.

We left her yard and strolled up Southeast Second Street and passed a small-plates joint called the Daily Green. At Southeast Fourth Avenue, we turned left, walked by the Downtown Little Free Library on a heading toward Main Street. It was a Monday morning and traffic was brisk with workers heading to their jobs and students making their way to classes.

At some point, our hands brushed and she reached out to me and grabbed hold and didn't let go while we continued walking, as if we were a couple.

"You know, you could take a vacation," I said. "It wouldn't be running away. Come on down to Goodland, hang out on the boat for a while, kick back. Put your troubles behind you."

"I can't leave. I've too much to do."

"From what you've been saying, it sounds like you don't have a lot of work left. I'm sorry about *The Agi-Gator*. The only reason I'm here is because my own paper folded. I know how it feels."

"Yeah. It's heart-breaking. But I've got enough material in the can for one final edition. A farewell edition. Then it's 30."

Thirty is old-fashioned newspaper talk for "the end." Back in the days of Remingtons and Underwoods, reporters typed their stories on sheets of paper that had to be pasted together. At the bottom of every page they would type —more— as a signal to the copy desk that additional pages were coming and to keep their paste pots open. On the final page, they'd type —30— at the bottom to signify the story was concluded.

"I knew you were preparing for a final edition, but I guess it hadn't dawned on me that it would be right now," I said.

"I hadn't either, until I talked to Marv the other day. He's been good about the rent, but I'm a couple months behind. He can't float me much longer. He hasn't given me a deadline, yet, but he will."

"Your house?" I asked.

"My house and my office."

We walked a bit more then I asked, "So what will you do?"

"I'm working on some things."

"Working? That's all you do is work. You know, you could single-handedly wreck the stereotype we millennials have so undiligently created for ourselves."

"Even millennials gotta eat. Besides, taking off and hanging on your boat *would* feel like running away. And it wouldn't be very effective, would it? He's got my number. Literally. He can reach me anywhere." She stopped and patted her back pocket. "Ha. Except right now. I forgot my phone."

"You said he. But we have the Amy-parrot connection. So maybe she?"

"He, she, it. We should just call the stalker *they*, that's the new gender neutral pronoun."

"But *they* is plural."

"Not if we say it isn't."

"You think you got problems now, wait till a pack of angry grammarians comes after your ass."

"Shush."

I looked around, figuring she must be concerned we were being overheard. But we had the sidewalk to ourselves.

"Why shush?" I whispered.

"A shush of grammarians. Not a pack."

"Is that a thing?"

"Absolutely."

"If you say so. But, seriously, any more thoughts on who the culprit could be?"

"I don't know what to think. I always assumed Amy took off on her own, ran away from a bad situation—for her, anyway. That the blood on the floor, the tip to police, all that was her being a little shit, fucking with me. I've never thought she was kidnapped or anything like that. But now, I don't know. This is all so twisted. What I do know is that if the goal is to mess with my head, it's working."

"Speaking of messes, what was with the reference to shit and bit in the last message?" I asked.

"No clue. I guess we're going to have to go find out."

We had walked past St. Francis House when a tall blonde in a blue business suit stopped and said, "Oh, how cute." She looked at me. "May I pet her?"

I turned to Tess. "Can she?"

"Smart ass. She means the dog."

The blonde looked back and forth between us, confused.

"The dog's a he," Tess said. "He's being silly."

The blonde bent down and gave Fred a scratch behind his ears. "Are you silly?"

"I meant him, this lunk here," Tess said, jabbing me in the ribs.

"Oh, are you silly, too?"

"Only on Mondays."

She scrunched her brows, now thoroughly perplexed, then turned and kept walking.

Tess said, "Now I get why you have Fred. He's a chick magnet."

"Fred's a charmer, no doubt."

She squeezed my hand. "The newspaper is right around the corner, you wanna see it? Could be your last chance."

"Lead on."

We turned north on Main Street and in half a block we were across the street from *The Agi-Gator's* small storefront office. Through the large picture window I could see a couple of reporters at their desks hammering away at laptop computers.

"That's Denny and Marissa," Tess said. "They're both J-School students. Juniors. I sure hope there will be jobs for them when they graduate."

"There will be if they're good."

Suddenly, Denny looked up and saw Tess and I through the window. He was holding a telephone receiver in his hand and began waving it at Tess, signaling her to come inside.

"You have land-lines?' I asked.

"Comes with the internet connection. We better cross over, Denny looks frantic."

We waited for a break in the traffic, then Fred and I followed her across the street and into the small newsroom. The kid named Denny thrust the phone at her.

"Hello?" she said.

Tess's face empurpled and her knuckles turned bone white as she crushed the receiver in her fist. "You motherfucker!" she yelled, then dropped the phone and charged past me out the front door.

I tossed Fred's leash to the kid. "Watch him," I said, and raced after her.

She'd stopped on the sidewalk, turning left, then right, scanning for something, someone.

"What is it?" I asked.

"That cocksucker. It was him. He followed us. He's around here somewhere."

I whipped out my iPhone, punched up the camera, and began

145

shooting pictures of everyone I could see: men and women on the sidewalks, people behind storefront windows, drivers and passengers in cars. If it was human, I took a picture.

As I was shooting, I was also paying attention to anyone holding a cell phone. A college-aged student, male, was walking southward across the street, yakking out loud, earbuds in place, no doubt on the phone. That wouldn't be him. Tess was no longer on the receiving end of the stalker's conversation. To my left, north on Main, nearly to University Avenue, another guy held a phone in his left hand, glanced in my direction then quickly turned away and cut to his left onto a side street. I said to Tess, "Go back inside." Then I ran up the street after him.

I hooked a left on Southwest First Avenue and found myself on a busy two-lane street flanked by diagonal parking, most of the spaces full. I jogged westward past a café toward a vacant lot. I did a quick three-sixty, but didn't see him. Across the street was a ramen joint, a grill, a nightclub, and dozens of pedestrians milling about. He was gone.

I checked the Camera Roll on my phone. I caught a photo of him right before he'd turned the corner, a guy in a checkered shirt and jeans, but his face was turned away. Enlarging the picture, it became increasingly grainy and useless even after I edited it to sharpen the image.

Tess was sitting behind her desk in her small office when I returned, her eyes rimmed in crimson, her cheeks still flushed.

"I lost him," I said. "And, honestly, I don't know who he was. Just some guy with a phone in his hand."

She nodded.

"So what did he say to you?"

She took a deep breath, calming herself. "He said, and I quote: 'Tick tock, Tick tock. Play my game you stupid sot.' "

"It was a man's voice?"

"Definitely."

"And he called you a sot?"

"Yes. Like he knew my history. He seemed tense. Upset. His voice seemed strained."

"Because you weren't on your way to St. Augustine already?"

"I don't know."

Marissa and Denny walked into her office. Denny handed Fred's leash to me. "What's going on, Tess?" Marissa asked.

I interrupted. "Your phones, they record caller IDs?"

Denny shook his head. "No, these are hand-me-downs, real old school."

"What exactly did he say to you when you answered the phone?"

"Not much. He said, and I think this is verbatim, 'Call your boss inside, I want to talk to her.' That's when I looked up and saw the two of you on the sidewalk."

"Who is this guy? What's going on?" Marissa again.

Tess crossed her arms and nodded her head, making a decision. "Alex, I think we could all use some coffee. Would you mind? I'll fill these guys in while you're gone."

I started to say something, but caught the expression on her face and knew I needed to keep my mouth shut. We were in her office, with her employees. She was the boss. She'd tell them what she thought they needed to hear, but probably no more. Hopefully, they wouldn't insist on writing a story about it, which would be extremely awkward for her. Although from what she had said earlier, they only had one edition left to do so.

But even if she could keep the lid on it at her own paper, she had no control over other news outlets.

Florida has one of the strongest open records laws in the country, and that includes public—and press—access to police reports. Ever wonder why so much weird news comes out of Florida? It's not only because the state is overrun by whack jobs, which it is. It's also because all the weirdness police respond to is readily available thanks to the state's Sunshine laws.

The cops had responded to a possible break-in at her house, which would generate a police report. It was possible that report might be overlooked in the flurry of daily police calls, especially if it glossed over how a missing ring was found dangling on a Vulcan, which would dramatically elevate the weirdness factor.

Still, the police investigation occurred at the home of a woman who had been arrested for punching a cop, and a year ago had been detained when her roommate went missing, and who was the editor of a local alternative newspaper. Tess Winkler might not be a local celebrity— not in a major college sports town—but she wasn't an unknown, either.

If some enterprising reporter at *The Gainesville Sun* or *The Independent Florida Alligator*—the college newspaper—or a local television station ran across the police report there would be nothing Tess could do about it other than to refuse to comment. And she would have allowed her own paper to be scooped.

Tess Winkler, the woman who insisted on reporting her own DUI arrest out of a concern for journalism ethics now needed more than anything to avoid the news media. The secret she was hiding must be very damaging to put herself through this.

All of which meant that although under ordinary circumstances she should have called the police, I knew she wouldn't. That would generate yet another police report, perhaps enough to tip the scales.

By the time I got back to the newspaper office, four coffees in a cardboard drinks carrier in one hand, a bag of doughnuts in another, Denny and Marissa were back at work and Tess was at her desk.

Back in the glory days of newspapers, copyboys prowled newsrooms distributing coffee and cigarettes to reporters as they banged away on their typewriters. Now they're called interns and smoking is banned. I'd interned once at the *Austin American-Statesman* and was highly skilled at coffee distribution. I dropped off cups to the interns at their desks along with a doughnut each, then took the rest of the stash to Tess's small office where I plopped into an uncomfortable gray metal folding chair in front of her desk. Fred was curled in a corner, snoozing next to a stack of old newspapers.

"Just for the record," I said, "I'll point out, again, that you ought to call the cops. But I get why you don't want to. Still, shit keeps happening to you, it may be hard to stay out of the news."

She pried the white plastic top off the coffee and took a sip. "I know. I gave Denny and Marissa a sanitized version. Told them I may have a stalker, but we have to keep it quiet. I said we don't want to spook this guy before we can catch him. It's possible they may infer I was implying that's what the police want."

I shook my head. "I'm sorry, Tess. This has got to be miserable for you."

"I also called Demerest, told him I wasn't going to file a complaint, but I wanted him to know."

"What's his take?"

"He's concerned this guy is getting more aggressive. He's worried about my safety."

"You should be, too."

She nodded. "Don't let this cool, calm exterior fool you. He also asked if you could send him the pictures you took."

I nodded. "Sure. Give me his email."

I'd scored a handful of small half-and-half containers at the café and poured a couple into my coffee. I'd asked the dude at the counter to leave room for cream, and, unlike the Starbucks baristas, who never do, he actually did. Who says customer service is dead?

Tess said, "Demerest also said he knows somebody who may be able to help us—a psychologist at the university. He's going to try to arrange to have her meet with us today, to war game this a little better using her expertise."

"It would be a nice change of pace to know what we're doing," I said.

"Yeah, knowledge is good."

CHAPTER 20

LATER THAT AFTERNOON, Tess, Jazzy, Demerest, Bristol, and I were huddled in Tess's living room listening raptly to a gray-haired woman in jeans, tennis shoes, and a green Sigmund Freud tee shirt. Her name was Harriet Skinner, and she was an assistant professor of psychology at the University of Florida who had done her doctoral thesis on stalkers. Demerest had worked with her on a couple of cases and talked her into joining us at our war council.

"Stalkers, in the simplest sense, want something," she was saying. "And while no two individuals are alike, as the cliché goes, for purposes of this conversation we'll break stalkers down into a handful of generalized categories."

She began ticking them off on her fingers:

"Intimacy seekers are one type. Remember the man who was haunting Shania Twain? People like him, they latch onto someone, believe that person is their one true love, and harbor the delusion that their love is reciprocated. They usually have no actual acquaintance with the victim whatsoever. They're obsessed.

"Then there is a subset of the intimacy seeker who behaves similarly. They truly believe the target of their affection is the love of their life, but they understand that their victim may not actually love them back. And, again, they likely never have met."

She ticked off another finger. "Then there are the resentful stalkers who're out for revenge because they believe they've been humiliated or treated unfairly. Mark Chapman, John Lennon's assassin, he fits into this category."

Bristol grunted, "Jesus fuck," then bit her lip.

Dr. Skinner continued unperturbed by the interruption. "Predator stalkers spy on and want to control their victims, often physically, sexually, violently.

"All of these types reflect the neurotic nature of stalkers, and as you can see they can be dangerous. However, I think your stalker may fit best into this last general category."

The good doctor was guilty of burying the lede, but we had no option but to hang in there until she got to our guy.

"Finally, there is the rejected stalker, someone who seeks revenge for a break-up of some kind, usually a romantic partner. This is some-one who wanted a romantic relationship but was thwarted."

"And now wants to get even?" I asked.

"Yes."

"How does that play out?"

"That's unpredictable. As I said, no two people behave precisely alike. It appears your stalker is getting revenge by torturing Tess with all these phone calls and wild goose chases. It could escalate."

Tess said, "Wouldn't I have to know this person for him to be—what did you call it—a rejected stalker?"

"Yes, of course."

"Well, the only person I've rejected lately is my old roommate."

"That would be Amy, correct?"

"Yes."

"Well, if this stalker fits any of the usual patterns, and I think so, then I would say either the stalker is Amy, herself, or perhaps she is working with someone based on the voice you heard on the phone earlier today."

"And you don't think it could be one of the other kinds of stalkers?" Bristol asked.

She shook her head. "The reason behind creating categories such as these—and there are other groupings that are used—is to find a way to organize behaviors into patterns to be better studied, understood, and, hopefully, treated. In the real world, it is rarely that tidy and a stalker can exhibit symptoms and characteristics of overlapping categories."

She held up a finger, her way of holding her place in the conversation as she marshalled her thoughts. "For instance, there is a delusional disorder known as erotomania. Do you recall the woman who kept breaking into David Letterman's house, the one who stole his car? She claimed to be his wife and she genuinely believed Letterman was in love with her. I would categorize her as an intimacy stalker, the first grouping I mentioned. There are criminologists, using different criteria, who would call her love-scorned, which bears symptoms similar to our rejected stalker."

Tess shook her head. "This is all so confusing."

Dr. Skinner smiled. "People are complex, and our understanding of human behavior is imperfect. But for practical purposes, since you asked my opinion, and since we deal in probabilities and preponderances of evidence, I believe we are dealing with a rejected stalker."

She paused and tapped her chin. "Tess, if the man hadn't called you today, my shot in the dark would be that our stalker was your former roommate. But the messages you've received do refer to Amy in the third person. He's talked about stealing something from Amy that he knows you want back. There's a strong connection there. We are looking for someone who is powerfully motivated. Therefore, my guess is that Amy is the woman behind the curtain."

"If it were a woman on the phone today, you wouldn't have any doubts?" I asked.

"If we could recognize the voice as Amy's, this would be simple. But in this case it is the content and context of the messages that matter. The pattern is clearly that of someone who is trying to punish you, Tess."

"Harriet," Demerest asked, "could this be someone who is acting like a stalker, but who has other motivations for harassing Tess?"

She chewed on the knuckle of her index finger while she considered the detective's question. "That's clever. Anything's possible, I suppose, but that doesn't feel right."

We digested that for a bit, then I was struck by a stray thought, one of those stupid questions that, even if embarrassing, is better to ask than not.

"Could Amy be an Amos?" I asked.

"What do you mean?" Dr. Skinner replied.

"Our line of reasoning points to Amy. Yet the only real-life contact we've had with the stalker was a man's voice on the phone. One possibility is that Amy has a man working with her. My question, and I know it may seem foolish and perhaps politically incorrect, is this:

"I'm wondering if Amy could have had sexual reassignment surgery. If that would explain her masculine voice—if, in fact, this is her. It's been a year since she disappeared. Now this happens out of the blue. Could she have been spending that time to, you know, undergo treatment to become a male."

"Wow. That's coming out left field," Bristol said.

"Just because Amy was a lesbian does not mean that she identified as a male," Dr. Skinner said.

"Yeah, I know. And I don't want to come off like a troglodyte. I almost didn't ask the question because I know it invites scorn. But, doctor, is it possible someone could be so obsessed, so determined to overcome unrequited love, so desperate they would do something as radical as that?"

"Oh, God," Tess said. "Oh, God in heaven." She was holding her face in her hands. She started to say something else, her lips parted, but nothing came out.

Bristol, who was sitting beside her, put her arms around her. "Hey, you okay?"

Tess shook her head, then turned to me. "I guess I'd forgotten about this, put it out of my mind. But I remember the last time we spoke, right before I left for that weekend in Tampa, the weekend she disappeared. Amy was upset. I'd told her that if she didn't stop pestering me, didn't stop making all these sexual innuendos, that I'd have to ask her to leave."

Tess stood up and walked into the kitchen, leaned on the table, then returned to face us.

"The last thing Amy said... she was screaming... she said, 'If I grew a dick, then would you love me?'"

She put her hands on her hips and shook her head. "Of course, I never took that seriously. It was ridiculous. I figured she was being insulting, getting back at me because I'd had a few guys over, kind of rubbed it in her face, I suppose. But I never thought she'd actually do it."

Demerest said, "Let's not get ahead of ourselves here."

"Amy wasn't butch," Bristol said. "I don't know about this."

"I would caution all of you about stereotypes," Dr. Skinner said.

"I didn't mean that in a bad way," Bristol said. We all looked at her. "Yeah, okay, I get it."

The psychologist was scowling at Bristol, and I felt the need to step in since I was the one who brought it up. "Doctor Skinner, I apologize if the question seemed stupid or maybe even insensitive, but if I've learned anything it's that once a question occurs to me, I need to spit it out."

She turned to me and smiled. "Spoken like a scientist, Mr. Strange. The boundaries of knowledge are not expanded by the timid."

Jazzy, who had been her usual sphynx-like self, sitting quietly and observing the conversation behind her magenta shades, jumped in: "Should we try to smoke him or her out?"

Dr. Skinner chewed on that for a minute then said, "Our operating theory is that this stalker wants Tess to love her. And since Tess has rejected her—or possibly him—he or she is angry and wants to get back at her."

"Besides Tess standing on a street corner as bait," I asked, "how would we lure this asshole into the open?"

That prompted an eyebrow raise. I assumed it was in reaction to my profanity.

"Well, I guess asshole isn't a clinical term."

She smiled. "We prefer terminology that avoids phrases like crazy, deranged, and, as you put it, asshole. But between us chickens, our stalker is all of the above."

That got a snort from Demerest. Tess was chewing her lip. Bristol was saying something to herself as she got up from the couch and walked into the kitchen, but I couldn't make it out.

"What was that?" I asked.

She shook her head. "Never mind. My first language is mumble."

Dr. Skinner raised her hands to her chest and scratched around the perimeter of Sigmund Freud's face between her breasts. She saw me staring at her and laughed. "Sometimes an itch is just an itch, Mr. Strange. Mosquito bites."

I understood. I'd been fighting the urge to claw my ankles, which were scabby with no-see-um scars.

"You know, if you're right, Mr. Strange..." Dr. Skinner paused and gathered her thoughts. "It seems unlikely—it does not at all fit the ordinary profile—but if you *are* correct and Amy Duffy has gone through sexual reassignment, that would be a radical personal decision. She would not do that unless she hoped—and expected—to reunite with Tess, not just punish her."

Tess asked, "So how do we get him out in the open?"

"One way would be to make your stalker jealous."

"Jealous? How?"

Dr. Skinner nodded toward me. "He might be adequate."

Adequate?

155

Tess mulled that. "You know what? I think there's a chance he already is. His tone of voice this morning. I told Alex, it wasn't like the recordings. He seemed upset. Maybe because he'd seen us together?"

The professor nodded. "That could be."

Tess thought about it for a few more seconds. "This idea, could it be dangerous?"

"Very possibly. I worry about escalation. You are dealing with someone who could be highly emotional and unpredictable."

Exposing Tess—or any of the rest of us, for that matter—to danger didn't sound like the best idea I'd ever heard. In fact, it sounded like the perfect way to make Jazzy's palm-reading prophesy come true. I'd checked my to-do list earlier. Dying wasn't on it.

"Any alternative ideas, doctor?" I asked.

She thought about that for a few beats then nodded. "Your stalker is enjoying this, playing cat and mouse. From your description, it sounds as if he wants to run you around for a bit, make Tess dance for him or her—God, why can't we invent a decent gender neutral pronoun besides *it*?"

"Try *they*," Tess said.

"They? They is plural."

I looked at Tess. "See."

She ignored me. "You're saying I should play along?"

"If you do, Tess, there's always a chance your stalker will slip up, make a mistake that allows you to identify him/her/it. The more you play along, the more likely hubris will set it. That's when you could catch a break."

Or get our necks broken.

I didn't like this suggestion one iota. Not only was it risky, it had no clear objective—largely thanks to Tess's secretiveness. But I didn't see a better alternative.

Oh, theoretically, I could have just walked away from it all. Told myself: Not my circus, not my monkey. But that wasn't going to happen. Not just because it would be disloyal and cowardly, but because the stalker had accomplished at least one thing—he/she/it had aroused my curiosity. Where did all this lead? There seemed to be only one way to find out.

I checked my watch. If we left right away we could easily make it to St. Augustine before dark. But it had been an emotionally exhausting day for Tess, and while I was willing to go along with this strategy, I didn't feel like jumping through the stalker's hoops at that very moment.

"First thing tomorrow. Who's up for a road trip?" I asked.

"I don't see how I can get away," Tess said.

Demerest shook his head. "I talked to Jack Turner. Told him you weren't filing a formal complaint, but that he should be aware. He said they'll send cars around, keep an eye on the neighborhood. Even so, we know this guy's followed you. Here's the problem. If you *don't* go, he'll probably know. If we want to catch this guy, I don't think you have a choice but to play along with this. At least for a little while."

"Tess, let me help," Bristol said. "It's been a while since I've been at the paper, but I can babysit for a few days, buy you some time."

Tess shook her head. "I can't ask you to do that. You've got your own job."

"Yeah, but I don't have any showings scheduled for this week. Got some contract stuff I can work on anywhere on my laptop. I'm shepherding a closing for the week after next. The most I might have to do is head out for inspections and such. It'll be no big deal. I can handle it. And, besides, it will only be for a few days."

"What about you, Jazzy?" I asked.

I wasn't sure where her head was at. She'd tagged along with me to Florida, but couldn't have anticipated any of this craziness. Or could she?

Her gaze lingered on Tess, then she finally said, "It's just the two of you. I stay here. I watch the house. Take care of Fred." Then she slipped off her wraparound sunglasses and offered a small, sad smile. "I'll be here when you and Tess get back."

From her look and tone of voice, I was certain she'd had another vision. But I didn't want to ask her in front of everyone. She examined each of us in turn, first Bristol, then Tess, then finally me, studying us, as if seeing each of us for the first time.

"I'm going for a walk," she announced, and opened the front door. She looked back at me before walking out:

"Be strong, Strange Man."

CHAPTER 21

"Ed, did you know they grow algae here that eats people's brains?"

I was overdue to report to my editor, Edwina Mahoney, so I thought I'd start the conversation with some entertaining news.

"That could explain a lot about Florida," she said. "But you didn't call to tell me that. You've gotten yourself into something, haven't you."

"What? Me?"

"Spit it out, Alexander. Don't bury the lede."

"Well, boss, it's a bit of a shaggy dog story. It begins with a soothsayer in New Orleans. A trip to Florida in a casket. Losing, then recovering Spock..."

"Spock? Wait. Is he alright? You don't have that many friends, you know."

"He's fine. And don't forget, I've got you, babe."

"Spare me the Sonny and Cher. Then what?"

"Then my friend here in Gainesville..."

"Gainesville? You're not in Naples yet?"

"Goodland."

"Okay, the greater Naples area. You're still up in north Florida?"

"Why yes, and that's why I'm calling. I have this friend..."

"It's a woman, isn't it. With you, there's always a woman."

"She is, but we're not sure about her stalker. Let me fill in the details."

Normally Ed is great about listening. She was a terrific reporter in her day and a journalist's most important job is to pay attention to what people are saying. Her interruptions at the beginning of our conversation were uncharacteristic. She was probably just excited to hear from me, don't you think?

I ran down the events of the past few days. She only jumped in a few times, mostly to get more details on the Devil's Millhopper and the history of Annie Lytle School. I ended on our meeting with the University of Florida shrink and her assessment of the stalker.

I could imagine Edwina leaning back in her chair, legs propped up on her desk, heels kicked off, listening on the speakerphone while polishing her nails. She went with red, which matched her lipstick, which merged splendidly with her melanin-enriched epidermis. Before the *Phoenix Daily Sun* folded, she was one of a very few black newspaper editors in the country. She didn't get there by accident. Ed was one of the toughest, smartest and most profane journalists I knew. A real life Walter Burns.

"So, this university shrink, she thinks you should play this out, go galivanting around the state letting this little prick pull your weenie, all on the off-chance he might slip up and you can expose him, is that what you call a plan?"

"Not sure about the weenie pulling part, but, yeah, that's the result of the best strategic thinkers in Gainesville. It's better than the other alternative we discussed."

"What was that?"

"Well, one way to lure this dickhead out of the shadows might be to make him jealous, so at one point Tess and I talked about staging a phony wedding."

"Oh for Christ sake…"

"But our private eye, he said the cops would never go for it. That it would be too dangerous. There'd be no way to protect us. That this asshole might decide to pick Tess off with a deer rifle or something."

"And you, too, I imagine."

"Which would definitely put a crimp in my column production…"

"Speaking of which…"

"Yes, speaking of which, I haven't been entirely unproductive. I have a backlog of evergreen material that I've dredged up and in a little while I'll be sending you a batch of columns that should cover us while I'm, as you say, galivanting around the great state of Florida."

Edwina was quiet for a few moments then said, "Alex, in the long line of crazy shit you've gotten wrapped up in, this could be the weirdest yet."

"Well, boss, weird is the job, after all."

"Yes it is. And who better to do it, right?"

I wasn't entirely sure how to take that.

"And what will keep this madman from taking you out while you're on the road? Won't the two of you traveling together also make him jealous?"

"Yes. But there's his game. He wants to play it out. As long as we're doing that, we should be okay."

"And when the game ends?"

"I'm still working on that."

There was a pause, then she asked, "Have you spoken to your uncle about this?"

"Uh, no. Not yet."

"Leonard will throw a fit."

Leonard.

Ed's relationship with my uncle was a small, itsy-bitsy, miniscule sticking point between us. Apparently, Leo and Ed had briefly been an item while I was away at college. It was a fact that neither Leo nor Edwina disclosed when she offered me a job at his urging. I was and still am grateful for the opportunity, but a small—probably immature—part of me wishes I'd been hired on merit alone.

Ed and I had a frank discussion about that once, and her take on it was pretty direct: "Yeah, so somebody opened the door for you. That was your good luck. But you only get to keep this job if you earn it. So shut the fuck up and get back to work."

Like I said, frank.

Now she was considering what we were about to embark on, our weird trip around Florida. "Well," she said, "I see at least some upside to this crazy plan of yours."

"What's that?"

"You're new to Florida. By the time you're done with this non-sense, you should have a pretty good orientation on how crazy it is down there."

"Exactly."

"Assuming you don't get shot."

"Like I mentioned, I've got that backlog of material. So, you know, if something goes south you'll have some time to find a replacement for me and avoid *columnus interruptus.*"

"You're forgetting the cost and inconvenience of shipping your body home."

"I'll make arrangements to be cremated. Keep shipping costs to a bare minimum."

"Good boy."

Attack of the Zombie Amoeba

By Alexander Strange

Tropic©Press

TALLAHASSEE—News flash. Zombies are real.

The Florida Department of Health has issued a warning to avoid freshwater swimming due to an outbreak of what is being called the zombie amoeba.

It's scientific name is *Naefleria fowleri* and it is a single-celled organism that lives in warm lakes and ponds, untreated swimming pools and spas, well water, aquariums, and even dirt.

The amoeba usually enter the body through the nose or ears then migrate to the brains of their victims where they eat away. The result is almost always fatal.

The warning was issued this week after a 67-year-old tourist from Milwaukee succumbed to the disease. Robert Haiman had been riding his bicycle in Golden Gates Estates in southwest Florida when he was run off the sidewalk by an 88-year-old woman, Maggie June Hutsteader of Mankato, Minnesota, when her late-model Cadillac Deville jumped the curb.

Haiman plunged into the Golden Gate Canal, where he was rescued by construction workers who saw him thrashing about, drawing the attention of several alligators nesting in the drainage ditch.

"We got that poor old man out in the nick of time," Johnny B. Hawkins said.

But he was submerged long enough to become exposed to what is now being called the zombie amoeba. Haiman's partner, Bob Efferman, said he began experiencing headaches, nausea, fever, and dizziness, classic symptoms of the disease. He died five days later.

"Our advice," said Mary Hardesty of the Health Department, "is stay out of the water."

Are Florida's famous beaches safe? "The amoeba can't grow in saltwater," she said. "Just beware of the red tide."

STRANGE FACT: Only four out of 143 people known to have been infected with the zombie amoeba have ever survived.

Keep up with weirdness at *www.TheStrangeFiles.com*. Contact Alexander Strange at Alex@TheStrangeFiles.com.

CHAPTER 22

I PUSHED THE send button on the last of eight columns I'd written, then took Fred outside for a walk.

"Be gone a few days, pal," I said. "Jazzy will be here to keep you company. I expect good reports when I get back."

Fred actually stopped and sat down and looked up at me. He cocked his head and I swear he looked sad. And, while I realize it's illogical (and, perhaps, unfair) to impart to animals the characteristics of humans, it is also naïve not to appreciate that animals have powerful sensory capabilities and instincts that we don't know much about.

Dogs, for instance, have 300 million olfactory receptors in their noses compared to a paltry six million in humans. They experience the world through the sense of smell in ways we cannot imagine. Let alone their superior hearing. Who knows in what other ways animals have it over us. Sure, we have opposable thumbs. Which allows us to shoot guns, design nuclear weapons, and tweet. One thing I knew: Fred was a better person than some humans, especially certain tweeters.

Tess and I had huddled earlier that evening, making plans for our road trip. We assumed once we got started we would be hopscotching around Florida and that the pace might get frenetic. We talked about what to pack and where we would stay. We agreed we could share a room. After all, we were adults, nothing to be shy about. Which eventually drifted into a pleasantly meandering conversation about our relationship, what we thought our futures would hold, would either of us ever settle down, have families—you know, life, the universe, and everything.

"You're absolutely, positively my best guy friend," she'd said. "And we've even had sex. Course I was completely shit faced and barely remember it."

"You're not suggesting…"

"Ha!" she slapped me on my thigh. "Oh, hell no. It was entirely my idea. You did not take advantage of the poor, drunken college girl. If anything, it was the other way around."

"Well, that's a relief."

We were sitting on the couch and she began fiddling with the drawstring of her lavender running shorts, avoiding eye contact. Finally, she stopped and looked at me. "You know, we were talking about relationships, whether we wanted families of our own. I can't have that."

"What do you mean?"

"Six weeks after I got back from Austin I had an abortion."

Suddenly I felt my skin on fire and my vision narrowing. "You had an abortion?" It came out as a croak. "After Austin?"

"Yes. And it really messed me up."

It took me a few beats to process that, then I said, "Tess, I'm so sorry. You should have called me…"

"Called you?" Her eyes grew wide. "Alex, it wasn't you. I'd already missed my period before my trip to Texas. And even if I wasn't already pregnant, it was five days and nights at one of the great party schools of America. I adore you, but, uh, I was a very busy girl that week."

"So I can stop playing the theme song from *Mama Mia* in my head?"

She patted my thigh again. "Yeah, you can relax. I mentioned it for two reasons. The first is, we were talking about having families of our own. That can't happen now for me. There was a complication, a nasty infection, that, to make a hideous story short, means I can't have children."

"Oh, Tess."

She shrugged. "Well, I've no interest in starting a family anyway, so unless I have a change of heart, it's alright. Actually, I've no interest in any kind of relationship. I like living alone. I'm better that way and I'm pretty set in my ways."

"You saying it's time for me to hit the road?"

She nodded.

"Yes. But with me." She fiddled with her drawstring some more. "Alex, of all the guys I've known, you're the only one I've ever considered a true friend. You're the only one who reached out to me, to stay in touch, to show concern for me. I may never settle down. I don't think I have it in me. But if I ever do, and if it's with a man, I hope I get lucky enough to find a guy like you."

I could have said the obvious: She actually had found a guy like me—me. But that would be an invitation. It would open a door I didn't feel like walking through. Tess had called it. The chemistry is either there or it isn't. And I knew it wasn't there for her, either. Like Tess, I was uncertain who I was looking for. I'd know when I found her. But I appreciated the compliment. So I simply said, "Thanks."

She smiled then scooched next to me on the couch and grabbed my hand. "Best friends forever. Pinky swear."

She curled her little finger around mine.

"Come on, pinky swear."

"You're really not going to make me do this."

"Come on."

I relented, and we did it, locking it with our thumbs.

We sat in companionable silence for a little while, then I asked her, "So, all these years, there's been nobody special for you?"

She shook her head. "There was one guy. For a while I thought it might work out. But I was young and stupid and no, nobody special. The truth is, I've kinda worked at avoiding entanglements like that. I mean look at me. My nails are bitten to nubs. I haven't even shaved my legs this week. When have you ever seen me wear makeup?"

She was being much too hard on herself. "I think you're pretty without all that."

Her face softened and her eyes glistened. She pulled off her glasses, rubbed them, then smiled.

"Ya see. That's why you're my bestie. And it proves what Harry told Sally was dead wrong."

"You talking about that old movie?"

"Yeah. *When Harry Met Sally*. It's one of my favorites. Must have seen it a dozen times. Harry, he tells Sally that men and women can't ever really be friends. His famous line is, and I quote: 'The sex part always gets in the way.' But he was wrong. Look at us. We already did the sex part and we're still friends."

Later that evening, I called Uncle Leo. I could hear ice tinkling in a glass and barroom chatter in the background.

"You still at Kelso's?" I asked.

Kelso's Saloon is one of downtown Phoenix's most popular watering holes. Before I packed up and headed east, Leo and I would frequently meet there for drinks after work. I checked my Mickey Mouse watch. It was 10 p.m., so it would be seven o'clock in Arizona, which doesn't switch to Daylight Savings Time. This was later than normal for His Tortness to be hanging out at a bar.

"Yeah, I'm still downtown," he confirmed. "Let me step outside. It's too noisy in here."

A few seconds later he was back on the line. "That's better."

"What's the temp?" I asked.

"Nice. It's about a hundred, but the humidity is zero. I could hang out in this weather all day."

"And you're still out barhopping, why?"

"What? You my mother?"

"I'm not wearing army boots, so I guess not."

"Ha. Ha. Sarah's at a fund raiser. I stuck around for the reception then skipped out. I'll catch up with her after the dinner. My digestive tract is allergic to rubber chicken."

I updated him on my travels, about the night at the Millhopper, my trip with Jazzy to Jacksonville, Spock and the necklace, and the scavenger hunt we were about to embark upon.

"So, this psychic, she got any predictions on the playoffs?" March Madness was about to get underway, and knowing Leo he had money on the outcome.

"No. We've been too focused on all the craziness here. She has these visions, and I get the sense that whatever is going to happen over the next few days, it may not have a happy ending."

"Then get the fuck out of there."

"I can't."

"Why not?"

"I promised."

I heard the ice tinkling in his glass. "She worth it?"

"Doesn't matter. A promise is a promise. It's sacred. You taught me that."

"Now it's my fault."

"Yes. Entirely."

"But is she worth it, going through all this?"

Leo was nothing if not persistent.

"She's a friend. And she's desperate. But she's keeping some of this pretty close to the vest." I gave him a quick overview of the partial document pages we found, how Tess was worried they could be used as blackmail if she didn't retrieve them.

"So let me see if I've got this right," Leo said. "She wants you to trust her, but she doesn't trust you enough to level with you, that about it?"

"It's a little more complicated than that. There's someone else who could be hurt. She's trying to protect somebody."

"Have you considered the possibility that somebody might be you?"

"Meaning?"

"Maybe this thing she's trying to recover, maybe even knowing what it is could be life-threatening."

"You mean like 'if I told you I'd have to kill you,' that kind of dangerous?"

"Beats the shit out of me. But you better watch your back."

"That's impossible."

"Well, watch it anyway. This sounds like a total cluster fuck."

CHAPTER 23

TESS RECEIVED SOME good news the next morning before we hit the road. Her attorney called to tell her the assault charges had been dropped at Jack Turner's request. Somehow the local papers and TV stations hadn't stumbled onto the report of the bar fight and her arrest, so it seemed likely that the dismissal of charges would go unnoticed as well.

Bristol called from the newspaper and reported she was on the job. "I think I like this," she told Tess. "It feels like old times."

"Enjoy it while you can."

Jazzy borrowed Tess's bicycle and pedaled into town. This happened after announcing over morning coffee that she had made a life-altering decision:

"I'm quitting smoking."

This seemed to puzzle Tess. "What brings this on?"

"I need to get in shape."

"Planning on running a marathon or something?"

Jazzy offered a hesitant smile. "No. No marathon."

I, for one, was happy for her. I stood up from the table and fist bumped her. "Jazzy, I'm being as serious as I can be. Congratulations. Future Jazzy will thank Today Jazzy for this decision. My advice, get as much exercise as you can, keep working those lungs. After a few days, you won't want smoke in there."

Tess looked at me curiously. "How do you know? You're a jock. You've never smoked."

"I read a lot."

"Whatever."

Tess reached over to a rack on the kitchen wall and removed a small brass key off a hook. "This unlocks the chain to the bike on the front porch. Use it if you like."

Jazzy took it and walked toward the front door. As she crossed the threshold she paused and allowed her eyes to rest on me. She lingered like that for several seconds, which caught my attention, and when my eyes met hers a faint smiled crossed her lips. Then she closed the door behind her.

Tess said, "You know, I think your friend Jazzy may have a thing for you."

"Oh, come on."

"The way she looks at you. I think there's something there."

"That's ridiculous. She's old enough to be my stepmother."

They were, in fact, about the same age. And they both looked younger than their years.

"I can see why an older woman would go for you," Tess said, not letting it go.

"My youthful vitality, right?"

"You know, you're sorta scary. I mean, you're big, and you're kind of shiftless, no offense—I mean your big goal in life is to live on a boat, after all. Women my age, they probably are looking for more stability. But an older woman Jazzy's age—What is she, forty?—you represent adventure, maybe the excitement of youth she never had."

"Good to know. If this writing gig augers in, I'll become a cub to some cougar. Find me a rich one. Kick back."

"Happens all the time in Florida."

"That I believe. If shit happens, it's bound to happen here."

I gave Fred a nice scratch goodbye then said farewell to Spock. We tossed our bags in the back seat of the Sebring, lowered the top, and pulled out.

I purposely drove by Tess's office on our way through town. "Still there," I said. "At least for a while longer."

"Hey, it was a great ride," she said. "Think about it. A bunch of college kids start a newspaper and make a go of it for a decade."

"Not bad. Not bad at all," I said. "And the paper did some fine work, too,"

"Yes, we did."

"So, you have every reason to be proud. You can hang onto that as you plot your next moves."

She nodded.

"Speaking of which, any further thoughts on that subject?"

She sighed. "My parents have suggested I move home to Dayton for a while. Take time to regroup so I won't be rushed into making a decision I might regret later on. It's tempting. I mean, I know I wouldn't be the only millennial camping out at her parents' house, but, still, it feels like a failure. And their place isn't very big. They downsized after my brother and I left home."

"Tess, with everything we've been going through these past few days, I hadn't thought about your parents. They know about all this?"

"Oh, hell no. They would flip out. And my dad, he recently had a double-bypass. He doesn't need this stress."

Dayton's just north of Cincinnati, home of the sainted Reds. Oddly, for a lifelong fan, I'd never set foot in Ohio. But with the top down, I was wearing a Cincinnati ball cap, a black number with a big red C. Even though a fan, Tess didn't have a hat, so I'd loaned her one, a traditional red with a white C. If anyone we knew caught us in matching hats we'd be kicked off the cool-kids table and exiled to hang out with the dorks.

Of course, the reason space is a vacuum is because the Reds' bullpen sucks. And I suck when it comes to picking winners. My other team, the Dolphins, hasn't had a Super Bowl winning quarterback since Bob Griese. Tess—one of her minor flaws—was not a football fan. "Too many meetings, too many replays," she argued.

I had to admit she wasn't entirely wrong about that.

"I've got applications out all over the place," she said. "I don't suppose you guys are hiring, are you?"

The news service I worked for technically had no employees. All of us who labored there were partners in the venture, so the answer to Tess, unfortunately, was no.

After the *Phoenix Daily Sun* folded, Edwina Mahoney gave a handful of us a chance to buy into this new enterprise. We pooled our money and she was a genius at securing some grants from do-gooder foundations to help launch the operation. Leo fronted my share of the partnership. He said he'd rather loan me the money than allow one of his ex-wives to inherit it.

Edwina's first act was to purchase—for a song—a failing Florida news website that had overleveraged itself, which gave us a list of subscribers to jumpstart the operation. Since I was heading to the Sunshine State anyway, I loved the idea of working for news site named Tropic ⊚ Press, with its hurricane symbol embedded in the name. And I'd be doing that while living on a boat in the actual subtropics. How cool was that?

Cool for me. Not so much for Tess.

"We're not hiring right now," I told her. "Maybe in six months or so, if we can keep it going, we might be able to expand. But that won't help you with your immediate need."

"That's alright," she said. "Something will turn up."

I turned east onto University Avenue. In a few miles it would hit State Route 20 and from there we would link onto Florida 207, which led directly into downtown St. Augustine, about eighty miles away.

"You think he's out there, following us right now?" Tess asked, glancing out the side mirror.

"You could always lean over and nibble my ear. If we hear gunshots we'll know the answer."

"Or you'd drive us into a ditch. Seriously, though, where do you think he is?"

"I don't see how he can both tail us and get out front with all these messages unless he's already hidden them."

"I doubt that," she said.

I thought about that for a moment. "Good call. What's the life expectancy of a stuffed parrot before somebody random snatches it?"

"Graaakkk."

CHAPTER 24

St. Augustine

As the 207 enters St. Augustine it becomes South Ponce De Leon Boulevard and winds its way over the San Sebastian River. After crossing the bridge, I missed the turn onto West Castillo Drive, named for the Castillo de San Marcos, the brooding, ancient stone fortress whose cannons guard the city on the Matanzas River—haunted like every other tourist trap in town. Now, heading north on U.S. 1, I turned right as soon as I realized my mistake and we found ourselves on Cincinnati Avenue.

"I think this is a sign," Tess said.

"Better signage would definitely be helpful." (When you make a wrong turn, always blame the signs.)

Cincinnati dead-ended at San Marco Avenue, a.k.a. Highway A1A, and Siri directed us to turn left. We passed the ivy-covered Shrine of Our Lady of La Leche at Mission Nombre de Dios. I knew enough *Espanol* to know *la leche* referred to milk.

"Who's the milk lady?" I asked.

"Don't be rude. It refers to the Virgin Mary, how she breastfed baby Jesus. It's a lovely place."

"Huh."

"Women make pilgrimages here. They pray for help with troubled pregnancies, and to conceive."

"It work?"

"There are stories."

I'd recently read a medical study about how placebos actually *did* help people, that the simple act of believing can result in physiological changes that can be beneficial. Perhaps for some people a shrine like this could be, no pun intended, a genuine godsend?

"You know what Tess," I said. "If I've learned one thing in my brief time on this rock, it's that life can be cruel. People take comfort where they can find it. I don't see how anyone can fault that."

She glanced at me, a curious expression on her face. "You're actually being serious."

"I do that once in a while."

"You should do it more often."

I let that sit for a few seconds then said, "Okay, here's a serious question: Is this really where Ponce de Leon looked for the Fountain of Youth?"

She snorted. "That's a myth. And there are dozens of places around Florida claiming to be the real fountain."

"Oh, that's too bad. I was kinda looking forward to this."

"Tell you what, you want what could be the real deal? North of Naples is a town called Punta Gorda. They've got a fountain there that some people swear is what old Ponce actually found."

"Why am I expecting a punch line?"

"Because the punch line is this: The water is radioactive."

"Thou shitest me."

"I shitest thee not."

"People don't actually drink it then, do they?"

"They actually do. Even though it's got radium in it."

"Yikes."

"But there may be something to it. We did a story on it. The water is also high in magnesium, and that's good, especially for old people's hearts."

"So they get stronger hearts and they glow in the dark as a bonus. Nice. Saves money on night lights."

We turned right onto Williams Street, and shortly thereafter we were entering The Fountain of Youth Archaeological Park, which sprawls over fifteen acres along the Matanzas River.

Mantanzas, by the way, is Spanish for *place of slaughter*. It was immediately south of the theme park that hundreds of years ago conquistadores rounded up and executed a crew of shipwrecked Frenchmen blown ashore by a hurricane.

The park, like countless other businesses, attractions, and legends in Florida, has a colorful history, founded by a woman who called herself "Diamond Lil" McConnell. She bought the acreage in 1904 with cash and diamonds, possibly with loot from a Yukon expedition, and claimed it was where Ponce de Leon waded ashore, although there's no evidence to back that up. She also hired some guys to enlarge a well on the property and began charging people to drink its water with the promise of eternal life.

We dropped eighteen bucks each at the ticket counter and scored a map to the park. "Let's find some food, then we can figure out where to look," Tess said.

The map guided us to a restaurant called the Five Flags Café where Tess ordered a crab cake sandwich and an iced tea. I chose a blackened chicken quesadilla and a Diet Coke. We sat down on the same side of a green picnic table to look at the map together, which we did for a couple of minutes until Tess said, "Well, where the hell do we start?"

Fifteen acres is a lot of territory to cover, especially when you don't really know what you're looking for. The map showed something called a Spanish Watchtower; a Navigator's Planetarium; the Timucua Theater; a blacksmith exhibit; a Maritime Traditions exhibit; a statue of old Ponce himself; and the Spring House, which sheltered the alleged Fountain of Youth.

Hourly cannon firings startled visitors and flocks of roaming peacocks. The big guns commemorated the landing of Pedro Menedez de Aviles, the first Spaniard to set foot here. He was accompanied by 20 artillery pieces on the off chance the native Timucua Indians objected to illegal immigrants.

He put his guns to quick use after arriving, wiping out a settlement Frenchmen up near Jacksonville, thus ensuring that St. Augustine and not Fort Caroline would be North America's oldest surviving city and Florida's longest-operating tourist attraction.

"I'm starting to feel a little frustrated," she said.

"Me, too."

"That fucker, you think he could have been a little more clear on where we were supposed to look."

"I don't think his plan is to make you happy."

"If that's the case, it's working."

Tess knuckled her cheek, thinking. "Let's take another look at that poem."

I pulled out my notebook and read it aloud, softly so we couldn't be overhead:

> *Follow my lead,*
> *To more hauntin'.*
> *Splash a bit*
> *Near the youthful fountain.*
> *Your next clue*
> *Is in the shit*
> *Ain't no horse;*
> *Ain't no bit.*

Tess started to say something, then held up a finger while she finished chewing and then washed down her mouthful of crab cakes with a gulp of iced tea.

"He said *near* the fountain."

"So, you think we should wander over to the actual fountain first and look around there?"

"I don't know. This feels like we're off the mark. What's all that about shit and horse and bit. That sounds like a horse and buggy ride or something."

I looked at the map of the park. "Don't see anything about horsey rides."

We sat for a moment. I took a sip of my drink. She chomped on her sandwich.

"Tess, what if we got this all wrong. Maybe referencing the *youthful fountain* was primarily to direct us to St. Augustine. It says *near* the fountain, like you said. Maybe it's not inside the park at all but somewhere else. Is there some place with horses around here?"

"Hey, I paid a small fortune to get into this joint. I'm not leaving until I at least get to see some of it."

First stop was the Spring House. A sign at the well declared, "This spring was discovered in 1513 and was recorded a landmark in a Spanish grant."

"Sounds official to me," Tess said.

We snagged a couple of tastefully decorated white plastic cups and held them under the sign inviting us to TAKE A SIP.

"Feel any younger?" I asked.

"No but I feel like I swallowed a bunch of iron filings. God that water tastes bad."

She stared at me and cocked an eyebrow. "You haven't tasted it, have you?"

I shook my head.

"And why not?"

"I was waiting to see if it killed you."

"My hero."

We walked back outside and I said, "Maybe we should check the restrooms."

"Why?"

"Well, the poem said the next clue would be, and I quote, 'in the shit.'"

"So what are we going to do, check out every stall in the park? We'll probably get arrested, hauled off as perverts or something."

"And your better idea is what?"

She stuck her tongue out at me.

"How very Bristol-like of you."

"She gets all her best moves from me."

The pathway from the Spring House to the restrooms took us past the gift shop, which doubled as the park's exit.

"Wanna check there first?" I asked.

"On the way out."

The good news was the park was not especially crowded, and neither were the restrooms. After a few minutes, I had peered inside every stall, under the sinks, behind the trashcans, and managed not to get arrested or solicited. A few minutes later, I met Tess outside.

"This is idiotic," I said. "Anything findable in this place would be too obvious and there'd be no way to ensure someone else didn't get to it first."

She was shaking her head. "So now what?"

"There were a bunch of other tourist attractions on that main drag. Maybe one of them has horses."

"But the poem said there was no horse."

"Well, that certainly narrows it down. Not."

But then I thought about that and decided, for a change of pace, to set aside sarcasm and actually engage my brain.

"Right. No horse. No bit. But that wouldn't be referring to an auto parts store or a Publix, would it? It must be something or someplace where you would expect to see a horse, but for some reason there isn't one. Let's go look."

We blew through the gift shop on the way out, ignoring bottles of genuine Fountain of Youth Spring Water, shot glasses, magnets,

Christmas ornaments, collectible spoons, patches, and hand-painted statues of old Ponce, himself.

A couple of minutes later we pulled into a Howard Johnson's parking lot, figuring we might be on foot for a while and it would be as good a place as any to park the car. The motel was right on the main drag and if it got late enough we could crash there for the night.

"Let's go inside, first," Tess suggested. "Most of these places have maps and touristy info. Maybe we'll figure something out."

We walked through the double French doors into the lobby and to our right by a small archway was a stand filled with brochures. Tess grabbed a map and we sat down at a small round table and spread it out.

"Okay, this is soooo St. Augustine," Tess said. "See that tree outside, right in the middle of the parking lot by your car?'

"Yeah?"

"According to this," she stabbed a map with her finger, "it's the oldest tree in St. Augustine. Six hundred years old."

"So?"

"So, they've named it the Old Senator, which is a complete rip-off. The actual *Senator* was a tree in Longwood. It was a bald cypress, over a hundred-and-twenty-five-feet tall and huge at the base. And get this, it was supposed to have been over thirty-five-hundred years old. The oldest cypress in the world. It was alive when Jesus was born, when the Greeks and Trojans were fighting, when Stonehenge was being built."

"And you know this how?"

"I know this because it was on our original list for the *Weird Tour of Florida*."

"A tree?"

"Yes. Because this magnificent tree burned to the ground, and you want to know how?"

I had a feeling I was going to find out no matter what I said, but she was on a roll and I didn't want to be discouraging.

"Absolutely."

"It wasn't lightning. It had survived countless lightning strikes. No, it burned up when a woman built a campfire inside a hallowed out area of the tree. You wanna know why she did that?"

"Tell me."

She needed the fire to see while she was smoking meth."

I had to process that for a moment.

"Somehow, that is so Florida."

"Yeah, right? Anyway, calling this little old live oak in the parking lot here the Old Senator? Give me a break."

"Well I can see why that would be upsetting," I lied.

"Damn straight."

"Meanwhile, do we see anything that suggests horses on this map."

We scanned it for a few more minutes, then she jabbed the map with her finger again.

"Hey look. This is practically next door."

"What is it?"

"Old Town."

"They have horses there?"

"It's supposed to be historic. Maybe they do. It's right around the corner."

We stepped outside just as an open-air trolley full of tourists drove through the parking lot. The guide was telling the visitors all about the Old Senator. "This tree was here when Ponce de Leon took his first sip from the Fountain of Youth. He may have napped under its sheltering limbs…"

"It's not the real Senator!" Tess shouted.

The tourists stared at her perplexed.

"You're ruining a good story," I said.

"Yeah, yeah. Interesting if true. True if interesting." An old newsroom joke.

"You'd fit right into this place."

"Come on. Let's go and not find a horse."

CHAPTER 25

AND WE DIDN'T. Find a horse, that is. Which was good news, since we weren't looking for a horse, we were looking for a place without a horse. And this stands as Exhibit A for how much confusion bad poetry can sew.

Tess and I left the HoJo lobby, walked out to the sidewalk along A1A, past the huge sign with bold yellow lettering directing tourists to the entrance to "Ponce de Leon's Fountain of Youth. Where Legend Meets History. Cannon Firing Daily!"

"Been there, done that, tasted the water," Tess said. Then she cut her eyes toward me. "You never did, did you?"

"Never did what?"

"Never drank the water."

"Nope."

"That was stupid."

"How so?"

"Well, if it works, think about all the broccoli you wouldn't have to eat."

"Fair point."

A few steps later we were staring at the entrance to Old Town, a collection of ramshackle buildings that housed, among other establishments, Gator Bob's Trading Post, where a sign over the store notified alert shoppers that, for modest sums they could acquire ice cream, cold drinks, and gator heads. Flanking Gator Bob's was the Spice and Tea Exchange on one side and The Old Jail on the other. Cars, pickup trucks, and RVs stuffed the sprawling parking lot as did cheerful orange and green Old Town Trolley Tours buses and a hauntingly black Ghosts & Gravestones bus labeled the "Trolley of the Doomed—We'll Drive You To An Early Grave."

We looked around. There were no horses. Which was good. We were clearly hot on the trail.

The front of The Old Jail was decorated with life-like statues of a pair of inmates wearing black and white striped prison rags laboring in a flower garden. The black prisoner standing with a hoe in his hand was glancing off to his left, an anxious expression on his face, as if fearing a whipping. It was an eerie and repugnant reminder of Florida's and St. Augustine's shameful history of slavery and racial discrimination.

"Do you fucking believe this?" I asked Tess.

"Welcome to Florida. It ain't all beach blanket bingo."

"I think we're getting warm," I said after we'd wandered around a bit in fruitless exploration of the grounds. "We've found exactly what we're looking for—no horses."

"Let's walk over there," Tess said, pointing to a shop nearer the entrance, a blue clapboard building labeled the Oldest Store Museum. "I think I see a wagon."

We must have unknowingly walked right by it when we first entered the compound, bedazzled, as we were, by the prospect of owning our very own gator heads. A large red metal wagon, the size of a compact car, rested on the rims of four yellow wheels that presumably once were encircled by tires. In bold capital letters the words OLIVER SUPERIOR were painted on the side. A wooden sign, also with white capital lettering, was propped in the wagon's bed. It read: MANURE SPREADER. A red tractor seat was bolted to the front of the vehicle, no doubt where the driver would sit and direct the horses pulling the contraption.

Tess grabbed my bicep and squeezed in excitement. "Oh, wow, this has got to be it. This is exactly where there are no horses."

Then she looked up at me and squeezed my arm again. "Remind me not to arm wrestle you."

"Don't arm wrestle me."

"Thank you."

The question confronting us was simple: Where would an insane stalker hide bad poetry in an antique manure spreader?

I dropped to my hands and knees and crawled under the wagon, figuring the most logical place to hide a note, unnoticed and out of the weather, would be underneath.

And it was.

I rolled out from under the contraption with a small envelope that had been duct-taped to the spreader's underside. "This has got to be it."

Tess took it from me and began feeling it with her fingertips, as if trying to detect something inside.

"Whatcha looking for?" I asked.

She looked at me blankly then shook her head. "Oh. Nothing. It just felt empty."

"Huh. Well, is it?"

She held it up to the sunlight and we both could see the shadow of a slip of paper inside. Tess started to tear it open.

"Uh, forensics?" I said. "Prints? We talked about this, if you'll recall."

"Oh. Yeah. Fuck."

She shoved the envelope into the back pocket of her shorts. "We can open it in the car."

A few minutes later we were in the Sebring with tweezers that Tess had brought along just for this purpose. She extracted yet another half-page of a legal document with a hand-written message in small lettering on the opposite side:

YOU WHERE TO GO
TO FIND YOUR PRIZE

I slipped my reporter's notebook from the back pocket of my cargo shorts and transcribed the lines to the accumulating stanzas:

Your prize awaits
So don't be slow
Cut and paste
And it will show
You where to go
To find your prize

"Well," I said, trying to be cheerful, "that's the third stanza. Only seven more to go. We're a third of the way there."

"Thirty percent."

"Close enough for atomic weapons."

Tess carefully refolded the note, holding it on the edges, and slipped it back into the small letter-sized envelope. She did not show me the legalese on the opposite side of the paper and, demonstrating amazing restraint, I didn't ask. The silver duct tape was still affixed to the envelope, and she stuck it on the dashboard.

"Now what?" she asked.

"I don't suppose you have any samples of Amy's handwriting with you, do you?"

She thought about that for a second or two. "Might have some back at the office. We all filled out W4s for our tax withholding at the newspaper. There might be other things in the files there that we could try to match with this."

"Sorry, Tess. Should have thought of that earlier."

"Nobody's perfect."

We thought about that for a few beats then I said, "That seems too easy, doesn't it?"

"Maybe. Or maybe this is the slip-up we were hoping for."

The shadows in the parking lot were growing long and we would have to make a decision about next steps.

"So, now what?" I asked. "We drive back to Gainesville and wait for further instructions from this douche bag? Or do we camp out here?"

Tess grew an irritated look on her face and jammed her hand into her back pocket, extracting her cell phone.

"Goddammit. I'll bet this is him."

But it wasn't.

CHAPTER 26

I WAS SPRAWLED on a queen bed in our HoJo motel room giving my back a rest and catching up on Word Chums on my iPhone while Tess was furiously typing a response to the email she'd received.

The message hadn't come from our stalker, but from the publisher of a magazine in the Cincinnati area. They were looking for a managing editor and had posted the vacancy on journalismjobs.com, a media employment website. Tess had sent them a letter and resume weeks ago, but hadn't thought too much about it. She'd applied at dozens of newspapers, magazines, and online operations, and although this one held some hometown appeal and would put her close to her family, her first choice was to work for a real news operation, not a glossy monthly aimed at upscale suburbanites.

Before we checked into the motel room, we spent a few minutes dithering in the Sebring, discussing whether she should agree to a phone interview the next morning or not, and whether we should spend the night or drive back to Gainesville. She seemed unusually indecisive.

To me, the answer was obvious:

"You say yes, of course. You take the call. You can't pass up opportunities when you're job hunting."

"But how can I with all this going on?"

"Yeah, I get it. You're on overload. But you can handle this, Tess. Here's a suggestion: We check into the motel. You get a good night's sleep. I promise not to assault you…"

"That's a relief."

"And in the morning you can wash your hair, make yourself presentable…"

"Oh, I'm not presentable now?"

"That's not what I meant. It's a video call. I just figured you might want the extra time to get ready to call this guy…"

"Not a guy. A woman."

"Call this *woman* on Skype and be your normal, charming, unsarcastic self. Relax. Just because you agree to talk doesn't mean you have to accept an offer—if she even makes one. And odds are she'll have other candidates to talk to and that will take some time. Meanwhile, we'll wrap this up, find a convenient place to bury the stalker's body after we beat him to death, and you may have other offers to consider, too."

Despite my advice, Tess was unsure about staying over in St. Augustine. A night in her own bed would make her more relaxed for the interview, she thought. But if the stalker kept to the Weird Tour of Florida pattern, the next stop would be somewhere here on the East Coast, so that was an argument for sticking around. On the other hand, who knew when that asshat would contact us?

Neither of us much liked being toyed with like this and we spent some time debating whether we would kill him with our bare hands or if we should pummel him to death with garden implements—shovels came to mind because they would be handy for grave digging afterward.

"I kind of favor those small, foldable camp shovels," she said at one point. "They're small enough to carry around and they're handy for digging small holes for flowers."

I argued for a large, flat-edge coal shovel as it would make chopping off his head easier.

Then her phone buzzed again and it settled the question of whether to stay or go. This time it was a text message:

You're not done yet

I must report.

Head on down

To the Last Resort.

I asked, "What's the Last Resort?"

Tess opened the *WTF* magazine and pointed to the list. "It's a bar in Port Orange about an hour down the coast from here."

"So should we go now or wait until the morning?" I asked.

"Let's wait. I'm exhausted, physically and emotionally. And I need a good night's sleep if I'm going to do this interview in the morning."

So we checked into the motel, scored a ground-floor room with two queens, a small but clean bathroom, and free wi-fi.

Tess finished typing on her phone and hit the send button.

"Okay. I'm set for the interview for nine o'clock tomorrow. I tested the wi-fi signal and it's got enough bandwidth for the call."

"Good. Now to more crucial matters. Do you think 'gorup' should be a word?"

She slid off her bed and plopped down next to me, then peered at the game on my phone. "No. But 'group' is a word. Oh. But that won't work, will it?"

"No."

"How about 'guru'?"

"I don't have a second 'u'."

"But you've got a blank."

"But I don't want to waste a blank."

"Well, Zander, life's about choices."

Zander? I hadn't been called that since high school.

"Where did *Zander* come from?"

"It's your new Delta Tau Chi name. I just decided."

So now Jazzy and Tess each had their own nicknames for me. How nice.

"Well, I guess it's better than Flounder."

CHAPTER 27

Port Orange

STEP INTO THE Last Resort Bar and there she is—Aileen Wuornos, serial killer—a mural of her haunting face adorns the barroom wall, her image peers out from the labels of "Crazed Killer Hot Sauce" bottled and sold in her honor.

Sure that's in bad taste. It's insensitive, offensive, maybe even incontinent—so what? It's Florida. The only relevant question is: Can it be sold? And with a huge markup?

It was in this tiny saloon, a flat-roofed, one-story brick graffiti-magnet on the edge of U.S. 1 that Wuornos was arrested in 1991. That led to her execution a decade later for the murders of half a dozen men. In the one case that went to trial, her lawyer, whose nickname was Doctor Legal, argued that the victim was a drugged-up, drunken john who viciously raped her.

Two documentary films were made challenging the competency of her defense, the second of which was used as source material by the actress Charlize Theron in the movie *Monster*.

The rusting hulk of a truck trailer abutted the bar and advertised the Last Resort as "Home of Ice Cold Beer" and "Killer Women Where the Movie Monster Was Filmed." A black wooden door led into the bar's interior, hand painted with the saloon's name in white block letters.

Memorials were painted on the brick exterior: "In Loving Memory H.D. 'Heavy Duty.'" "World Famous Ted E. Bear," "Tattoo Jeff," "Big Dick Daddy," "Some Will Walk Through the Pearly Gates; Some Will Skate." That kind of place.

Wuornos was a rare female serial killer. She was reared in poverty and had been sexually abused. And because it's unusual that women are ever accused of multiple homicides, her arrest and murders became something of a sensation at the time.

A jury of her peers found her sane enough to be executed. As proof of the wisdom of that decision, Wuornos offered these as her last words before she was lethally injected:

"Yes, I would just like to say I'm sailing with the rock, and I'll be back, like *Independence Day*, with Jesus. June 6, like the movie. Big mother ship and all, I'll be back, I'll be back."

Tess had been uncharacteristically quiet earlier during the drive to Port Orange, so I'd tuned into a local radio station for some news:

- The president had proposed the creation of a new national holiday—Commander-in-Chief Day. He was offering his own birthday as the ideal date.
- In a special election to fill a Florida congressional vacancy, the Republican and Democratic candidates were preparing for a debate in which they both planned to argue they were the best pro-life candidate. It was a ultra-conservative district.
- A new scientific report concluded that if carbon dioxide levels got much higher, the earth's atmosphere would lose the ability to make clouds. Which, I guessed, would be bad news for farmers and a great boost to the sun screen industry.
- And ground was about to be broken on the site of what would soon be Florida's newest tourist attraction: GrifterLand,

celebrating con artists from the Sunshine State and elsewhere who had made history with their deceptions, lies, and cheating. For two-hundred-and-fifty dollars, you, too, could have a brick with your name on it at the entrance. Listeners were told where they could send their money.

"So, you gonna buy a brick?" I'd asked Tess as we rolled down the highway.

Shrug.

"Got plenty of sunscreen?"

Eyeroll.

"You voting in this election?"

Nothing.

Finally I got to the elephant in the car.

"So how'd your job interview go on Skype?"

"Fine."

"Fine, meaning you got the job and you're happy? Fine, meaning you think you're going to be offered the job, but you're having buyer's remorse? Fine, meaning you blew it? What does fine mean?"

"It went okay."

"Ah, that clears it up. Okay. Not fine. Okay."

I had been trying to humor her. But sometimes even your best material flops. It was a tough room. With one customer. That's how it goes sometimes. If I didn't know better I'd guess stress was a factor.

We pulled into a leaf-strewn lot on the side of the bar where a dilapidated wooden fence was festooned with myriad license plates, most from out of state. A cheery red Budweiser banner announced "Welcome Bikers" near another section of fence plastered with messages, among them: "Metro Detroit, Michigan—It's a White Thing."

"Remember that pep talk you gave me about being courageous and all," Tess said. "I'm thinking the better part of valor is for me to sit here and guard the car, with the doors locked, while you check this joint out."

"Bwaaakkk, bwaaakkk." It was my best-ever imitation of a chicken. It didn't faze her.

I raised the rag top and handed her the keys. I heard the locks click as I walked over to the front door.

I poked around the inside of the bar for a hot minute. Except for the bartender, I had it to myself. The ceiling was littered with handwritten notes from bar patrons, the walls were splattered with photos and plaques and memorabilia. A stuffed jailbird in black and white prison garb hung suspended from a cage next to an important notation on a beam announcing that "Stephanie-n-Tina Were Here." Photographs and sketches of Aileen Wuornos were scattered about. To the left a skeleton in formal wear, to the right a half-mannequin completely covered in graffiti. It was a visual riot. I'd need help trying to find a clue in all that.

"You looking for something?" the bartender asked. She was a large woman with silver hair and a tattoo of a spider on her left cheek and a very pleasant smile.

"I think I may have lost my babel fish last time I was here," I replied.

"Babel what?"

"Oh, never mind. That was on Bartledan. I have a friend out in the car. Be right back."

I wandered back outside checking out the entertaining tags painted on the bricks. Next to "Tattoo Jeff" I spotted something written in black felt-tip ink in small capital lettering. I pulled out my iPhone, took a picture, then rejoined Tess in the car.

"What was it like in there?" she asked.

"Oh, about half a dozen bikers, all pretty drunk and rowdy, one of them wearing a six-shooter on his hip. Long hair, lots of leather and tats, what you'd expect from a pack of Hell's Angels. Your kind of place."

"Uh huh."

"Check this out," I said.

I opened the Camera Roll app on my phone to the picture I'd taken of the writing on the wall. I spread it with my fingers to enlarge it and we read:

SO YOU CAN HIDE
ALL YOUR LIES

I pulled out my notebook and added this stanza to the growing poem. It now read:

> *Your prize awaits*
> *So don't be slow.*
> *Cut and paste*
> *And it will show*
> *You where to go*
> *To find your prize*
> *So you can hide*
> *All your lies.*

"All my lies," Tess said quietly. "Nice."

"I don't suppose you want to talk about this, do you?" I said. "It's only you and me. It would go no further. Cross my heart and hope to die."

Tess stared out the windshield. The view wasn't inspiring—a used car lot unimaginatively named Best Cars. I scanned the area, but saw no dealers advertising Second Best Cars. I figured they'd be the ones without wheels. Or engines.

"I know I can trust you," Tess said. "Maybe at some point. Not now. Okay?"

She turned to me and had a pleading look on her face.

"The guy you're protecting, I hope he's worth it."

Of course, I didn't know if it was a guy she was protecting. It was a bit of an old reporter's trick to get her to say something in response, maybe narrowing down the list of possible people she was trying to shield. If she had said, for instance, "not a guy," then it would have instantly eliminated the 152 million males in America, leaving only 157 million females to be considered.

Hey, you have to start somewhere.

She grabbed the remains of a cup of coffee and took a swig. We sat for a few minutes and reread the latest addition to the poem.

"We don't know where to go next do we?" she said.

"No, we don't."

"There was nothing else on the wall outside waiting for us?"

"Not that I saw."

"Could you look again?"

"Why don't you come with me. Two pair of eyes are better than one. Plus, I could use your help inside the bar. It's, uh, a little busy. Visually. And there was one room I would feel a little awkward poking around in."

That earned me a curious look then she got it. "The ladies room."

We stepped out of the car, locked it, walked back over to the building, and gave the exterior walls a thorough examination, hoping to find something I might have missed.

"He's trying to wear me down," she said.

"Yep. And from the sound of your voice it's working. I'd tell you to woman-up, but I know that would be pointless. We all have our breaking points, Tess. It's not your fault you're such a weenie."

She slugged me. Same shoulder as before. But not hard.

"What was it like inside, really?"

"Empty."

Without saying a word she turned and walked around to the front of the saloon, opened the black wooden door, and stepped in. I followed.

"I could use a drink," she told the bartender. "Got any Diet Coke?"

She nodded and I said, "Make it a double."

The bartender frowned, then said, "You find your fish?"

I shook my head. "Not yet."

If Tess heard that exchange, she ignored it. She was scanning the interior, her nose crinkled, maybe from the smell, maybe from the bar's distasteful exploitation of a deranged woman, perhaps out of frustration at the prospect of finding anything in the confused décor, if you could call it that.

"You looking for something, too, honey?" the bartender asked.

"Yeah, actually," Tess said. "Somebody was supposed to leave word on where I can meet him."

"Word?"

"Probably a note."

The bartender's face brightened. "Oh. Hey, maybe I can help you. Larry, he closed last night, he texted me and said somebody left an envelope for a woman named Tess. It should be around here somewhere. That be you?"

CHAPTER 28

The Dead Zone

WE WERE DRIVING inland on Interstate 4, which connects Daytona Beach to Tampa, but, more importantly, is the busiest route for the millions of tourists who flock to Florida each year to visit the park the rat built—Disney World.

I-4 leads to Mickey's Magic Kingdom, but it often also leads to the grave. Traffic studies show that it is the most dangerous roadway in America, racking up nearly one and a half fatalities per mile. And a stretch of the highway between Dayton Beach and Orlando is haunted.

It's called the Dead Zone because of the unusually high number of crashes and fatalities, but the haunting dates back to the 1800s when some early settlers died of yellow fever and were buried in what eventually became agricultural land. Farmers who dared tamper with the gravesites saw their houses burn down and even suffered mysterious deaths themselves.

The interstate was eventually built atop the graves—somebody forgot to move the bodies—and on the day the highway opened a tractor-trailer full of frozen shrimp lost control right over the gravesite becoming the first of many casualties on this deadly stretch of road.

I knew all this from the pages of Tess's special section and a bit of digging around on the internet. Today, however, our destination was not the Dead Zone nor the ghosts of ancient settlers, but the Cassadaga Spiritualist Camp near the town of Lake Helen, known as the Psychic Capital of the World.

No sooner had we ramped up onto the interstate and begun our journey to the land of spiritualists and mediums, than Tess announced she was "sick of this shit."

"I feel your pain," I said. "I've been wondering if we can't figure out a way to get ahead of this."

"What are you thinking?"

"Well, we seem to be following the order in your *Weird Tour of Florida* magazine. If you recall, I was the one who was nervous about assuming there was a pattern to this, but now it seems clear."

"So far."

"Sure, our stalker could change this up at any time. Still, what would be our next stop after Cassadaga?"

Tess dredged the magazine from her backpack and flipped it open to the centerfold and the map. "Next after Cassadaga would be Ashley's Tavern," she said.

"And that's where?"

"Down the East Coast a ways in a town called Rockledge. It's not far from Cape Canaveral."

"How about after that?"

"Hmmm. Let's see. Spook Hill. That's in Lake Wales. Then the Skunk Ape Research Headquarters in Ochopee, then Our Lady of Clearwater, then the Gravity Research Foundation monument in Tampa."

"Is Skunk Ape the longest gap?"

"Not following you."

"So, the next two stops, Ashley's Tavern and Spook Hill are still up around this part of the state, right?"

Tess was checking out the map in her lap. "Yeah, sort of. After those two, the Skunk Ape Research Headquarters is way south, all the way down southeast of Naples, which would be at least a couple hours driving, mostly on back roads. That what you mean by gap?"

"Exactly."

"After Skunk Ape, we shoot all the way up Interstate 75 to Clearwater, probably another two-and-a-half hours, so both of those are the two longest uninterrupted stretches we're facing."

"Assuming we continue with this pattern."

"Assuming that, yes. Where you going with this?"

"Okay, brainstorm with me for a minute. If the stalker is operating solo, he has to stay ahead of us—just ahead of us—dropping off these clues. That is, assuming we're right, like we talked about before, and he won't want the clues lying about too long before we get there since somebody else could find them. We still on the same page with that?"

"Well, that's a pretty big assumption. But it's not unreasonable."

"Okay. Then what if we anticipate his moves? What if we assume he'll keep following the map, and we skip ahead and catch him in the act? We could bypass Spook Hill, for instance, and just wait for him at this Skunk Ape place. Or skip the Skunk Ape and ambush him in Clearwater. He'll be on those long drives so we'd have plenty of time to beat him to the next stop that way."

She thought about that for a minute then shook her head. "Too risky. He might be watching us at each stop, waiting to make sure we got the clues before moving on."

She rubbed her hands together thinking it through for a few seconds then said, "In fact, I'd bet on that. He's probably getting his rocks off watching us jump through these hoops. Likely taking pictures, maybe video. I'll be her jerks off to them every night."

"Okay, that's a little graphic, but I see your point."

"And, besides, that would mean we skip a stanza of the poem, which could be crucial."

"So if we want to get ahead of him, we'll need some help."

"Demerest?"

"That's what I was thinking. If we can talk him into staking out, say, the Skunk Ape place, or the Clearwater location, he could catch this asshat in the act. We could reverse the paradigm. Instead of us *following* the stalker, we'd be herding him into a trap."

"But how would Demerest know who to look for?"

"Look for a guy with an envelope and duct tape sneaking about. Or maybe a parrot."

"I'll call him."

But she didn't have to. He called us.

CHAPTER 29

Cassadaga Spiritualist Camp

"D2's gone missing."

"Is that good news or bad news?" I asked.

Tess frowned. "Not sure. But Demerest says the police may want to talk to me. That's why he called. He was giving me an early warning."

"The cops want to talk to you because of that fight at the biker bar?"

"That. And since he's Amy half-brother and since the last person to see her alive was me, they may not like that kind of coincidence."

I nodded. "True that. Cops hate coincidences." So do journalists, for that matter, but Tess already knew that.

"Well, I've got an alibi," she said. "I've been with you the entire time."

"I don't know. I'm a pretty heavy sleeper. You could have snuck out of the motel last night, driven to Gainesville, killed him with that camp shovel you've got hidden away, buried him, and gotten back in time for breakfast. You have been kinda grouchy today. Maybe from lack of sleep?"

"Nah. It's just that time of month."

"Thanks for sharing."

"Not *that!* The rent's due."

"Oh."

"So what's the scoop on D2? Somebody call the cops?"

"Yes. Demerest said the police got a call this morning. Darnell didn't show up for work yesterday or today. His boss over at the car dealership got worried, drove over to his apartment, thinking he might be sick or something. D2's car's missing. And it looks like nobody's home."

"Cops look inside his place?" I asked.

She nodded. "Landlord let them in. All his stuff is still in the apartment. Neighbors have no clue, didn't report anything unusual. There's nothing out of the ordinary except Darnell isn't around. And despite being a complete fuckwad, he apparently has been a reliable employee and paid his rent on time, according to the landlord."

"So, he's been missing ever since we hit the road on this scavenger hunt."

She nodded. "Yeah, I guess so."

I processed that for a couple of minutes then said, "Let's say Amy's the stalker. Is it possible she might have recruited D2 to help her?"

"Beats the shit out of me. But why would he risk his job? Why not call in sick or take vacation or something? Just vanishing like this sounds sketchy."

Everything about this misadventure was sketchy, but she had a point.

Tess had told Demerest about our idea of getting ahead of the stalker. He liked it, but didn't fancy driving more than five hours down to Ochopee, the little town outside Naples where the Skunk Ape Research Headquarters was located. He suggested ambushing the stalker in Clearwater, and Tess readily agreed.

The call markedly improved her attitude. "I'm better now. I don't like feeling out of control, being pushed around. Now, we're the hunters."

When the stalker called Tess at her office, I'd rushed outside and shot several dozen photos of everyone on the street nearby. I'd shared them with Demerest and with Tess. But even though she didn't recognize anyone, it occurred to me they still might be useful.

"At least Demerest has those pictures I shot in case the bad guy is one of the people who were outside the newspaper," I said. "Might help him spot our guy up in Clearwater."

"That would be good."

Tess's phone buzzed again. She looked at the screen, expecting the police, but it was Bristol.

"Hey, girl, how's my newspaper?" She punched the call onto her speakerphone.

"It's a little drafty," Bristol said.

"What's that mean?"

"It means somebody threw a brick through the window last night. I got here later than usual this morning. I think it's possible I was overserved last night. And when I showed up there was a gaping hole in the plate glass."

"Jesus fucking Christ."

"Yeah. I called Marv. He's got some guys coming over with plywood to seal it up. But I gotta tell you, he's not a happy camper."

"He's probably pissed about the rent on top of everything else."

"Funny thing. He did mention that and asked where you were and I told him you were on an assignment, which I guess is kinda true. He wants you to call him."

"Okay, I will."

"But there's more. He also told me that when he got to his office this morning he discovered somebody had been messing with his spare keys. You know how he keeps them in envelopes labeled in alphabetical order? They were all mixed up."

"Oh, crap. How about the keys to my house?"

"That's the thing. He put them in a separate place, so you're okay there, but he's convinced that's the reason someone was going through his desk."

"He call the cops?"

"He said he's going to."

"So who would know to do that?"

"He's thinking it's the college student who works Saturdays. He's going to give his name to the cops to track him down. He tried to call him but got no answer."

"Bristol, do I need to come home?"

"Well, it's certainly getting fucked up around here. You heard about D2, right?"

"That he's missing?"

"Yeah."

I jumped in. "Bristol, have you been in touch with Jazzy? If someone was trying to get the keys to Tess's place, we need to alert her."

"Dammit, you're right. You got her cell?"

"She doesn't have one."

"Fuck. Fuck. Fuck."

Tess said, "You got your hands full. I'll call Demerest back and have him swing by and check on her."

"Good. Call me later. The guys with the plywood are here." Bristol hung up.

While that conversation was taking place, I had pulled into the Cassadaga Spiritualist Camp and navigated to a public parking area adjacent to the Colby Memorial Temple and the Caesar Forman Healing Gazebo on Marion Street.

Were it not for the signage advertising certified mediums and healers, spirit encounters, meditation gardens, and a crossroads sign pointing to Mediumship Way and Spiritualist Street, it would look like a normal small Midwestern village. Clapboard houses, screened-in porches, curtained windows. Never mind the plaque celebrating the founder of the village, one George P. Colby, "a trance medium (who) worked with several Spirit guides."

While Tess made calls to Demerest and Marv, I stepped out of the car and stretched my legs. I pulled my reporter's notebook from my back pocket and reread the notes I'd transcribed back at The Last Resort after the bartender handed Tess the envelope.

Who left that envelope? Did he—or she—leave a name? We asked the bartender to call Larry, the overnight guy who'd left her a message about the note. He didn't pick up. Probably still asleep. So we had no clue who left it.

Another piece of the puzzle was inside the envelope, once again on the back of a half-page of a legal document directing us to this place, once again in rhyme and verse. And once again, I did not ask Tess to show me the legalese on the other side of the note and she didn't offer. The handwritten note read:

> *Get one*
> *with the Spirit.*
> *And when you*
> *are near it*
> *You'll find a*
> *perturbance*
> *At the back of*
> *Emergence.*

It rhymed, but otherwise it seemed our mad poet's gifts for verse were deteriorating. The word "spirit" told us our next stop was Cassadaga. That was the easy part. Then I'd googled the word "emergence" and this is what I learned from Wikipedia:

"In philosophy, theories that emphasize emergent properties have been called emergentism. Almost all accounts of emergentism include a form of epistemicor ontological irreducibility to the lower levels."

That certainly cleared things up. All we had to do was capture any outstanding epistemicor ontologies and beat the living shit out of them.

Tess stepped out of the Sebring still holding her cell phone. "Demerest is heading over to my house right now to make sure Jazzy's alright."

"Good."

"Yes, that's good news."

"Let me guess, there's also bad news."

"Yes. Marv says I'm bad for his blood pressure. He loves me. And he wishes me well. But he's not running a charity. I've got two weeks to clear out of the office and the house."

"Fuck me! Two weeks? That's crap. What's he expect you to do, pitch a fucking tent? Give me a break. What a bastard. We'll bury him next to D2. We'll hang him by his microscopic testicles and let Fred lick him to death. We'll feed him to the no-see-ums..." I went on like that for a while until Tess was laughing so hard tears dripped off her chin.

She walked over to me and put her arms around me. "You *are* my bestie. Thanks."

I hugged her back then said, "Now what?"

"It's not all that bad. I've got two weeks. Plenty of time to wrap this up, put out a final edition, throw my stuff in a U-Haul, and head to Dayton."

"Dayton?"

"Yeah. I've been thinking about it. I can at least store my stuff at my folks' place. Who knows, maybe that job in Cincy will pan out. If not, I can still use Dayton as a base of operations until I get things sorted out. At least I'll have a roof over my head."

"Wow."

"Yeah, wow. Now let's figure out where this *emergence* is."

We strolled up Stevens Street to a bookstore and gift shop and walked in. A woman with silver hair, unadorned by makeup or jewelry but possessing the clearest most unblemished skin I'd ever seen on an older person, was standing behind the checkout counter.

Around her in the little shop were crystals, and jewelry, and statuettes, and herbs, and potions, and books about feng shui and astrology, and magazines, and buddhas, and candles—lots of candles.

"I have a question," I said.

"Hmmm."

"I see a lot of signs about mediums. They talk to dead people, right?"

She gently shook her head. "Anyone can talk to the dead. You're a medium when they talk back."

"Oh."

I let that lie for a few moments then said, "One more question. If I said the word *emergence*, would that mean anything to you?"

"Is that really something you would say?"

"Let's assume so."

She thought about that for a little bit then said, "Oh. Do you mean the magazine?"

"Magazine?"

She pointed to a rack by the door. "Over there."

There were a handful of periodicals in the rack: *Psychic World*, the *Mountain Astrologer*, *Sage Woman*, *Yoga*, *Reiki*, *Spirituality & Health*, *Buddhadharma*, *The National Spiritualist*, and, finally, a half-dozen copies of the *Sedona Journal of Emergence*.

The magazine's cover featured a beautiful sunrise over the planet Earth shot from outer space with headlines such as :

A Magnetic Polar Shift
Is Happening—
An Opportunity for
Global Cooperation

and

GUIDANCE AS YOUR SPIRIT SELF
BECOMES YOUR DAY-TO-DAY SELF

Our mad poet had said our clue would be at the "back of Emergence." I pulled one of the magazines out of the rack and flipped to the back inside cover. It featured a full-color advertisement for something called the Cosmic Awakening Conference featuring Thunder Beat and The Sexy Skulls. I wasn't sure what that was, but if it was a band I wanted their tee shirt.

"You see anything, Zander?" Tess asked.

"Not this copy. Let's look through all of them." We pulled them out of the rack and started paging through the magazines, one-by-one. They were over a hundred pages each, so we looked at the back inside covers first, taking the poem the stalker had left Tess literally.

And it paid off.

Once again, the note was handwritten on the back of a piece of a legal document. Tess started to pull it out of the magazine and I jerked it away from her.

"Forensics?"

"Oh. Fuck. Right."

I carried the magazine over to the saleslady at the counter and plopped down my credit card.

"Did you find what you journeyed here for?" she asked. She was speaking formally, maybe it was supposed to be spiritually. Who knows? I was a stranger in these parts. But when in Cassadaga, do as the trance mediums do.

"The true journey is the one within," I replied in my best effort to sound sincere.

She frowned at me, and I hurriedly scrawled my signature on the credit card receipt and stepped outside.

I started to ask Tess a question, then realized the answer was back inside the store. I handed her the magazine and told her I'd be right back.

The silver-haired woman at the counter appraised me as I stepped back inside. "Has your inner journey taken you back here so soon?"

"It has. And I have a question."

"Let me consult the stars and see if I am in a place where I can answer." She closed her eyes, pressed her palms together as if in prayer.

Then, after a brief moment, peeked out of one of her eyes and a brief smile flitted across her lips. "Why, I believe I am."

I put my palms on the counter, took a breath, and said, "You know, that may have been discourteous of me, earlier. If so, I apologize. Sometimes I try too hard to amuse myself."

She smiled, a wide, friendly grin. "How very gentlemanly of you. Apology accepted. Now how can I help you?"

"Did you notice us examining a note in the back of that magazine?"

"I did."

"Someone left it there for us. By any chance, did you see the person who did that?"

She frowned. "I've been here all day, since we opened, and we've had dozens of people wander in. I'm not always standing right here. I watch over the whole store, put things back where they belong. I don't see every little thing. So, it's possible, but I didn't notice that."

"I don't suppose you have closed circuit TV?"

She shook her head. "But I could consult the spirits for you if you like."

I shot her with my thumb and index finger then turned to leave. "I must continue my journey."

"Safe travels, Alexander."

I froze. How did she...

"Your credit card."

I shot her again and left.

Tess was sitting on a park bench, the magazine open to the back cover, rereading the note. She looked up when I approached.

"I was hoping the sales lady might have seen someone messing with the magazines earlier today, but she didn't"

"Figures."

"Meaning?"

"Meaning this asshat is throwing us a curveball. Check this out."

The message was in tiny block letters, once again handwritten with a black felt-tip pen:

Half man,
Half skunk,
Half ape.
Get there soon,
Don't hesitate.
Look in the boat
That don't float.
Then find the shed
Or you'll be dead.

Tess shook her head. "What the hell does that mean, anyway, half man, half skunk, half ape?"

"It's a riff from *South Park*. You've seen the episode, haven't you, about the ManBearPig?"

"Uh, no."

"It's my favorite. Al Gore's in it. Anyway, that's the joke, half man, half bear, half pig. This asshole has a sense of humor. I think I'm starting to like him."

Tess looked around for something to throw at me, couldn't find a rock big enough, so she rolled up the magazine and took a swing. I let her chase me around for a bit hoping she would burn off some tension, then I stood still and she whacked me on the shoulder. Yes, the same shoulder. I'd probably need rotator cuff surgery.

"Wubba Lubba Dub Dub," I said.

"What?"

"That's Bird Person for 'I'm in great pain.'"

"And a Bird Person is what?"

"Where have you misspent your youth?" I asked.

"Recovering from alcoholism, running a business, getting knocked up, having an abortion, being stalked. And you?"

"Watching *Rick and Morty*, of course." I pointed to the tee shirt I was wearing.

"That's a pickle," she said.

"Yes. Pickle Rick. He turned himself into a pickle so he didn't have to go see a shrink. Season three."

"It's a cartoon."

"And your point is?"

"It's a cartoon."

"You know, we really need to work on your connection to popular culture. Anyway, what were you saying about a curveball?"

"He's directing us to the Skunk Ape Headquarters. It's over four hours away."

"That's the curveball?"

"No. The curveball is he's violating the list. We should be going to Ashley's Tavern and then to Spook Hill before we go all the way down to Ochopee. He's skipping right over both of them."

"He's mixing things up. Trying to keep us off balance."

"And where the hell is the next stanza in the poem? I looked all through this magazine. There's nothing."

"You sure?"

"Yes, it isn't in here," she said, slapping the magazine against her thigh.

"Well, this is your call, Tess. What do you want to do."

"I don't think we have a choice. We drive to Ochopee."

We walked back toward Marion Street where the car was parked. Tess was glum. Me, too. For a little while, we were back in control, turning the tables on the puppet master, setting a trap. Now this. As we got to the car I froze.

"I don't fucking believe it."

"What?"

"Check it out."

Sitting on the hood was a blue parrot.

CHAPTER 30

On the Florida Turnpike

Siri said it was a 265-mile drive from the Calladaga Spiritualist Camp to Skunk Ape Research Headquarters. The fastest route would take us back onto Interstate 4 southbound until it linked with the Florida Turnpike, where we would continue onto state and county roads around Lake Okeechobee and eventually intersect with U.S. 41, the two-lane linking Tampa and Miami, a.k.a. the Tamiami Trail.

The predicted travel time of four-and-a-half hours seemed optimistic to me given we'd be driving through Orlando and all the heavy tourist traffic clogging highways around The Rat. And why we had to be there before eight o-clock struck me as odd—but what wasn't?

We'd lingered in Cassadaga for about a half hour and I had to gas up the car before we set out, so even if I put the pedal to the metal, didn't get pulled over, and drove non-stop, it seemed unlikely we could actually beat this moron there. He had too long a head start to compensate for. But we could try.

"Tell me about this place we're headed to," I said to Tess.

"You've heard of the Skunk Ape, right?"

"Sure. He's related to Bigfoot, only he lives in the Everglades."

She looked at me curiously. "And you know it's a joke, right?"

"People say that about the ManBearPig, too. Until he tears their ears off."

"Are you ever serious?"

"You'll know all about serious if you're attacked by the ManBearPig. Or the Skunk Ape, for that matter."

"Jesus. Anyway, Skunk Ape Headquarters is this tourist trap out in the boonies on the Tamiami Trail in this itsy bitsy town, if you can even call it a town."

"Ochopee?"

"Right. That's Seminole for the word 'farm.' Anyway, there's not much there, but it's also home to the country's smallest post office, which is kinda cool."

"I read about that. It used to be a barn or something?"

"Or something. But now it's a full-service post office. And the Skunk Ape Research Headquarters is a stone's throw away. About the only research they do is searching through tourist's wallets. They sell tee shirts and hats and trinkets. They've got statues of the Skunk Ape, plaster of Paris footprints, that sort of thing."

"You sound skeptical."

"Zander, please."

The next two lines in the developing poem had been squawked out by the stuffed blue parrot:

"Graaakkk.

"Halfway home,

"You're on the move."

Presumably the stanza after that would find a word ending in "ove" to rhyme with "move." But at the rate this was dragging on neither of us held any hope that we would discover our final destination until the last two lines.

I turned on the car radio and scanned for a news station, eventually picking up WIOD in Miami. A Florida man had been arrested for dressing as a pirate and firing black-powder flintlock pistols at passing vehicles in the Keys. Police arrested a Palm Beach man for biting off his neighbor's nose when he refused to give him a cigarette. A half-dozen bottlenose dolphins washed up in Ft. Lauderdale and wildlife ecologists said autopsies revealed their stomachs were filled with plastic bags and straws. The president, who was spending the weekend playing golf in Florida, jumped into the special congressional election by endorsing the candidacy of a guy named Aaron Landry who…

Tess reached over and turned the radio off before I could hear the rest of the report.

I turned to her. She looked away, stared out the side window.

Sometimes I'm not entirely stupid. I kept my mouth shut. Something was up. If she wanted to talk about it, she would. Me pestering her wouldn't help. We drove along in silence for about ten minutes, me glancing repeatedly at the rear view mirror for cops, keeping the speedometer as high as I dared.

I glanced over at Tess. She was now staring directly out the windshield, her arms clenched across her body. Silent.

I continued my strategy of staying mum. It's actually a good interviewing technique. Most people can't handle it. They feel the social necessity to fill the empty air. You can learn a lot by being patient, giving people the chance to do the talking. And it burns zero calories.

Finally, she broke down.

"Landry. Aaron Landry. He's the Republican candidate in that special election."

I nodded, said nothing.

"He's why we're doing this."

Keeping my mouth shut seemed to be an effective strategy. I stayed with it, figuring she'd explain herself. But after a couple of miles and a couple of minutes it was clear she was channeling a Sphinx.

I'd been wondering what it was that Amy could possibly have stolen that would have Tess so uptight. We all have our secrets and they make us vulnerable. But more often than not, they involve our feelings, our fantasies, our histories—less so actual physical objects. What could be in this contract that would be so awful if it were disclosed? Something from her past, of course. Evidence of some sin or misjudgment. Ever since the first piece of the puzzle came to light—that half-sheet of contract at the Devil's Millhopper—I'd been cross-matching the possibilities with my limited history of Tess. This might be the missing piece of the puzzle. I took a flyer:

"Was he the father?"

She swiveled her head and appraised me, but still said nothing.

"Did he ask you to have the abortion?"

She took a deep breath and exhaled. "No, he didn't. That was my choice. I didn't even tell him I was pregnant until it was over."

"Was he upset about that?"

"No. He was relieved, actually. He's a lawyer. And he'd just gotten married. And he had political ambitions."

"And he was a Republican."

"Yes, but not Republican enough for some people. The first time he ran for the state legislature he lost in the primary election to a right winger with loads of support from evangelicals. So he reinvented himself as this family-first, pro-life guy, and the next time he won."

It wasn't hard to connect the rest of the dots at that point. "And the last thing a pro-life, family-first candidate needed was for the voters to learn he'd cheated on his wife, knocked up his girlfriend, and she had an abortion."

She nodded. "It would destroy his career."

I exited the Florida Turnpike at the Yeehaw Junction toll plaza and navigated my way to U.S. 441 and continued aiming the car south toward the Everglades.

Tess was staring straight ahead, clamming up again, so I prompted her:

"This legal document we're piecing together, it's related to all that, right?."

She nodded. "Hush money."

She said it softly, and I wasn't sure I caught it. "You said hush money?"

"Like that deal between Donald Trump and that porn star, Stormy Daniels. It's a contract. He was afraid I would tell on him, which was insulting."

"He paid you?"

"He was very matter-of-fact about it. To him it was a simple business deal. Take the money, keep your mouth shut. I was desperate. The paper was going under. I needed cash."

"Not to be crass..."

"Fifty thousand dollars. But with a two-hundred-and-fifty-thousand-dollar penalty if the contract were disclosed."

I was speechless and we drove on in silence for a few minutes.

"So, what, he shows up one day with this contract, out of the blue?"

"I was shocked. But, obviously, not so shocked that I didn't take the money."

"And that's why you've been so secretive, the penalty?"

"Not just that. The whole thing is humiliating."

I glanced at her and she was rigid, staring out the windshield, hands clasped tightly in her lap. She had to see me looking at her, but she didn't turn, refused eye contact. But I wanted to keep her talking.

"You were young and desperate and you took the money."

"Yes. Indirectly. He had an LLC—a limited liability company—and that's what he wrote the check on. It didn't go to me; it went to the *Agi-Gator* and was styled as a charitable donation. We'd set the newspaper up as a non-profit—and was it ever—so he even got a tax deduction out of the deal."

I saw a flash of blue in the rear-view mirror and for a nervous moment was afraid I'd picked up a cop, but it was merely a reflection. I was doing eighty-five and dialed it back a bit.

"Just to be clear, this thing Amy stole from you, it's this nondisclosure agreement?"

"I *have* to get these pages back."

I digested that for a few seconds, realizing she hadn't actually answered the question, but I let that pass. "But even if you collect all the pieces on this scavenger hunt, there's no guarantee that will be the end of it."

"I know."

"Tess, this doesn't feel like it ends well."

"I have no clue how this will play out. And I agree, it doesn't seem like a happy ending. But what else can I do?"

We let that sit for a few minutes, then I asked:

"Who else knows about this?'

"I've never told anyone. Not until now."

"This Landry guy, he know about any of this, that the document is missing?"

She shook her head. "Not as far as I know. I haven't talked to him. And I have no intention of talking to him. In fact, he made me promise never to reach out to him. It's not in the paperwork, per se, but I promised I'd never contact him again."

"This is fucking bogus. This document is terrific blackmail material. But why bother you? You've got no money. The stalker should be blackmailing this Landry turd."

She didn't respond for a few seconds, then finally she said, "Zander, I have to be clear about something else."

I glanced at her. She was running her hands through her hair. She did that when she was stressed, and this certainly qualified as a stress-rich moment.

"I don't hate Aaron. He didn't ask me to have an abortion. That was my decision. Yeah, he cheated on his wife. But I knew he was married when I slept with him."

"That's awfully fair minded of you.

"What can I tell you? I'm a journalist."

"Yes you are. And as a journalist you should be asking yourself the same question I just did. Why *isn't* he being blackmailed? In fact, he may be and he simply hasn't told you."

She thought about that for a few beats then said, "I think Amy is our stalker. Maybe working with someone. Maybe Darnell. In which case, her motive is what that psychologist told us—revenge, against me, and maybe an irrational hope of reuniting. Could she be blackmailing Aaron? I think he would contact me if she was."

"There's something else we should talk about," I said. "You're putting yourself through a lot doing this. If it were disclosed that you'd had an affair with him and an abortion, it would be embarrassing for you, but it would be a career ender for him, right? In fact, if he took a tax deduction for essentially bribing you, it could be a felony."

"You know, Zander—and please don't take this the wrong way—but you don't have a mother and father and brother and cousins and all the rest like I do. Can you imagine the shame I would have to endure? What it would do to my parents? Their own daughter, a minor league Monica Lewinski? I can't allow that, not just for my own sake but theirs."

She was right, of course. I was untethered by family except for an uncle who was both a father figure and best friend. Except for Leo, nobody on this earth had any expectations of me. No hopes or dreams that would be shattered if I screwed the pooch. Nobody whose heart would be broken.

"Tess…"

She put up her hand. "You don't have to stick with me. I know you've been helping me because you wanted to protect me. Because you are a loyal friend. But…"

"But now that I know this also is about giving cover for some undeserving, hypocritical politician…"

"Right. I'll understand if you want to beg off."

Which we both knew wasn't going to happen. I wouldn't abandon her. We'd been through too much already not to see it through. If not out of a sense of loyalty, then out of a much more basic instinct—pure curiosity. I had to know how all this would end.

"So, you want out?" she asked.

"And not see the Skunk Ape? Have you lost your ever-loving mind?"

CHAPTER 31

Ochopee

SIRI SAID THE Skunk Ape Research Center was ten minutes out, which would get us there right at sunset, plenty of time to prowl around before it got too dark.

"How dangerous is a Skunk Ape, anyway?" I asked Tess.

"Zander, please."

"No, really, have there been any confirmed kills?"

She sighed and began reading from her *Weird Tour of Florida* magazine. "According to the crack team of journalists who wrote this guide—some of whom were even sober at the time—there have been no deaths directly attributed to the Skunk Ape. However, lots of people wander in the 'Glades and never come back out."

"We likely to see one while we're here?"

"Not very. Skunk Apes live in the air pockets of alligator dens, underground. That's why they smell so bad. According to this, those hidey holes are not well ventilated and Skunk Apes do not use deodorant."

"So if we stay downwind we can smell them coming. That's good to know."

"A guy name Dave Shealy is one of the owners of the Skunk Ape Headquarters and he wrote a pamphlet called the *Everglades Skunk Ape*

Research Field Guide. In it, he says one way to find a Skunk Ape is to put out bait. He recommends deer liver."

"Where would one find deer liver?"

"Inside a deer, I guess. He also says not to put bait too close to highways and that it's illegal to use leg traps or tranquilizer darts."

"Well then, how do you catch one?"

"Nobody has."

"They're wily, these Skunk Apes. We better find the note this asshole has left for us and get out before dark."

"Good call."

We pulled into an empty parking lot, the attraction having closed at five o-clock. I'd hoped we might catch our stalker in the act, but he must have beaten us here and left. It had always seemed unlikely that with his head start we would have somehow gotten here before him.

White capital lettering on a lime green metal building declared it SKUNKAPE HEADQUARTERS. A red and white sign warned of DANGEROUS REPTILES, presumably referring to a small zoo in the back filled with snakes, gators, and other scaly critters.

Being the eagle-eyed journalist that I am, I immediately spotted a huge problem.

"Uh, Tess."

"Yes?"

"You see that sign on the building?"

"Of course."

"Do you notice an inconsistency?"

"No. What?"

"Well, here we are at the official Skunk Ape Research Headquarters, the *epicenter* of Skunk Apedom, and the official sign spells Skunk Ape as one word, not two words like here in your magazine. I think we've found a typo."

"Jesus Christ, Zander."

"Hey," I insisted. "Accuracy, accuracy, accuracy. And this is a proper noun."

"No it's not a proper noun. If it was Harvey the Skunk Ape, it would be a proper noun. Skunk Ape, either as one word or two, is like lion or dog. It isn't capitalized."

"We're going to have to agree to disagree. I'm going to argue it is a fanciful appellation and, therefore, should be capitalized. But in any event, either you or the people running this place got the spelling wrong."

"Or maybe there is no universally agreed upon spelling. We may never know the exact spelling until we can interview an actual bona fide Skunk Ape and ask him."

"Spoken like an editor."

"Thank you."

"Who won't admit she fucked up."

She stuck her tongue out at me.

A photo in the *WTF* guide showed a hulking statue of the Skunk Ape on a platform in front of the headquarters, but that evidently had been rolled back into the building lest some yahoo in a pickup snatch it to decorate the front lawn of his single-wide.

But at the adjacent Trail Lakes Campground, another Skunk Ape statue holding an upright and empty kayak greeted visitors at the entrance. The Skunk Ape was much too large to fit into the kayak, so, presumably, the humans who once occupied it had become a suitable substitute for deer liver.

"The poem mentioned a boat. You figure this is it?" Tess asked.

"A kayak is a boat and it's the only one I see." We walked over and looked inside. Resting on the bottom at the stern was a single sheet of paper, a color printout showing Tom Hanks and Meg Ryan in a friendly embrace, a photocopy of the DVD cover from the old movie *You've Got Mail.*

Tess reached into her back pocket and fished out her cell phone. She shook her head. "No emails from our stalker," she said.

"Damn."

"Is there any chance this could be random?" she asked. "A coincidence?"

I was holding the sheet of paper by a corner to ensure we didn't smudge any possible prints. It looked unweathered, fresh. "That's hard to believe. This looks like it was just dropped here."

And then it dawned on me that this would be the perfect opportunity for the stalker to get a picture of us standing around puzzled, dumbfounded about what to do next. Smile! You're on Candid Camera.

Trying not to appear too obvious, I began scanning our surroundings. I looked across the road, then up and down the highway, but we had the area to ourselves, not even a passing car. A tall archway led into the adjoining campground. I looked beyond it. Maybe if he were photographing us I'd spot the glint of light off a lens. Or perhaps movement as he skulked about. But I saw nothing.

"What are you doing?" Tess asked.

So much for not being obvious.

"Looking for a psychopath."

She spun around, a full three-sixty. "Where, where?"

"Nowhere, apparently."

That earned me a dirty look.

"Okay," I said. "Back to this clue. Maybe he's not talking about email. Maybe snail mail?"

"Snail mail?"

I looked at her. She looked at me. We both had the same thought.

"The post office?"

We piled back into the Sebring and took a second look at the poem he'd left for us in the back of the magazine:

> *Half man,*
> *Half skunk,*
> *Half ape.*
> *Get there soon,*
> *Don't hesitate.*

Look in the boat
That don't float.
Then find the shed
Or you'll be dead.

"The shed," I said. "This post office down the road. Is it really that small?"

"Let's find out."

I pulled back out onto the Tamiami Trail and in less than a minute we were parking in the gravel lot outside the nation's smallest post office.

A plaque outside the outhouse-sized structure declared that it had once been an irrigation pipe shed belonging to a tomato farmer. In 1953, after a fire destroyed Ochopee's general store and post office, the postmaster, one Sidney Brown, commandeered the shed to keep mail deliveries going, and it has been in operation ever since, both as a post office and a ticket station for the Trailways bus line.

Except now it was closed.

I walked up to the little building and spread my arms across the front of the structure. My reach was nearly as wide.

"Wow, this really is tiny."

A sign next to the closed and locked door listed it's operating hours. "Uh, don't call me crazy, but what day is it?" Tess asked.

"Friday," I said, then pulled out my phone and doublechecked to be sure.

Tess pointed to a placard that showed the post office hours. It was open Monday through Friday from 8 a.m. to 10 a.m. and then from noon to 4 p.m. The Saturday hours were from 10 a.m. to 11:30 a.m., but a small sign had been placed over Saturday and it said CLOSED.

"Great. We're stuck here for two days?"

"Or I guess we can drive back to Gainesville then turn around and come back on Monday," Tess said.

I thought about that for a moment, then said, "Maybe we should check in with Bristol and Demerest, that might help us decide."

Tess dialed the detective and he answered on the first ring. She put him on speaker.

"Where you at?" he asked.

"Down near Naples," I said. "Dangling participles. Anything new there?"

"Yeah, couple of things. First off, Jack Turner asked me to relay a message to you, Tess, when you checked in. He understands that you're out of town and have been since Darnell Duffy disappeared, but he still wants to question you about it. You've got his card, but just in case, here's his number. He said to call any time. My advice is to do it sooner rather than later."

He recited the number and I wrote it down in my notebook.

"I'll call him," Tess said. "What's number two."

"Good news, maybe. Yours isn't the only place that got vandalized. Another broken window a block over. Cops are thinking maybe it was some drunk college kids."

"They think it's unrelated to all this?"

"Like I said, good news of a sort. But that sounds a bit too easy to me. I wanted to break into your newspaper, maybe I'd throw a brick into another store front, too, make it look like vandalism, not a burglary."

"Bristol didn't say anything about stuff being stolen."

"No, she didn't. But I'm thinking it might be worth another look. Maybe when you get back. You'd notice something missing none of the rest of us would."

I didn't imagine Tess would share with Demerest what she had told me about the nondisclosure agreement, and she didn't. I asked the detective if he'd checked on Jazzy, and he had.

"Everything was fine at the house. She seemed okay, not stressed. I encouraged her to get a pre-paid cell phone in case she had an emergency, but I got the feeling she doesn't plan to do it."

"Figures," I said.

Tess updated Demerest on our travels and read to him the latest updates on the poem.

"He's really messing with you," he said. "We won't know where this ends…" He paused and I assumed he was counting the number of stanzas. "…for five more stops."

"And we're no closer to figuring out who he is," I said.

"And the two of you traveling together hasn't prompted any more phone calls, no direct contact, I gather."

Tess confirmed that. "We're debating whether we should come back to Gainesville for a day or hang out here and wait for the post office to open. Any thoughts on that?"

"Nothing happening here. You're where the action's at. I sure as hell wouldn't want to drive ten hours back and forth for nothing."

Demerest said he still was willing to stake out the drop site in Clearwater, but we agreed there was no point in locking in that plan until Monday when we saw where we would be directed next. Now that we were off the numerical order of the *Weird Tour*, who knew where that would be?

Next, Tess dialed Bristol. She didn't pick up after half a dozen rings, so Tess dialed again and she finally answered. There was a lot of clatter and loud voices in the background.

"Let me guess, you're at a bar," Tess said.

"Ten-four. Thunder Hog. It's ladies night and there are quite a few women here but I wouldn't vouch that any of them qualify as ladies, me excluded, of course."

"You get the window fixed? The paper okay?"

"Yes. Marv ordered replacement glass and it should arrive on Tuesday. In the meantime you have a lovely piece of half-inch plywood where your window used to be."

"Marv get anywhere on his key drawer? He track down his weekend guy?"

"He told me he was going to call the police, but, honestly, I haven't checked back with him on that. But when he came by to inspect the window repair, I told him he needed to replace the lock on your house again. He gave me some shit and I got in his face about it a little, told him it was his responsibility, that he was the one who had been negligent, yadda, yadda, yadda. He wasn't happy, but he did it. I've got your new key waiting for you."

"And Jazzy has one?" I asked.

"Yes. I made a copy for her and one for me."

"Thank you for doing that, Bristol," Tess said.

"Got your six, chick." She was a little slurry and a little loud. I checked my Mickey Mouse watch. It was nine o-clock. My guess was she'd been hammering them down for a while.

"Did Marv tell you he's evicting me?" Tess asked.

"What?"

"Yeah, he's given me two weeks' notice. I've got to vacate both the office and the house."

"Fuck me. What a prick."

"Yeah. We'll talk about it some more later. Zander and I got to roll."

"What's a Zander?"

"Alex."

"Alex is Zander?"

"Yeah, you know, like Alexander only different."

"Whatever."

Tess closed the call and we looked at each other. I had the interior light on in the car. It was dark outside and we seemed to have this corner of the Everglades to ourselves.

"What's your pleasure, Tess?"

"I'm sick of driving. It's late. Things seem to be under control there. I think we should wait it out."

"Your wish is my command."

I cranked the Sebring and pulled out on the Tamiami Trail heading west.

"Where you taking me?' she asked.

"How do you feel about spending the night in a glamorous Florida marina?"

CHAPTER 32

Goodland

GOODLAND IS A half-hour drive from Ochopee. When Tess and I arrived, the town's most famous watering hole, Stan's Idle Hour, was still in full swing. The parking lot was littered with Harleys and pickup trucks, and the outdoor seating area bustled with bikers, tourists, and locals eating and drinking and listening to live music.

By then we were both famished, so before heading down to the marina and the *Miss Demeanor*, we crashed the party, ordered burgers and a Cuba Libre for me and a Coke for Tess.

"Now this is my kind of place," she said, taking in the rowdy crowd from our seats at one of the brightly painted picnic tables outside the sprawling concrete dance floor. Lots of tats, long hair, cowboy boots, jeans, cutoff shorts, a couple of feathered boas, and a decibel level rivaling an airport on-ramp.

Stan's anchors Buzzard's Bay South, which is home to other eateries and drinkeries, too, including the Little Bar and the Crabby Lady. But Stan's is what put Goodland on the map.

Drop by Stan's on a Sunday afternoon and you'll be witness to one of the most bizarre dance spectacles in North America as women flock to the stage to do the Buzzard Lope, the climax of which occurs when they all flop down on their backs and wriggle their feet in the air in a crazed imitation of drunken vultures.

The bandstand was sheltered under a tin roof held aloft by telephone poles painted in pinks and purples. A buzzard, perched on a guitar, graced the top of a metallic weather vane on the roof's peak. Stan's had the riotous and chaotic feel of the Last Resort only it was bigger, mostly outdoors, had live music, and instead of celebrating a serial killer it hosted the annual Mullet Queen festival.

By the time we downed our burgers and I finished my second drink, the place was thinning out and the band was finishing it's last set.

"I guess we better find the boat," I said. "They'll probably be closing up soon."

Buzzard's Bay South is really just a sheltered cove off Goodland Bay, part of the Ten Thousand Islands that dot Florida's southwest coast from Marco Island down to the Keys. Goodland, itself, is a small village that sits on a spit of land jutting into the bay off the much larger Marco Island, all part of the greater Naples area.

Look at a map of the state, and it appears as if a gigantic shark took a nasty bite out of the southwestern tip of the Florida peninsula. Naples and Marco Island are the last towns of any size right above that wound. After that, it's all Everglades.

Uncle Leo had told me I'd find the *Miss Demeanor* right by Stan's Idle Hour. I had reasonably assumed he meant the boat was docked there. Imagine our disappointment when the few watercraft tied up outside Stans and the Little Bar bore no resemblance to a converted fishing trawler. I'd recalled the *Miss Demeanor* being roomy—a characteristic of trawlers—about forty feet in length. But the boats tied up at the piers were much smaller pleasure craft.

"Uh, Zander, I'm not seeing this yacht of yours," Tess said. "You sure we got the right marina?"

The bartenders were closing up, and one of them walked over, presumably to shoo us off. But he'd overheard a snippet of our conversation and asked, "You guys looking for something?"

He had shaggy gray hair, multiple piercings, and a concerned look on his face.

"Yeah," I said. "We seem to have misplaced a boat."

"You sail over today?"

"No. It's my uncle's. We were going to spend the night on it, but I don't see a trawler anywhere."

"Trawler? Is that kind of like a tugboat?"

"I suppose so. It has a large cabin, so, yeah, it is kinda like a tugboat."

"Is that it?"

He pointed to a large shadow in the weedy lot between Stan's and the Little Bar. There was an unlocked gate in a chain link fence separating Stan's from the lot and we walked through it. I shined my iPhone's flashlight on the watercraft and immediately noticed three things:

The first was that the boat was propped up on oil cans and bricks in a crude sort of drydock.

The second were the words *Miss Demeanor* painted in black lettering on the dingy hull.

The final thing I noticed was a gaping hole in that hull right below those letters.

"Dear God."

"You expect us to spend the night in this?" Tess asked. "Wow. You really know how to show a girl a good time."

"There's a ladder propped up on the other side," the bartender said. "Some guys were here earlier this week. I think they were hooking up electric and water or something. I was curious about that since it's been here for a while. You say your uncle owns it?"

"Yeah."

"And he didn't tell you?"

"Uh, no."

The bartender cackled all the way back to Stan's.

I turned to Tess. "Uh, look, we can find a motel someplace and…"

She was shaking her head. "Ah, come on Zander. Where's your sense of adventure. You said I could spend the night at a marina. This is sorta near a marina."

She began circumnavigating the boat while I continued to stare at it, paralyzed. Leo had a mischievous sense of humor, but this was beyond the pale.

"Hey, here's the ladder," Tess shouted. "Come on. Let's climb aboard."

We did.

CHAPTER 33

WE AWOKE TO the sound of seagulls and pelicans squabbling over a bucket of fish guts that had been thrown into Buzzards Bay South. This was soon accompanied by the cacophonous clanking of empty beer cans cascading into a dumpster at the restaurant next door.

This was not how I had envisioned my mornings beginning aboard the *Miss Demeanor*, my new home in the Sunshine State. Was it so unreasonable of me to assume the trawler would actually be in the water, floating like a normal boat?

When Leo had invited me to "go on down and live on my boat," he had neglected to mention that, after a few martinis too many, he'd slammed into a pier puncturing the hull, nearly capsizing it. He also neglected to mention that because of the boat's age—I think it may have been used by Noah—that it might be a while before parts could be found to make it seaworthy again.

Awakened by the clatter outside, I rolled out of the forward berth. Tess was still asleep and the sun was painting the early morning clouds in pastel shades of pink and orange. I stepped up into the galley and poked around the small pantry in hope of finding some coffee, even instant, to clear out the cobwebs—I'm pretty useless until I get a couple of cups in me. But the cupboard was bare.

I thought about that briefly and concluded it was probably a *good* thing. Conditions were Spartan aboard the *Miss Demeanor*, which was bad enough. Food left onboard would have attracted unwanted critters making staying overnight unbearable.

The trawler had two sleeping berths. The largest, forward under the bow, was surprisingly spacious. Big enough for a bookshelf full of old detective novels, a small chest of drawers, and a queen-sized bed.

Leo left the books, which was nice. But no pillows, sheets, or blankets. I really didn't have a right to complain—after all, I was deeply in his debt to have a place to crash rent-free at all—but I felt badly for Tess.

The aft berth, by the engine compartment, was less luxurious and I had suspicions about how well ventilated it would be. Tess had suggested a game of rock, paper, scissors to decide who would sleep where. Being the consummate gentleman, I demurred and told her she could have the larger bed. We debated that for a while and finally concluded we could share the queen bed, Tess promising not to attack me, and me promising not to put up a struggle if she changed her mind.

She didn't.

In fact, she was still sound asleep, and I was thinking it would be nice if I could figure out how to score some coffee and doughnuts before she got up. I fired up my cell phone and saw that the nearest restaurant serving breakfast was the Crabby Lady on the other side of the cove. But it wouldn't be open for another hour. The nearest doughnut shop in Marco Island would be about a half-hour round trip.

The seagulls cranked up their squawking again, and I heard Tess moaning down below. "Where am I?"

"You are aboard the luxury yacht *Miss Demeanor*," I said cheerfully. "I was contemplating a coffee and doughnut run. Be gone about half an hour. You good with that?"

When she didn't answer, I ducked my head back into the berth and saw that she had fallen back asleep. I had worn my shorts and tee shirt to bed. I laced up my running shoes, locked the cabin door on my way out, and walked over to the Sebring, which I had left parked in Stan's lot overnight.

Most of my stuff was still at Tess's house in Gainesville. I hadn't anticipated making it all the way to Goodland, and we both had only packed overnight bags. Facing a weekend layover, it occurred to me we might want to find a coin laundry before our clothes began standing up of their own accord. We'd need towels, too. And sheets. And soap. And coffee. And a coffee pot. And rum. And Cokes. It dawned on me that a significant portion of our day today would be spent shopping.

Tess was already up and scanning her phone when I climbed the ladder back aboard the trawler. "I've come with provisions," I announced.

She looked up and smiled. "Coffee. I need coffee."

"With cream. And chocolate filled croissants."

"Thanks. I sent Jack Turner a text, told him I'd be available all day to talk."

The trawler had a small lounge with a wraparound couch and a pedestal table on a cylindrical post that could be pulled from a recessed slot in the deck. I set the coffee and pastries down, pried open the lid on my coffee, and took a sip. It was still warm, if not hot, after the fifteen minute drive back.

"I'm thinking we need to get a few supplies today if we have time for a little light shopping," I said.

"I always have time for shopping, especially when I'm spending someone else's money."

I told her what I had in mind, including my idea that we might want to find a laundromat.

"Well, you're going to need these things, anyway," she said. "And, besides, I bet we can get it all and still spend less than we would if we'd crashed at a motel for three nights. I'm an amazingly frugal shopper. You'll be glad you had me along."

While we ate, I did some exploring online and came up with a plan of attack. "Okay, how's this? First stop, find someplace cheap and get some bed linens, soap and towels. Second stop, there's an L.A. Fitness in Naples. Let's hit the gym then the showers…"

"You a member?"

"Yes. I joined in Phoenix and I think I can get you in for free."

"Groovy."

"Then we go round up all the other items on our shopping list using your frugality superpowers. Maybe find a nice place near the water—not overly expensive, mind you—for a late lunch or early dinner, then head back here. How's that sound?"

"Sounds like somebody is a little OCD."

"An inherited family characteristic. You should see my uncle."

"As far as dinner goes, we can grab another burger at Stan's," she said. "And it *is* right on the water."

"Fine by me. I just don't want you getting stir crazy."

"I like it here. I even like your boat. I mean, sure, it needs a coat of paint and it would be nice if it floated and all. But this is kind of fun. It's like camping out. And, honestly, I've got to say I think this is the first time since all this craziness started that I actually feel relaxed. No way that asshole can find us here."

It was a lovely sentiment, and her sense of relief was contagious. But when we finally pulled back into Goodland with a convertible full of kitchen supplies, food, sundries, and a disassembled mannequin, I felt a cloud of dread enveloping me. I knew, really knew, that somehow, no matter how irrational it might be, that we would return to some spoiler, a note duct-taped to the hull or a talking parrot hanging from the yard arm.

I opened the gate to the weedy lot that was the *Miss Demeanor's*—and my—new home and gazed around for signs of trouble. Nothing taped to the hull. No stuffed birds. We climbed aboard and the door was still secured.

Tess's instincts had proved out. We had at least one day of peace.

She poured Cokes, splashed some rum in mine, and then sat in the lounge and said:

"Before you put her together you have to give her a name."

I'd never named a mannequin before. Didn't even know they had names. And I'd certainly never assembled one.

"How does Mona sound?"

Tess began making faux orgasm noises. " Ooooh. Yeess, Uh. Uh. Uh. AAAHHH."

"Pay no attention to her, Mona. She's being crude, rude and socially unacceptable."

"I specialize in that. But why Mona?"

"When I first saw her, the way she's looking out of the corner of her eyes with that slight upturn of a smile. It reminded me of the Mona Lisa."

"You're such a fucking liar. You picked her because she had the biggest boobs."

"Well, there's that."

While shopping we had run across a women's clothing store that was going out of business. Everything in the store was half off, and Tess made a bee line to it, scoring some shorts, shirts, a bikini, and a pair of sandals.

There were a half-dozen naked mannequins perched about the showroom, and on a whim I asked the saleslady if they were going out the door, too. Don't ask me why. Maybe I thought she could keep Spock company. And I really was reminded of the Mona Lisa. Her lifelike eyes were freakishly penetrating.

The saleslady checked with the owner. "Everything's gotta go," she said.

"How about ten bucks?" It was a joke. I figured that would be the end of it.

"Sold."

While Tess was ringing up her purchases in the store, I figured out how to disassemble the soon-to-be-named Mona and walked her various pieces—arms, legs, torso, head, and stand—out to the convertible and plopped them into the back seat. If we got pulled over, I could only imagine the conversation we'd have with the cop.

"So, you plan on having her lounge around in her birthday suit?" Tess asked. She was removing her new garments from a shopping bag and holding them up for closer inspection.

"Uh, no. That would be perverted. I'm having second thoughts about this decision already. What will the neighbors say?"

"You mean all those tattooed bikers over at Stans? You better keep her hidden or they'll be swarming over to have their way with her.

"Swell."

"What do you think?" Tess asked, holding her bikini bottom across her waist.

"I think it's tiny. And tiny is good."

By then, I had Mona assembled, and Tess was giving her the once over.

"Don't go falling in love," I said.

She threw her bikini at me. "You know what would be great. We should dress her up as a pirate. Maybe we can even find her a sword at a toy store or something."

"This cove is called Buzzards Bay South. That has a piratical ring to it, doesn't it?"

"Piratical? Is that a word?"

"It is now."

We had one more day to kill before the Ochopee post office would open. I told Tess I might spend it writing some columns for the news service, adding to my stash of evergreen material in case this dragged on much longer. She said if I would loan her my car, she'd finish getting supplies for the boat and finding appropriate attire for my new shipmate.

After dinner—burgers once again at Stan's—we sat out on the foredeck in lawn chairs and enjoyed the cool evening breeze wafting shoreward from the Ten Thousand Islands.

"It's nice here," Tess said. "I think Fred and Spock will like it."

"You think Spock and Mona will get along?" I asked.

"Famously. But you might want to separate them during Pon Farr."

Pon Farr is an affliction that occurs every seven years, a blood fever that forces Vulcans to mate with someone with whom they are mind-melded. Spock and I had been together for many more years than that and I had yet to see him become feverish.

"I don't think cardboard Vulcans get the Pon Farr," I said.

She looked at me skeptically. "I'm just saying. You never know what might happen when he gets a load of those hooters of hers."

"Hooters? You're going to set women's lib back a century with talk like that."

"I'm a modern, sophisticated, bisexual woman. I can say whatever I want."

"I wouldn't dare."

"I certainly hope not."

"But that's a double standard."

"Of course it is."

We eventually retreated back into the trawler's cabin. Tess crashed early. She was beat, both physically and emotionally. I poured myself another Cuba Libre and sat down with my laptop and my notebook and began to write.

Chimp DNA a Pain in the Butt

By Alexander Strange

Tropic⊚ Press

MIAMI—Six women who subjected themselves to plastic surgery at a clinic here have filed a class-action lawsuit claiming that materials used in their Brazilian butt lifts were contaminated with defective chimpanzee DNA.

The clinic, Amazon Rejuvenation and Spa, widely advertises that its "breakthrough" sculpting technology implants DNA from "genuine Brazilian chimpanzees" to provide "a fuller, rounder and better contoured" derriere.

Male chimps are known to go ape over the rear-ends of females in heat. "They think their pink butts are the most wonderful sight in the word," said zoologist Melford Topps of the Florida Center for Primate Studies. But Topps cautioned that the idea of using chimpanzee DNA in a human "sounds risky" and, besides, "the only chimps in Brazil are in zoos. Chimpanzees are native to Africa."

In their lawsuit, the women, identified as Jane Doe 1 through 6, contend that since their surgeries, their buttocks periodically become inflamed and swollen and that these events seem to coincide with their menstrual cycles.

This has caused great discomfort and embarrassment, the lawsuit says, and has interfered with the women's "conjugal relations."

"We're not interested in being the butt of any jokes," says their attorney, Anthony Shoemaker in a press release. "This is another example of the assembly-line cosmetic surgery crisis in South Florida. My clients have been irreparably harmed, not only by the irresponsible conduct at this clinic, but by state regulators who aren't doing their jobs."

An attorney for Amazon Rejuvenations, hoping to get this monkey off his client's back, said the keister clinic takes the women's complaints seriously. "We will get to the bottom of this," he promised.

STRANGE FACT: Humans eat more bananas than monkeys. Of course, bananas taste better.

Keep up with weirdness at *www.TheStrangeFiles.com*. Contact Alexander Strange at Alex@TheStrangeFiles.com.

CHAPTER 34

UNCLE LEO WAS lecturing me. He thought I was being hare-brained participating in this wild goose chase with Tess. And while I hadn't shared the details of Aaron Landry's non-disclosure agreement, I told him Tess had finally leveled with me.

"So what's it about?" he asked.

"Can't say, Leo. I promised."

"I'm your lawyer. You can tell me anything."

"You're an officer of the court."

"So what you're telling me, by not telling me, is that this is a real hairball."

"It's complicated."

"No doubt. But why do you trust her?" he asked.

"I've got no reason not to trust her."

"Absence of evidence is not evidence. You haven't caught her lying, I get that. But is there any hard evidence that what she's told you is the truth?"

Fair question. I hadn't actually seen the contract. But I couldn't imagine why she'd make something like that up. That seemed preposterous. Leo was simply being over-protective.

I'd called him while I was holed up aboard the *Miss Demeanor* catching up on my columns while Tess went shopping. My intention had been to give him a ration of shit about the condition of the boat, but I found myself recounting events on our weird tour of Florida since we'd last spoken.

"Don't you and Edwina belong to some outfit, Cynics Anonymous or something?" he said, not letting it go. "What would they say about this?"

"Well, first of all," I said, "Cynics Anonymous is make believe. Secondly, the fact that she confided in me shows she's dropped her shields, that she trusts me."

"Or she's playing you."

This is where I could have gotten angry. Not only was Leo criticizing what he saw as my poor judgment, he was insulting Tess, and he didn't even know her. But here's the thing: When Leo jumps on my case, he's not being spiteful, he's coming from a place of genuine concern. Not only do I respect his opinion, I have to admit I have this lingering adolescent need for his approval. He's the closest thing to a father I will ever have, and for the entirety of our relationship he has always tried to do what's best for me. So, instead of getting all pouty about it, I took a deep breath and tried to see if we couldn't reason our way through this.

Was she playing me? Well, she was affectionate, but in a non-romantic way. She wasn't the least bit flirty, showing no interest in resuming any kind of sexual relationship. But she did continually reinforce how we were friends, even made us pinky-swear on it. She gave out lots of hugs and continually reminded me how much she appreciated my help. But was all that calculated or genuine?

"You could look at it two ways, I suppose," I told Leo. "If I were able to step out of myself and replay the past few days, I could see how you might interpret some of her behavior as manipulative. But I can also see how it could be interpreted as the real deal. And that's what I think it is."

Leo chuckled. "Not a binary. She can like you and use you at the same time. I really do think you need to get your cynicism topped off."

"You're saying she's playing Irene Adler to my Sherlock."

"Except Sherlock Holmes always knew she was a con artist. And she knew he knew. It was playful at the same time it was poignant. I don't see that here. All I'm saying is watch yourself. You're assuming the best of this woman. And for your sake I hope you're right. But you don't need me to tell you the first rule of journalism."

"Right. Never assume. If your mother say she loves you, make her prove it."

"Correct. And think about this: You're a pro-life politician who put his dick where it didn't belong and now you want to bribe an old girlfriend into silence. Do you leave her a copy of a contract? Something she could use against you?"

"I guess that would depend on the language in the contract, whether there was anything there that could be used against him."

"Well, if there's not, why go through all of this?"

"I guess I won't know until I see it."

CHAPTER 35

Ochopee, Monday morning

TESS AND I were in the gravel parking lot of the Ochopee post office waiting for it to open. We'd buttoned up the *Miss Demeanor* with all its newly stocked provisions, and were packed and ready to head on down the highway to wherever the insane rhymester directed us next.

We'd gambled that the next clue would be waiting for us when the doors to the shed-sized office swung open. We'd feel like—and, in fact, would be—idiots if there was nothing waiting for us.

I'd left Mona, sword in hand, pointed at the cabin door. "Anybody tries to break in here," I told her, "do your pirate thing, make them walk the plank." She offered no acknowledgement of those instructions, but buccaneers are notoriously taciturn.

While I'd hung around the boat the day before, Tess had ventured back into Naples with the goal, among other shopping destinations, of finding suitable attire for Mona. She returned with a bagful of items from a Goodwill and a fishing supply store up in Bonita Springs.

"Okay," she announced proudly after she had climbed back aboard the trawler. "I think we've got Mona covered. Literally."

She pulled out a pair of black, baggy culottes that she held up to our naked mannequin. She eyeballed the fit for a minute then declared them to be "perfect."

"I looked everywhere for a striped shirt, you know the ones with black and white horizontal lines like the pirates used to wear?"

"You mean like prisoners?"

"Yes, exactly. But Goodwill didn't have any. I also went to a place called St. Matthews House. It's a homeless shelter and they have a lovely store to help raise money. But I struck out there, too. Then I decided to go shopping up in Bonita Springs, and I found this."

She held up a black tee shirt with a white drawing of a shrimp on it and in large letters:

MASTER BAIT & TACKLE
"YOU CAN'T BEAT OUR BAIT"

"Well, that certainly looks like a shirt any pirate would be proud to wear," I said.

"I know, right?"

At Walmart, she also scored a black wig and a rubber, but realistic, sword to complete the ensemble. We spent the next hour dressing Mona, wrestling the slacks over each of her legs, then removing her head and arms and reattaching them so we could pull the shirt on over her torso. It was a tight fit.

"What do you think?" she asked, obviously delighted with her fashion decisions.

"I think you're right," I said. "I'll need to keep Spock away from her during Pon Farr."

While Tess had been shopping, Gainesville police detective Jack Turner had called her back about David Darnell. As Frank Demerest had reported, Darnell went missing approximately the same time Tess and I began this clown fiesta of a road trip. There were no signs of foul play at his apartment and his car was gone, suggesting he had taken off voluntarily.

Ordinarily, that would be enough for the police to drop it, but Turner still asked Tess a handful of questions about when she had last seen D2 and what the altercation in the bar had been about.

"He was respectful," Tess said. "But the combination of Amy's disappearance and now her brother going missing has got his antenna up. He had me on the phone for about half an hour. And he wanted to make sure he could reach me again if need be."

"In all fairness, Tess, I can't blame him, can you?"

"No. I get it. It's weird."

"You think D2 is in on this?"

"Awfully coincidental he blows town the same time we do, don't you think?"

I agreed. I'd asked Tess if she'd learned anything useful from the detective.

"I did. He was surprisingly willing to talk. I think he may like me, or he's being clever and doing the good-cop routine. He told me Darnell drives an orange Camaro. That shouldn't be too hard to spot. I haven't noticed one on this trip, have you?"

I shook my head.

"They've BOLO'd it but haven't gotten any hits so far. He also mentioned that they got a warrant for his cell phone calls. He wanted to know if my number would be on the list. I told him no, but given what we're going through I asked him to give me a call if he found anything interesting that might affect what we're doing."

"I'll bet that went over well."

"He surprised me. He said he would."

"He wouldn't be sending out a Be On the Look Out notice and getting a search warrant if they didn't smell a rat. Be careful what you say to him."

She promised she would. Then dropped this nugget:

"His employer at the car dealership says Darnell has been taking classes at Santa Fe College."

"What's that?"

"Local community college. Darnell's boss said he's starting there then hopes to transfer to Florida, that after all these years he wants to get his degree."

"So?"

"So, you recall Marv saying that the weekend help he had was a college student?"

"You thinking…"

"I told Jack he should run a mugshot past Marv and see if it's him."

"Now that would be interesting."

At 8 a.m., the doors to the little post office swung open and Tess and I walked up to the closet-sized shack.

"We're expecting a letter," she said to the postal clerk. "Not sure, but it might have been deposited on Friday, probably in the drop box in back. I don't suppose you've had a chance to check it yet, have you?"

The clerk, her name was Shannon, said she would check, and five minutes later Tess was handed an envelope postmarked Ochopee, Florida addressed to her at General Delivery.

I pulled a pocket knife from my glove box and handed it to Tess to slice open the envelope, once again taking care to minimize smudging any prints. Tess had scored a small box of surgical gloves during her shopping expedition, and had snapped a pair on as soon as we returned to the car.

She pulled another half-page of the nondisclosure agreement from the envelope, once again handwritten on the opposite side of the contract with our latest poetic instructions, the longest ones so far:

> *Four more clues*
> *Await you now.*
> *Five stops hence*
> *You'll have them all.*
> *I made no copies;*
> *Trust me, LOL.*

When you're done
You'll be clear.
Then we'll meet;
I'll be near.
To hand to you
In a flash
How you made
All that cash.

That was followed by the next four stanzas of the poem we were assembling:

SOON YOU'LL SEE
THE PLANETARY COURT
THEN OFF TO MARY,
THE TRIP'S NOT SHORT.
OBEY THE LAW;
GRAVITY'S A BITCH.
JUST ASK THE SPOOKS;
DON'T MISS A HITCH.

We both stared at the stanzas realizing the game had changed.

"He's picking up the pace," Tess said. "We've got directions to the next four stops."

"Yeah, it sounds like he's already hidden the next pieces of the puzzle, but these clues seem really vague. I hope this isn't like St. Augustine where it takes all day to sort each of these things out."

Tess nodded. "Yeah. And we need to get after it. The longer they lay around the more likely someone else will find them."

"What's the next stop?" I asked.

"Well, that's the thing. He's gone completely off the map now. The next clue is for a *planetary court.*" She glanced at me, a look of concern on her face. "I'm a little worried. I have no idea what that is."

"That like a basketball court or a tennis court?" I asked, unhelpfully, from the annoyed look I got from Tess.

"Let me think."

"Maybe a planetarium?"

"Shhhhh." She wagged her index finger and closed her eyes. "Give me a sec."

While she sat trancelike, cogitating, I reread the poem in its entirety again. Some of the later references seemed self-evident, but I could find no connection between "planetary" and the ten stops on the *Weird Tour of Florida* list.

Suddenly, Tess opened her eyes and she said: "Got it!"

"Tell me while we're rolling," I said.

"Turn left. We're taking the Tamiami Trail north up to Estero."

"What's an Estero?"

"A town, north of Bonita Springs. The area was originally settled by a cult. I'll tell you all about it while we drive."

"I'll drive, you talk. What's with the last half of the instructions, the part before he gave us the final four stanzas?"

"You mean the part about no copies?"

"No. You already told me it can't be copied, that the contract's on special paper. I'm talking about where he mentions flash and cash. What does that mean?"

She reread the poem aloud, lingering over the last two stanzas:

> *To hand to you*
> *In a flash*
> *How you made*
> *All that cash.*

"I'm not sure," she finally said. "It's not directional. It's like he's describing what will happen at our last stop, when he hands over the final piece of the document. I get the cash reference, the hush money Aaron made me take. Does flash mean quickly?"

I didn't have a clue, so I kept my eye on traffic and let her continue to sort it out.

"Zander, this is actually a little frightening. Could flash mean an explosion?"

"Or maybe he's going to take a picture of you using a flash and then blackmail you with it."

She crinkled her brow with that. "Maybe."

"Or maybe it's nothing more than bad poetry. Tell me where we're going."

"Koreshan State Park."

"What's a Koreshan?"

"A cult. They believed the planet was hollow and we live inside it, that's the clue. The use of the word planetary."

That was confusing. "But Koreshan State Park isn't on the map."

"No, not the one we published. I mentioned before we originally had a list of about fifteen places we wanted to include but narrowed it down to ten. This was on the original list, but didn't get drawn from the hat."

"Who would know that?"

"That's the thing. It would have to be somebody who was there at the very beginning."

"That means it's Amy."

"Or somebody Amy talked to. I don't see how this narrows it down."

"Or it's Amy. What are the next stops after this one. Let's see if we can figure out how long this is going to take."

She'd folded the *WTF* magazine to the map page and pointed to the Tampa Bay area.

"After Koreshan State Park, the next stop is in Clearwater. That's the Virgin Mary reference. That was on the original map. There's a building there where the glass oxidized and people swore the discoloration looked like the Madonna. It's was a big sensation. They say more than a million people came to pay homage. They set up a monument of some sort outside. Then some kid shot the window out with a slingshot, and that was it for the Virgin Mary."

"Only in Florida."

"Right?"

"Well, I guess you better text Demerest and let him know our Clearwater ambush is off," I said. "The clue's already there."

She sighed. "Yeah. I'll do that right now. Dammit. I was really looking forward to that."

When she finished typing, I asked, "Where to after Clearwater?"

"He refers to gravity. There's a monument on the campus of the University of Tampa celebrating something called the Gravity Foundation. Funny story with that. Anyway, after we leave Estero, it's a two hour drive up to Clearwater. Then about half an hour over the Courtney Campbell Causeway to Tampa, then the final stop, also on our map, is Spook Hill in Lake Wales. That's another hour away."

I'd been keeping a running drive-time tally in my head as she talked. "We're looking at four hours on the road not counting potty breaks, lunch, and gas stops. Call it six hours."

"Sounds right. So, if we get lucky, find these clues right away, we should be able to do all of this today."

"Which will leave—what?—one final piece of the puzzle?"

"Yes, the final clue should be at Spook Hill, and that should also have one of the two critical pages to the document, either the top half of the first page or the bottom half of the last page."

So far, most of the legalese on the backs of each of the handwritten notes had looked like ordinary legal boilerplate, at least in the brief glances Tess had shared. But the top half of the first page would include the names of the parties in the agreement, Tess and Landry, and the last page would show their signatures.

The Tamiami Trail had widened to multiple lanes as we entered Naples. At the heart of downtown—the posh Fifth Avenue South— the road bent ninety degrees northward through the city. Tess said the park we were headed to was about a mile past a sprawling shopping mall called Coconut Point.

"So tell me about these hollow planet people," I said.

CHAPTER 36

En route to Koreshan State Park

"So, THERE WAS this doctor in upstate New York, shortly after the Civil War. His name was Cyrus Teed and he was doing all these experiments, trying to turn lead into gold by using electricity. Apparently, during one of his attempts he damned near electrocuted himself and he was never right in the head again, if he ever was in the first place."

Tess was summarizing the history of the Koreshan Unity, the cult that had settled in Estero near the turn of the last century. "Anyway, Teed claimed to have seen this woman who revealed the secrets of the universe. According to her, the Earth is hollow and we live inside the planet. The sun, moon, sky—all inside."

I liked that idea. "So if the space aliens attack, we'll be protected."

"No, there are no space aliens because there is no outer space. The whole universe is inside the earth."

"But then what's on the outside of the earth?"

"There is no outside, that's the whole point of the religion."

"And people bought into this?"

"Yes, they created this entire community. That's what the park is, where we're going, the dormitories and other buildings. It was a real town filled up with true believers."

"Awesome."

"Right. So Teed is damned near killed by one of his experiments and has this electric vision. He changes his first name from Cyrus to Koresh. Interesting footnote here. A guy with the last name Koresh a hundred years later was the leader of yet another screwball religious sect called the Branch Davidians."

"You talking about that massacre in Texas?"

"Right. David Koresh was the guy in charge and when the ATF tried to enter his compound—it was outside of Waco—that's when the shooting started. Finally the FBI was called in to break up the siege and 75 people were killed."

"So did this guy make up the Koresh name, too?"

"Yes. I did the write-up on all this for the magazine. Koresh is derived from Persian and it means farsighted."

"So, if you're a whack-job prophet shopping for a stage name, Koresh is pretty popular."

"Evidently."

"So, back to the Koreshans. The planet is hollow, that was their core belief, pun intended."

"They also believed in reincarnation, among other things. They preached that if you led a celibate life you would be reborn."

"How'd that work out?"

"When Cyrus Teed finally died, his followers left his body in a bathtub for two weeks seriously thinking he would come back to life."

"Like Jesus."

"Exactly. But after a couple of weeks the smell was ghastly and they finally planted him in a tomb that, a few years later, got washed out to sea in a hurricane and nobody's seen good ol' Cyrus since."

"So the whole gig was a scam."

"Not really. There was no real science behind it, of course, but it wasn't your typical Florida flim-flam job, either. These people drank the Kool Aid. It was their whole lives. To them it was a religion as genuine to them as Christianity, Islam, or the Force."

"And where are we supposed to be looking when we get there?"

By then, Siri was telling me I would be turning west onto Corkscrew Road in half a mile and a few yards after that we'd be at the park's entrance.

"You mean where in the 135 acres of settlement and campgrounds and hiking trails will we find our next piece of the nondisclosure agreement?"

"Yes, that."

"I got no fucking idea."

CHAPTER 37

Koreshan State Park

WE PAID OUR five dollars to enter the park, and because it was early we appeared to be the only visitors in the settlement area, which is where we figured the clue would have to be—in, on, or around one of the handful of historic buildings.

"What are we looking for?" I asked Tess.

"Don't think it will be a parrot this time."

We'd scored a printed guide to the park. It was a letter-sized sheet of white paper with a list of attractions and park programs on one side and a pair of maps on the other. One map showed the larger state park with picnic spaces, boat ramps, playgrounds, and such. The other highlighted a list of historic buildings along a walking trail.

"Check out Number 2 on the map," I said. "It's a building called the Planetary Court."

"What?" Tess snatched the map out of my hand. "Holy cow! This is it. I thought the clue was the word *planet*, that it referred to the hollow planet thing, but this really, truly says *Planetary Court*. What a break."

The park's setting was enchanting with towering pines and palms that reached into the cloudless azure sky. We paused in a large open space between settlement buildings to get our bearings and I gazed heavenward toward the cloudless sky.

"Call me crazy," I said, "but I sort of get it. How, if you let your imagination go, this would feel like being inside an enormous sphere."

"You're crazy."

A white gravel pathway led to the entrance of the Planetary Court, a two-story yellow clapboard building with wraparound porches on both the ground level and second floor. It had been the home to the seven women who were in charge of the settlement, the Sisters of the Planetary Court.

The park was well curated, and a glass-enclosed display outside the building showed the photos and biographies of the original sisters: Virginia Andrews, Rose Gilbert, Evelyn Bubbett, Eleanor Castle, Berthaldine Boomer, Ella Graham, and Henrietta Silverfriend.

Tess pointed to the photograph of Eleanor Castle. "She's a distant relative. How's that for a small-world moment."

It was a little challenging to tell for sure in the aging black and white photograph, but Eleanor Castle seemed to have the same light brown hair as Tess. It was cut short and it suited her. She had high cheekbones and full lips and an expression on her face that seemed to say, "I know something you don't know." She was beautiful.

"I think you take after her a little bit," I said.

Tess studied the photograph a few seconds then said, "Thank you."

"She was a professor of languages before she came here," I read from the sign. "Maybe that's where you get your interest in journalism."

"They did have their own newspaper," she said. "*The American Eagle.*"

"You know, Tess, it's easy to make fun. Well, it's certainly easy for me. Hollow planet, reincarnation, and all. But I've got a different feel for this place now that I see pictures of the real people who lived here."

She nodded. "I like it when you're sincere. It suits you."

I couldn't let that go, so I said:

"That doesn't change the fact they were insane."

"Of course not."

"I mean, come on. We all know the world is flat and it rests on four elephants who, in turn, stand on the back of a giant space turtle."

"And the space turtle is being chased by Schrödinger's cat."

"Exactly."

We approached the structure, not sure what we were looking for, keeping a sharp lookout for something that would seem out of place. Maybe a DayGlo orange message spray painted on the side of the building—LOOK HERE FOR CLUE—or something else equally obvious. It's good to have hope.

A set of six steps led up to the porch, which was elevated off the graveled foundation by a couple of feet. A series of narrow boards, four deep, framed the base of the porch, preventing anything larger than a lizard or a mouse from crawling under the building.

The gravel on the pathway leading to the dormitory widened at the foundation, encircling the entire structure, creating a rocky divide between the building and the grassy yard. The gravel was bleached white by the sun, which by then was rising over the trees and warming the air—pleasantly for the moment, although the Weather Channel said the high would hit an unseasonable 91 and that there was a chance of thunderstorms.

We paused about twenty feet in front of the building. "See anything that draws your attention?" I asked.

"Hmmm."

Tess dropped down on her hands and knees and peered along the gravel. I scanned the walls and roofline. Would our stalker have hidden the clue inside? We might never find it there. Inside, the clue would have to be secluded it in such a way that the staff wouldn't notice. How would we ever find it?

I crouched down next to Tess, hoping a different perspective might be helpful.

"Check this out," she said, still on her hands and knees. "To the left of the steps. The gap between those boards and the gravel is a little larger there. All the rocks are white except for that one, do you see it? Or am I imagining things?"

I walked to the spot she had pointed to. "Here?" I asked.

She signaled me with her hand. "A little to the right."

I lowered myself to the gravel and peered under the slats. And there it was, a stone, larger than the others, and it was gray, not bleached white.

Our stalker, it seemed, had cornered the market on hollowed-out hide-a-key rocks.

CHAPTER 38

Clearwater, Tampa, Lake Wales

THE BUILDING WAS a three-storied, glass-curtained heap, the kind of boring, nondescript structure you would associate with a bank or a mortgage company, not a church.

Yet it was the headquarters of Our Lady of Clearwater, which the double glass doors identified in white lettering as "A Division of Shepherds of Christ Ministries." If a religious order was going to be a division of something, as opposed to, say, a parish, then operating out of a building that looked like a savings and loan was probably a good fit.

Indeed, before the shepherds took the place over, it had belonged to the Seminole Finance Company. That was before the glass exterior became stained with age and relentless sunlight, and somebody figured a sixty-foot-tall discoloration in the shape of an elongated rainbow was really a visage of the Virgin Mary.

Tess was showing me a photo of the window before it had been vandalized, and I suppose it did conform to the traditional profile of the Madonna in her long scarf. But it could just as easily have been a condom.

"You say more than a million people showed up to look at this?"

Tess nodded. "That's a fact, Jack."

"What if they'd said it looked like a rubber instead of Jesus's mom. Probably wouldn't have been as big a draw, huh?"

She scrunched her nose, took another look at the photograph, then said, "Well, I see your point. And, I can't see hundreds of thousands of people flocking here with their lawn chairs to gaze at a dick hat, even if it were rainbow colored."

"And isn't contraception considered evil by the church?"

"I can't tell you; I'm not Catholic. All I know is that there was at least one time that I should have used one and didn't, and now we're here."

Here was next door in a Toyota dealership lot on busy U.S. 19, the main artery that feeds traffic through Pinellas County, from St. Petersburg to the south, through Clearwater and up to Tarpon Springs to the north, We'd pulled in, found an empty parking spot next to some used Corollas, and walked over.

"We got lucky down in Estero, maybe this will be a snap," Tess said.

It was.

Maybe our stalker was getting as tired of this silliness as we were. It was another rock, this one resting inside a small arched brick enclosure sheltering a statue of Mary, Joseph, and baby Jesus.

"It's hard to imagine thousands of people hanging out here," I said. "We've got the place to ourselves. Except for that flock of crows on the roof. Man, they're noisy. Maybe they don't like us poking around here."

"Murder."

"Whose murdered?"

"The crows. It's not a flock, it's a murder of crows."

"Oh, yeah, I knew that. In honor of Edgar Allan Poe."

That kid with the slingshot should have been scaring the birds, not aiming at the building. He didn't just shatter some glass, he demolished a major money making machine.

"Maybe he was from the Baptists or Mormons or something," I said.

"Who?"

"Little David, the kid with the slingshot, the one who destroyed this Goliath of a tourist trap."

"We need to get you some food," Tess said. "You're starting to lose it."

Two burgers and a pair of Diet Cokes later, we were crossing Courtney Campbell Causeway, which connects northern Pinellas County with Tampa.

"This kinda reminds me of driving to Key West," Tess said, "crossing over all this water."

"Never been."

"You'll have to go. I love the Keys. Hey, when you get your boat fixed up, give me a call, I'll cruise down with you."

Tess had the magazine on her lap and was reading about the Gravity Research Foundation, our next stop on the University of Tampa campus.

"There was this dude named Babson who created this foundation. He hated gravity. He claimed his sister, who I guess drowned, was really killed by gravity. Here's the actual quote:

She was unable to fight gravity, which came up and seized her like a dragon and brought her to the bottom.

"That was from an essay he authored titled *Gravity—Our Enemy One.*"

"And the alternative would be what? No gravity, so we could all float around like in outer space using suction toilets and eating through toothpaste tubes?"

"They don't actually use suction toilets, you know."

"Schrödinger's cat does."

She ignored that.

"Babson set up headquarters at some place called New Boston because he thought it was far enough away from large metropolitan areas to survive World War III, and he sponsored a batch of little monuments around the country, including the one we're going to."

"Seems kinda lame if you ask me," I said. "How'd it ever make the cut? Surely there's weirder stuff in Florida than this."

"That's what you get when you draw names out of a hat."

It's a quick drive across the causeway into downtown Tampa, and Siri said the monument we were looking for—about the size and shape of a large tombstone—was across from the campus library. We pulled to the curb in a no-parking zone and stepped out of the convertible. We'd dropped the top to enjoy the fresh air while we crossed Tampa Bay. It was now early afternoon and starting to warm up, but still pleasant.

The anti-gravity marker had been erected on a landscaped corner surrounded by pampas grass and bushes. It's purpose was engraved in stone: "...to remind students of the blessings forthcoming when science determines what gravity is, how it works, and how it may be controlled."

We crossed the street and stood before it. Tess jumped up—and then back down—I suppose to make sure gravity was still working.

"Gravity's not a suggestion, Tess," I said. "It's a law."

"You're so wise."

We looked around for yet another hollow rock. It would have been the ideal place for one amid the mulch and grass of the landscaping.

"I wonder how many students pass by here every day," I said. "Hundreds at least. Anything obviously out of place would be noticed immediately."

"We've been lucky so far," Tess said. "I'm kinda surprised we haven't hit a snag before now."

"Even if this one's already been found, it might not be the end of the world, right? Aren't we figuring it's the last two, the top half of the cover page and the signatures on the last page that will be the most important?"

"It would be meaningless to anyone without those pages, that's for sure."

We looked around a bit, Tess exploring in one direction up the sidewalk, peering into the shrubbery; me the other way. After about ten minutes of this we hadn't found anything, although we had attracted the passing attention of wandering students. One squadron of co-eds stopped Tess and asked if she needed help. Rather than blowing them off, she said:

"We're on a scavenger hunt, and someone was supposed to leave a note for us around here."

That got a laugh out of the girls. One said, "We'll help," then they fanned out and joined us in the search, poking about in the pampas grass and bushes.

That lasted about a minute, then they wished us luck and skittered off to class.

"This is a bummer," Tess said.

I agreed. "We could just take it down the road."

"We do know where the next stop is," Tess said. "But I'm worried we might miss something important. Can we look a little bit more?"

We'd come up empty-handed prowling the ground near the monument, so I took a step back to give the area a wider view. Maybe I'd spy something unusual from a different perspective.

The Moorish minarets of Plant Hall towered over the one hundred-and-ten-acre campus creating the unofficial icons for Tampa that you see on all the tourism brochures. A few yards to the east, the meandering Hillsborough River separated the college from the downtown skyscrapers, a divide that allowed the lushly landscaped campus a degree of serenity in the midst of a sprawling, bustling metropolis.

A mature oak tree dripped Spanish moss directly behind the anti-gravity monument. I recalled the last time our stalker hid a clue in a tree we found a parrot. I squeezed behind the monument and looked upward, but didn't see any colorful stuffed birds.

The students who'd been passing by earlier were now all in class, so I asked Tess to steady me as I clambered atop the headstone, stood up, and prepared to hoist myself onto the tree's lowest branch. Maybe if I climbed up in there I'd see something that eluded us from below.

But as I did, I looked up and saw, not in the tree, but under the overhang of an adjacent one-story building, a flash of silver. It was duct tape.

Theoretically, it's about an hour drive to Lake Wales, but traffic in downtown Tampa was brutal and it took us more than a half hour to drive across town. Which gave Tess time to share Spook Hill's history.

"Looks like gravity is the theme of the day," she said. "Spook Hill is supposed to be haunted—something about an epic battle between a warrior Indian chief and a monster alligator. They fought to the death, which left the place littered with ectoplasm, I guess, because now when you approach it, your car defies gravity and rolls uphill."

"Uh, huh."

"It's an optical illusion, of course. But people love it."

"Hey, when you can get a million people to stare at the image of a condom on a sheet of glass you can sell anything."

"You're too cynical."

Not according to Leo.

She read some more then said, "It's real popular with kids. In fact, there's a school next door and it's named—are you ready for this?—Spook Hill Elementary. Casper the Friendly Ghost is the school mascot."

Nothing much looked friendly, however, when we finally arrived.

Lake Wales police cruisers, lights flashing, blocked the entrance to the hill area on Fifth Street. I pulled over onto a side street leading to the elementary school.

"Wonder what this is about?" I said.

"This could make poking about a little challenging. I don't suppose you brought your cloak of invisibility, did you?"

"No. I took it to the cleaners and haven't seen it since."

I put the top up and we locked the Sebring then walked over toward the cruisers where a couple of uniformed officers were loitering. A bit further away, off the road in an adjoining field near a pond, there were more cruisers, two Polk County sheriff's cars, a couple of unmarked vehicles, and what looked like a crime scene investigation van.

As we approached the uniforms blocking the road, I pulled out a business card identifying myself as a reporter.

"Hi, guys," I said. "We're reporters. Here's my card. Can you tell us what's going on?"

The shorter of the two cops took my card, gave it a brief look, then handed it back. "You'll have to talk to the chief if you have any questions."

"He around?" Tess asked.

The cop nodded in the direction of the activity by the pond.

"So, we should walk on over there?" I asked optimistically.

That got me the look, the look all cops learn at the academy, the one when translated from policespeak to English said, "Go ahead, give me a reason to cuff you, better still, shoot you."

The taller of the two uniforms spoke into his shoulder mic. I couldn't make out what he was saying. He took a few steps away, yakked some more, then walked back over to us.

"I'll need to see some ID. For both of you."

I looked at Tess. She looked at me. We both shrugged and dug out our driver's licenses. Shoulder Mic took them and walked a few steps away again and began gabbing on the radio some more.

"What do you figure this is about?" I asked Tess.

She gave her head a slight shake. Her lips were pursed, obviously tense. She wasn't liking this one bit. Neither was I.

Shoulder Mic walked back over. "Someone will be here in a minute." He didn't return our licenses. I thought about insisting, then thought better of it. The smart play was to be patient. Maybe the chief wanted to know who he was talking to. That wouldn't be unreasonable.

While we waited, I checked out the archway over Fifth Street spelling out Spook Hill in white ghostly lettering. A black and orange sign on the side of the road, held in place by a white ghost—not Casper—repeated the legend of the warrior chief and the gator.

In a few more minutes, one of the unmarked cars by the pond began rolling our way. It pulled up short of the street, stopping in the grass.

The day had gone so smoothly, I should have known it was too perfect. Nothing is ever that easy. We were so near the end of this ridiculous scavenger hunt. The prize we'd been searching for was so near our grasp. Now this.

The car door opened, and the last person I would have expected to see stepped out.

It was Jack Turner.

CHAPTER 39

Lake Wales

"I WONDERED IF you two would show up," Turner said. He took our driver's licenses from Shoulder Mic and handed them back to us. "I've been trying to reach you, Tess."

She grew a perplexed expression and dug the cell phone from her back pocket. "Well, shit. It's on silent mode."

"Little out of your turf aren't you, detective?" I said.

He didn't reply, just gave us the once-over, not the usual dead-eye cop stare, merely observing, assessing, maybe waiting for us to put the pieces together.

"It's Darnell Duffy, isn't it?" I said.

"I suppose the two of you can validate your whereabouts during the past forty-eight hours," Turner said, not responding to my question.

I thought about that, then dug into the front pocket of my cargo shorts and pulled out a receipt from a Mobile station in Naples.

"Here's a gas receipt that will place us down in Collier County. We had dinner the past three nights at Stan's Idle Hour in Goodland and I paid with my credit card. Those receipts are in my backpack. We also spent the last two days shopping in Naples. I also have receipts for those purchases. We stopped at the post office in Ochopee this morning before heading up this way. The clerk at the post office can validate that. Tess had a General Delivery letter waiting for her and the clerk had to find it for her. She'll remember us. That good enough for now?"

He looked at the receipt and handed it back to me. "Who keeps gas receipts?"

"I do. I keep records of everything."

"He's a little OCD," Tess said.

Tess turned toward the field and all the activity around the pond.

"Is it Darnell? Is that why you're here? Is he…is he.. " She couldn't spit it out and finally pointed and said, "over there?"

"This is really interesting," Turner said. "Both of you assuming it's Darnell."

"Well, he's missing, right?" Seemed like a reasonable leap of logic to me.

"Yes. And he still is."

Tess and I glanced at one another, then back at Turner.

"You do have a corpse over there, right? That's what this looks like."

He nodded. "But not Darnell."

"Then why are you here?" Tess asked, then started to add another question when the implication hit her.

"Oh, no."

That could only mean one thing: It had to be Amy.

"I'm going to ask you to identify the victim, Tess."

But Turner wouldn't allow us to view the corpse out by the pond and he wouldn't confirm who the victim was, although we were certain there could only be one reason why he would have been called down from Gainesville. He was being stiff and formal, as if he were talking to strangers.

Or suspects.

He said that as soon as the CSIs were through photographing the site, the medical examiner would transport the body to the county morgue in Winter Haven, a half-hour away. Tess would be asked to ID the body there and sign a formal statement.

"How'd she get out there, by that pond?" I asked Turner.

"You know perfectly well I'm not going to answer that."

"Hey, I'm not asking as a reporter. We might be able to help."

"That would be a nice change of pace. How about I ask the questions."

Actually, we learned it would be a detective from the Polk County Sheriff's Office who would be leading the interrogation. When we arrived at the morgue, the detective—his name was Samuelson—tried to escort Tess back to the examining room by herself, but she objected.

"He's coming with me," she said, nodding toward me. The detective ignored that and touched her elbow to point her in the right direction, but she jerked away. Samuelson, middle aged and slightly overweight, gave her a patient, condescending look. I imagined him with a cut lip if he touched her again. But he wasn't stupid.

"No problem," he said. "You both can come."

The morgue actually served Highlands and Hardee counties as well as Polk. Florida organizes its medical examiners that way, especially in the rural areas. The morgue was part of a complex of white and gray buildings with green roofs set well off Winter Lake Road. Inside, it was modern, stainless steel, brightly lit, and smelled of chemicals.

An assistant medical examiner lowered the sheet covering the body down to the neck. It was gruesome. The bullet had entered her face at the bridge of her nose causing an ungodly star-shaped swelling around the entry point, blackened with dried blood. Her eyes were simply gone. Apparently eaten by insects. It was horrific.

Tess gasped, threw her hands to her mouth, and began sobbing.

I put my arms around her shoulders and drew her into me. My heart was hammering and I felt the room closing in. I'm not sure I was steadying Tess as much as I was using her to keep my own balance. We stayed like that, huddled together, for a few seconds, then she abruptly wrenched free and ran out of the examining room.

I followed right behind her, trailed by Turner, and Samuelson.

"We'll need to get a statement from you," Samuelson said to her back as she fled. "There's a form to sign."

Tess dropped down to the lobby floor, held her head in her hands, and began wailing.

"No, no, no, no, no."

I whirled on Turner.

"You could have told her before we got here, Turner. What the fuck were you thinking?"

"It's standard…"

"Oh, come on."

I felt a hand on my chest. It was Samuelson, pushing me back. Without realizing it, I had edged up on Turner. Edging up on cops, especially cops with Glocks on their hips, has historically not been a premium move for anybody interested in longevity.

"Take it easy, pal," the Polk detective said.

I backed away and bent down beside Tess and held her in my arms,

The body on the gurney was not Amy Duffy. We had assumed incorrectly.

It was Bristol Kreuger.

CHAPTER 40

Winter Haven

THE NEXT SEVERAL hours were a blur. We left my car at the morgue and were driven over to the sheriff's office, nearby. We were placed in separate interview rooms and tag-teamed by Samuelson and Turner until late in the afternoon.

It's standard procedure to interview crime witnesses separately. That lets police compare their stories and look for inconsistencies. Anticipating we would be questioned apart from one another, Tess and I had war-gamed what we would say while we drove from Lake Wales to the public safety complex in Winter Haven where we now were.

"Tess, the scavenger hunt is over," I'd said. "We're dealing with a homicide. You have to tell the police everything. You can't leave anything out."

"I still need to protect Aaron."

"I'm sorry, but you can't. Not anymore. You leave out anything, it's the same as lying to the police. That's a felony."

"I'll risk it."

"Well, good for you. You're willing to risk me going to prison, too, are you?"

"Oh."

She was quiet for a few seconds, working it through.

"Dammit. I should never have told you."

"Tess, even if you hadn't told me about Landry, it would still be obvious you were withholding evidence in a murder investigation. I'm sorry, but you can't protect him anymore. Besides, that's the last fucking thing you should be worrying about now. We need to find this killer."

That came out more harshly than I intended—and that was before I knew the victim was Bristol. But after a week of being run around like a puppet on a string and dealing with Tess's secrecy, I was more than a little frustrated. I'd tried to be a good sport about it. I thought there was every chance that, in the end, she'd get her contract back and we'd be able to file all this away as a bizarre memory.

But no more. Now somebody had lost her life.

Tess made one final plea. "I'll tell them I had a financial arrangement with Aaron. I'll tell them that's the reason for all this, my desire to get that contract back. How it was stolen. That it included confidential information. Our suspicion that Amy took it. All of that. I'll give them the notes, the poems. But I don't want to get into the details of the contract. That's not really relevant. I'm going to insist on talking to my attorney if they push me that."

"And what do you expect me to do?" I'd asked.

"I won't ask you to do anything that would get you in trouble. I kept the details from you until recently. You just learned who the contract was with. You haven't seen the contract."

"All that's true. But what if they ask me what I know about the contract's details?"

"Go ahead and let them know I told you it was a nondisclosure agreement. But if they want specifics, tell them to talk to me."

The questions during the several interrogation sessions were pretty straightforward. They wanted the history of the misadventure, dates and times of where we'd been, the last time we'd spoken to Bristol, the nature of that conversation, that sort of thing.

"What's so important about this contract?" Samuelson asked, a question repeated later by Turner.

"I asked the same question when all this began," I told him. "Tess wouldn't say. Said it was private information she didn't want anyone to know about."

"You're telling me you drove all over the state just on her word?"

"Yes, that's what I'm telling you."

I expected him to push me on that, and then I would have a decision to make. Would I deflect, and tell them to talk to Tess about specifics? Or would I spill the beans? But he didn't ask. Which at the time I figured meant he'd already gotten Tess's answer. Instead, he switched gears.

"So this stalker, he has the contract, he's feeding it out a half-page at a time, using it to blackmail Ms. Winkler, intimidate her into doing all this?"

"Yes."

"Any idea who would do that?"

"No direct information. But given the kinds of details we received in the instructions, I believe it has to be somebody who worked on Tess's newspaper, and she thinks it's her old roommate, Amy. Maybe with help from her half-brother. But that's just speculation."

The most challenging question came from Turner: Why the hell didn't we come to the police before things went haywire?

"We thought maybe we could ferret out who was behind this on our own," I replied. "It seemed like low-level harassment. We didn't have an identifiable suspect, only our guesses. Who could have predicted this? And what the hell was Bristol Krueger doing in Lake Wales?"

By then, I think Turner was feeling a little guilty about how he'd mishandled things with Tess. We were alone in an interview room and he turned off the recording system.

"Look, here's the thing," he said. "Both you and Tess have confirmed it's been a couple of days since you spoke to Bristol."

I nodded. I'd told him the last time that we had heard from her, she was in a bar, the Thunder Hog.

"I'm sure you could tell in the morgue her body was out there by that pond a couple of days. The flies had gotten to her. You saw her eyes."

"Was she killed there?"

Turner was quiet for a moment. "We don't know for sure. The ME will have to weigh in on that."

"Wherever she was murdered, the earliest that could've happened would have been after Tess called her," I said. "Tess's phone will have a time stamp of that call, by the way."

"Yeah, we got that."

"Okay. So the last time we talked to her she was at the Thunder Hog. Sometime thereafter—precise time of death to be determined, I suppose—Bristol gets shot in the face. For the sake of argument, let's assume that takes place in Gainesville. Then her killer drives her here. Why here?"

He'd already thought of that, I assumed, but perhaps it was useful to hear someone else say it. Or maybe he was trying to trick me into talking too much. But I didn't think so. They hadn't Mirandized us. The recorder was off. We weren't under arrest.

"The 'why here' question is the key," I said. "It points to the stalker. I guess that's obvious. He would have been here to leave the latest installment to the puzzle. Speaking of which, did you guys try to find it?"

Turner said, "The sheriff has his people looking all around the lake for evidence. He said they're going to go over every square inch, all the way back to the road."

I thought about that. Why would the stalker, having murdered Bristol, still be running around distributing pieces to the puzzle? That seemed insane. And maybe that was the answer. But if he bothered to travel all the way to Spook Hill and leave Bristol's corpse, why would he do that without dropping off the next clue, perhaps the most important clue, the one that would tell us where the final half-page of the nondisclosure agreement would be found?

Insane or not, that wouldn't make any sense. There had to be a clue out there somewhere.

What was it that Sherlock Holmes said?

Once you eliminate the impossible, whatever remains, no matter how improbable, must be the truth.

"You're looking everywhere?"

"Yes."

"And so far, nothing?"

Turner brow furrowed. "What are you thinking?"

"In the morgue, Bristol was still fully clothed."

"So what?"

"Maybe you should look there."

Turner stared at me for a few seconds, then rose from the table and left the room. A few minutes later, he returned. "I told Samuelson what you suggested. He's calling the ME right now."

"He still around?" I asked, glancing at my watch.

"Yes. They agreed to do the autopsy tonight. I don't know if they started yet. I doubt we'd get that kind of cooperation up in Gainesville. There are some advantages to small towns, I guess."

After a few minutes, Tess was escorted into the room and the two of us were left alone while the cops compared notes.

"You okay?" I asked.

Her eyes were red, but she appeared to have cried herself out. "No. I don't think I'll ever be okay again. What am I going to tell Bristol's parents?"

She dug the heels of her hands into her eyes for a few seconds, then lowered them and stared at me.

"This is all my fault. I got her killed. I don't know how it happened, but knowing Bristol she found something or talked to someone or jumped into somebody's shit. You saw her in the woods at Devil's

Millhopper. She was dying to be a hero. Now she'd dead. I as good as killed her by getting her involved in this."

I reached across the table to hold her hand, but she withdrew it and crossed her arms tightly across her chest and hung her head.

"I am such a fucking idiot."

I kept my peace for a few minutes, then I said:

"Tess, with all due respect for what you're going through, you didn't get Bristol killed. You didn't pull the trigger. Whoever stole that contract from you and concocted this stupid scavenger hunt, did this. You're a victim. Don't blame yourself."

She didn't respond, evidently uninterested in my efforts to assuage her feelings of guilt. Maybe I was trying to absolve myself, too. After all, I had aided and abetted her throughout this clown fiesta. At any point in time, I could have brought this madness to a halt, dropped a dime, called Turner. Staged an intervention. But I hadn't. I'd gone along for the ride. And now we were here.

We sat there in silence until there was a knock at the door and Turner stuck his head in. He nodded toward me. "Got a sec?"

Tess hadn't looked up, head hanging, lost in her grief.

"I'll be right back." I said.

I stepped out into the hallway. Turner's face was strained. "The ME called back. You were right. Jesus God this is so sick."

When the ME started the autopsy, Turner said, the first thing he did was strip her clothes off. Standard operating procedure. That's when he found two lines of poetry written on her chest in black felt-tip marker.

"What did they say?"

He shook his head. "I couldn't tell you even if I knew; they haven't shared that information yet."

"But they will, right?"

He nodded. "I'm sure they will."

"How about a paper note or copy of a document. They find that?"

"No."

"The two lines that were written on Bristol. They complete the poem that was supposed to lead us to the final stop on this fucking tour."

"Well," Turner said, "I guess the tour's over now."

The tour *was* over. But the final pages of the document were still out there somewhere, perhaps in the hands of the killer. Had he—or she—followed through and hid it somewhere? Did that even matter anymore?

"Has someone called Bristol's folks?" I asked.

"I don't know if that's happened yet, but it will. Sometime soon if not already."

I thought about things for a moment then asked: "This going to be Polk County's case or yours?"

"That's over my pay grade. I've reported in. For the time being, it's Polk's because that's where the body was discovered. But like you said, she was from Gainesville and there's every chance she might have been murdered there, so I'm sure we'll be working together on this."

"And Darnell Duffy is still missing."

"Still in the wind."

"And the final page of the contract is also still missing, and the coroner has the key to its whereabouts."

Turner considered that then nodded his head.

"Yeah."

CHAPTER 41

Gainesville

IT'S ABOUT TWO hours from Winter Haven to Gainesville, and we passed that time mostly in silence, arriving at Tess's house about 10 p.m. The lights were on inside. I'd called Demerest and told him we were returning. He said he'd be wait up for us.

During what little conversation we had during the drive, I told Tess that neither Samuelson nor Turner had tried to pry details of the contract from me. "How much did you tell them?" I'd asked.

She'd shaken her head. "The less you know the better. I never should have told you anything about it in the first place."

"Well, do they know about Landry at all?"

"Don't, Zander. Just don't"

So I didn't.

Tess flung the car door open the instant it rolled to a stop and marched toward the house, her movements stiff, robotic. But before she got there, the front door swung wide, silhouetting Jazzy, who stepped onto the porch and wrapped her arms around her. Tess didn't have a chance to fight off the embrace, even if she'd been so inclined. She let Jazzy squeeze her tightly, and after a few moments, she seemed to wilt in her arms and I could hear her snuffling.

Jazzy took her by the hand and led her into the house. "Your bed's made down," Jazzy said. "You need to get some rest now. Tomorrow will be another day."

She walked Tess into her bedroom and a few minutes later emerged and shut the door gently behind her.

"How is she?" I asked. It was a naive question. Maybe I was hoping for some reassurance.

Jazzy shook her head.

While she attended to Tess, Fred ran over and pawed my leg. I picked him up and scratched him behind his big floppy ears. That earned me a lick on the face.

"Good to see you, too, pal. You been a good boy?"

"Gerrrufff."

"Awesome."

We joined Demerest, who was seated at the kitchen table holding a can of Swamp Head IPA. There were three other empties on the table. He'd had the good sense and decency to leave Tess alone. Like Jazzy said, tomorrow would be another day.

But I wanted to work some things out with him. He offered me a beer, but I declined.

"Coffee's fresh," Jazzy said. I poured a cup and sat down.

"What do you know that we don't know?" I asked.

"It's been a busy evening. Amy Duffy has contacted the police through an attorney. She wants to come in."

I felt my heart skip a beat. Hadn't seen that coming.

"Where is she?"

"Don't know, but it's a local lawyer, so she must be nearby."

"She confess?"

Demerest shook his head and held up his hand. "All I know is that the state attorney's office is now involved. I'm told they're setting up a meet. I have no idea what her lawyer told them. I'm lucky to know what little I do."

"So we don't know if she's the killer."

"No. But, she's been missing for a year and she shows up now? That can't be coincidental. That doesn't mean she's the trigger puller. But she's got something to say, so maybe this will be cleared up tomorrow."

"And Darnel's still AWOL."

"Far as I know."

"So she could know something about that."

"Maybe. Or it could be something else."

We heard Tess's bedroom door click open, and she walked into the kitchen wearing her pink pajamas and her bunny slippers. She plopped down at the table.

"Walls are thin. I heard all that."

"Coffee?" I asked.

She nodded. I got up and poured her a cup, added a dash of milk from the fridge, and dropped in a sugar cube. Fred was giving me a hopeful look, so I grabbed one of his treats from a Ziploc bag on the counter and tossed it to him. He caught it in mid-air.

"Have you been keeping up with Jack Turner?" I asked Demerest.

"I can't reveal my sources."

I smiled. "Of course not. But you know what we found down there at Spook Hill, out by the pond, all that, I assume."

"And maybe a little more. A few details have emerged while the two of you were on the road."

"Yeah, about that. I'm kind of surprised they let us go."

He shook his head. "You both will be material witnesses at some point, but nobody thinks you're good for Bristol's murder. But you may need to lawyer up. There's a lot of unhappiness about your not coming clean about this earlier, especially you, Tess."

"I know."

Demerest stared at her for a few seconds, then said, "Tess, you're not responsible for Bristol."

"People keep telling me that."

She turned to me, expressionless, then took a sip of coffee.

"Speaking of Bristol," I said. "Anything on her whereabouts after we talked to her at the bar?"

"Witnesses said she was yakking it up with a guy there," Demerest said. "They're trying to get a positive ID on him. But she took off with him in a big hurry."

"I don't suppose it was Darnell."

"No. But it might be somebody who worked with him. Maybe. It's been a while since I heard anything on that front."

We chewed on that for a bit then I said, "Is it possible that this guy Bristol met, he might have told her about Darnell, maybe where he was, and that's how this came down?"

Demerest shrugged his shoulders. "We'll find out."

"Any more news from the medical examiner in Winter Haven?"

Tess glanced at me. "What?"

I hadn't told her about what the coroner had revealed.

"They found a message," I said.

"Where?"

I hesitated to tell her, but she'd have to hear it sometime. "Handwritten on Bristol's chest."

Tess's eyelids fluttered and she wobbled. Demerest reached her first and steadied her. Jazzy came around the table and knelt down beside her as Tess lowered her head to the table. She was sobbing. I found a clean dish towel and wet it with ice water and handed it to Jazzy, who applied it to the back of Tess's neck. After a minute, Tess straighten up, took the dish towel from Jazzy, and wiped her face.

"What the fuck," she said. "What the actual fuck."

I turned to Demerest. "Your source tell you what was written?"

He shook his head. "My guess is he won't."

"Because?"

"Because there is a killer on the loose, and this is something only the killer would have seen."

I got it. Anyone who's ever watched a cop show on TV would get it. The police never give up information that could directly link a suspect to a crime. Basic procedure. And Turner knew Demerest was working with us and he wouldn't put him in an awkward position like that.

Jazzy, who was still kneeling next to Tess, suddenly stood up turned toward the door.

A moment later, the doorbell rang.

Fred growled and Demerest pulled a Smith & Wesson from his hip and walked to the door. He looked through the peephole, then stepped to the side of the door and said in a loud voice, "Hands where I can see them."

I stood up and placed myself in front of Tess and Jazzy.

I heard a woman's voice outside, and Demerest swung the door open.

Even though I'd never seen her before, I knew who it was:

Amy Duffy.

CHAPTER 42

SHE WAS MEDIUM height with dark hair, tight fitting black yoga pants, running shoes, and a loose fitting blue and orange University of Florida sweat shirt. Her hands were raised in a don't-shoot-me pose. Demerest gestured her inside with his right hand, his left hand still holding the revolver by his side, then immediately closed and locked the door behind her.

I heard a guttural sound behind me and turned to see Tess rising from the table, her face empurpled, fists clenched. Jazzy reached out to grab her arm but Tess shook it off and she charged toward the front door.

I grabbed Tess around her slim waist and pulled her off her feet. She screamed and struggled, whipping back and forth like a rattle-snake trying to free herself from my grasp, but I held on.

Amy lowered her hands and stood beside Demerest, motionless, waiting for the punishment that would come the instant I released her former roommate. Then she said "Tess" in a hushed, contrite voice.

Tess stopped struggling and stared at her. Her breathing slowed. Then she looked up at me. "Let me go."

"No."

"I promise I won't hurt her."

"I don't believe you."

Jazzy stepped beside me and put a hand on my back. It was hot, as if she were feverish.

"You can let her go," she said.

So I did.

Demerest gestured Amy toward the couch with his revolver and she sat down, balanced on the very edge, and looked up at Tess.

"I'm here to apologize for all the crazy shit you've gone through."

"And for Bristol?" Tess asked, her voice tight. She walked over to the door and leaned against it. Demerest took a step back from Amy and stood beside Tess.

Amy paused then shook her head. "I just heard about that. My lawyer told me."

"You saying it wasn't you?" I asked.

Again another pause before answering. "I had nothing to do with that. The first I heard she'd been killed was a little while ago." She held her hands out, palms up, a gesture of openness. "Tess, I swear to God, I don't know what happened to Bristol. I came here to talk about it."

I walked over to the occasional chair nearest Amy and stood behind it. Using the chair back as cover, I pulled my iPhone out of my cargo shorts and turned on the recording app. Amy, who had eye-lock on Tess, didn't notice. Under Florida law, it is illegal to record conversations without the consent of those involved, but legal niceties were the least of my concerns.

"You're saying you didn't pull the trigger," I said. "But this entire fiasco has your fingerprints all over it." It was an assertion, not a question, but I wanted to see if she would deny it. She didn't.

Once again, she paused before answering. It was like talking over the radio to someone on the moon, waiting for the signal to cross outer space.

"Partly my doing. I didn't steal your stuff, Tess. But I knew about it and where you had it hidden in your room. And I'd told Darnell about it. So when he came to get my things, he snuck in there and snatched it. He took the friendship ring I'd given you, too."

She hesitated again, perhaps trying to sort out how much to reveal. Or not. "I didn't ask him to steal anything. But I did ask him to find the ring. I wanted it back."

"You could have told me you wanted the ring back," Tess snarled. "You knew damn well I had no use for it."

"I know. But I was avoiding contact with you. It was part of my therapy. When I asked Darnell to get it, I assumed he would ask you for it. It didn't occur to me he would steal it."

"How did he know what ring to grab?" I asked.

Amy looked at me curiously. "Didn't you see it?"

The truth is, I saw the ring on a chain around Spock's neck, but I didn't inspect it closely. I certainly didn't want to touch it and smudge any prints.

Tess interjected: "It had both our names on it."

"Okay, but then why did Darnell break into here and bring the ring back? You tell him to do it?"

Amy was wringing her hands and she ran her tongue over her lips before answering.

"No. When Darnell told me what he did, I became very frightened. I realized then what he was doing wasn't just annoying but threatening. He was stalking you. I begged him to stop, but he told me to go to hell. That's when I knew I needed to come back here, to get in his face, make him quit."

"So why the wild goose chase?" I asked. "Why run Tess all over Florida?"

She took a deep breath and slowly exhaled. "Let me back up, okay? I was upset with you, Tess. When you left for Tampa that weekend, I was so distraught, I thought about killing myself. I even cut my wrist a little bit, thinking maybe about committing suicide. That's where that blood in the kitchen came from."

She held up her left arm, the palm of her hand facing Tess, showing the mark on her wrist. Tess was impassive, arms crossed, scowling, not the least bit interested in Amy's scar tissue.

"I chickened out, but when I left town, I dimed the cops, figured I'd make your life miserable. That was stupid and mean and I'm sorry. Looking back, I realize now how out of my mind I was. I drove to California, and my aunt got me into rehab to dry out. I promised myself I'd stay clean and that I would never return to Florida and that I would never have any contact with you again."

She hesitated, collecting her thoughts.

"But then Darnell called."

She stopped and rubbed her eyes and was quiet for a few more moments, and I became concerned she might lose her resolve. So I prompted her:

"You said Darnell called. It was about the contract?"

She looked at me curiously for a seconds, then at Tess. Finally, she nodded. "Yes."

She paused again as if she were calculating exactly what to say next. Getting her story straight.

"Darnell had this *great idea*. He has all these get-rich schemes. He figured you and Aaron Landry would do anything to make sure none of this never saw the light of day, so he was going to blackmail both of you. But he wanted to punish you, first, Tess. I tried to talk him out of it. Told him he'd end up in prison. That he wasn't thinking clearly, that he needed to clean up his life."

She paused and shook her head. "That part didn't go over well."

"The clean up his life part?" Demerest asked.

"Yes. He thought I was lording it over him, that I'd done rehab and stayed clean. That I was acting like I was better than him or something. He wouldn't let it go. Kept badgering me, saying I was only partially cured, that I needed conversion therapy, that this Florida preacher, Lee Roy Chitango, had some kind of camp to reverse homosexuality. Anyway, I finally talked him out of his blackmail scheme, but he had this stuff on you, Tess, and he was bound and determined to use it. To punish you."

"Why me? What did I ever do to him?"

Amy shook her head. "You don't remember? Really?"

Tess had a blank look on her face and shook her head. "I have no idea what you're talking about."

Amy shrugged. "No surprise. Why would you remember? Darnell's a nobody." There was an edge in her voice.

Darnell's a nobody.

It hung there like an accusation, the inference being Darnell wasn't the only nobody in Tess's world. As if it were some fault of Tess's.

"I've lost count of the number of times he's repeated it. You were at the Purple Dolphin, it was one of our planning sessions, where we cooked up the idea for *The Agi-Gator*. Some of us were underage, using fake IDs, everyone but you had one. You kinda slipped in with the rest of us. You remember that?"

"I guess. What's your point?"

"Darnell approached you, offered to buy you a beer, said he could get you a really good driver's license, asked you if you'd like to go somewhere and talk. And you laughed in his face and said, 'Get away from me you little bastard. I don't hang out with lowlifes.' You remember that?"

"No. But if you're suggesting I brought this all on myself by by telling your idiot brother to buzz off you can go fuck yourself."

Amy leaned back, shook her head slowly, and resumed full contrition mode. "No, of course not. Darnell's not right. He hasn't been in, like, forever. And he hates gays. And Jews. And blacks. And Muslims. He's become this bigoted white supremist. But my point is that he's hated you for a long time and he says you're the reason I'm a lesbian. And he really, really didn't like you calling him a bastard. Because, of course, he is. Neither of us know who are fathers are. I couldn't talk him off of that."

I wasn't sure how much of what Amy was telling us was truthful and how much was embellishment. Everything about this conversation seemed staged. As if she were remembering lines she rehearsed, pausing to stay on script. But she seemed to be building an argument that, she, too, was a victim in all of this, which was hard to swallow. Too much of what we'd been through had to have originated with her, not the least of which were the destinations on the *WTF* map and, especially, those that never made publication, like Koreshan State Park. Darnell would have known nothing of those things.

So I put it out there: "Then why the scavenger hunt? That had to be your idea."

Amy blinked several times before replying. "Who are you, exactly?"

Tess said, "He's my friend. Answer the question. The scavenger hunt. Your idea?"

"Yes, that's right. I can't deny that." She paused, gathering her thoughts, figuring out how to frame it to her advantage, I assumed.

"I thought I had to give Darnell something. I went along with his Tess-hating thing as a way to get him off blackmailing. And then, and this is the really awful part, I kinda got into it, the idea of running you ragged. Maybe not so much to hurt you, Tess, but just because engineering it turned out to be a kind of release."

"I call bullshit," Tess said.

Amy stared at Tess, bit her lip, then said, "Yeah, okay, fair point. But I never thought it would lead to any of this."

"So you admit you're the mastermind of all this craziness." I said.

Amy nodded. "I played a part."

"But you're saying you didn't encourage Darnell to break in here?" I asked.

"No. That was his own idea. He was very proud of himself. Thought it would terrify you. He saw it playing out like a scene in a horror movie, imagined you returning home to find it. He really got off thinking how terrified you would be. He told me he had planned to hide outside to video record it through the window. But then something happened. He said there was this tall guy. You, I guess. He said you went outside and started walking around the house. You scared him and he ran off."

Demerest jumped in.

"So how'd Darnell get in here?"

"He said he found a key. That's all I know."

"When did you return?" Demerest asked.

"A week ago. I drove back. I didn't want to be seen in Gainesville, so I booked a room at a motel in Micanopy. I tried to talk sense to Darnell, but by then he'd done all this preparation, had it all plotted out. Of course, my fingerprints were all over it, him using the *Weird Tour of Florida* guide as a map for this insanity."

"But he didn't," I said. "He veered from the map, took us to different places."

She nodded. "Again, my bad. I'd told him about our argument, Tess. About how I resented your taking over the production of the magazine. He figured that would be part of the revenge."

"And you couldn't talk him down?" Tess asked.

"No."

"You have an attorney and you're meeting with the police," I said. "When did you decide to do that?"

"I have a friend, she's a lawyer here; we were undergrads together. I called her yesterday and told her all about this and asked for her advice. Darnell had stopped answering my phone calls and when I went by his apartment, he was gone. I was afraid of what he might do next, how all this would end. I asked my lawyer friend if I should go to the police, turn my own brother in? She made arrangements for us to visit somebody in the state attorney's office tomorrow."

She was wringing her hands and staring at the ceiling while she spoke, avoiding eye contact.

"Anyway, a little while ago she got a call from her contact in the prosecutor's office. Said the police were looking for Darnell in connection with Bristol's murder. She told me we shouldn't wait, we should meet at the police station tonight. That I could be charged with being a... what did she call it?... an accessory before the fact. That the sooner I turned myself in, the better it would be for me."

Jazzy, who had remained in the kitchen during most of the

291

conversation, stepped over and asked, "What does that mean? Accessory before the fact?"

"It's the same thing as an accomplice," Demerest said. He was staring down at Amy. "She could be charged with murder."

Amy shook her head. "No!" It was not quite a shout, but it was emphatic. "I told my attorney that I had no part in any violence. I mean, this isn't going to be easy for me, but she says if I turn myself in voluntarily, it will work out okay."

I could not imagine any way she was going to be okay, but there was no point debating that. "I have a final question for you, Amy," I said. "Did you see the clues, the poems?'

She hung her head. "Yes. I wrote them."

Tess groaned and rolled her eyes.

Amy turned on her: "Hey, I wasn't a fucking English major like you, alright?" It came out sharp, brittle. So much for contrition.

"So, Amy, you wrote the clues sending us on this clown fiesta of a road trip," I said. "Did you also write the final clue, the one we haven't seen?"

"Yeah, did you?" Tess said. "The one handwritten on Bristol's chest?"

Amy opened her mouth, then closed it. Finally, she said, "I wrote them all. On my phone. And sent them to Darnell."

"Fine," Tess said. "Where was the last stop?"

Amy lolled her head a bit then looked at Tess. "The last stop? Where it all began. The Devil's Millhopper."

CHAPTER 43

DEMEREST INSISTED ON escorting Amy to the police station. The two of them had just left, and it was a relief to have her out of the house. It was a minor miracle that Tess hadn't found some way to kill her. In hindsight, I realized that's why Demerest had stationed himself next to Tess during the conversation. He wasn't blocking the door, as it seemed, he was protecting Tess from doing something she'd later regret.

Probably.

We were seated back at the kitchen table. I was on my third cup of coffee. I wouldn't have slept anyway.

"Any thoughts on where D2 might be hiding out?"

Tess squinted her eyes and thought about that for a few beats. "I murdered somebody, I'd be running as far away from Florida as I could get."

"In an orange Camaro."

"I guess I'd be stealing some new wheels first."

Jazzy said, "Yes, but you're not insane. He is. That might make a difference."

I took in Jazzy. Had she seen any of this before in one of her visions? Her gaze met mine, those clear brown eyes with flecks of gold.

"Have you…" I began.

She leaned across the table and held out her hands, palms up, an invitation I couldn't refuse. She squeezed.

"Strange Man," she said. "Just remember. There's more to the world than meets the eye. Your job is to tell the truth of it all."

She released my hands, then reached up and removed her turban. Then she slipped off her wraparound sunglasses and set them on the table. She stood up and walked out the front door, closing it quietly behind her.

Tess and I looked at one another, no doubt both wondering what all that was supposed to mean.

"Cigarette break?" Tess asked.

"Said she quit."

We sat there staring at one another for a minute or two, drained, physically and emotionally.

"Right before Amy left, for a moment there it looked like she was going to approach you," I said. "She started in your direction then stopped. I'm sure you noticed that."

She nodded.

"It was awkward. It looked like she wanted to give you a hug good-bye or something. It was weird. Good thing Demerest was in between the two of you. From the look in your eyes, I think you might have throttled her."

"She's not right in the head. You can see it. She's crazy as her fucking brother."

"I think you may be right."

Tess did her hands-through-her-hair routine then said, "I really have no recollection whatsoever about that scene in the Purple Dolphin Amy described. D2 offering to buy me a beer. Or me insulting him."

"Why would you?"

She shrugged.

"Look on the bright side," I said.

"What's that?"

"You had him pegged as a lowlife even then. Excellent character judgment on your part."

She shrugged.

"How much of what Amy said do you believe?"

"All I know is Bristol's dead and she wouldn't be if it weren't for that bitch. They're going to nail her, aren't they?"

"Oh, yeah. She's fucked."

I thought about that, then shook my head.

"You know, Tess, she should be smart enough to understand that. She's either incredibly naïve if she thinks she can rat out her brother and walk away from all this, or she was lying through her teeth."

"I vote for lying."

Then why did she leave willingly with Demerest? Something didn't fit.

I glanced out the front window, expecting to see Jazzy on the porch burning down a coffin nail. But she wasn't there. I wanted to have a word with her. Before we'd left on this last leg of the scavenger hunt, she'd had one of her spells. Had she foreseen any of this? Did she know about Bristol?

I couldn't imagine her not saying something if she had, but I wanted to hear it from her.

I walked to the door, swung it open, and was greeted by a yellow moth flapping around the front porch light, but no New Orleans palm reader. I stepped out into the front yard and looked up and down the street. It was deserted.

What the hell?

When I stepped back inside, Tess was standing in the living room, one hand on the back of an occasional chair, the other rubbing the back of her neck.

"You don't think…" I started to say.

"Think what?"

"You don't imagine she went down there, to the Millhopper, do you?"

"How would she get there?"

We walked back outside and Tess pointed to the porch railing.

"My bike. It's gone."

"Oh, fuck."

CHAPTER 44

The Devil's Millhopper

WE ENTERED THE park much as we had a few days earlier, leaving the Sebring across the street and traversing Northwest Fifty Third Avenue on foot. We spotted the bicycle immediately upon entering the visitor's lot, leaning against a tree.

My first impulse was to call out Jazzy's name, but Tess and I had discussed that on the brief drive over and agreed we would operate on the down-low. We weren't sure what Jazzy was up to, but the determined manner in which she left the house and her final words to me made it clear she had a plan, and we agreed we shouldn't do anything that might disrupt it and place her in jeopardy.

"It's like she's had another vision," Tess said. "She seems so fatalistic about all this, don't you think?"

By then, the reality of Jazzy's attacks of *deja vu*—or whatever they should be called—were no longer in question. They were genuine. Whether they foretold the future was another question entirely, but she believed they did, and her sincerity was convincing.

I told Tess, "At one point during our drive here from New Orleans, I got a little annoyed with her. I said, 'Hey, mystery lady, tell me what's going on, or I'm dropping you at the nearest bus station.' And she just smiled that all-knowing smile of hers and said:

"'Won't matter. Your car will break down. Again. Or you'll get a flat tire or t-boned or run out of gas. Something will always happen. Like when your alternator blew up and you forgot Spock and you had to come back to New Orleans and get me. You can't change fate.'"

"Jeeez."

Before we left her house, Tess grabbed a pair of flashlights that she kept in case of power failure—basic hurricane preparedness. I also had a lantern in the trunk of my car, but it had an ultraviolet bulb in it instead of a white light. It's how I tracked down scorpions in the Arizona desert—they glow an eerie iridescent green under a black light, which makes them easier to hunt at night than during daylight.

I carry a folding knife in my backpack. I dug it out and slipped into my pocket. A knife isn't much of a weapon—certainly not against a pistol—but I felt a little better having it on me.

Tess phoned Demerest to let him know where we were heading, but the call rolled over to voicemail. She then texted him. The message was the same both times—meet us at the Devil's Millhopper.

I didn't expect to see Demerest waiting for us when we got there, and he wasn't. It would take a while to get Amy turned over to the police.

"Should we hang here and wait for Frank to show up?" Tess asked.

"Why don't you stay here," I said. "Wait for him, then the two of you can catch up with me."

"You're going ahead by yourself?"

"Jazzy's here somewhere. I'm afraid for her. I have to find her."

"And leave me alone?"

Oh.

"Okay. You're right. I'll escort you back to the car. You can wait for Demerest there where you'll be safe."

"No. We should wait together. Here."

That wasn't going to happen. Jazzy was out in the darkness somewhere all alone. I was not going to wait for the cavalry to come to the rescue. Every second I hesitated would increase the danger she might face.

"I'm going, Tess. You can come with me if you want. Or you can go back. Make a decision. But I'm going."

She hesitated then said, "Fine. Let's go find her. But let me try to reach Demerest one more time." She called and once again the call went unanswered.

"Text him, tell him to catch up with us."

She did.

We worked our way past the deserted park ranger's office and concession stand to the gravel trail that led to boardwalk. We stopped at the hollowed-out pignut hickory tree where the first clue had been hidden, and rooted around inside just in case that's where D2 might have left the final piece of the puzzle. He hadn't.

"Where the hell in this park would he have hidden it?" Tess whispered.

"No clue. Let's focus on finding Jazzy."

A wooden boardwalk with a series of stairways leads to the bottom of the sinkhole. Rather than wander aimlessly along the topside trails, it seemed more reasonable—if anything about this misadventure could be considered reasonable—to follow the boardwalk as it descended the 120 feet to the lake at the bottom.

Befitting a scary movie, a half-moon was waxing behind scattered clouds allowing us to see our way without having to turn on the flashlights. Would David Darnell be hiding somewhere nearby? Is that why Jazzy beelined over here?

We arrived at the first set of stairs and paused. There were a total of 232 steps to the bottom, to where the devil dragged his victims to hell. We were utterly quiet, listening for the sound of human voices. Nearby, a small twig rustled, a slight scraping sound, not the crack of a bigfooted human on a fallen branch; maybe a raccoon or rabbit in the underbrush. There were croaking sounds from below, the mating calls of frogs. But not too many. It wasn't a chorus, merely the occasional *hello, any other amphibians around?* We also could hear the whisper of water pouring into the lake from the many small streams that fed it.

As we began our way down, I could feel a light mist on my exposed arms and legs as the temperature gradually dropped the lower we descended the stairs, the Millhopper creating its own micro-climate. Heat rises, cooler air descends. From our position, it was too dark to see to the bottom, but I guessed we might find the lake enshrouded in fog when we arrived.

Two more sets of stairs and we paused again. Same routine. We stood utterly still, this time for a couple of minutes, breathing quietly, not speaking. Then it dawned on me, like an embarrassed patron in a movie theater, that I hadn't silenced my cell phone. I squeezed Tess's arm and leaned in and whispered. "Our phones. We need to silence them."

She whispered back, "Duh."

I dug into the front left pocket of my cargo shorts and felt around for the button on the side of my iPhone and pushed the switch to silent mode. Wouldn't that have been embarrassing if it had gone off right as we were about to sneak up on Darnell Duffy? And I pushed that switch in the right direction, didn't I? Dammit. I stuck my hand back in, gently felt around on the side of the phone. Forward turned silent mode off; backward turned it on. I didn't dare take it out, lest the phone light up and give us away.

"Okay. I got it."

Tess leaned in. "You're sure."

"Yes, I'm certain."

"No message from Demerest?" I whispered.

She shook her head. "I'll feel the phone vibrate if he calls or texts back. Nothing so far."

I could hear the nervousness in her voice. Which was perfectly understandable. Here we were deep in the woods in the middle of the night, vulnerable, with maybe a stone-cold killer skulking around nearby, armed only with a pair of flashlights, which we didn't dare turn on. Maybe we could use them as clubs. Against a guy with a gun. About as useful as my pocketknife.

On the other hand, while I could sense Tess's anxiety, most of the self-loathing and grief that had gripped her earlier seemed to have been supplanted by the utter terror of what we were doing. Better to be doing something than lying about feeling sorry for herself. Even if it was reckless.

We were down another flight of stairs and I could smell the water below us. Small waterfalls cascading into the lake were becoming louder, drowning out some of the night noises from the top of the pit.

Then we heard it. The crack of a branch being stepped on. It wasn't nearby, maybe another forty or fifty feet below us, perhaps near the bottom of the descending boardwalk. We froze and crouched down, both of us straining to see movement in the dimness ahead.

I put my mouth to Tess's ear and whispered, "Maybe you should go back up, wait for Demerest."

She shook her head.

"I'll keep on going," I whispered. "But I've got a bad feeling about this. Maybe calling for backup would be smart. If you can't reach Frank, call 911."

"I won't leave you."

She said it, then stood up, ending the conversation. Of course, I could have pressed the issue, even gone back up with her, but I couldn't leave Jazzy here alone. So we pushed on, each step closer to the water below and the entrance to the devil's lair.

The clouds thinned, and in the unfiltered moonlight we could see more clearly ahead now. We were only a few dozen yards from the bottom. I'd been wrong about the fog. The water was visible, blue-green, and it was covering the bottom of the stairway and a small observation platform whose railings were missing.

"What's with that?" I whispered to Tess.

"Hurricane damage. They're going to be shutting this down soon to rebuild the stairways."

"Is the water always this high?"

"No," she whispered. "It can get even deeper than this after a big storm. Water runs downhill, Zander. Gravity's a bitch."

We'd gone as far as we could without wading onto the submerged platform. We gazed around, using the moon for light. I peered back up the stairs. Nobody had followed us. Across the submerged platform the stairway re-emerged from the lake. The ascending steps appeared to be dry. Nobody had waded through the water and continued upward, not recently anyway, or they would have left watery footprints in their wake.

And then we heard another branch snap, this time on the side of the ravine right beside us.

We whirled and standing there was a man with a pistol in his hand.

I heard Tess suck in her breath. Then she said:

"Hello, Darnell."

CHAPTER 45

HE WAS POINTING the revolver at us, waving the barrel side to side as if deciding which one of us to shoot first. I've had a gun pointed at me before. I didn't like it then, and liked it even less now. Is this what Jazzy had foreseen? My death at the hands of a lunatic at the bottom of a mysterious sinkhole? What an idiot I was walking into this. We should have waited. I should have listened to Tess. I'd foolishly done the very thing I'd scolded Brandy for—playing the hero. Now it was too late.

Darnell's teeth were clenched, like Clint Eastwood in *Dirty Harry*. Tough guy. He had us absolutely pinned down. He was just out of my reach, on higher ground, and we were sandwiched by the boardwalk's guardrail and the submerged platform.

This was the first time I'd seen D2 face-to-face. But I recognized the plaid shirt. I'd seen it on the guy running away from us on Main Street. At least that piece of the mystery was now solved.

In the movies, this would have been the perfect moment for a melodramatic speech, for him spill his guts about all the ways he'd been wronged, what a pervert Tess was, how clever he had been manipulating us to this spot. But he was looking fidgety and I figured we had only seconds left to live.

"Your sister, she's at the police station right now," I said.

As I spoke, I stepped in front of Tess, putting my body between her and the gun. I wondered, fleetingly, if she could swim. That might be the only way out of this mess. Jump in the lake, hope he missed, swim as far away as possible under water. Maybe in the darkness we could escape. Maybe I could distract him so that at least Tess could get away.

He turned the gun fully in my direction and sighted down the barrel, not holding it sideways like in a gangster movie. Better to aim, better to hit his mark—me.

Why had I been so impulsive? We never should have come down here by ourselves. No weapons. Phones turned off. We should have waited for Demerest. And where the hell was he?

My eyes were riveted on the gun. I recall having a fleeting notion that maybe I'd be able to detect when he was about to pull the trigger and dodge the bullet. Which was absurd, but it might be fair to say I wasn't thinking coherently in that moment.

But I did notice Darnell's hand begin to tremble, if only a little, which was unnerving. And I wondered if maybe he was as nervous as we were. I nudged backwards, pushing Tess closer to the guardrail of the boardwalk. I felt her hands on my back, a natural reaction to someone who's pushing you toward a drop-off. Then I heard her whisper:

"Oh."

She understood.

"We called the cops before we came down here, Darnell," I managed to say through the panic that gripped me. I tried to make it come out calm, and mostly it did. "They're on the way. You're trapped. They've got you for killing Bristol. Maybe you can cut some kind of deal, avoid the needle. But not if you do this."

Darnell cocked his head slightly, seemingly surprised at the reference to Bristol. He squinted his eyes, and opened his mouth to say something. I could feel Tess moving behind me, sliding slightly sideways, toward my right where the railing ended by the submerged portion of the boardwalk. She was going to make a break for it.

I braced myself to jump in the opposite direction, draw his fire so she could get clear. Maybe, if I were fast enough, and lucky enough…

Then Darnell's face came apart, silhouetted from behind in a flash of brilliant yellow light and thunder and smoke. He collapsed undramatically in a tangled heap.

I expected to see Demerest behind him. But no. Standing there, a semi-automatic pistol in her hand, was his sister, Amy.

I heard a thump behind me and whirled to see Tess collapsed on the boardwalk, a plume of red blossoming from the side of her tee shirt.

"Jesus fucking Christ! Tess! Tess, talk to me!"

Her eyes were squeezed shut in agony and she was groaning. I pulled her tee-shirt up revealing a jagged bleeding gash in her side. Either the bullet had passed through Darnell's head and struck her, or she'd caught shrapnel from his exploding skull. That step she took, trying to get ready to jump. It had exposed her just enough to get hit. Dammit!

I wrenched the handkerchief from my back pocket and pressed it on the wound, but it quickly became blood-soaked.

"What have you done you crazy bitch," I yelled at Amy.

What had I done?

She was staring down at us from the edge of the embankment, emotionless, the pistol loosely dangling by her side, smoke still leaking from the barrel. She had a vacant expression on her face.

"I saved you," she said.

I tore off my tee shirt, wadded it up, and pressed it against the seeping wound. "Tess, can you hold this here?" I took one of her hands and laid it atop the compress, but while her eyes were open she was unresponsive, staring wide-eyed at Amy in disbelief.

I ripped off my belt, slid it under her, and tightened it over the tee shirt to hold the makeshift compress in place.

"I saved you, Tess," Amy said again in a high-pitched voice. "Darnell. He was bad. He would have ruined you."

Amy raised the gun and pointed it in my direction to cover me, then knelt down by D2's splayed body. She dug her free hand into the back pocket of his jeans, rooted around, then her fist came out holding what appeared to be a thumb drive.

"I've got it, Tess. You're safe now."

I glanced down at Tess. Her eyes were closed. I placed my hand on her neck. I could still feel her pulse.

"Amy, I'm going to reach into my pocket and get my cell phone. We have to call an ambulance."

"No!" she shouted and steadied her aim on me. "I'll take care of Tess. I'll take good care of her."

Keep her talking...

"Where is Demerest?" I yelled. "What have you done to him?"

Amy ignored the question. "Darnell said you were tall, but you're bigger than I thought. Still, I can't imagine what she sees in you."

Keep her talking...

"What's on the thumb drive, Amy? What's worth killing your brother for?"

She cocked her head and lowered the gun.

"You don't know?"

Keep her talking...

"I know about the contract. How Aaron Landry made Tess promise not to tell about her abortion."

Amy switched her gaze from me to Tess.

"You little liar."

She raised the gun, arm fully extended, and sighted down the barrel.

That's when I heard the scream. At first I couldn't tell where it came from. It seemed to penetrate the air around us, a loud banshee-like screech that echoed off the Millhopper's walls. Then I saw a blur of movement behind Amy. She had the gun pointed straight out in front of her and she flinched at the noise the instant she pulled the trigger. The shot went wild, the bullet splashing into the water over the submerged boardwalk.

And then Jazzy flew into her, hitting Amy square in the back in a flying tackle that launched both of them over the boardwalk into the lake below, sending a cascade of water atop Tess and me.

Tess groaned.

"Tess, Tess, can you hear me? I need you to hold this here." I put her hand back on top of the compress.

She cried out in pain and her eyes fluttered open, but she didn't respond to my directions. I turned to the lake, but Jazzy and Amy had not resurfaced.

"Tess, you gotta help me here."

Nothing. She'd passed out again.

I cinched the belt a little tighter, then rose and jumped feet first into the water, my old lifeguard training instinctively kicking in, knowing better than to dive headfirst without knowing the depth. The lake was deeper than I imagined so close to shore and I went completely under. I bobbed back up, took in a huge gulp of air, then dove back down. Between the darkness and the murkiness of the water, I couldn't see a thing.

I resurfaced and glanced back at Tess. She hadn't moved. A few yards away in the darkness I could heard the water churning. Perhaps it was Jazzy and Amy struggling right beneath the surface. I launched myself in that direction and dove again, thrashing about under the water, reaching out blindly into the darkness desperate to find them.

Suddenly, I was jolted by a shockwave, as if someone had detonated a bomb underwater. Immediately thereafter I felt myself being pulled away from the shore as if in the grasp of an invisible and overpowering hand. It was a frightening current—a tremendous force, like a riptide—sucking me toward the center of the lake. I stroked hard against it but could feel myself losing the battle.

By then, my blood oxygen was becoming depleted and I kicked back to the surface to get another gulp of air. As my head emerged from the water, the current grew more powerful. I glanced over my shoulder into the Millhopper and in the moonlight saw the outline of an enormous whirlpool, a counter-clockwise swirl that seemed to have stirred up a phosphorescent reaction in the water. The concentric rings of the whirlpool were glowing, a faint but visible blue. And growing larger with each rapidly passing second. The air was filled with the cacophonous roar of rushing water.

"Jesus Christ, Strange, get the hell out of there!"

I turned back toward the boardwalk. It was Demerest, blood dripping down the side of his head, kneeling over Tess.

"It's a goddamned vortex, you fool, get out of the water," he screamed.

I ignored him and dove back down, reaching into the gloom, desperate to bump into a submerged human, preferably Jazzy. The water was shallower now and rushing toward the whirlpool in the center of the rapidly receding lake. It took all my strength to keep from being sucked along with it.

Stay down, don't give up, don't quit until you find them.

But this time, I didn't have to come up for air. In a few moments, I found myself on my hands and knees in mud gasping for breath. All the water that had covered the bottom of the Devil's Millhopper's had drained into a huge hole that had opened in the center of the lake bed.

Taking Amy Duffy and Shirley DuMont, a.k.a. Madam Jazzabelle, with it.

CHAPTER 46

Four Weeks Later

NEITHER JAZZY NOR Amy's bodies were ever recovered.

Geologists from the University of Florida concluded that the same forces responsible for the creation of the Devil's Millhopper eons ago caused the sudden collapse in the sinkhole's center that drained the lake. Acidic groundwater had eaten away at the limestone under the lakebed creating a new cavern, and when the roof of that underground cave collapsed, the water overhead swirled into it.

The newly collapsed cave under the Millhopper wasn't that large in and of itself, but it was linked to countless underground tributaries and it was through them that the lake water was ushered away along with the bodies of the two women. Any attempt to find them would be pointless, scientists said.

The vortex that formed in the lake with the cavern's collapse was so powerful that it swept vast amounts of mud, sand and rock into the cave. It was a miracle that I did not end up entombed with Jazzy and Amy. Indeed, so much sediment was washed into the newly formed hole that it sealed itself completely and the lake soon began refilling. If you visit there today, you would never know.

This scientific explanation for the women's disappearance did little to dissuade those who saw it as confirmation that the Millhopper was, indeed, a gateway to hell. And that it was the handiwork of Beelzebub, himself, drawing Jazzy and Amy into his infernal lair. Always a popular tourist destination, the Devil's Millhopper skyrocketed into the Number One ranking in popular lists of the most haunted places in Florida.

Surgeons removed a bullet fragment from Tess's side, and it took her a month of hospitalization and rehab to get back on her feet. I had climbed out of the muddy lake bottom and carried her in my arms halfway out of the Millhopper before paramedics arrived to take over. One of her doctors later told the *Gainesville Sun* that if she had arrived at the hospital any later she would have bled out.

It wasn't until the medics carried Tess away that the enormity of what had just transpired finally hit me. I'd just witnessed a man's face explode, a woman shot, and two other women drown. Jazzy, my crazy friend Jazzy, had saved our lives. She had seen it all coming. And I could do nothing to save her.

I collapsed on the steps of the Millhopper's boardwalk, put my head in my hands, and wept.

I don't know how long I sat there, but eventually I felt an arm around my shoulder. It was Demerest.

"Come on, son, let's get out of here," he said. "What's done is done. There's nothing more to do."

While Tess was healing, her two-remaining staffers put the finishing touches on the final edition of *The Agi-Gator*. It included a story about the murders of Bristol and Darnell Duffy and the bizarre end of Jazzy and Amy. It's last headline, originally intended to chronicle the newspaper's demise, also served to record those deaths:

—30—

Tess's landlord, Marv, turned out not to be a candidate for The Very Worst Person Ever and extended her lease until she got well. And he was also able to identify Darnell as his part-time weekend employee using a photo provided by police.

Frank Demerest's physical injuries were minor, but the blow to his ego was worse than the one to his head. Amy had gotten the drop on him when they parked outside the police station, clubbing him in the face with her pistol and stealing his car.

Demerest had been negligent. He should have searched her. He never should have let her get the better of him. He'd gotten rusty and now he felt guilty about it. Those beers he had beforehand couldn't have helped his performance, either. Because of him, Amy, Darnell, and Jazzy were dead. Or so he reasoned.

I thought he was being too hard on himself. "Have you stopped to think what would have happened if Amy hadn't ambushed you? Darnell was about to shoot Tess and me when Amy showed up."

"Sure," he said. "But I gotta wonder if Jazzy wouldn't have tackled him instead of Amy and how that would have turned out."

My counter-argument was that Darnell was not a small man. Jazzy might not have been able to take him down. Who knows how that struggle would have played even if I'd been able to reach him armed, as I was, with only a flashlight and pocket knife.

"But Jazzy might still be alive," he'd said.

I didn't think so. I believed it was always going to turn out this way. That's what Jazzy would have said, what she wanted me to understand. I don't pretend to fully grasp her visions, but I know they were real. And I know she was resigned to her fate. She expected it. By her own decisions and actions, she made it happen.

Forensic tests showed that Amy's semi-automatic was the same gun used to kill Bristol. They found it in the mud by the boardwalk. Unlike its owner, it hadn't been sucked into the underworld. Darnell's pistol, recovered beside his body, was unregistered.

Jack Turner tracked down the guy at the Thunder Hog to whom Bristol had talked the night she was murdered. He was, in fact, a co-worker of Darnell's, and he confirmed that he had given Bristol directions on where she could find him.

What happened after that remains a matter of speculation. Since Amy's pistol was the murder weapon, either it had been in Darnell's possession at that time, or Amy was with him and one or the other pulled the trigger. Turner thinks either way, Bristol's body was transported from the murder site to Spook Hill and dumped when the last of the clues was planted.

Autopsy results showed that in addition to the bullet wound, Bristol had suffered severe laryngeal trauma—blunt force injury to her throat—most likely caused in a struggle that would have been life-threatening in its own right had she not been shot.

The placement of the final clue in the scavenger hunt—the words written on Bristol's chest—must have been a last-minute improvisation and likely the result of the wheels coming off the entire insane enterprise, Turner surmised.

Which also raised the question of who the real ringleader was.

I'd given Turner a copy of the recording I made of Amy when she confessed at Tess's house. She had tried to paint herself as a model of contrition and had thrown her brother under the bus. But that didn't square with what happened at the Devil's Millhopper that night. My instincts tell me that Amy was the puppet master.

But that, in turn, raised a further question: Why did she come to Tess's house? What was with the apology?

Demerest and Turner agreed to talk off the record on the afternoon following my testimony before a grand jury that had been empaneled to investigate what the local papers and television stations were calling the Night at the Millhopper. I had lawyered up, and upon the advice of my attorney, and with Edwina Mahoney's consent, I elected not to write about all this until now.

As Edwina told me, "Put this in the file, wait for the dust to settle, you may even get a book out of it."

We were sitting on the patio of the One Love Café, not far from the sinkhole, sheltered from an afternoon shower that would help the lake refill.

"It was a Glock, nine millimeter," Turner said.

"You remember that baggy sweat shirt she wore?" Demerest said. "You remember how when she sat on the couch she never leaned back, she was always on the edge? I think she had the piece jammed into the back of her pants the whole time. I should have searched her."

Why was she there? They could only speculate. Maybe to kill Tess, then use the gun to kill her brother and make it look like a suicide, pinning everything on him. Or maybe to kidnap Tess, then kill her brother.

I told them the second theory might be closer to the truth based on what I saw at the Millhopper that night. How Amy kept saying she was going to take care of Tess. She was clearly out of her mind. My theory is that once Amy pulled the trigger on her own brother, she snapped. She'd parked her sanity at the curb and joined the circus.

But why didn't Amy go for it while she was at Tess's house? Because Demerest was there with a gun, Turner believed. We'd gotten lucky. It could have been all over right then. Amy was forced to improvise.

"We're thinking she had already arranged to meet Darnell at the Millhopper," Demerest said. "Probably would have shot him then with the Glock, made it look like a suicide, cover her tracks. But all that fell apart."

Tess and I met for a drink the evening before I testified. I ordered a Cuba Libre. She had an iced tea. She told me to take good care of Mona, that she was concerned Spock might have designs on her. I assured her that Spock was without qualification the most honorable cardboard space alien I knew. It was mostly lighthearted conversation like that.

At first.

Then I placed the thumb drive—also known as a flash drive—on the bar.

The color drained from her face. She stared at it for a long moment then met my eyes. "Where did you get that?"

"Amy dropped it when Jazzy tackled her. You were unconscious when she fished it out of Darnell's back pocket."

"I see."

"It's what that final clue was all about, wasn't it." I'd memorized the line:

"*To hand to you
"In a flash
"How you made
"All that cash.*"

She started to reach for it, then hesitated. She looked at me. "You've listened to it, haven't you."

I ignored that.

"You knew all along what the reference to *flash* meant. A flash drive. That's what the scavenger hunt was all about, recovering this." I tapped the thumb drive. It was a black SanDisk with red lettering.

"The contract. It was just paperwork showing Landry made so-called donations to the newspaper and wanted to remain anonymous. You both needed copies of the paperwork for tax purposes. You didn't give a damn about that, never did. It was always about recovering the recording on this thing.

"You were lying through your teeth the entire time. You lied by omission by not telling me the real reason we went galivanting around the state. You lied when you said Landry pulled a Stormy Daniels, paid you hush money, that it was all his idea."

I shook my head. "It's wasn't Landry at all. It was you. You were blackmailing him. It's all on the recording. You'd been draining him for years and finally he had enough. He told you he couldn't pay any more. That's when the newspaper started going in the toilet, right?"

She sat motionless. Waiting for me to continue. I obliged.

"So why'd you tape him? Why'd you keep this? You figure maybe you could start the blackmail all over again someday, maybe if he was elected to Congress where he'd have more to lose? You plan on using him as your personal gravy train for the rest of your life?"

She continued staring.

"Just out of curiosity, Tess, how much money were you able to wring out of him? So far?"

She snatched the thumb drive off the bar and gripped it tightly.

"Wipe that smug look off your face, Zander. You have no idea what I've gone through. It must be nice to sit there, so judgmental, so privileged. I would have expected you to at least extend me the benefit of the doubt."

"What else was a lie, Tess? Was Landry even the father?"

"What? You think it was you?"

"Was I?"

"What an ego you have."

I took a deep breath and thought about what I wanted to say.

"Tess, I know you played me. And I should hate you for it. But I don't. I've thought about this, and I realize I can't take it personally. You can't blame a scorpion for stinging. I blame myself. I let myself be taken in by how you reached out to me. I wanted to believe you, to be your friend. To have you as a friend. I brought this on myself through my own naivete."

I slugged down the remainder of my drink.

"Thanks for the lesson. I'll never make that mistake again."

I rose from the barstool and stood over her.

"Any final words? Anything you want to say?"

A tear leaked from the corner of her right eye. Was she playing back *Wrath of Kahn* or *Spider-Man 2*? Or did she have her own trick to generate tears

Or was I just being cynical?

"I did use you," Tess finally said. "But I wasn't lying about our friendship."

She was good. She was very good.

The flash drive was still in her fist, clutched in a death grip.

"Tess, I'll take that, if you like. Destroy it so you'll never be tempted again. Without it, you can make a clean start. Put this behind you."

She stood up, stepped away from me, but held on tightly to the flash drive. The look on her face was neither anger, nor resentment, nor regret. Just cold indifference.

Then she walked out of the bar and didn't look back.

In the following weeks I completed my relocation to Goodland and began operations as a weird news reporter based aboard the *Miss Demeanor*. A more ideal location might have been Miami or Key West—the true epicenters of weirdness in America, perhaps the entire Milky Way. But home—and in this case, my office—is where the boat is. And this boat was going nowhere until that gaping hole in its hull was repaired.

But while Goodland was headquarters, my job took me around the state. Recently, I was in Fort Myers attending a press conference hosted by the Rev. Lee Roy Chitango. He announced a lottery for people willing to join him aboard the Ark II to escape the coming End of Days. Tickets cost thousands, but the Sermonator took VISA, Discover, and Master Card. And he encouraged believers to enter more than once.

And I'm busy trying to track down the secretive social avenger as Mister Manners. He's become something of a folk hero, punishing hero, punishing people who fail to use their turn signals, under-tip, over-honk—that sort of annoying behavior. The police in several cities have been trying to find him for months. But with the help of some students at the University of South Florida—they've started this fan club of sorts and call themselves the Army of the Strange—I think I'm closing in on him.

I've gotten to know a few of my neighbors in Goodland, including a nice elderly lady who lives in the nearby Drop Anchor Mobile Home Park. She watches Fred for me when I'm out and about. The boat's air conditioning is working now, which in the tropics is a must. Fred and Mona get along and Spock is his normal unsocial self. Uncle Leo has promised that he and *Numero Cinco* will be down to visit as soon as hurricane season is over.

While most of my travel outside Goodland is for business purposes, I've found a poker room up at the dog track in Bonita Springs where I've kept my Texas Hold 'Em skills fresh. Met a cop there, a fellow player, that I hope to cultivate as a source.

I also have a return trip to New Orleans on my schedule.

I gathered all of Jazzy's things when I left Gainesville and have kept them in the carpet bag she brought with her to Florida. I'd been reluctant to go through them, but the other day I finally did. Her journal was in the bag, the one from which she deduced her name when she woke up in the back room of Madam Jazzabelle's on Royal Street.

I paged through her entries, largely a recollection of her daily activities, which also included notes describing her bouts of *déjà vu*.

The attacks are coming less frequently now as I have begun to accumulate a clearer picture of what lies ahead. I am resigned to my fate. There will be no stopping the coming events; I am at peace.

And then this:

Alexander, you are reading this because my story had ended. Please know that while the memory of my life is short, your being a part of it has been a great joy. The world is a strange place. Go tell its story truthfully.

—Your once and always friend, Jazzy

P.S. If the opportunity presents itself, please return this journal to its rightful owner. Thank you.

CHAPTER 47

New Orleans

THIS TIME, I avoided crossing the River Styx by flying instead of driving.

There are zero non-stops between southwest Florida and the Big Easy, so I caught a dawn-thirty Delta flight out of Fort Myers with a layover in Atlanta en route to Louis Armstrong International Airport. After landing, I taxied straight to Café du Monde in the French Quarter. I was devouring sugary beignets and chicory-laced coffee on the covered patio while enduring the cacophony of a riotous jazz band on the sidewalk in front of the restaurant.

If you've come to New Orleans for peace and quiet, you've come to the wrong place. There is music everywhere. Always. Blowing out the doors of saloons and restaurants, bellowing from street performers and parades, rattling PA systems in the stores. If you are the kind of person whose ability to concentrate is disturbed by loud noises, just hang it up and have a drink, because this place is all about distraction.

But I hadn't come to deliberate, but to deliver a journal. To its rightful owner, as Jazzy had instructed.

And who would that be?

Jazzy said she'd found the diary beside her when she awoke, her memories vanished, in the back room of Madam Jazzabelle's. And that's where I was heading. Before booking my flight, I called to ensure the little shop of prophesy was, indeed, still open. After all, the last time I was here there was an eviction notice on the front door.

The woman who answered my call assured me that not only was the shop still in business, Madam Jazzabelle, herself, would be there to read my palm and discuss my future whenever I decided to show up.

Now a veteran of Florida's unpredictable weather, I had an umbrella stuffed in my backpack. I carried it always. I popped it and held it in my left hand as I crossed Decatur Street to protect me from the shower that began falling from the overcast skies. In my right hand, I was toting Jazzy's carpet bag, still filled with her belongings.

I cut through Jackson Square, past St. Louis Cathedral, to Royal Street. Two blocks later, my shoes a little damp but otherwise successfully protected from the downpour, I stepped into Madam Jazzabelle's.

A middle-aged African-American woman was sitting at the round table in the middle of the room. She wore a flowing silver and garnet robe that ordinarily would have been stifling in the Louisiana heat and humidity, but the AC was on full blast and I actually felt a chill as I entered the shop.

At least I assumed it was the temperature.

Unlike Jazzy, this Madam Jazzabelle didn't wear a turban. Her hairless scalp was as smooth as a crystal ball. She was slender and had penetrating eyes, brown with gold flecks just like Jazzy's. And she was giving me a curious look with those eyes.

"Hello, Alexander," she said.

How did she know? I have no idea. Maybe she'd traced my caller ID and looked me up on Google. Or maybe she didn't need to.

I walked over, dropped the carpet bag on the floor, then pulled the diary out of my backpack and sat down.

"I believe this may belong to you."

She glanced at the journal, took it from me, and laid it on the table. "Thank you."

"You'll note in the final entry that my friend—I called her Jazzy, but she believed her real name may have been Shirley Dumont—asked me to return this to its rightful owner. Is that you?"

"Yes. It is my journal and I am Shirley Dumont."

"Jazzy…" I paused. I felt my throat tightening a little bit. "Jazzy said she woke up behind the curtain one day. She had no memory of who she was. She took the name and history in this journal as her own. She didn't know what else to do."

The woman nodded and her eyes glistened.

"She always was such a troubled child," she said. "She had these terrible seizures. I was worried about her when I asked her to watch the shop for me." She paused, her eyes far away for a few heartbeats. "I was in Europe for a few months. The first real vacation I've ever taken. Melika promised to watch over things while I was gone."

"Melika?"

She nodded. "My niece."

I knew the police had tried to track down Jazzy's next of kin and that they had placed calls to New Orleans PD in that effort. But I hadn't heard whether those efforts were successful. The handoff to the cops in New Orleans had wrapped it up for the police in Gainesville, and they lost interest thereafter.

"The police were able to reach you? They told you? I didn't know who to call."

She nodded. "Yes."

We sat quietly for a minute. It wasn't uncomfortable. Then she said:

"I wonder. Would you be willing to tell me about Melika, what she and you were involved in, how it ended?'

"Yes, of course."

She nodded, then rose from the table and walked to the front of the shop, locked the door, and flipped the OPEN/CLOSED sign.

"Would you like something to drink?" she asked.

"In the worst way."

"Have you ever tried Dixie? It's not as terrible as Budweiser, but it's the worst I've got."

She poured us each a glass. I took a sip. She was right.

"Before I begin, can you tell me something?" I asked.

She nodded.

"Jazzy had these visions, *déjà vu* attacks she described them, in which she saw the future. I gather you knew about that."

She nodded again.

"Do you believe they were real? That she actually could visualize future events?'

She was silent for the longest time, looking at me intently. Finally, she said:

"I have wondered about that her entire life. And my answer is, I do not know. But I do know she believed they were real. I believed—I still believe—she was being truthful."

She paused then asked, "And you?"

"Let me tell you the whole story."

It took a couple of hours. The real Shirley DuMont was a patient listener and it was apparent from the outset that she wanted as many details as possible.

I started with our first encounter, how Jazzy had held my left hand and foreseen death.

"I assumed she was talking about me," I said. "Looking back, and doing my best to recall her exact words, I now realize she wasn't referring to me at all. I believe she was seeing her own demise. I just happened to be there, a catalyst for one of her seizures."

"And a participant."

"Yes. And a participant."

About an hour into recounting the story, Madam Jazzabelle cocked her head, hearing something outside her door, and held up her hand. She stepped into the drizzle, and in a few minutes returned with two Lucky Dogs.

While we were eating, she glanced down at Jazzy's carpet bag that

I set by the table. She reached in and pulled out the red turban. She held it in front of her, examining it. Then pulled it close to her face and took in the scent of her lost niece. Then she gracefully placed it on her head.

I concluded the story with my final conversation with Tess, her seizing the flash drive and walking out without a word.

I remembered the look on Tess's face, gripping the thumb drive tightly in her fist, the prize she had been willing to sacrifice so much for—trust, integrity, friendship, and, ultimately, people's lives. It was not a look of contrition, but victory.

Madame Jazzabelle gazed up at the ceiling, processing all she'd heard, then asked me:

"You let her go? After all she was responsible for. Bristol's death. Melika's. All of it?"

Her tone was neutral and her face a mask disguising whatever emotions were hidden underneath.

I'd buried the lede.

"Did I say that?"

She was giving me a curious expression now. Waiting for me to spill it.

"I debated with myself about what I should do after I listened to the recording and read the contract on the flash drive. I talked to my uncle. He's a judge in Phoenix. His answer was legal. It was evidence in a murder. Withholding it would be a felony. Then I thought about what Jazzy would say, and I remembered your niece's words to me. She said my job is to *tell the truth of it all.*"

Madam Jazzabelle had a confused expression. "But you gave the thumb drive back to her."

I slowly shook my head.

"I put a thumb drive on the bar. A look-alike. I wanted to give Tess a final chance to explain herself. I was willing to give her that last benefit of the doubt. I thought, perhaps, there might be this big reveal, that she would share some secret reason for all she had done that would be, if not entirely exculpatory, as my uncle would say, at least offer some forgivable justification for her behavior."

"And did she? Did she offer a reason?"

"No, she didn't."

I paused, collecting my thoughts.

"Ever since I literally crossed the River Styx, I've thought about the story of Achilles, how despite his mother's best efforts even he had his vulnerabilities. We all do. Sometimes we discover them the hard way."

Madam Jazzabelle nodded. "We do. It's how we face them that defines us."

"If it hadn't been for Jazzy, the lesson for me might have been 'trust no one.' It's a journalism trope. But she cautioned me against becoming too cynical. She told me my job was to seek the truth and tell it. And you can't do that if you go around assuming everyone is a liar or a cheat. I'm inclined to give people the benefit of the doubt. Just like I gave Tess. I've been told it's a weakness. What Jazzy wanted me to understand is that it also can be a strength."

Madam Jazzabelle nodded. "To be unafraid to face the world despite your vulnerabilities."

"Yes. To be mindful of them, understand where and when to keep my guard up, but to carry on. It's as if Jazzy knew I'd be at this cross-roads and she was advising me, helping me make the right decision."

Madam Jazzabelle ran her hands over the red turban, a gesture I had seen Jazzy do countless times, then reached into the carpet bag and extracted the wraparound rose-colored sunglasses and put them on. She looked at me and offered a gentle smile.

"You turned the real thumb drive over to the police."

"Yes, I did."

She smiled again.

"She knew you would."

I nodded. "I think so, too."

I took one long, last look at Madam Jazzabelle. Then I rose from the table and turned toward the shop's entrance. There was nothing left to say. Through the front window I could see the rain still splattering the sidewalk on Royal Street. I'd left my umbrella by the door. I bent down, picked it up, and reached for the door handle. But as I did, she spoke:

"Be strong, Strange Man."

I froze. Jazzy had said those exact words to me. I turned around.

The room was empty.

—**30**—

Acknowledgements

I owe a deep debt of gratitude to many people in the creation of this book. Foremost to my friend Alexander Strange, for allowing me to tell this story and for his comprehensive notes that made it possible.

I have written this in first person, with Alex as the protagonist, as this is his tale to tell. I am merely his scribe. Why didn't Alex write it himself? As he told me, "I'd rather have a colonoscopy than write a book."

Many of the details of this story flow from the audio recordings Alex gave to me (including the entire final conversation at Madam Jazzabelle's in New Orleans). Other sources of information include police reports and interviews with Third Eye investigator Frank Demerest, Gainesville Police Detective Jack Turner, Polk County Sheriff's Detective Bob Samuelson, retired Gainesville real estate agent Marv Mannheimer, and Professor Harriet Skinner of the University of Florida.

During the course of creating this narrative I did from time to time fill in gaps not covered in interviews and notes, particularly when trying to relate Alexander's internal dialogues. He's reviewed all this, of course. When I asked him if he saw anything that troubled him in my extrapolations, he replied, "close enough for non-government work."

If I have introduced any errors, I blame it on the internet, innate slothfulness, and the *Weird Tour of Florida* magazine produced by the young and ambitious staff of the former *Agi-Gator*.

The names of some characters have been changed to honor confidentiality requests and to avoid troublesome lawsuits. Other details have been obfuscated for similar reasons here and there throughout the narrative.

Special thanks to Edwina Mahoney, for her assistance and guidance and for her permission to use examples of *The Strange Files* published by Tropic ◎ Press. Also, thanks to all who assisted me in preparing this for publication, especially my capable first reader, Sandy Bruce; insightful editor, Logan Bruce; and my talented web designer and reader, Kacey Bruce. Also a shout-out to my International Thriller Writers coaches Donald Maass, Gayle Lynds, Meg Gardiner, and F. Paul Wilson for their continuing inspiration and priceless guidance. As well as the assistance I've received from my ITW Master Craft classmates over the years and my wonderful colleagues at several writers' groups with whom I have belonged. And a tip of the hat to Annisa Karim for her help navigating the wilds of Gainesville and the Devil's Millhopper.

ABOUT THE AUTHOR

J.C. BRUCE IS a journalist, teacher, and author living in Naples, Florida. A lengthy newspaper career included serving as an editor, managing editor, or reporter at the *Naples Daily News*, the *Dayton Daily News*, *Tribune* Newspapers in suburban Phoenix, the Longview, Texas *News Journal*, the *Austin American-Statesman*. the *Miami Herald*, the *Palm Beach Post*, the *St. Petersburg Times* (now the *Tampa Bay Times*) and the *Tampa Times* (now deceased).

As the journalist-in-residence at Wright State University, young impressionable minds were subjected to instruction in Bruce's classes on the basics of reporting, editing, and feature writing. Some of those students are now committing journalism for a living.

Affiliations, present and past, include: Mystery Writers of America, International Thriller Writers, Sisters in Crime, the American Society of News Editors, the Society of Professional Journalists, Investigative Reporters and Editors, the Press Club of Southwest Florida, the League of Women Voters, NAACP, the Dayton Literary Peace Prize, and juries for the National Journalism Awards and the Pulitzer prizes.

CPSIA information can be obtained
at www.ICGtesting.com
Printed in the USA
BVHW030632191120
593707BV00001B/1

9 781734 290325